PRAISE FOR THE NOVELS OF JOE WEBER

Dancing with the Dragon

"The action is brisk. . . . A solid accomplishment for thriller readers."

—*Booklist*

DEFCON One

"Chilling and credible . . . an ominous, nightmarish scenario of how World War III could happen."

—STEPHEN COONTS

Primary Target

"A chilling scenario of global warfare . . . The suspense never stops."

—W. E. B. GRIFFIN

Targets of Opportunity

"Some writers get better with age; Weber is among them."

—*Library Journal*

Other Books by Joe Weber

DEFCON ONE
SHADOW FLIGHT
RULES OF ENGAGEMENT
TARGETS OF OPPORTUNITY
HONORABLE ENEMIES
PRIMARY TARGET
DANCING WITH THE DRAGON

ASSURED RESPONSE

A NOVEL

JOE WEBER

BALLANTINE BOOKS • NEW YORK

2005 Presidio Press Mass Market Edition
Published by The Random House Publishing Group

Originally published in hardcover by Presidio Press, a division of the Random House Publishing Group, a division of Random House, Inc., in 2004.

www.presidiopress.com

ISBN 0-345-47255-1

Manufactured in the United States of America

OPM 9 8 7 6 5 4 3 2 1

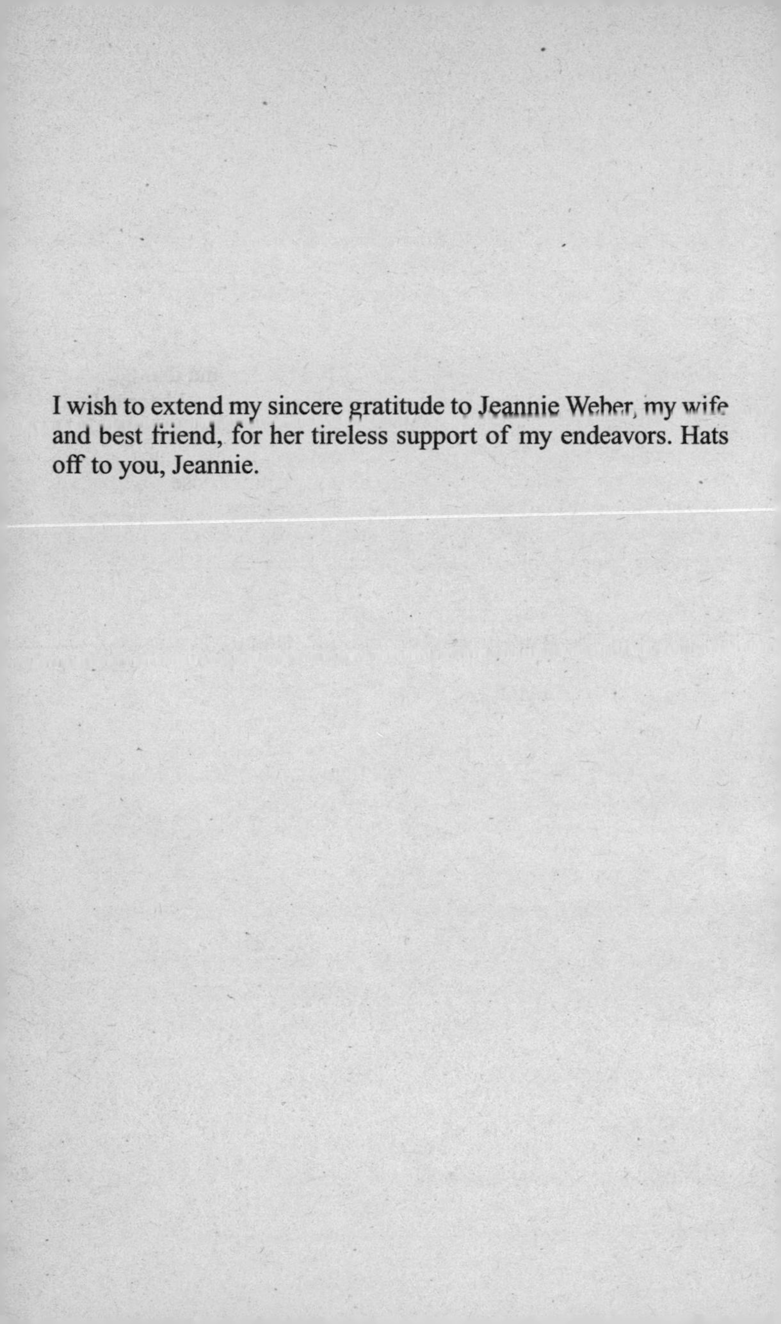

I wish to extend my sincere gratitude to Jeannie Weber, my wife and best friend, for her tireless support of my endeavors. Hats off to you, Jeannie.

Dictators are people who attempt to accomplish by calculated brutality and aggression what they lack the intelligence and magnanimity to consummate.

—Lewis Mumford

1

Dulles International Airport

Located twenty-five miles west of Washington, D.C., the sprawling airport and the inhabitants of the busy aerodrome were gearing up for the usual morning rush hour. Airliners and corporate jets were beginning to form long conga lines on the taxiways, while throngs of business passengers and vacationers were being packed into airplanes. Hardly an airline seat was to be had and, having exhausted their patience while clearing security, passengers' tempers were growing shorter by the minute.

In the concourse used by British Airways, senior members of the Dulles management team were playing host to Brett Shannon, the U.S. secretary of state. His large entourage of State Department functionaries, Washington dignitaries, and a few close friends were receiving VIP treatment from the airport staff.

Enjoying his late fifties, Brettford Earl Shannon had huge jowls that dominated his wide face. A large man, he was partial to tailor-made oversized business suits, brightly colored suspenders, and black wingtip shoes. Wire-framed glasses highlighted his long aristocratic nose. Shannon's sonorous voice boomed above the others as he held court prior to boarding a new British Airways Boeing 777.

Secretary Shannon and his key staff aides, plus the chairmen and ranking members of select congressional subcommittees, a handful of Shannon's fraternity brothers, a sextet of security personnel, and a baker's dozen of well-known journalists, were about to depart for London's Heathrow International Airport.

The mood was deliciously jubilant. Shannon's guests chatted and smiled as they mingled with the convivial crowd.

Although the possibility of an airliner's being hijacked in the United States was greatly reduced since September eleventh, some members of the delegation were still uneasy about commercial air travel. Privately, they admitted their preference would have been their usual conveyance aboard a jet operated by the 89th Airlift Wing at Andrews Air Force Base. Others—who felt more confidence in the current airport and airline security systems—were taking their spouses on the historic trip.

In London, Shannon would spend the night at the Dorchester and then sightsee and shop the next forenoon. After a casual lunch at the hotel, he and his group would board the new Cunard ocean liner *Queen Mary 2,* the grandest floating palace in the world. An authentic transatlantic liner, the unrivaled Cunard flagship featured British White Star Service and extravagant accommodations. The streamlined *QM2* showcased the latest in shipbuilding technologies for the twenty-first century, including the powerful Rolls-Royce four-pod propulsion system.

To a person, Shannon's guests were excited about the relaxing six-day voyage from London to New York City. Two couples from Shannon's college days even brought freelance cinematographers along to record the memorable experience.

Secretary Shannon looked forward to holding a "floating summit" with fellow statesmen from major European and Middle Eastern countries, including their host, the United Kingdom of Great Britain and Northern Ireland, the Russian Federation, the Islamic State of Afghanistan, the French Republic, the Arab Republic of Egypt, the Federal Republic of Germany, the Kingdom of Saudi Arabia, and the Republic of Turkey. The stunning attack on the World Trade Center and the Pentagon had created a global movement that had recently culminated in the development of the Terrorism Coalition Council (TCC).

During their cruise, the U.S. secretary of state, along with the foreign ministers and other officials of the TCC, would focus on immediate measures to eradicate terrorism on a worldwide basis. Shannon had known that once the problem was under some degree of international coordination and control, networking between nations to maintain an intelligence net over the terrorists would be much easier.

Although it was an ambitious undertaking, Shannon felt confident that continued progress could be made if the coalition countries worked as a team to achieve their mutual goals. Messages received at the State Department suggested that a majority of leaders were enthusiastic about the initial effects of the TCC and desired to accomplish even greater results.

The summit aboard the regal *Queen Mary 2* was in the initial planning stages when British Airways generously offered a special charter flight from Washington's Dulles Airport. The overture would make the entire trip uniquely British.

After the grand cruise from England to the Empire State, the group would be guests of the president and first lady at a gala White House state dinner. The following day, many members of the delegation would be returning to their respective countries. Others planned extended vacations at various locations across the United States, Canada, Mexico, South America, and Hawaii.

When the boarding call was announced, Shannon led his cortege to the waiting airliner. After being cordially greeted at the entrance to the plane, the secretary made his way to his reserved seat in the spacious First Class section. Shannon's immediate staff joined him in the forward cabin. Two of the seats would remain vacant, allowing the secretary to visit casually with various dignitaries during the long flight to Heathrow.

The ranking members of Congress were comfortably ensconced in the New Club World section of the airplane, while the remaining passengers were seated in the New World Traveler area.

Shannon removed his rumpled suit coat and gave it to a charming flight attendant, one of eighteen assigned to this flight.

"Welcome aboard, Mr. Secretary."

"Thank you, nice to be aboard," he replied, with a friendly smile, as he took his seat. "How's the weather in London?"

"Actually, it's quite pleasant for early summer, mild evenings and no mention of rain in the forecast."

"Good." Shannon loosened his tie and unbuttoned his shirt collar. "I just hope it's cooler than it is here."

"Oh, I assure you, it is." She had worked hard to overcome the broad accent of south London. "Would you care for something to drink?"

"Sure. Champagne would be fine."

"Champagne it is," she said, with an easy smile.

While everyone settled into their comfortable seats, Shannon accepted a glass of Dom Perignon and stretched his long beefy legs. He glanced at his new Rolex wristwatch, a self-indulgent gift expressly for this momentous occasion: *6 A.M. We'll be in London around 6:15 P.M. with plenty of time to prepare for the prime minister's reception.*

After takeoff, Shannon and his fellow travelers enjoyed a smooth ride while they perused their breakfast menus. They finished the light meal while the airplane climbed to its cruising altitude of 37,000 feet and accelerated to 0.84 Mach.

Two hours later came the pièce de résistance. Specially prepared for this occasion, the first course of the elaborate meal consisted of various hot and cold hors d'oeuvres. Shannon indulged himself with Gougère Puffs, a hot cheese pastry from the Burgundy region of France. He accepted another glass of champagne and studied his embossed menu.

BRITISH AIRWAYS

WORLD CLASS SERVICE

Hors d'Oeuvres with Appetizer Wines
Cream of Leek Soup
Cucumber-Watercress Salad
Standing Rib Roast with Yorkshire Pudding
Potatoes au Gratin
Sliced Parsnips and Carrots
Sherry Trifle or Crème Brûlée with Raspberries
Earl Grey Tea or Demitasse
Café Brûlot or Coffee

After the meal, Shannon invited two senior members of the U.S. delegation to join him for tea. The men promptly took their seats across the aisle. Known to be a man who did not mince words, the secretary of state wanted to finalize their strategy for handling the details of the summit before they arrived in London.

Shannon thoroughly relished his cabinet position—primarily for the prestige it afforded, but also because of the perks and personal attention he received. He desperately wanted this meeting to be another milestone in his illustrious career. The men mapped out their detailed plans and then returned to their seats for the final phase of the flight.

By the time the triple-seven came to a smooth stop at Heathrow, everyone had smiles on their faces, including the gracious flight attendants. The passengers agreed the standard of service on the flight was truly impeccable, first rate in every category.

Now it was time for Secretary Shannon and his delegation to prepare for the prime minister's reception at the Dorchester. The prestigious hotel overlooking Hyde Park and the boating lake known as The Serpentine was a favorite of the well heeled. Shannon looked forward to the evening and the multitude of photo opportunities. He was always treated well by the British press, and he expected this evening would be no exception. And, of course, the American journalists accompanying Shannon had been carefully selected to project the best image for both their secretary of state and the TCC conference.

Queen Mary 2

Renowned for her generous size and truly majestic style, Cunard's reigning monarch was about to get under way from Southampton, Britain's second largest commercial port. Corks were popping in the Champagne Bar as passengers toasted a bon voyage with crystal flutes. The 5 P.M. sailing to New York City was a festive affair that highlighted the beginning of another glamorous Atlantic crossing.

Indeed, affluent travelers from an earlier era had coined the word *posh* (port out, starboard home) to describe the preferred cabin location when sailing from London or New York City. Many booked their cabins and suites years in advance, including passengers who circled the globe each year on a worldwide adventure. Some even brought their personal assistants along to attend to their every need.

A bastion of civilization and luxurious surroundings, the Cunard flagship fulfilled with calm assurance an atmosphere that is best depicted as splendidly British. From her maiden voyage, the one and only *Queen Mary 2* consistently set the highest standard for transatlantic service.

Aboard the culturally sophisticated *QM2,* informal dress for meals required jacket and tie for men, cocktail dress or dressy pantsuit for women. Formal dress signaled a tuxedo, or at minimum a dark business suit with a conservative tie and black shoes, evening gowns or other formal attire for women. On rare occasions a celebrity or Hollywood notable would defy the dress code, but the majority of guests appreciated the commitment to maritime excellence.

In the intimate atmosphere of the Queen's Grill Lounge, Brett Shannon, the consummate bachelor, was engaged in lively conversation with his fellow passengers. The elegant watering house was reserved exclusively for travelers who selected the most lavish accommodations. Secretly, Shannon was thrilled to be where tycoons, royalty, sports legends, movie stars, and other world-famous celebrities routinely gathered to enjoy the privileged realm of ocean travel.

He had been equally thrilled by the prime minister's warm reception at the Dorchester, truly the embodiment of goodwill and fellowship. The evening was a genuine success, with many old friendships renewed and new friendships formed. In addition to the camaraderie, Shannon was pleasantly surprised that a few original ideas were advanced about curtailing international terrorism.

The Queen's Grill Lounge was almost filled to capacity while the captain and his seasoned crew prepared to get under way. Basking in the limelight of the moment, Shannon played to the other passengers. He regaled them with stories about the White House and life inside the Beltway. They, in turn, seemed to enjoy rubbing elbows with the powerful and influential U.S. secretary of state.

Shannon took in a deep breath of unbridled satisfaction and slowly let it out. Tonight he would relax and enjoy the great ship's unmatched elegance and traditions. Tomorrow would be soon enough to address the complex issues awaiting the international members of the Terrorism Coalition Council.

When the spectacular liner slipped her moorings and got under way on her six-day voyage, some of the members of the U.S. and British delegations left the lounge to walk along the observation deck. While the resplendent liner gathered speed, the strolling passengers absorbed her faint rhythms and breathed in the fresh sea air. For one and all, the excitement was contagious.

Once the liner cleared the channel leading to Southampton, she would pass the Isle of Wight before proceeding southwest through the English Channel to the deep waters of the Atlantic. The captain and his senior officers never tired of these back-and-forth voyages between New York City and London. There were always interesting passengers aboard the *QM2,* and engaging sea stories to share over a pint of lager in the neighborhood pub.

Concluding a lengthy stroll on Deck 7, Secretary Shannon and his senior staff repaired to the Queen's Grill for cocktails and dinner. The elegant restaurant was well known for its epicurean masterpieces. After the sumptuous feast, Shannon and his fraternity brothers gathered at the Chart Room for a nightcap. The cabaret singer spent the better part of an hour entertaining them with marvelous renditions of Gershwin tunes.

The Queen Mary Suite

The sun was well above the horizon when Brett Shannon opened his eyes and looked around his extravagant quarters. It took a few seconds to orient himself to his surroundings. The pleasant memories of the previous evening flashed through his mind. *This is the way to travel: the only way.* The gentle motion of the ship, combined with the alcohol, had produced the most restful sleep he could remember. Located on the forward port side of Deck 10, Shannon's room, the Queen Mary Suite, was among the *QM2*'s most lavish accommodations. Forward of his spacious quarters were the Queen Anne Suite and the Queen Victoria Suite, widely considered to be among the finest accommodations on the ship. Across from Shannon's quarters was the Queen Elizabeth Suite.

He ordered chilled orange juice, Kona coffee, and fresh croissants from room service and began preparing for the conference. Forty-five minutes later, Shannon finished his juice, shaved, and slipped into one of his business suits.

The secretary joined members of his staff for a final briefing before they joined their counterparts. He intended to keep the meetings short and focused—three hours in the morning, followed by a leisurely lunch, then two hours in the afternoon—for three days. After that, everyone would be free to enjoy the remainder of the voyage.

Fort Worth, Texas

Scott Dalton was taking in the stylish decor in the legendary Reata at Sundance Square. Located in downtown Fort Worth's premier dining and entertainment district, the highly acclaimed eatery was a landmark name among Southwestern restaurants.

With its Old West motif, Texas-sized furnishings, and original murals, Reata was a favorite gathering place for local legends, cowboy poets, millionaire cattlemen, oil barons, and genuine rodeo hands. Today's lunch crowd, some dressed in business attire and some wearing cowboy chic, was colorful and animated.

Scott and Jackie had arrived at Dallas/Fort Worth International Airport the previous evening to be in position for an early morning flight department audit for a corporate client.

When they completed their review, they briefed the company CEO and his vice president of operations on their findings, signed the necessary documentation, and then headed for the restaurant to kill some time. At two o'clock, they were scheduled to take delivery of their new airplane at Fort Worth Meacham International Airport, situated five miles northwest of downtown Fort Worth.

Scott surveyed the other patrons and then turned his attention to Jackie. Slim and athletic, Jackie Sullivan was Scott's partner, in life as well as in their corporate aviation consulting business.

Noticing Scott's attentive eyes, Jackie turned the tines of her fork down and placed it across her plate. As was her custom, she left a small amount of her entrée and side dishes untouched.

"Dessert?" Scott asked.

"Thanks, but I can't eat another bite."

"They're famous for their pecan pie."

"I'm saving myself for this evening." Her gray-green eyes sparkled with anticipation. "Monterey, here we come."

"And tomorrow we're off to Hawaii," Scott confirmed.

"Off to Hawaii in our *own* jet." She reached for his hand and gently squeezed it. "No more long lines, security hassles, or missed connections, no air rage, and no lost luggage."

"Say hallelujah," he said, with a smile.

Scott Johnston Dalton, a former U.S. Marine Corps Harrier pilot, was a descendant of a Confederate general and the son of a retired marine corps brigadier. Standing six feet tall, he had dark hair, broad shoulders, and piercing blue eyes that exuded confidence.

After his active duty commitment to the marine corps, Scott reported to the Central Intelligence Agency for initial training. During his stint at the Agency, he gained recognition in a short period of time. However, the internal politics and turf wars finally drove him out of the organization. Regarded as one of the CIA's best and brightest, Scott's impending departure from the Agency was noticed at the White House.

The president and his closest adviser had watched Scott develop into a first-rate counterterrorism expert. They did not want to lose his blend of marine corps and CIA training, natural flying ability, honed parachuting skills, and other extraordinary capabilities. He was a highly dedicated, motivated, and resourceful operative. Hartwell Prost, the president's national security adviser, was dispatched to offer Dalton a plum position, albeit a dangerous one. After mulling the offer and weighing the odds, Scott accepted the challenge. He would be an off-the-record covert operator working directly for Prost.

As a private citizen with no ties to the U.S. government, Scott would conduct special operations on behalf of the White House. Only President Cord Macklin, Hartwell Prost, and his senior aide would know about the clandestine arrangement. Dalton would be operating outside the boundaries of congressional-oversight requirements that often hamper covert CIA operations.

Scott would be free to circumvent the obstacles that might prove embarrassing to President Macklin, the departments of Justice and State, the Central Intelligence Agency, or the Pentagon. His primary objective on any assignment was to leave no fingerprints, no record of any kind, and certainly no sensational headlines. If anything went wrong, Macklin and Prost would disavow any knowledge of him. The risk factor was high, but Prost assured him the reward was commensurate with the risks.

Scott had met Jackie by chance at an elegant restaurant in Georgetown. She was unaware that Scott was a former CIA counterterrorism strike-force team leader. Likewise, he was unaware that Jackie was a clandestine intelligence officer with the Defense Human Intelligence Service. Their initial conversation was about being former military fighter pilots. They had spent the majority of the evening exchanging their humorous experiences in the service, and afterward, when Scott invited Jackie to go sailing the following weekend, she accepted. Much to his disappointment, he was called away two days later for a covert operation in Buenos Aires. He attempted to contact Jackie at her home, but her phone recorder was not working.

While Scott was on assignment in Argentina, his maid discarded the cocktail napkin on which he had scribbled Jackie's unlisted telephone number. When Scott returned to Washington, he continued to frequent the dining establishment where he and Jackie met. Unfortunately, the dark-haired beauty never reappeared.

By happenstance, they were reunited less than a year later by Hartwell Prost. He enlisted their collective assistance to rescue one of Jackie's closest colleagues at the Defense Human Intelligence Service. Working alone, under deep cover, Jackie's friend was trapped in Lebanon, surrounded by hard-core terrorists in the Bekaa Valley.

After Scott and Jackie returned from the hazardous rescue mission, they explored the idea of joining forces to capitalize on their combined skills. Scott needed a dedicated and qualified pilot to assist him. He and his partner had to think alike, instinctively knowing what the other person was going to do at any given moment.

Working under great stress and pressure, they had to have implicit trust in each other. There was no question in Scott's mind: Jackie was that person. After surviving the Bekaa Valley operation, they solidified their mutual trust and allegiance. The chemistry between them was beyond improvement.

Jackie was an unusually gifted aviator in both fixed-wing and helicopter aircraft. Her clandestine background, language skills, high-speed driving ability, calmness under fire, and military training as an F-16 fighter jock made her perfect for the job.

After discussing the concept at length, they approached Hartwell Prost with their suggestion. Three days later, aboard *Marine One* en route to Camp David, Prost presented the idea to the president, who endorsed the merger.

Operating as The Dalton & Sullivan Group, Incorporated, Jackie and Scott formed a legitimate aviation-consulting firm located near Ronald Reagan National Airport and hired a full-time secretary to mind the office. Mary Beth Collins was a bright, vivacious self-starter who had the office humming from day one.

Between special assignments and sensitive field operations for Prost, Scott and Jackie conducted their consulting business in a professional manner. Subtleties from a few new clients confirmed what they suspected from the day their firm was incorporated. The growing business was getting good press from someone with a lot of influence at the highest level of the U.S. government. Undoubtedly Hartwell was behind the steady increase in blue-chip clients.

Jackie studied Scott's face. "You look like you're ready to launch from the catapult in Zone-Five burner."

"Is it that obvious?" He smiled and shifted in his seat.

"Yes, but I don't blame you. I feel the same way: can't wait to get my hands on *our* plane."

He checked his watch. "It's not like we take delivery of a new Gulfstream One Hundred every day."

She raised an eyebrow in good humor. "It's probably normal to be anxious, to want to finalize the deal before we wake up and find out it was only a dream."

"Don't say that," Scott said, with a nervous laugh.

"Well, it *is* going to happen." Jackie leaned closer to him and spoke in a whisper. "We earned it, in spades, and we're going to put it to good use."

"For business *and* pleasure," he added.

"Our magic carpet."

Scott smiled with pure satisfaction. "No more torture sessions at the hands of the baggage screeners."

A mild sigh of relief escaped Jackie's lips. "That and being crammed into a seat designed for a skinny ten-year-old girl."

The couple had earned large fees for completing three dangerous operations for Prost. The sensitive missions involved the People's Republic of China and were critical to U.S. national security. Prost arranged to have the multimillion-dollar checks hand-delivered to Scott and Jackie's personal representative at an offshore bank on Grand Cayman.

Between rum punches and working on their tans, the duo disbursed funds to several investment accounts in the United States. After a five-day vacation on Grand Cayman, Scott and Jackie made arrangements to pay for their new corporate jet. When the transaction was verified, they departed the island paradise for Gulfstream 100 initial training at FlightSafety International located at the Greater Philadelphia/Wilmington Learning Center, New Castle, Delaware. There they received their type ratings and were qualified to fly as PIC (pilot in command) in the Gulfstream 100. Afterward, they returned to Washington, caught up on their mail and phone messages, and then left the following evening for Dallas/Fort Worth.

A midsize jet with an IFR (instrument flight rules) range of 2,950 nautical miles/3,400 statute miles, the Gulfstream 100 is capable of flying nonstop from New York to Los Angeles, or San Francisco to Honolulu, with ample fuel reserves.

They considered a number of jets, but only the Gulfstream 100 met their primary criteria: safety, speed, range, payload, and low operating cost. With an Mmo (maximum Mach) of .875, the corporate jet could cover a lot of territory in a short period of time.

Normally unflappable, Scott's anxiety was growing by the minute. "What do you think?" he asked Jackie. "Want to head to the airport and watch our new plane arrive?"

"Actually, I've been ready since sunrise," Jackie conceded, reaching for her handbag. "Let's get this celebration under way."

"Ditto." Scott signaled their waitress and handed her a credit card. He looked at Jackie and smiled. "Why don't you take us to California, and I'll take the helm to Hawaii?"

"Deal." She returned the smile. "Diplomacy. You're showing steady improvement."

"I aim to please."

Scott waited for his credit card, signed the tab, and then slid Jackie's chair back. "Let's go get our plane."

"On second thought"—she hesitated and caught his eye—"perhaps *you* should fly the first leg."

She can't be serious. "What's the catch?"

"No catch." She appraised him closely. "Just thought I might christen the bar and celebrate our inaugural flight."

"Your choice."

Khaliq Farkas studied the facades of two circa 1880s buildings in the Sundance Square complex. He adjusted an air-conditioning vent in the Buick and lit another American-made cigarette. He placed a remote-control unit on the front seat next to his 9mm Smith & Wesson and waited. Considered one of the world's most dangerous and elusive terrorists, Farkas was a merciless, pathological product of a radical ideological culture, a culture that began shaping his views and beliefs when he was three years old.

Over a period of years, the forcible application of prolonged and intensive indoctrination induced a regimented sense of hatred and cruelty in the teenage Farkas. Extremist political, social, and religious beliefs were deeply ingrained in his young mind. By the time Khaliq Farkas turned sixteen, he had killed his first three infidels with a car bomb.

During the next fifteen years, Farkas and various special action cells of Hezbollah (Islamic Jihad) were responsible for numerous bombings, kidnappings, assassinations, hijackings, extortion plots, money-laundering schemes, and plane crashes.

Operating as a direct extension of Osama bin Laden's al-Qaeda, Farkas had eliminated a number of Jewish religious and political leaders who had close ties to the United States. With strong encouragement and considerable financial backing from bin Laden, Farkas and an accomplice had even attempted to assassinate the U.S. president, an assault that had changed the way *Air Force One* operated.

With Osama bin Laden's influence greatly diminished, Saeed Shayhidi was now calling the shots and providing a continuous flow of operating funds to a handful of terrorist organizations. Farkas, the leader of the most experienced group, was poised to continue his personal jihad against the United States until "Western imperialism" and the cultural pollution of the "Great Satan" were driven from the Persian Gulf. But first the field general had another mission to accomplish, one he had dreamed about for a long time.

Scott Dalton and Jackie Sullivan had caused Farkas much anguish and professional embarrassment, having single-handedly quashed several of his terrorist attempts. Farkas knew he must eliminate the possibility of their involvement *before* Shayhidi's far-ranging plans were set in motion. With revenge paramount in his mind, the feared terrorist was parked only seventy yards from the couple's rental car.

Although no one in Farkas's operation was sure who the mysterious Americans worked for, they were thought to be either special operatives from the CIA or members of some hush-hush experimental military unit. There was one thing Farkas did know: the pair had to be eliminated before they caused more damage.

The American operatives had come to Saeed Shayhidi's attention through his close connections with other extremist groups, foreign and domestic spies, espionage specialists, and well-organized Southeast Asian allies, including the Chinese-based "Four Seas" Triad gang. Jackie and Scott became target number one on many of the bad guys' radarscopes, but trying to get reliable information about them proved to be difficult.

Zheng Yen-Tsung, a senior aide to a former Chinese prime minister who chaired the National People's Congress, had encountered the two operatives in China and sent a detailed description and a sketch of Sullivan and Dalton to half a dozen leaders of major terrorist organizations, including Shayhidi. The description, sketch, and reward for information about the Americans was disseminated to informants throughout the New York City, Newark, Philadelphia, Baltimore, and Washington, D.C., areas.

Zheng spelled out in graphic detail how Dalton and Sullivan had exposed a secret Chinese weapons system. Recuperating from a gunshot wound inflicted by Dalton, Zheng explained that the two operatives must be removed. Through the efforts of Zheng, the People's Liberation Army was offering $7.8 million for the assassination of Sullivan and Dalton.

By chance, the Iranian taxi driver who drove Scott and Jackie from a Georgetown restaurant to Reagan Airport thought he recognized the elusive couple. When he asked them which airline they were flying, Scott confirmed they were booked on American Airlines. In a pleasant manner, the driver tried to cajole the couple into revealing their destination and where they would be staying that evening. When Jackie and Scott deflected the inquiry, the driver formed a new plan.

After he dropped the Americans at the airport, the driver—"on assignment" from an Islamic group—parked his cab and jogged to the terminal building. He checked the departing flights and discovered the last American Airlines flight was scheduled to leave at 7:16 P.M. Flight number 1991 was a nonstop departure to DFW.

He immediately went to the nearest pay telephone, called his contact in Fredericksburg, Virginia, gave him the detailed information, and made arrangements to collect the reward if the couple turned out to be the operatives targeted for assassination.

When Khaliq Farkas was notified at his headquarters in Idaho, he contacted two associates living in the Dallas area. He faxed sketches of the operatives and instructed the men to meet the flight at DFW. The subordinates would confirm Scott's and Jackie's identities and then follow them to wherever they were staying. Farkas ordered his men to remain vigilant until he arrived to relieve them.

Next, Farkas communicated through an intermediary with Saeed Shayhidi. He passionately lobbied for permission to assassinate the pair. Shayhidi gave his approval to proceed with the operation but stressed that it should not interfere with their primary objective. Farkas was a crucial part of their plan. Shayhidi could not risk the possibility of having him captured or killed before the operation was under way. Farkas assured his go-between the assassinations would be uncomplicated and the task would in no way interfere with the master plan. Nothing would be jeopardized by his side trip to Dallas.

Late in the evening, therefore, Farkas gathered his bomb-making equipment and boarded a chartered Citation III bound for Dallas's Love Field. En route, he called his associates, who met American Airlines Flight number 1991. The suspected operatives were staying at the Dallas/Fort Worth Airport Marriott. Due to increased security at airports and airport hotels, it would be foolish to try anything at DFW. Although Farkas preferred not to conduct business in the light of day, he would have to terminate the Americans after they left their hotel.

With the air conditioner running at maximum capacity, Farkas waited for his unsuspecting prey to return to their car. He smoked another cigarette and then extinguished it in the overflowing ashtray. Growing impatient, he was relieved when he saw the couple emerge from the Sundance Square complex and approach their rented Lincoln Continental. *Okay, stay relaxed. Wait until they're inside the car.*

Dressed in navy-blue slacks and a camel-colored silk blouse, Jackie could pass for a top fashion model. As they made their way to the Lincoln, she shifted her purse to her right shoulder. "This time tomorrow we'll be en route to Hawaii."

Scott glanced at the clear Texas sky. "Actually, we'll be getting ready to land in Honolulu."

"Are you sure you don't want to get up before dawn, get an early start?"

"Positive," he said firmly. "Let's take it easy and relax. Remember, we don't have to rush to the airport."

"You're right, I'm still in airline mode."

Farkas rested his finger on the trigger of the remote-control unit and waited for the couple to enter the Lincoln. A faint smile crossed his ruddy face as Scott and Jackie neared their car. *Look at them—not a care in the world.*

Without warning, a police officer approached Farkas's car and tapped his knuckles on the driver's window. Startled, Farkas's right hand prematurely triggered the potent explosive. The shiny Lincoln was instantaneously engulfed in a huge fireball, at the same moment that Farkas reached for his Smith & Wesson.

He shot the stunned patrolman twice, shifted the Buick into gear, and floored the accelerator. Shards of the driver's window shattered along the street. He fishtailed around a corner, bounced off a parked car, and disappeared in heavy traffic.

Sonofabitch! He was furious, banging the steering wheel and cursing nonstop. The beginnings of fear crept into his mind. It was all he could do to force himself to slow down and blend in with the other cars. *How can this be? Has Allah put a curse on me?*

The thunderous, reverberating explosion lifted the heavy Lincoln three feet off the pavement, ripping it to pieces. Scott forced Jackie to the ground and sprawled on top of her, trying to protect her from the falling debris. Metal parts and glass flew in every direction, ricocheting off parked cars and raining down on the street. Even sheltered by other automobiles, Jackie and Scott could feel the heat from the blast thirty yards away.

His ears ringing, Scott automatically reached for his 9mm Sig Sauer; then, realizing the threat was gone, he shoved it back into its concealed holster. He helped Jackie to her feet, and they stared in silence at the demolished car. The main bulk of the Lincoln, frame, engine, transmission, and three wheels, was sitting at a 45-degree angle to the parking space. The pavement underneath was scorched a charcoal-brownish color. One tire was burning while the other three smoldered, sending a thick plume of black smoke billowing into the blue sky, which drifted away on the warm Texas wind.

Still shocked by the deafening explosion, Scott took Jackie by the shoulders and surveyed her from head to toe. "Are you okay?"

She swallowed once, looking dazed. "Yeah, I think so, but I can't hear." Jackie brushed herself off and wiped a trickle of blood from a superficial wound on her forearm.

Wide-eyed, Scott stared at the smoking wreckage for a few seconds, then turned to Jackie. "That was close—*Sweet Jesus.*" He looked around the immediate area. "Any ideas?"

Still coming to grips, Jackie glanced at the wide pattern of smoking debris. "Zheng Yen-Tsung has to be involved."

"Yeah, he doesn't give up easily."

"Are you sure you didn't kill him?"

"Yes, I'm sure. I shot him in the leg."

She recalled an earlier encounter with Zheng Yen-Tsung. "Think about the—what did Hartwell call the bomb under our car in Pensacola?"

"A Wile E. Coyote bomb," he said, in a louder than normal voice. "It would have blown us into the Gulf of Mexico."

"Well, it's certainly Zheng's MO."

They walked toward the bystanders gathering around the remains of their rental car. Jackie and Scott noticed another group of people hurrying to assist someone lying on the pavement. Scott glanced down the street. "There's an empty police car parked over there. Where's the cop who belongs to the car?"

"Good question."

A moment later, a young man yelled that a police officer was shot. A woman running toward the scene responded that she was a doctor.

Jackie looked at the downed patrolman. "I don't know how this went down, but he probably saved our lives."

"I'd bet on it." Scott watched while the physician worked to stem the bleeding from the policeman's wounds. "I hope he pulls through."

"Yeah, what a nightmare."

Scott saw another cruiser, lights flashing and siren screeching, pull up behind the empty patrol car. The officer jumped out and ran toward his fallen colleague. Behind the cruiser, a Fox News television van came to an abrupt stop.

Scott turned to Jackie and lowered his voice. "The last thing we need is national news exposure."

"That's *exactly* what we don't need."

They watched an ambulance race toward the chaotic scene, followed by two fire trucks. The firefighters carefully approached the smoldering car and began extinguishing the blaze. A muffled explosion from the Lincoln startled the bystanders and the firemen.

Jackie opened her handbag and retrieved her satellite phone. "We better let Prost know what happened. The FBI needs to jump on this as quickly as possible, put a lid on it before it goes national."

"You're right." Scott watched the ambulance drive away, lights flashing and siren emitting a piercing warning signal. "Zheng isn't going to give up. He'll try again."

Jackie nodded. "We have to be prepared for him day and night, never let our guard down."

"We better focus on tracking him: get on the offense and stay focused."

"I agree," she said evenly. "We have to take the fight directly to him, keep him guessing and under pressure, force him to make a mistake."

Scott gave her a puzzled look. "Something seems strange, out of focus."

"I'm not following you."

"Why would Zheng risk entering this country again? He knows the FBI and many other jurisdictions are waiting to pounce on him."

"Maybe the guy isn't firing on all cylinders," Jackie offered, handing Scott the satellite phone. "He's like a hubristic little poltergeist, a shadowy ghost we can't seem to shake." She opened her handbag and retrieved a small package of tissues. "Try Prost while I go brush the glass out of my hair."

"What if it wasn't Zheng?"

"Then we have a huge problem." She motioned toward their smoldering car. "That wasn't a coincidence."

3

The Winslow Estate

The sprawling European-style mansion in Maryland was home to Hartwell Huntington Prost IV, the president's renowned national security adviser and close friend for many years. The manicured grounds and immaculate residence reflected the comfortable lifestyle of the owner, one that included Harvard Law, triannual vacations to exotic destinations, and a pristine 82-foot Hatteras motor yacht moored next to a palatial second home in Palm Beach, Florida. Prost's family heritage of wealth and privilege dated back to the early 1800s, when Earl Digby Gardiner Prost founded a banking and investment empire in Boston.

Intelligent and clinically analytical, Hartwell Prost was the president's closest aide and most trusted confidant. Considered a Renaissance man by most of his associates, Prost was a soft-spoken gentleman who appeared to be the quintessential Ivy League college professor. Although he was the consummate well-mannered man, Prost was best known for his unyielding adherence to his principles. When warranted, he did not hesitate to take anyone to task, including the president of the United States.

Wearing his ever-present tam-o'-shanter, Prost sat astride one of his prized Appaloosas. He had just completed a thorough inspection of his 37 acres of property in prime Maryland hunt country. After a chat with the groundskeepers, Hartwell gently steered the horse to the private avenue leading to his home. Halfway to the residence his satellite phone rang. He brought Curly to a stop under the long canopy of trees and answered the call.

"Prost."

"Mr. Prost? Scott Dalton."

"Scott, how are you?"

"Could be better." Dalton brought him up to date on the assassination attempt. He told Hartwell that Zheng Yen-Tsung might be behind it, although it was speculation at this point.

"I'll call Jim Ebersole and have him look into it." Ebersole was the current director of the FBI. "We'll make sure nothing unfavorable gets into the press."

"Thank you, sir. We appreciate it."

"No problem." Hartwell urged Curly to continue walking. "I

must say, the possibility that Zheng might be in the country surprises me."

"Same here. Wouldn't think he'd have a chance of getting in with the increased security."

"Right." Hartwell patted Curly on the neck. "The INS is watching everyone like a hawk."

"Then again, we know he's capable of beating almost any system."

"True, he *is* well connected." Reflecting on the administration's continuing efforts to suppress international terrorism, Prost elected not to bring Dalton into the loop on the latest intelligence reports. Like everything else, satellite phones could be monitored. "When you and Jackie have an opportunity, why don't you plan to visit me here at Winslow."

"Sure. Is it urgent?"

"Yes, I would say so. We've had some disturbing news, and I'd like to discuss it with the two of you in person. We may be looking at another project in the immediate future."

Project was Hartwell's euphemism for covert operation.

"Yes, sir." *Forget Hawaii.* "How about late tomorrow afternoon?"

"That sounds fine. Plan on dinner here."

"We'll be there."

After Scott finished his conversation with Prost, he handed the phone to Jackie. "We're clear on the bomb deal, but we may be reporting for duty in the near future."

She rolled her eyes heavenward. "It figures. What's the latest?"

"He asked us to visit him at home."

"When?"

"I suggested late tomorrow afternoon." He braced for the inevitable storm surge.

Her hands on her hips, she didn't blink an eyelash. "Pardon me, but the last time I checked, Maryland wasn't en route to Hawaii."

"I know." Scott raised both palms in a calming gesture. "I suggest we take delivery of our plane, fly to Monterey, have a great dinner, and take in the nightlife. Tomorrow morning we'll head for Baltimore and find out what's on Prost's mind."

In her heart, Jackie knew the request was important. Her voice was tempered with disappointment, but she smiled. "Here we go again. Perfect timing."

"Hey, depending on what happens in Maryland, we can reschedule our departure. That's why we have our own jet. Flexibility to travel whenever we want."

A cool smile edged her lips. "Okay, I'll buy that. We *are* going to Hawaii as soon as possible, right?"

He smiled in return. "No argument from me, but responsibility *is* the nature of our business."

"How well I know," she said, resigned to the inevitable. "Did Hartwell say what he wants to discuss?"

"No, no details over the phone, but I would bet it has something to do with the ongoing terrorist situation. Probably some new development we aren't aware of."

Jackie remained quiet for a moment and then shook her head. "I don't know whether to laugh or curse."

"What?"

"Do you realize we don't have any clothes?"

"It crossed my mind."

"We don't have anything except what we're wearing."

Scott tried unsuccessfully to keep a straight face. "All those endless hours shopping with you, the new custom-made luggage, the shoes, the wardrobe update, and the . . ." He trailed off, laughing. "And now everything has been incinerated or blown halfway to Dallas."

"I don't think it's funny," she managed to say, before she had to smother a laugh. "You may think it's funny, but our en-route charts and approach plates are charcoaled confetti like everything else. So are our new life raft and the laptop."

"Hey, don't worry about it." He draped a reassuring arm over her shoulder. "We'll get new charts at the FBO. Besides, we won't need a life raft this trip."

She raised a brow. "We can only hope."

Scott watched the firemen hose down the blackened, twisted

wreck. "Let's grab a taxi and do a little shopping before we go to the airport."

"Yeah, all we need is everything," she deadpanned.

"Let's be thankful for what we have."

"I know." Her grin changed to a wide smile. "I'm a tad short on patience at the moment."

The crowd was dissipating when Jackie and Scott began walking toward Sundance Square to call a taxi. Scott reached into his pocket and tossed something into a trash container. "Sayonara."

"What was that?"

"The keys to our rental car."

When Jackie and Scott arrived at Texas Jet, their gleaming G-100, N957GA, was already sitting on the ramp waiting for them. They paid the cabdriver and hauled their meager luggage to the airplane. Three representatives from Gulfstream walked out of the fixed-base-operator's lounge to meet the new owners.

The aircraft's sleek fuselage and long curved wings reinforced the feeling that the Gulfstream 100 was a hot performer. With the engines mounted on each side of the tail and winglets accentuating the tips of the wings, the G-100 was the picture of aerodynamic efficiency. It could take off at a maximum gross weight of 24,650 pounds on a standard day (mean sea level, 760 millimeters pressure, 15 degrees Centigrade) and climb directly to 41,000 feet.

The wings and the bottom of the long fuselage were bright metallic red. The tops of the cabin, engines, and tail were white, as were the winglets. The side number was emblazoned in red on the sides of the white engine nacelles. The staff at Gulfstream's headquarters had done their job well. N957GA was shining like a diamond with new tires all around.

The spotless interior was stocked with a wide variety of snacks, soft drinks, and adult beverages. The cabin consisted of a four-seat club arrangement with two additional seats and a comfortable couch across from the galley. A totally enclosed stand-up lavatory with hot and cold water taps was located at the back of the cabin.

Jackie decided to stow their duffel bags in the roomy passenger cabin. Along with new clothes, shoes, and toiletries, they also had purchased two laptop computers to replace the one destroyed in the explosion.

Most of the reams of paperwork involved in transferring ownership of N957GA had been completed ahead of time. After everything else was signed in Texas Jet's conference room, Scott and Jackie thanked the Gulfstream representatives. They posed for the obligatory photographs next to the jet and shook hands with the smiling company officials.

Jackie ordered fuel, checked the en-route weather, filed an instrument flight plan to Monterey, and completed a thorough preflight check of the plane. Scott purchased the charts they would need and called Sporty's Pilot Shop. He ordered a new chart case and a complete set of IFR en-route high altitude charts and terminal procedures publications. The order also included a new top-of-the-line quick-inflating nine-man life raft and nine twin-cell airline-type life vests.

Once they boarded their new jet, Scott activated the electrical power, checked ATIS (automatic terminal information service), and called Clearance Delivery. After he copied their instrument clearance and read it back to the controller, Jackie was ready to start the right engine. She placed the throttle in IDLE detent, placed the fuel switch in AUTO, and pushed the START button. Scott called Ground Control for permission to taxi.

While they taxied to the active runway, Jackie exercised the thrust reversers and set the flaps to 12 degrees. Scott started the left engine and completed the takeoff checklist, including computing their V-speeds, and then called the tower for permission to take off.

After they were cleared, Jackie checked the panel for anomalies and taxied onto the centerline of the runway. She rolled her eyes toward Scott. "You ready to rock and roll?" she asked with a grin.

"Flog it."

Jackie pushed the throttles into the takeoff detent. The

AlliedSignal TFE-731 turbofans rapidly spooled up, and the rudder was effective almost immediately. The lightly loaded G-100 accelerated almost like a fighter plane. Jackie eased the yoke back at Vr (rotation speed) and placed the nose smoothly in the takeoff attitude. When the jet was safely airborne, the landing gear was retracted, followed by the flaps as the airspeed increased.

The airplane quickly reached 200 knots and Jackie reduced power to level off at their assigned altitude of 3,000 feet. Once cleared to continue their ascent, she set the throttles in the climb detent. Flying at precisely 250 knots, the jet was climbing over 3,000 feet per minute through 10,000 feet.

She glanced at Scott. "Pinch me."

"I feel the same way, keep waiting to wake up."

"Think I'll just hand-fly it."

"You're the chief."

The Fort Worth Center controller cleared the G-100 on course and directed them to climb to 35,000 feet.

Scott keyed the radio. "On course and up to three-five-oh, Fifty-seven Golf Alfa."

After Jackie leveled the plane at 35,000 feet, she watched a Southwest Airlines Boeing 737 pass over them going the opposite direction at 37,000 feet. She could not remember a day in her life that had been punctuated with such contrasts. The images flashed through her mind like a slide presentation, ending where it began, with their demolished rental car engulfed in flames. She forced her thoughts back to the present. "What's our plan for dealing with Zheng Yen-Tsung?"

"It may not have been him."

"If it wasn't him, we had better find out who it was, like ASAP."

"Gulfstream Nine-Five-Seven Golf Alfa, climb to and maintain Flight Level three-nine-zero."

Scott keyed the radio. "Up to three-nine-oh, Fifty-seven Golf Alfa."

While Jackie initiated a gradual climb, he organized their charts for Monterey. "Let's see how much information Hartwell and Jim Ebersole come up with, and then we can formulate a sound plan."

She tweaked the altitude select to 39,000 feet. "The sooner, the better."

They were handed off to Albuquerque Air Route Traffic Control Center near Clovis, New Mexico, and then switched to Los Angeles Center north of Flagstaff, Arizona.

Lost in his own thoughts about the car bombing, Scott looked out the side window and took in the beauty of Lake Powell and its surrounding vistas. They remained silent as the jet raced the setting sun. The Gulfstream was slowly losing the contest.

The activity in the cockpit increased when they neared the restricted air space north of Edwards AFB. Los Angeles Center rerouted N957GA down a jet airway to an intersection east of Monterey and then cleared the G-100 for the approach to Runway 28-Left at the Monterey Peninsula Airport.

Located at the southern end of Monterey Bay, the historic city is well known for its Monterey Jazz Festival. It is also a favorite retreat for artists and writers. Monterey formed the background for several novels, including John Steinbeck's *Tortilla Flat* and *Cannery Row.*

With the airport in sight, Jackie canceled IFR and made a visual approach to a soft landing on the trailing link main gear. She taxied the plane to the Monterey Jet Center, a popular quick-turn fixed base operator for corporate jets en route to Hawaii or Asia. The friendly professional staff helped them secure the airplane for the evening and provided them with a complimentary crew car.

After checking into the Monterey Plaza Hotel, Scott and Jackie refreshed themselves and went to the Duck Club Restaurant for dinner. The sun was dipping below the horizon when the couple left the restaurant. Hand in hand, they strolled along Cannery Row, finally stopping at a park bench. They sat down and took in the view of Monterey Bay while the shimmering sun disappeared.

"You've been unusually quiet this evening," Jackie noted, leaning next to him. "What's on your mind?"

"How close we came. . . ."

"Same here—can't shake it."

He cast a lingering look at the tranquil bay. "If we assume Zheng Yen-Tsung was the bomber, either he was personally tracking us or someone was feeding him information about our whereabouts."

She turned to him. "I don't want to think about it tonight, okay? We need a distraction."

"Yeah, enough of this," Scott said, rising to his feet. "Let's go find some entertainment."

Monterey Peninsula Airport, California

Carrying a heavy load of jet fuel, over 9,100 pounds at the threshold of the takeoff roll, N957GA was wheels-in-the-wells the next morning at 7:32 A.M. Pacific Time. Scott had filed an instrument flight plan from Monterey nonstop to Baltimore Washington International. Prior to takeoff, he had made arrangements for a rental car at Signature Flight Support, BWI's fixed base operator.

The 2,130-nautical-mile trip would be a breeze for the Gulfstream 100, especially with an assist from the jet stream. There were thunderstorms brewing over Kansas and Nebraska, but they would not develop fully until later in the day.

After a couple of altitude holds for conflicting traffic, the G-100 was cleared to climb to 41,000 feet. When they leveled off at their cruise altitude, Scott set the power for .82 Mach and studied the avionics suite in the state-of-the-art cockpit.

"Would you like some coffee?" Jackie asked, unfastening her seat restraints.

"Sure, thanks."

She stepped into the passenger cabin, went to the galley, fixed two cups of the Monterey Jet Center's freshly brewed coffee, and handed one to Scott. Returning to the cabin, Jackie sat down in the four-seat club arrangement and fastened her seat belt. She lifted a lightweight table from the enclosure in the sidewall next to her seat.

Unfolding the table, she energized one of their new laptop

computers and brought up the *Fort Worth Star-Telegram*'s Web site. Jackie scrolled down the front page and read only part of the article about the car bombing near Sundance Square in downtown Fort Worth before she unsnapped her seat belt, grabbed the laptop, folded the table, and headed for the cockpit.

"Are you ready for some good news?" she asked.

Scott eyed her distrustfully. "I'm always suspicious of good news this early in the morning."

"I just checked the Fort Worth paper. The policeman who was shot is going to be okay."

A smile flashed across his face. "That's good news—great."

"One round grazed his cheek and the other went through his left shoulder. He's resting comfortably, and the doctors expect him to make a full recovery."

Scott drank the last of his coffee. "We need to see if he can ID Zheng Yen-Tsung from the photos we have."

"Good idea."

"Anything about the investigation who rented the car or why it was blown to kingdom come?"

"Just a second." She quickly scanned the rest of the article. "The FBI is investigating the incident, which they suspect was a case of mistaken identity on behalf of the bomber." She paused and placed a hand on his shoulder. "You're going to love this. 'The couple who rented the Lincoln returned to their home in Alabama and were not available for comment. The FBI said their names were being withheld and would not be made available while the incident is being investigated.' "

Scott glanced at her. "Which means the incident will be under investigation until everyone forgets about it."

"Thank you, Hartwell."

"Speaking of Hartwell, let's try the satcom system. Give him our ETA and add thirty minutes for the drive from the airport."

"I'll take care of it," she said, turning to leave.

"Oh, one other thing," Scott said. "Would you mind canceling our reservations in Hawaii?"

"I canceled them while you were in the shower."

"Gulfstream Nine-Five-Seven Golf Alfa, contact Salt Lake Center on one-three-four point three-five; good day."

Scott keyed the radio. "Salt Lake Center, thirty-four thirty-five; Fifty-seven Golf Alfa."

He checked in with the center and wrote a note to pick up a good bottle of wine on the way to Prost's home.

"We're all set," Jackie said, stepping into the cockpit. "The satcom system works like a dream."

"How's Hartwell doing?"

"Zachary answered the phone. He said Mr. Prost is on his way home from the White House. He will deliver our message the moment Mr. Prost arrives."

Queen Mary 2

On day five of their voyage, Brett Shannon and members of his staff were enjoying tea in the Winter Garden. Afternoon tea is served with white gloves, a tradition of Cunard's White Star Service. Shannon and his aides were partaking of an assortment of scones, finger sandwiches, fresh cream cakes, and warm Darjeeling. Grown in the mountainous districts of northern India, the tea was worthy of the high standards set on the *QM2.*

Relieved that the summit on international terrorism had been a reasonable success, the secretary of state was sampling a wide variety of activities on the ship. He had attended an enrichment program about wine appreciation, perused the quaint library, indulged himself with a seaweed treatment at the Canyon Ranch SpaClub, practiced his golf swing in a simulator, played shuffleboard, visited The Planetarium, and bought presents from a wide variety of Mayfair Shops.

Tonight would be the last hurrah before the mighty ship arrived in New York the next morning at 8 A.M. sharp. Shannon and his staff would dine in the elegant Britannia Restaurant and then assemble in the Royal Court Theatre to watch a Broadway musical. Afterward, they would adjourn to the Commodore's Club for a nightcap while they listened to jazz.

Although he was a wealthy man in his own right, Brett Shannon relished the knowledge that U.S. taxpayers were footing the bill for the extravagant cruise, including the considerable bar charges. Shannon believed that only the best things in life were good enough. He found that especially true when someone else was picking up the tab.

4

Khartoum, East Africa

Khartoum, the capital of the Republic of the Sudan, is located south of the confluence of the Blue Nile and White Nile rivers. Long a hub for international terrorists, Khartoum serves as a safe haven, meeting place, and training center for al-Qaeda (the Base).

A military Islamic fundamentalist regime, Sudan also plays host to the Palestinian Islamic Jihad, Hamas, the Lebanese Hezbollah, the Egyptian Gama'at al-Islamiyya, al-Jihad, and the Abu Nidal organization known as Ghanem Saleh. Other Islamic extremist factions of lesser notoriety have called Khartoum their headquarters for over three decades.

Sudan does more than provide a safe haven for terrorists; Sudan is *the* place to secure a base for organizing terrorist operations. Everything is available to the groups, including weapons, forged travel documentation, and false identification papers. It is a refuge for international fugitives who have been linked to bombings, assassinations, kidnappings, hijackings, and various other atrocities around the world.

A grayish-pink twilight was settling over the sprawling city of Khartoum when a gleaming Boeing Business Jet began its final approach to the international airport. A hybrid of the popular 737 airliner, the privately owned BBJ was a graceful combination of airborne office, conference center, executive stateroom, galley, and entertainment/ dining room.

Equipped with a self-contained air stair under the forward entry door, satellite communications, and computer capability, the airplane combined a work environment with the ambiance of a comfortable vacation home. Capable of nonstop flights over 6,000 nautical miles, the spacious aircraft was considered an ultra-long-range time machine for business leaders.

Saeed Shayhidi, an Iranian shipping magnate, oil trader, investment banker, and international power broker, had recently purchased the lavish corporate jet through a third party based in Bermuda. The negotiations, like many of Shayhidi's transactions, were time-consuming and nerve-racking. Before the deal was finalized, Shayhidi managed to whittle over $2 million off the asking price for the Boeing.

Shayhidi, a multibillionaire, typically enjoyed badgering his opponents to the point of exhaustion. In this instance his adversary was a hard-nosed hard-drinking aircraft broker. The act of haggling was one of Shayhidi's favorite sports: the intellectual version of fencing. Both men would duel again when Shayhidi's newer, larger BBJ-2 was ready for delivery. It would have more powerful engines, a larger passenger cabin, and greater storage capacity in the lower lobe.

The money Shayhidi saved on the initial purchase of the BBJ went into an interior completion that re-created the atmosphere of his château in the Graves district of the Gironde. Not surprising, the wine served aboard the BBJ came from the vineyard adjacent to his château.

The eldest son of a wealthy hotelier who retired in London, Shayhidi was not unlike many successful entrepreneurs. Ivy League–educated, he was extremely shrewd and pernicious. Though hopelessly narcissistic, he was a brilliant tactician in the boardroom. As one might expect, regardless of the location, time, or circumstance, Shayhidi required painstaking care from his throng of personal attendants.

There was another side to Saeed Shayhidi, a much darker side. Unknown to his associates in the business world and the political arena, Shayhidi's influence reached far beyond the boardroom. He was a master terrorist with an obsessive passion that enveloped every aspect of his psyche: the passion to rid Muslim-inhabited lands of Western control and influence.

An entirely new breed of terrorist leader, Shayhidi was less dependent on state or political sponsorship and more dependent on his own sizable financial empire. This understated leadership arrangement was accomplished with a minimum of one or two intermediaries, allowing him to remain a comfortable distance from the disreputable individuals who actually carried out his orders.

Shayhidi's hatred of Americans and their culture began during his first year at Princeton University. Initially, the transformation was insidious, but it rapidly began to affect every aspect of his life. Shayhidi's fiery personality and cantankerous attitude provoked uneasiness and annoyance among his fellow students. By the beginning of his sophomore year both students and faculty, for the most part, quietly shunned the wealthy Iranian. Two weeks into his junior year, Shayhidi desperately wanted to leave school and return home to Iran. Much to his dismay, his father insisted he remain at Princeton and receive a proper education. Grudgingly, he stayed the course and became a recluse.

During the many years after Shayhidi's graduation from Princeton, his disdain for the American people expanded to include contempt for their powerful military. Over a period of five years, with no direct ties to Osama bin Laden, Khalid Sheikh Mohammed, Bassam Shakhar, or any other prominent Islamic zealot, Shayhidi managed to recruit dozens of key members of al-Qaeda and other well-known terrorist factions. With Bassam Shakhar dead from a massive stroke, and the al-Qaeda organization in disarray, Saeed Shayhidi felt compelled to accept the mantle of authority and leadership in the jihad against American imperialism.

Shayhidi's lieutenants, like himself, were well educated, neat, and wholesome-looking. They were a diverse group of individuals representing many nationalities, dressed in expensive clothes from top-drawer designers in Europe and America. The men—and women—comported themselves as successful people. Polar opposites of the archetypical Middle Eastern terrorist, this coalition of operatives could easily pass for executives from multinational corporations. They were as skilled at acting as they were ruthless in carrying out their deadly attacks.

Saeed Shayhidi's approach to terrorism discarded the medieval mind-set that so many of his counterparts desperately clung to. Unlike other militant extremists, Shayhidi would never descend to carrying AK-47s around the desert or taking refuge in dismal caves. He laughed at the notion of roaming the bumpy strife-worn crossroads of Central Asia with an entourage of ragamuffins.

To the contrary, Shayhidi carefully crafted the persona of a nonreligious no-nonsense business titan. In stark contrast to his fundamentalist colleagues, he almost always had a beautiful woman on his arm. He would often take five or six striking women on lavish European shopping sprees, staged for public consumption. European tabloids, concentrating on sensational news and gossip, always covered these excursions.

Shayhidi dined with royalty, played golf with heads of state, and entertained Hollywood's elite on his yacht. He sponsored private economic summits with the most powerful men and women in the world, none of whom suspected his involvement with terrorism.

He lived in the lap of luxury with unrestrained gratification. Always clean-shaven and impeccably attired, he maintained distinctively different penthouses in Hong Kong, London, Paris, and Sydney. Because he spent much of his time traveling, he leased spacious suites in some of the most prestigious hotels in the world. Suites and other services in his family-owned hotels were, of course, complimentary.

His meticulously constructed homes were stately in size and design. One of the imposing residences contained a narrow indoor river running through a rain forest, a bird sanctuary, and an extensive art gallery that showcased Pablo Picasso, Jean Dubuffet, and a variety of French beaux arts. The mansion had three indoor waterfalls, four guest suites with his-and-her bathrooms, two gourmet kitchens, and two Japanese arched bridges leading to a lagoonlike swimming pool surrounded by powdery white sand.

Shayhidi was instrumental in bringing the ruthless Khartoum-Moscow-Beijing coalition together to fully take advantage of Sudan's vast energy resources. With generous succor from Communist China and the Russian Federation, he intended to drive the United States and its vaunted military, the "God-less West," out of Muslim-dominated countries and out of the waters of the Persian Gulf. Beijing and Moscow were quite pleased to help, viewing this as an opportunity to keep the U.S. military off balance.

While Russia and China "fully cooperated" with the U.S.-led war on terrorism, they quietly funneled money and arms to augment Shayhidi's terrorist organization. The complex financial web, which included Middle Eastern and South American banks, front companies, charities, and underground brokers, provided hundreds of millions of dollars for his jihad against the United States.

Unlike many of his predecessors, Shayhidi and the experienced leaders of his terrorist cells would take no credit for the devastating attacks they were planning. The anonymous assaults in the contiguous United States were designed to leave the U.S. president, authorities at the CIA and the FBI, law enforcement professionals, and the Pentagon brass in a quandary.

Washington would be unable to assign responsibility for the violent and destructive attacks, thereby neutralizing or reducing any military retaliation or economic sanctions. The master plan, the Destiny Project, had been in the developmental stage for over six years.

Unfortunately, Operation Iraqi Freedom scrambled the time frame of Shayhidi's ambitious plan. Incensed by the overthrow of Saddam Hussein and what the regime change portended, Shayhidi had to confront the future. He was determined to destroy the Americans' ability to restructure the Middle East in the mold of Western democracy.

The United States had to be annihilated, reduced to utter ruin, with no political effect, no measurable military force, and no relevance in shaping the world order. Now, after many months of reorganizing his priorities, Shayhidi's highly detailed Destiny Project was ready for implementation.

On board his plane in Khartoum, Shayhidi would meet with his senior leaders to initiate a concerted effort to wreak havoc on the Americans and their military forces. To Shayhidi's way of thinking, the well-orchestrated attack on the World Trade Center, the Pentagon, and the crashed jet in Pennsylvania, while a rousing success for the cause, stopped far short of achieving his ultimate objective: the total destruction of America.

Now, after training more homicidal recruits and energizing hundreds of sleepers in the United States, Mexico, and Canada, it was time to capitalize on their first perceived triumphant victory over America. Shayhidi and his followers fervently believed this was the opportune time to finish the job. Time to paralyze the United States and bring its people to their knees in total submission to Allah.

It was the intent of Shayhidi and his coterie of cell leaders to cause disruptions so severe and to generate such psychological terror throughout the United States that the vast majority of Americans would cower in fear. Shayhidi was brazenly confident the American people would then confront President Macklin and demand an immediate cessation of hostilities toward any Muslim country.

Gulfstream N957GA

The flight to the East Coast was pleasant, and the jet touched down at Baltimore Washington International a few minutes before 3 P.M. local time. Clearing the runway, Scott taxied the airplane to Signature Flight Support. When the aircraft came to a halt, a customer service representative drove their Avis rental car to the cabin entrance.

Although the Gulfstream 100 had enough fuel for the short flight to Dulles International, N957GA's new home airport, Scott purchased 250 gallons of Jet A as a courtesy to the fixed base operator.

The Winslow Estate

When Scott and Jackie arrived at the residence of Hartwell Prost, his butler of long standing answered the door. A trim distinguished-looking gentleman with impeccable manners, Zachary always had a genial smile to offer guests.

"Miss Sullivan, Mr. Dalton—what a pleasure to see you again."

"It's good to see you," Scott said, while Jackie extended her arms.

Zachary responded with a gentle embrace. "Please come in. Mr. Prost is on the veranda."

"How have you been?" Scott asked, as Zachary led them through the expansive foyer.

"I've been splendid," he replied, without turning around. "Thank you for asking."

They followed Zachary to a roofed back porch extending half the length of the mansion. When Jackie and Scott stepped outside, they detected the distinctive whiff of mesquite smoke.

Hartwell was sitting in an Adirondack chair, sipping a beer and puffing on a Cuban cigar. Next to him was a wooden tub filled with assorted brands of beer buried in ten pounds of crushed ice. The brick four-by-eight-foot grill was loaded with an array of barbecue selections, including beef, chicken, ribs, and turkey. The mesquite smoke, mingled with their host's favorite barbecue sauce, gave off a pleasing scent that whetted the appetite.

The serving table was loaded with several side dishes, Spode bone-china dinner plates, freshly polished silverware, finger bowls, and stacks of cloth napkins the size of kitchen towels. Hartwell's chef, a large raw-boned woman with a pronounced Bostonian accent, tended the barbecue and the simmering pot of baked beans. Though Molly McCallister never attended a formal culinary school, she could match any chef de cuisine in quality of preparation and presentation.

Hartwell extracted two beers from the sea of ice, placed them on the table, and dried his hands on a towel. He stood to greet his guests and reached for Jackie's hand. "How was the flight?"

"Great, smooth as silk," she said, with a wide smile.

Hartwell shook Scott's hand firmly. "So you're the captain of your own bird now?"

Scott chuckled. "Yeah. But the *real* captain is shorter than I am."

Hartwell laughed good-naturedly. "I hope you're hungry."

"Starved," Jackie admitted, surveying the abundant array of food. "Looks like we'll have enough for seconds."

"Molly never runs short of food," Hartwell said, with a hint of pride. "After one of her spreads, Zachary and I eat leftovers—at least three days' worth."

Without fanfare, Scott placed a bottle of 1987 Chateau Montelena Cabernet Sauvignon on the dining table.

Hartwell opened the beers and handed the first one to Jackie.

She raised the palm of her hand. "Thanks, but I'll stick with iced tea. We have to fly home tonight."

"Nonsense," Hartwell said, handing Scott a beer. "You can stay in the guest lodge and head home tomorrow."

Scott caught Jackie's quick smile. "Sounds great," he said. "I'll call the FBO and tell them we'll be staying overnight."

Jackie handed him her cell phone while he fished the Signature Flight Support business card out of his wallet.

"Don't worry," she said, under her breath. "I packed a bag for us. It's in the backseat."

"You think of everything."

"Someone has to," she said, with an innocent look.

When Scott had completed his call, they fixed their plates and enjoyed the old-fashioned barbecue dinner. Old-fashioned that is, except for Scott's Cabernet and a bottle of Côtes-du-Rhône wine from Hartwell's private stock.

After the meal, Molly and Zachary cleared the table while Hartwell charged his guests' wineglasses. "Let's take a walk."

Scott and Jackie picked up their glasses and followed their host. Hartwell led them past the swimming pool and the tennis court and seated them on the raised deck of a large ornate gazebo. He cast a look across the pond at the two horse stables and, with his gaze still fixed in the distance, he began the conversation.

"I'll bring you up to date, and then we'll explore our options regarding Zheng Yen-Tsung. A Dallas police officer found the vehicle we believe Zheng was driving."

"Are you sure it was Zheng?" Jackie asked.

"No, but the vehicle was stolen and then abandoned at Love Field. It's a white Buick Century identical to the one witnesses described. The window on the driver's side was blown out, and there were two streaks of blood on the driver's door. We're betting it will match the blood of the Fort Worth policeman."

Scott caught Hartwell's eye. "As it stands now, we really don't know if it was Zheng?"

"True. And that leads me to the next subject. Are you familiar with the name Saeed Shayhidi?"

Jackie recognized the name. "Isn't he the billionaire shipping mogul?"

"One and the same." A smile of satisfaction crossed Hartwell's face. "We have hard evidence that he recruited terrorists from the al-Qaeda network. This came from two senior al-Qaeda leaders recently captured near Khost, Afghanistan."

"What's Shayhidi's profile?" Scott asked.

"He's a clever and cautious man who takes great pains to conduct his affairs in stealth mode, but he's made a few mistakes recently." Hartwell retrieved a fresh cigar from his shirt pocket. "Prior to the assault on the World Trade Center and the Pentagon, Shayhidi was recruiting key members of al-Qaeda and key figures from other international terrorist organizations."

Hartwell's mouth quirked in wry remembrance of the secret meeting in the Canadian Maritimes. "Just before the Osama bin Laden–Taliban campaign, the Russians agreed with us on the deployment of tactical nuclear weapons near Afghanistan: actually, at the military air base in Dushanbe, the capital of Tajikistan, along with three other locations in the area."

He paused to light his cigar. "In turn, we assented to Russia's deploying several tactical nukes around Chechnya. One of our CIA retirees, a savvy Central Asian expert named Dennis Stambaugh, was recruited to oversee the Russian deployment. Stambaugh was having a late-night dinner with the senior Russian nuclear expert when the Russki, well into his cups of vodka, bragged about his former military boss selling suitcase nukes to one of Shayhidi's right-hand men.

"That was our first big break." Hartwell inhaled the aromatic smoke and slowly released it. "The National Security Agency has been using an updated version of Echelon—the name is still classified—let's just call it Echelon Two. They're using it to monitor Saeed Shayhidi's e-mail and phone conversations to three members of his terrorist network."

Jackie, who was knowledgeable in the world of electronic monitoring, was surprised by the unexpected disclosure. "I didn't know they had a new version of Echelon. Must be an incredible leap forward for NSA to keep it under such tight wraps."

"Oh, it's a quantum increase in technology," Hartwell said, with a knowing smile. "The new system is designed to deal with some of the thorny encryption problems we ran into with the earlier version. It still has some bugs, but we're slowly working them out."

Hartwell flicked ashes from the end of his cigar. "Shayhidi has no idea what we know, but I can assure you we have a major problem brewing."

Jackie and Scott exchanged a questioning glance.

"Echelon Two, our unmanned aerial vehicles, and our space-based assets have produced a windfall of intelligence about another campaign of terror aimed at America, even more ambitious than the attack on the World Trade Center and the Pentagon. The primary link in the chain of evidence clearly ties Shayhidi to these planned attacks."

Hartwell reached into his pocket for a piece of paper, which he unfolded. He handed Scott a picture of Shayhidi that included his physical description and information about his ties to various terrorist-related crimes.

Hartwell finished his wine. "From what we know—again using the technology of Echelon Two, satellites, various recon assets, and unmanned aerial vehicles—his terrorist cells in the United States are preparing to embark on an all-out assault on American soil. And, we believe he is preparing to bring in hundreds of reinforcements for the sleepers who are already here."

Jackie had a question. "Can't we stop them at our borders?"

Hartwell sighed. "We're still being invaded almost daily by members of Hezbollah, Islamic Jihad, Hamas, and other terrorist organizations."

"The border problem should have been fixed by now," Jackie insisted.

"They're making progress, but it's like one person trying to plug forty holes in the dike. It's going to take a lot more people and assets. According to the CIA, hundreds of 'freedom fighters' are pouring in every month. The newcomers are distributing an 'Encyclopedia Jihad' that contains elaborate bomb-building instructions and other advice for newly trained insurgents."

"The Montreal connection?" Jackie suggested.

Hartwell nodded his head in frustration. "Yes. That's a serious problem for us. In the last few years, Canada has become a Disneyland for terrorists, estimated to be five to six thousand strong." He leaned forward in his chair. "Many of them, including female Tigresses with degrees from MIT, Stanford, Brandeis, and other prestigious schools, are arriving in Montreal. They make their way to the Canadian Rocky Mountains on the western side of the Continental Divide. From there, they filter across the border at night and disappear into Washington, Idaho, and Montana.

"From what we know, they live inconspicuously. Canadian law enforcement officers recently apprehended two Islamic extremists outside the Sunnah al-Nabawiah Mosque in Montreal."

"The ones with the explosives?" Jackie asked.

"That's right. One of them, Ahmed Abun-Nasr, was a member of Egypt's Vanguards of Conquest. Abun-Nasr has assassinated three Egyptian politicians who were outspokenly pro-American. Shayhidi is one of his supporters.

"At any rate," Hartwell continued, "these two thugs had counterfeit U.S. visas, fake birth certificates, and phony Social Security numbers. They also had a station wagon filled with enough high explosives to bring down the Empire State Building, and—"

"What about the Border Patrol agents?" Scott interrupted. "Have we added more officers to that area?"

"About eighty as of yesterday, including three dozen more FBI agents disguised as vacationers or locals. But the border is still so poorly staffed that terrorists and explosives are slipping through on a daily basis. In the area we're most concerned about, there are close to sixty smuggling corridors, heavily used day and night, that have had their electronic motion and heat sensors destroyed."

Scott shook his head. "That's amazing, just *amazing,* after the World Trade Center and the Pentagon. We have over nine thousand agents patrolling the two-thousand-mile Mexican border and what—three hundred, maybe four hundred agents for the Canadian border, almost three times as long?"

"Close to four hundred agents," Hartwell said. "There are some places that aren't even patrolled. Many crossings in sparsely populated areas are closed at ten P.M. and left unattended until the next morning."

Scott looked at him and shrugged. "Terrific. Put out the orange cones and head to the tavern."

"That's about it. Some of the sectors don't have jail space for illegal aliens, so they're released to await trial."

"You're joking." Jackie's eyes were wide in disbelief.

"I wish I could joke about it," Hartwell said. "The agents call the process their 'catch and release' program."

"While America sleeps," Scott said, with a touch of sarcasm.

"The president is working on the problem as we speak. As you know, our relationship with the Canadian government since the war in Iraq hasn't been exactly cozy. President Macklin and the homeland commander-in-chief are dealing directly with the Immigration and Naturalization Service and senior Canadian authorities. We're going to use forces from marine, army, and National Guard units to help patrol the Canadian border until we can train more agents."

He hesitated. "At the other end of the spectrum, heavily armed Mexican soldiers and Mexican police are increasingly crossing our border to provide cover for illegal immigrants and drug smugglers. Violence is spiraling out of control. As this is happening, Border Patrol agents are resigning in droves.

"The drug problem is especially prevalent along a hundred-mile stretch of desert between the Organ Pipe Cactus National Monument and the Coronado National Forest. Mexican drug smugglers account for eighty percent of the cocaine and fifty percent of the heroin that reaches the streets of America. During the past three weeks, heavily armed Mexican soldiers, inside our border in Humvees, have fired on Border Patrol air units near Copper Canyon, California, and Vamori, Arizona."

"And we're not doing anything?" Jackie asked.

"As of tomorrow afternoon or evening, depending on how long our meeting with the Mexican ambassador lasts, National Guard troops will be assisting Border Patrol agents along critical areas of the Mexican border. Mostly crossing points."

Scott's curiosity was aroused. "What about the Posse Comitatus Act?"

"It's a genuine concern," Hartwell admitted. "Under the circumstances, many people on Capitol Hill are calling for a congressional review of the act. Involving the military in domestic policing is going to offend a lot of people, but the president has to do what's best for all the citizens.

"On top of everything else," Hartwell went on, "we have a serious problem brewing in our own backyard, our southern flank, Central and South America. Latin American countries are teetering on the brink of financial collapse and total chaos. Crisis seems endemic to that region, and it's getting worse by the day.

"The biggest threat to the region is terrorism orchestrated by the pro-Castro, pro-Iraq radical regime in Venezuela. Terrorism and terrorist training camps are spreading like wildfire throughout Central and South America. The instability is moving many struggling countries into an anti-American, anti–free-market direction.

"Elements of Hamas and the Iranian-backed Hezbollah have established terrorist operations in the tri-border area of Paraguay, Argentina, and Brazil. The region has become a haven for Islamic extremists, who have bombed Jewish and Israeli compounds in Buenos Aires."

He seemed tense. "In addition to that breeding ground, Hezbollah and al-Qaeda are extremely active in training terrorists in the tri-border area of Colombia, Ecuador, and Peru. We have clear evidence that many common-border terrorists from both regions are making their way by seagoing freighters to Vancouver, British Columbia, and then coming across our border in eastern Washington State."

Hartwell's expression hardened. "This terrorism problem is the reason I wanted to visit with you in person. President Macklin and I want to keep this information quiet until we're ready to make our move."

He cast his gaze across the wooded hills. "Homeland security is a priority at the White House and at the Pentagon. We don't want to create any undue public anxiety. The Twin Towers and Pentagon catastrophes are still on people's minds."

"They're certainly on mine," Jackie said.

Hartwell puffed on his cigar and continued. "As a supplement to our undercover FBI agents on the ground, we would like the two of you, using a civilian helicopter, to concentrate on tracking these illegal infiltrators from the time they leave Canada until they reach their destination—or destinations. See if you can figure out where they're gathering and, most important, what their plans are."

Jackie and Scott shared a concerned look.

"What do you think?" he asked, sensing their lack of enthusiasm. "You seem concerned."

"We'll do the best we can," Scott said with a frown. "As you know, they slip in and out of the shadows like ghosts. Don't know how effective we'll be at tracking them."

"Just do your best. See what develops." Hartwell tapped ashes from his cigar. "We're using a great number of other assets, but we know there is no substitute for on-site human intelligence. President Macklin and I appreciate your situation reports, the direct unfiltered truth. Your sit-reps are a real contrast to the watered-down assessments we receive through various bureaucracies."

Scott and Jackie made momentary eye contact, but neither said anything. Both suspected not all the cards were on the table.

Their host exhaled a long stream of cigar smoke. "As usual,

we'll provide anything you need: weapons, equipment, intelligence information, et cetera: just say the word."

Scott was already thinking about some of the base weapons of a SEAL platoon's firepower. "We like the H and K P9S, the Smith and Wesson 357, and the H and K MP-five submachine gun."

"Just make a list," Hartwell said evenly. "One other thing. If you locate any terrorist cells, we prefer you *not* act unilaterally, unless your lives are in danger. We want to have plenty of backup before we take them on."

"Understood," Scott said, and then hesitated. "How closely is the president working with the INS?"

"Very closely. After the latest developments, he and General Jamison are working directly with the Canadians and the Immigration people."

Scott spoke bluntly. "Sir, forgive me for asking, but couldn't the FBI handle an operation like this?" He didn't wait for an answer. "Is there a bigger problem?"

Hartwell vacillated a few moments, staring at the wooden deck beneath his feet. He slowly raised his head. "Actually, there is a *much* bigger problem," he said wearily. "I was going to wait until morning, after the president's daily brief from the CIA, to discuss it with you." He locked gazes, first with Jackie and then with Scott. "This is so confidential that only a handful of people know about it."

Silently, Scott and Jackie exchanged another glance.

"Four days ago, a U.S. Border Patrol agent stumbled onto a special-action cell of terrorists crossing the Canadian border close to the junction of the Idaho–Montana state line. There was a shoot-out and the agent killed three terrorists while he was calling for backup. When another agent arrived a few minutes later, he discovered his friend had died from gunshot wounds."

"How can you be so sure they were terrorists?" Scott asked.

Prost lowered his voice. "They left behind a Russian-manufactured suitcase-size nuclear bomb."

"You're kidding!" Jackie blurted.

"No. It's probably like the one Scott discovered on board *Sweet Life*. Only this one has definitely been modified."

"How so?" Jackie asked.

"The timing device has been moved to accommodate a fabricated band of steel, actually four bands, that encompass the weapon. The bands, which were not installed, appear to be a brace of some kind."

Scott met Hartwell's eyes. "Maybe they were used to attach the bomb to the shipping container, some kind of protective device."

"We don't know, but they're round; they intersect at opposing poles at forty-five-degree angles and bolt to the bomb."

Jackie's mind conjured images of nuclear weapons being detonated in the heart of New York City. "Do we know if any other nukes have slipped into the country?"

"Yes, we do," he answered in a hushed voice. "Through Echelon Two we know the terrorists who were killed were members of one of seven teams smuggling nukes across our borders. Each team was responsible for one bomb. We don't know where the other six groups are hiding."

The three sat in silence for a moment while the gravity of the situation impacted Jackie and Scott.

Hartwell finally broke the silence. "We have solid information, corroborated by intelligence on the ground, that these nukes originated in the Ukraine. A company named Yuzhmash, Ukraine's largest rocket maker, has a close defense-technology relationship with Syria and Iran. What we don't know is whether the bombs came from Syria or Iran. At any rate, we've been able to connect these seven nukes directly to Khaliq Farkas."

"Farkas?" Jackie and Scott said in unison.

"Yes. Farkas is working for Saeed Shayhidi. On Shayhidi's orders, Farkas will activate the other six cells. We believe that time is near. That's why we need the two of you involved in this operation. Like I said, only a handful of people know about this. We want to keep this totally contained, away from Congress and possible leaks to the media. Don't want to spook the public or cause Farkas to go underground."

Hartwell allowed them to absorb the revelation. "Sure, the FBI can help to a point, but if push comes to shove and we locate these nukes, we don't want to have to get a search warrant. We can't afford to get tied up in legal quicksand and have the news hit the media."

Scott and Jackie nodded their understanding.

"As we receive more information, I'll be feeding it to you. For now, we want you to familiarize yourselves with the northwestern states where the terrorists are coming in." Hartwell took a long drag on his cigar. "The bottom line: find Farkas and the nukes before Shayhidi activates the other six cells."

5

Queen Mary 2

Led by Islamic extremist Muftah al-Hamadi, the four terrorists posing as Saudi royalty arranged their passage on the *QM2* with counterfeit documents and certified funds. They left their adjoining Queen Anne and Queen Victoria suites shortly after 3 A.M. Al-Hamadi, mindful of the terror and chaos his brethren had inflicted on New York City and the Pentagon, intended once again to shock the financial capital of the world.

Two of the Islamic radicals would go to the ship's bridge while the other two would make their way to the ship's main air-conditioning plant located in the machinery spaces. The team going belowdeck would first kill the watch standers and then neutralize the security system for the flexible propulsion system. Their next target would be the closed-circuit television system monitoring the engineering spaces.

Between them, the terrorists possessed enough sarin to kill

everyone on a dozen *QM2*s. One of the most feared and most lethal of nerve agents, sarin is an odorless, tasteless, and colorless substance that can be inhaled or absorbed through the skin. This operation would make the Aum Shinrikyo's sarin attack on the Tokyo subway system pale in comparison.

Highly trained and totally dedicated to Saeed Shayhidi's cause, the four men had fanatical frontline mentalities. They were prepared to die for Shayhidi and his full-scale jihad against the "Great Satan."

For Shayhidi and his growing legions of followers, assassinating the U.S. secretary of state, along with key members of the U.S. Congress and leaders from countries allied with America, would be sheer ecstasy.

The irony was part of the elation. The unsuspecting conferees would die after having attended a summit intended to curtail international terrorism. Al-Hamadi's colleagues and Shayhidi would salute the four dedicated terrorists as conquering heroes and martyrs.

When they reached the ship's bridge, Muftah al-Hamadi and his partner used handguns with silencers to quickly dispatch the crew on watch. With sarin already flowing through the entire air-conditioning system, al-Hamadi chained the hatches leading to the bridge and rang up flank speed. The revolutionary Rolls-Royce four-pod propulsion system could propel the city-at-sea to a speed of 30 knots.

Before they were finally overcome, al-Hamadi and his associate sabotaged the primary and secondary communications equipment. They knew the navigation suite was preprogrammed to take the mighty ocean liner directly to New York City.

Traveling at top speed, the 1,132-foot *Queen Mary 2* would be well ahead of her scheduled docking at the Twelfth Avenue Passenger Ship Terminal. Regardless of the exact point of impact in the Big Apple, the high-speed arrival of the 150,000-ton ship would be an event etched in history.

When he succumbed to the nerve agent, there was no doubt in al-Hamadi's mind. Saeed Shayhidi and Allah would be proud of their efforts to help vanquish the infidels. They would be remembered as gallant warriors, admired and respected for their role in the never-ending war against the West.

The Queen Mary Suite

A growing sense of uneasiness awakened Brett Shannon from a restless sleep. He sensed something was wrong and glanced at his travel clock on the night table. The clock's face was blurred. He reached for his glasses: It was 3:14 A.M.

Shannon felt a subtle vibration in the hull of the world's grandest ocean liner. It would have been more difficult to perceive if he hadn't been accustomed to the velvety-smooth ride. But the vibration was real and it was becoming more pronounced by the second. *Maybe they're trying to outrun a storm.*

His nerves were on edge, and he felt chest pains when the *QM2* unexpectedly shook from bow to stern. The motion wasn't violent, but it certainly wasn't normal. As her speed continued to increase, Shannon could tell the Cunard flagship was plowing through rough seas and plunging into choppy waves.

While he tried to calm himself, Shannon forced his mind to think more clearly. Still not fully awake, he reached for the phone. The line was dead. The short hairs on the back of his neck began to rise. He sat up, turned on the night-light, and momentarily lost his balance when the ship lurched to one side and then righted herself.

His hands trembling, Shannon quickly pulled on a pair of trousers and donned a sport shirt. He hesitated a moment and then gingerly opened the door to his suite. As he stepped into the deserted passageway, Shannon felt a wave of panic sweep over him. His security guard was on his hands and knees, barely able to move.

Shannon's own forehead was damp and his breathing was shallow and ragged. *What's happening?* He walked to the nearby elevators and stabbed the buttons several times. They were not working. Shannon backed against a bulkhead, afraid to move, afraid of the unknown. His mind was trying to sort through the various possibilities. Why was the phone dead and why were the elevators not operating? Nothing made sense, especially the rough ride and the sudden increase in speed. *Someone needs to tell us what's going on.*

Shannon turned toward the stairway and froze in mid-stride when he saw a familiar couple staggering up the steps. *Nerve agents. Omigod.* In shock, the revelation hit him a second before the disheveled man spoke.

"Don't go down there," the man said, and coughed several times. He was having difficulty breathing and his wife was suffering convulsions. "Everyone below this deck is dead or dying," he said, in a weak, whispery voice. "We have to get fresh air." His wife suddenly passed out and the man collapsed to his knees.

Reeling from adrenaline shock and absolute panic, Secretary Shannon raced forward in the passageway leading to the Queen Anne Suite and the Queen Victoria Suite. They were locked.

Shannon had no way of knowing the former occupants were dead or dying by their own hand in the machinery spaces and on the bridge of the ship. He pounded on the door and no one answered. He had to get in and break the windows. Maybe the fresh sea air blowing through the suite and down the passageway would save him.

He was kicking in the door of the Queen Anne Suite when a member of his staff opened his door.

"Brett, what's going on?"

"We've been gassed. Get everyone up!"

"What?"

"Just do it, George! The ship is filling with nerve gas!"

"Oh, God, no."

Other people began poking their heads out, wondering what the racket was about. Many wondered why the ship was plowing through rough waves and going so fast. Their surprised looks turned to fear when most sensed a serious emergency.

Five more kicks and Shannon was inside the elaborate suite. But something was wrong. His production of saliva suddenly increased and his nose began to run. He felt a tremendous pressure on his chest, making it difficult to breathe. Tripping over a small table, he fell sideways, landing heavily on his right arm.

When he struggled to get up, Shannon felt pain in his eyes when he attempted to focus across the room. Seconds later a headache developed and his head began to throb. He felt tired and his tongue was thick. Random thoughts began flashing through his mind, adding more confusion to his inability to concentrate.

George hurried into the suite and knelt beside him, but Shannon's staff member was himself experiencing the initial symptoms of the nerve agent.

"Geor, you hafa help me."

"I can't do anything—can't do . . ." George stared at his boss for a few moments and then awkwardly sat down next to him. He was familiar with the autoinjectors containing the combined antidotes HI-6 and atropine, but it was too late for that remedy. The fast-acting sarin had already killed most of the passengers.

Shannon began hallucinating. His staff member looked like a multi-eyed creature that had come to kill him. "Get away from—get back aw way—"

"Okay."

Shannon experienced extreme nausea and coughed twice before paralysis claimed his respiratory muscles. Seconds later, his central nervous system ceased functioning and he died of suffocation. George remained by his side, awaiting his own death. Through teary eyes, he folded his hands and began praying for his family.

The lone survivors of the attack were a doctor and his bride near the bow of the *QM2*. They had decided to take a stroll after finishing their room service breakfast at 2:45 A.M. The newlyweds remained at the bow after they observed scores of people pouring out on the decks, yelling for help.

While the ship was accelerating, the couple watched more than three dozen passengers stumble out of hatches leading to the bow. All of them fell and crawled until their last death rattle. The honeymoon couple surmised what had happened, but they were powerless to help the dying victims.

The frightened pair were soaking wet from the cold spray coming over the bow, but neither of them budged. Entering the ship would mean certain death, obviously a cruel and agonizing one. Suffering from the first stages of hypothermia, the newlyweds knew they were in for the ride of their young lives.

The Winslow Estate

Fast asleep in Prost's guest quarters, Jackie and Scott were startled awake by the loud thrashing of helicopter rotor blades. Scott reached for the small lamp on the nightstand between their queen beds. *Something must be wrong.* Unfamiliar with his surroundings, he fumbled for the switch, turned on the light, and picked up his wristwatch. "It's almost four-fifteen. What the hell is going on?"

Jackie tossed her covers aside and sat up. "There's some kind of problem."

They crawled out of their beds and went to the window facing the dimly lit helicopter pad. A VH-60 Sikorsky Black Hawk from marine corps squadron HMX-1 was gently settling on its landing gear.

"It's a marine white top," Scott said.

"Not a good omen at this time of morning."

The VIP helicopter was on the ground less than twenty seconds when Hartwell Prost appeared out of the shadows and got on board. The power came up and the VH-60 leaped into the air, turned on its axis, and headed in the direction of the capital.

"We better get dressed," Scott suggested. There was a knock on the door. "I'll get it."

Zachary, his usual smile absent, was standing outside. "I'm sorry to bother you, Mr. Dalton, but there's been an emergency. What it is, I don't know, but Mr. Prost would like you and Miss Sullivan to make yourselves at home here until he can contact you."

"Okay." Scott darted a look at Jackie and then eyed Zachary. "Do you know where he went?"

"Yes, sir. He was called to the White House."

"Thanks, Zachary."

"Yes, sir." The butler saw the kitchen lights flick on and knew Molly would have fresh coffee brewing in a matter of minutes. "Would you and Miss Sullivan care to have breakfast?"

Scott looked at Jackie.

"Just coffee and juice for me," she said.

"Same here." Scott rubbed his eyes. "We'll be up in a few minutes."

"Yes, sir. We'll have it ready."

As Zachary turned to leave, Scott closed the door, turned on the television, and adjusted the volume. "Better see if we have any breaking news."

Jackie covered her mouth and yawned. "Let's get dressed and go have coffee."

The White House

Minutes before the secretary of defense arrived at the Oval Office, President Cord Macklin was awakened. He was told about the perilous situation aboard the *Queen Mary 2*. A dying passenger managed to use his satellite phone to call the coast guard and report the emergency. The man explained that hundreds of passengers and crew members were afflicted by a suspected chemical or biological agent. He also mentioned the ship was traveling at a high rate of speed. After that, his speech became slurred, followed by a spate of coughing and then silence.

Macklin put on fresh khaki slacks and a golf shirt, combed his hair, and headed straight for the Oval Office. His face was pale when he walked into the brightly lighted room. "Have a seat, gentlemen."

Secretary of Defense Pete Adair was waiting, along with Air Force General Les Chalmers, the chairman of the Joint Chiefs of Staff. Overhead, they could hear the marine corps helicopter carrying the president's national security adviser.

"What can you tell me?" Macklin asked, as he walked to his desk and dropped into his seat. "Any word from Brett or any of our other folks?"

General Chalmers deferred to Secretary Adair, his immediate boss in the chain of command.

"Sir, we haven't heard directly from anyone aboard the ship. We don't know any more than your basic briefing."

"How much time do we have?"

"The ship was scheduled to arrive in New York at eight A.M."

"That figures," Macklin declared. "If it's running at a faster speed than normal, we really don't know *how* much time we have."

Adair looked at his wristwatch. "According to our calculations, the ship is approximately ten to twelve miles southwest of East Hampton."

The president sighed. "What are we doing to get some answers?"

"General Chalmers?" Adair prompted.

"Sir, we have a coast guard helicopter approaching the *QM2* as we speak. We expect to hear from the air crew in a matter of minutes. The coast guard is sending warnings to all shipping in the path of the liner. They're being told to alter course and be on the lookout."

"Has there been *any* communication with the ship, other than the passenger on the satellite phone?"

Chalmers paused while Hartwell Prost entered the Oval Office.

"No, sir. We haven't been able to raise anyone, and there hasn't been any other communication from the ship. We think terrorists may have taken over the ship. They're probably holding the crew and passengers hostage."

"Or," Prost interjected, "based on the jihad planned by Shayhidi, everyone's dead or incapacitated and no one is controlling the ship."

An uneasy silence drifted over the office.

Hartwell looked at General Chalmers. "Where Brett Shannon and our other friends are concerned, we'd better plan for the worst."

The president rose from his chair. "Let's adjourn to the Situation Room so we can have direct contact with all the players."

The Dolphin

Operating from the deck of the Reliance-class cutter *Dependable,* the coast guard search-and-rescue Dolphin helicopter HH-65A was nearing the area where the crew expected to rendezvous with the *Queen Mary 2.* The two pilots, the flight mechanic, and the pararescue jumper (known as a PJ) were using night-vision goggles to search for the ship.

The pilot, Lieutenant Commander Jeffery Bergman, coupled the four-axis automatic pilot to the flight controls for hands-free operation while he devoted his full attention to scanning the horizon.

"There she is!" flight mechanic Petty Officer Earl Nogart yelled. "Eleven o'clock, just coming into view—that has to be the *QM Two.*"

"I see her," Bergman said, slightly altering course. He disengaged the autopilot and began a slow descent. "Let's keep a close eye on this baby. Could be armed men on deck."

Lieutenant Tim McLain studied the oncoming ship. "Something's out of whack. They would never cruise at high speed in these seas."

They circled the liner once and then moved closer to the stern. Bergman slowed the Dolphin to match the ship's speed while they trained the spotlight on the *QM2* and moved along the port side. The sun deck and the other exposed decks were littered with bodies.

"Judas Priest!" the flight mechanic said under his breath. "There are hundreds of bodies and no sign of life anywhere."

Petty Officer Stu Clements, the pararescue jumper, was stunned. "Man, I ain't never seen anything like this."

Appalled by the tragedy, Lieutenant McLain keyed the intercom. "They've struck us again—sorry bastards."

Bergman positioned the helicopter close to the bridge. They trained the searchlight on the windows and slowly moved across the span of the bridge. It was eerie not to see faces staring back. Whatever the cause, the ill-fated crew and their passengers had suffered horrible deaths.

"No sign of life," McLain said, with a lump in his throat. "What a terrible disaster. And it isn't over."

Bergman keyed the intercom. "I'm afraid you're right. New York City, brace yourself."

"Again," McLain added in a tight voice.

Bergman eased the helicopter toward the starboard side of the bridge. "This is unbelievable—unfathomable."

McLain stared at the bodies. "How could human beings hate so much they would fly airliners into the World Trade Center—or kill everyone on an ocean liner?"

Bergman shook his head in disbelief. "It's beyond comprehension."

McLain glanced at the pilot. "I'll contact our ship and give them the news."

Queen Mary 2

The doctor and his bride yelled and waved frantically at the helicopter, but to no avail. In desperation, the pediatrician took off one of his deck shoes and heaved it toward the top of the bridge. It fell short, forcing the doctor to move a few yards closer.

"Down here! Look down here!"

He leaned back and threw the other shoe as high and as far as he could. "Down here! We're down here!" *Don't leave us behind.*

Lieutenant McLain thought he saw something bounce off the front of the bridge. "Stop—stop! I just saw something."

"Where?" Bergman asked.

"Turn the light on the bow."

The pilot inched the helicopter forward as the searchlight flashed across the deck. He spotted two sets of flailing arms. "I'll be damned! We have survivors but we don't have enough room to land—too many obstacles."

"And we don't have a bullhorn with us," the copilot added. "We can send Clements down with the basket."

"Hang on a second." Easing the helicopter away from the ship, Bergman turned the controls over to McLain while he contacted the cutter *Dependable.*

6

The White House

After receiving the shocking news from the coast guard helicopter crew, President Macklin looked at his advisors. "Gentlemen, any suggestions? The helicopter is getting low on fuel and we're running out of time."

Hartwell Prost spoke first. "Sir, we have to place the two survivors on the back burner for the moment. Our first priority has to be stopping the ship before it plows into something along the Hudson River and contaminates everything from Wall Street to Yankee Stadium."

The president leaned back in his chair. "The rescue swimmer?"

"A possibility," Prost allowed, "but he has to volunteer."

Macklin nodded. "I agree."

"What if he can't get to the bridge?" Pete Adair objected. "What if he dies, and we accomplish nothing?"

"What if he gains access to the bridge and stops the ship, averts a disaster?" the president asked.

Macklin turned to General Chalmers, his close friend from football days at the Air Force Academy. "Les, any suggestions?"

"The passengers and crew are already dead. *Sink* the damn ship." The chairman of the Joint Chiefs of Staff was clearly uncomfortable. "Sir, we don't have time to get people out there who have the proper training and equipment to handle a contamination situation like this. It just isn't possible."

"I understand." The president accepted a fresh cup of coffee and sat quietly for a moment before looking at Chalmers. "Les, do we have enough assets available to sink the ship before it reaches New York, if the rescue swimmer can't get to the bridge or if he becomes incapacitated?"

"Yes, sir. We have a carrier—*Truman*—steaming about seventy-five miles northeast of Norfolk. It's headed toward the *QM Two* and they're loading ordnance at this time. I expect the Hornets to be launched in the next thirty to forty-five minutes."

The president tapped the ends of his fingertips together. "Let's see what the rescue swimmer's decision is."

Pete Adair was holding his temper in check. "Mr. President, I think we should get the survivors off the ship and let the Navy sink it as quickly as possible. We don't need to risk killing the rescue swimmer. The ship is a death trap."

"I understand your position, Pete."

Adair was not going to be deterred. "We've already lost Secretary Shannon, the entire top tier of our diplomatic staff, their colleagues in the Terrorism Coalition Council, and several members of Congress."

Another period of awkwardness engulfed the room.

Macklin broke the silence. "If the swimmer is willing to go aboard, I say we give it a try."

The president turned his attention to Prost. "Hartwell, what do you think, any chance?"

"Well, the odds are stacked against him, but there's always a slim chance he could get to the controls."

Macklin nodded to Les Chalmers. "Let's see what the swimmer says."

"Yes, sir."

The president hid his emotions as he tried to fathom the mind-numbing loss. "Hartwell, I'd like you to develop a short list of State Department replacements and get Jim Ebersole to vet them as soon as possible."

"I'll get right to it."

"And make sure Brad Austin's name is on the list," the president said firmly. "He's sharp."

Austin, a former state legislator and well-known marine corps fighter pilot from the Vietnam era, was currently serving as the undersecretary of state for global affairs.

Prost nodded. "My recommendation: Place Austin at the top of the list. He was Shannon's go-to guy."

"I agree," Macklin said. "Let's expedite the process, keep things moving as fast as we can."

"Yes, sir, but first I have another recommendation."

The president looked puzzled. "Let's have it."

"Sir, in my opinion, you should get the British prime minister on the phone and tell him why we're about to sink the *QM Two.*"

Macklin's neck muscles ached from the tension. "Let's see if we can get the ship stopped first—and we won't have to sink it."

"As you wish."

The Dolphin

Lieutenant Commander Bergman looked Stu Clements in the eye. "It's your decision; take a minute to think about it."

"Sir, I've made up my mind. It's my job, and we don't have a whole lotta time left."

Bergman felt a tinge of anguish. "Okay, but be extremely careful."

"Yes, sir." Clements wavered a moment. "Should we get the two survivors aboard before I try the bridge?"

"We don't have the fuel."

"Yes, sir," Clements said, slipping into a strop. The modified horse collar was used by PJs and downed military aviators.

Bergman maneuvered the helicopter over the ship's sun deck while Clements eased out of the hatch and began his descent.

Unsure of what was going on, the doctor and his wife shivered while they stared at the man dangling from the helicopter. They wondered why they were being ignored.

Clements was about to reach the sun deck at the same time

Lieutenant McLain was on the radio requesting another helicopter.

Although the rain-swollen clouds were low, the early morning sky was turning gray and the visibility was rapidly improving.

Considered an excellent aviator, Bergman held the Dolphin as steady as he could in the gusting wind. As he quickly learned, it was impossible to hover precisely in one spot.

Clements tried to stabilize himself a few seconds before his feet touched down on the *QM2.* He stumbled and then slipped out of the strop. The pilot climbed a few feet to keep the horse collar away from the ship.

Making his way to the bridge, Clements completed a radio check to Earl Nogart. When he reached the hatch leading to the bridge, Clements tried without success to open it. He pulled harder and forced it open an inch. *Uh-oh, we have a problem.*

Clements keyed his radio. "Earl, the hatches to the bridge have been chained shut from the inside."

"How strong, how thick are the links?"

"They're heavy-duty, big time."

"Stand by."

"Roger that."

Nogart conferred with the pilots and keyed his radio. "Okay, Stu, return to the sun deck and we'll get you out of there."

Silence.

"Stu, are you there?" Nogart fought the onset of panic. "Answer me, Stu. What's happening down there? Talk to me, buddy."

"Man," Clements said and then gagged when he reached the sun deck. "I don't feel so good. Can't breathe and I have something . . . something wrong with my chest, and . . ." He trailed off.

"Answer me, Stu!"

Nogart saw his friend stagger across the sun deck, stumble twice, and collapse to his hands and knees. He crawled a few feet, fell sideways, and then lay motionless.

"Stu, get up, you can make it!"

The flight mechanic swallowed hard. *Oh, shit.* He turned to the pilots, who saw what happened. "He's down. Have to go get him!"

"Negative," Bergman commanded. "Then we'd have both of you down there, no way."

"But, sir—"

"You can see how fast it hit him."

"And we're critical on fuel," McLain added, scribbling a note to the two bewildered survivors on the bow.

Bergman added power and spoke to Nogart. "Secure the hoist. Have to get out of here." *God forgive me.*

"Jeff," McLain said, "if you'll hover over the bow, I'll have Nogart drop a note to the folks."

"Okay, but let's make it quick."

Flying as smoothly as possible, Bergman hovered over the bow while the flight mechanic wrapped the piece of paper around a wrench. Nogart tossed it out a safe distance from the couple, but the downwash from the main rotor blades ripped the note loose. The message was blown over the side as the doctor tried to catch it.

"Shit," McLain said as he gave the couple a thumbs-up. *Hang in there—don't give up.*

Bergman turned the Dolphin around and headed straight for the cutter *Dependable.* "Let's hope we make it back."

McLain checked their fuel. "We're looking at a dual flame-out, be suckin' fumes in a couple of minutes."

Glancing at the fuel quantity, Bergman cringed. "Call the ship, give 'em our position, and have them head for us at flank speed."

The White House

Although he agonized internally, President Macklin showed no emotion when the bad news arrived that the ship could not be stopped from the bridge. "Les, check the status of the carrier."

"Yes, sir."

The president turned to Pete Adair. "How long until the other helicopter reaches the ship?"

"About thirty-five, maybe forty minutes. It's coming out of the Coast Guard Air Station on Cape Cod."

Macklin sighed and looked away. "When will the *QM Two* reach the waters directly off New York?"

Adair gave him a ballpark figure. "According to my calculations, one hour and ten minutes, plus or minus a few minutes."

The president's jaw muscles began working back and forth. "This, my friends, is going to be one difficult day."

USS *Harry S. Truman*

With Carrier Air Wing Three embarked, and her flotilla of surface escorts and the attack submarine USS *Boise* (SSN 764) positioned around her, the mammoth Nimitz-class aircraft carrier *Harry S. Truman* (CVN 75) was proceeding north-northeast at 27 knots in the Virginia Capes Operating Area. The offshore warning areas for air, surface, and subsurface units extends from just south of Nantucket Island, Massachusetts, to Charleston, South Carolina, and eastward for more than 200 nautical miles into the Atlantic Ocean.

Powered by two Westinghouse nuclear reactors and four steam turbines producing 280,000 shaft horsepower, the 100,000-ton warship could attain speeds of more than 30 knots. Using her four steam-powered catapults, she could launch an aircraft every twenty seconds. With her entire air wing of more than eighty combat aircraft aboard, the carrier was home to approximately 6,000 crew members.

Truman was at flight quarters and the 4.5-acre flight deck was humming with activity. The day was dawning under dark skies and numerous rain showers. The combination of leaked oil, jet fuel, and hydraulic fluid made the wet flight deck extremely slippery.

The red-shirted ordnance technicians were loading the last of the general-purpose, free-fall Mark-84 2,000-pound bombs on four F/A-18 Hornets from VFA-105, the navy fighter/attack squadron known as the "Gunslingers." The F/A-18 Hornets, the same plane flown by the navy's famous Blue Angels flight demonstration team, are twin-engine, all-weather fighter/attack aircraft.

Four marine F/A-18s from the "Checkerboards" of VMFA-312 were also receiving 2,000-pound bombs. Like the navy aircraft, the marines were allotted four bombs to a plane. Two additional "Gunslingers" Hornets were being readied and would be spares for the primary strike force.

Soaked from a heavy rain shower, purple-shirts were fueling aircraft at the same time yellow-shirts were directing airplanes around the treacherous flight deck. The plane-guard rescue helicopter, an SH-60 Seahawk from the "Big Dippers" of HS-7, lifted off and took up station on the starboard side of *Truman*'s island.

An E-2C Hawkeye twin-turboprop all-weather command and control aircraft taxied to the port bow catapult. The mission this morning was critical for the VAW-126 flight crew: Find the runaway *QM2* and provide guidance and communications relay for the fighter planes. The pilot of the Hawkeye brought the power up and made her final checks while the straining airplane shook violently. Satisfied that everything was in order, she flicked the master switch for the external lights. The Hawkeye was instantly bathed in a surreal layer of red and green lights.

Seconds later, after completing his final safety checks, the catapult officer knelt down and touched the flight deck. A young petty officer pushed the launch button, and the E-2C accelerated down the flight deck and disappeared in the gloom.

Two KC-130 Hercules from Marine Aerial Refueler/Transport Squadron VMGR-252 at Marine Corps Air Station Cherry Point, North Carolina, were en route to provide "gas" for the thirsty fighters.

Cautiously, the navy F/A-18s began taxiing forward to the bow catapults. The flight leader, Salty Dog 406, was directed to the starboard cat while his wingman taxied to the port catapult.

The number three and four Hornets were in trail as they taxied up the wet, greasy deck aft of the island. Without warning, Hornet number three lost his left brake. The pilot immediately dropped his tailhook to indicate to the deck crew and plane handlers that he had a problem; then he shoved on the brakes and reached for the ejection seat handle between his thighs. The right tire slid a few feet and then seized, turning the jet almost 90 degrees.

Lieutenant Commander Mark Seaborn in Hornet number four couldn't stop in time. With the brakes locked, he slid into the right side of his flight leader. The collision knocked a 2,000-pound bomb loose from the number three aircraft and ruptured a fuel tank, spewing highly flammable jet fuel onto the armored flight deck. The fuel ignited and rapidly spread flames under the two aircraft.

In the blink of an eye, the ensuing conflagration enveloped the fighter planes. In desperation, both pilots ejected moments before one of their bombs exploded, setting off yet another bomb. The two explosions sent shrapnel flying in every direction, wounding several deckhands.

Carried in their parachutes by the strong wind over the deck, the aviators landed safely in the churning wake of the carrier. Reacting instantly, the pilot of the plane-guard helicopter was hovering over them in a matter of seconds, and they were rescued with minor injuries.

Truman's skipper, keeping an eye toward the chaos on the flight deck, slowed the carrier to a crawl to lessen the force of the wind.

The powerful explosions turned a section of the flight deck into a blazing inferno and ripped two holes in the decking. Two crewmen were blown over the side of the ship and were quickly recovered by the plane-guard helicopter.

Working spaces immediately below the flight deck became death traps when the volatile fuel vapors ignited. Although sprinkler systems cut in automatically in the affected compartments, three men died and another seven were injured in the firestorm.

The deck was littered with debris from the two fighters and other damaged aircraft. Firefighters had the blaze under control in less than seventeen minutes, and the wreckage was quickly shoved overboard.

In the meantime, the two Hornets on the bow catapults were launched before *Truman* began slowing. The two spares were waiting behind the marine fighters positioned aft of the accident site. One of the marine F/A-18s was slightly damaged from flying pieces of shrapnel, but it was safe to fly and the pilot was eager to launch.

The tragic accident delayed the remaining strike aircraft from getting airborne in a timely manner. But the first two Hornets were in the air, and the commander of the air wing hoped they were carrying enough ordnance to sink the ship.

After *Truman* regained speed, the rest of the F/A-18s, including the two spare Hornets, were launched. The stragglers were now joining their flight leaders in preparation to rendezvous with the two marine corps KC-130 tankers.

Coast Guard Cutter *Dependable*

Lieutenant Commander Bergman was stabilizing the HH-65A Dolphin over the ship's landing platform when the starboard engine flamed out from fuel exhaustion. The other engine quit a few seconds after the helicopter plopped onto the cutter. The Dolphin was quickly secured to the slippery deck.

Bergman and his shaken copilot were speechless for a few moments. They felt a deep remorse over the loss of Petty Officer Stu Clements. Bergman also felt guilty about jeopardizing the lives of the rest of his crew. Another twenty seconds and they would have gone for a cold swim or crashed into the cutter.

But there wasn't time for soul-searching. While the deck crew hurried to refuel the Dolphin, Bergman was notified that the helicopter from the Coast Guard Air Station at Cape Cod, Massachusetts, had turned back because of mechanical problems. Bergman's helicopter was the closest to the *Queen Mary 2*.

With sufficient fuel in the tanks and a senior PJ on board, Bergman lifted the Dolphin off the deck and headed in the direction of the *QM2*. Less than a minute later, he and his crew were informed about the two fighters en route to sink the ocean liner. It would be a close race to rescue the couple stranded on the ship's bow before the fighters arrived.

Salty Dog 406

Commander Ben Rosenbaum, the commanding officer of VFA-105, unplugged his F/A-18 Hornet from the marine corps tanker when his wingman's plane was topped with fuel. Lieutenant Jon Worthington II joined on his CO's fighter while they turned away from the KC-130's refueling track. Worthington, an African-American, was the first in his family's history to graduate from college. He also was one of the best fighter pilots in the fleet.

Rosenbaum keyed his radio to check with the E-2C for vectors to *Queen Mary 2*. "Ringleader, Salty Dog Four-oh-six is up."

"Salty Dog Four-oh-six, Ringleader, roger," said the senior Hawkeye mission systems operator. "Come port to three-four-five . . . target is at your one o'clock for one-sixty."

"Three-forty-five for one-sixty, Salty Dog Four-oh-six."

The intercept was going to be close. A native of White Plains, New York, Rosenbaum knew the *QM2* was going to be south of Fire Island before his flight arrived overhead.

"Salty Two, comin' up on the power," Rosenbaum radioed, as he inched his throttles forward.

"Copy."

Queen Mary 2

Cold and shivering, Dr. Pace Woodbury and his wife, Robin, were holding each other closely. They were soaked from the drenching they were taking every time the ship's bow plunged into the heavy seas. Although the sky was overcast and dark, the visibility was increasing as the sun rose higher.

"What are we going to do?" Robin asked, kneeling down next to the bow railing. "It would be suicide to jump overboard."

"They'll be back." He looked at the bridge. "They were trying to get someone to the ship's controls, but he succumbed."

"Why would they leave us?"

He took a quick breath before another plume of cold water

rained down. "Low fuel maybe, but they had to get another person to help us."

She shivered and her teeth began chattering. "Can we survive if . . . if the ship runs aground at this speed?"

"Robin, the coast guard is going to be back. They aren't going to abandon us, trust me."

"I hope you're right."

"I am right."

Dr. Woodbury had doubts about the outcome, but he couldn't show any anxiety. Fear could turn to panic, and panic would sweep away logic and judgment. This was the time to demonstrate no emotion except calm and confidence.

"Just keep your faith," he said firmly, and then peeked over the bow railing. What he saw made his blood run cold.

She saw his eyes grow large. "What is it?"

He swallowed and started to answer as she rose to look over the bow.

Robin gasped when she saw the tops of New York City's tallest skyscrapers rising above the haze layer.

The Dolphin

After some initial confusion, Lieutenant McLain finally made contact with the E-2C Hawkeye. They handed him off to Commander Rosenbaum in the lead F/A-18 Hornet.

"Salty Dog Four-oh-six, coast guard Dolphin."

"Coast guard, Salty Four-oh-six."

McLain double-checked the time and keyed his radio. "Say your ETA over the *QM Two*."

"Ahh . . . looks like twelve, maybe thirteen minutes."

"Salty, we have two survivors on the ship."

"Say again."

"There are two survivors on the bow of the *QM Two*. We expect to be overhead in ten minutes."

"Roger . . . we'll back out of the throttle a tad."

"Copy."

Following vectors from the Hawkeye, Lieutenant Commander Bergman pushed the Dolphin to its limits while everyone searched for the ocean liner. The minutes were melting away when Petty Officer First Class Richard "Red" Bailey spotted the *QM2*. "Twelve o'clock, just coming out of the haze—kicking up some spray."

McLain keyed his radio. "Salty Dog Four-oh-six, coast guard Dolphin."

"Go Charlie Golf."

"We have the *QM Two* in sight, be overhead shortly."

"Roger, we're beginning our descent in one minute."

"Copy."

Commander Rosenbaum checked his fuel. "Ringleader, Salty Four-oh-six, do we have any air traffic in the area?"

"Negative, no contacts. The FAA is doing a great job of clearing the airspace around the ship."

With a *click-click* on the radio transmit button, Rosenbaum acknowledged the report. He glanced at his wingman. "Jon, you ready to start down?"

"Ready as I'll ever be, skipper," he replied in a guarded voice. "I can't *believe* we're doin' this."

Rosenbaum paused to contemplate the unprecedented attack. "I can't either, partner. Just concentrate and put your ordnance on target. Can't afford to goon this up."

"Roger that."

Rosenbaum eased the Hornet's nose down. "Ringleader, Salty Four-oh-six is out of Flight Level three-five-zero."

"Copy, come port five degrees."

Click-click.

"Call visual on the target . . . uh, the ship."

"Will do. Any reports on the ceiling?"

"Stand by."

"Copy."

The mission systems operator was back in seconds. "Uh . . . the last we heard was approximately eight hundred feet, two miles visibility in haze and light rain."

"Okay. What do you show, Charlie Golf?"

"About the same."

Click-click. Rosenbaum felt the tension building and glanced at his wingman. "Not exactly perfect weather for bombing."

"At least no one will be shooting back."

"We can't assume that the way things are going this morning."

The senior Hawkeye crewman keyed his radio. "Salty, the rest of your troops are on the way, just off the tankers."

"Tell 'em to buster!"

"They have the pedal to the metal."

Click-click.

"Tuck it in tight," Rosenbaum said to his wingman, seconds before their Hornets entered the tops of an endless expanse of thick, dark clouds.

With his eyes locked on Rosenbaum's plane a few feet away, Worthington was playing his stick and throttles like a violin. "Skipper, any closer and we'll have to take our jets to the paint-and-body shop."

The Dolphin

Listening to the fighter pilots and the Hawkeye controller, Bergman began slowing the helicopter and aligning it with the bow of the ship. He and McLain could see the look of exhilaration on the faces of the young couple.

Red Bailey positioned the basket and secured the line from the hoist. The basket was the preferred method of lifting civilians because it allowed for the least amount of risk in an otherwise risky situation.

Bergman maneuvered the Dolphin over the bow as it plunged

through the waves. Stabilizing the helicopter over the frightened couple, flight mechanic Earl Nogart began lowering Bailey in the basket. When the veteran PJ reached the deck, he jumped out. Bailey assisted Pace and Robin Woodbury into the basket. He seated them and then gave Nogart the signal to begin hoisting the couple. Suddenly, something didn't seem right. Bailey looked up at the same instant the hoist stopped. The basket was hanging twelve feet below the Dolphin, not going up or coming down. Paralyzed with fear, the doctor and his wife looked to Bailey for help.

Nogart tried everything he could to free the cable. It was no use. The hoist had malfunctioned and jammed.

"Sir, it's stuck!"

"What?" Bergman asked.

"The hoist is broken, won't go in either direction!"

Bergman looked to the north and saw the western end of Fire Island. He made a calculated decision and added power. "We'll take them to shore and return for Red."

The Dolphin gathered speed, but Bergman couldn't go too fast with the rescue basket swinging underneath the helicopter. The shocked couple gripped the sides of the basket and leaned toward each other. Neither dared look over the side at the cold, angry sea.

Bailey knew what his pilot was doing, but he was concerned about the inbound fighters. Warm and comfortable in his wet suit, he sat down and waited for the carrier-based Hornets to appear.

Bergman swore under his breath and keyed the radio. "Salty Dog Four-oh-six, coast guard Dolphin."

"Charlie Golf, Salty Four-oh-six."

From the sound of Bergman's voice, Rosenbaum sensed trouble.

"Salty, we have a problem."

"What kind of problem?"

Bergman explained the situation and estimated that he would be able to retrieve his PJ in approximately twelve to fifteen minutes.

Waiting to break out of the clouds, Rosenbaum glanced at his altimeter. "Okay, but we don't have much time."

"Roger that."

"Ringleader, Salty Four-oh-six, how are we looking?"

"Target—uh, the ship is eleven-thirty, thirty-three miles."

"Salty Four-oh-six." Rosenbaum again checked his altimeter as the jets descended through 7,000 feet at 1,500 feet a minute. "Salty Two, did you copy Charlie Golf?"

"That's affirmative."

"Okay, time is critical. We're going to strafe the ship until the helo returns, maybe punch a few holes near the waterline."

Worthington concentrated on flying in tight formation. "What about the rescue swimmer?"

"He's safe on the bow, no problem with him," Rosenbaum said, as the fighters passed 6,300 feet. "We're going to work on the stern, port side, nice and clean."

"Copy: stern, port side."

Click-click.

Each Hornet was fitted with a powerful M-61 rotary cannon mounted inside the nose of the aircraft. Equipped with six barrels, the Gatling gun could pour twenty-millimeter shells into a target at the rate of 6,000 rounds per minute. However, the gun carried only 568 rounds, requiring the pilot to shoot in short, accurate bursts.

A skilled aviator could work the cannon like an airborne buzz saw, spewing death and destruction in a confined area. You could smell the cordite and feel the gun through the airframe as the target was obliterated in front of your eyes. The experience was so mesmerizing that some pilots flew into the ground with their finger still pulling the trigger.

Descending through 2,000 feet, Rosenbaum began to slow his rate of descent. "Jon, we're not going to have much to work with, hard to achieve fifteen degrees nose down with an eight-hundred-foot ceiling."

"Any suggestions?" Worthington asked.

"Let's start as high as we can and *not* go below three hundred feet."

"Okay, but I'll be experimenting."

"That makes two of us."

At 900 feet, the Hornets began to break out of the clouds. They leveled at 800 feet under a ragged ceiling and low visibility. Rosenbaum saw the *QM2*'s wake directly in front of him and looked to the left. The jets were a half mile behind the ship.

Rosenbaum keyed his radio. "Okay, Salty Two, we're going to make a pass up the port side of the ship and commence a port turn. When we roll in on the stern, we'll arm 'em up. Coming off target, we'll safe the guns and begin a left-hand pattern. That way we won't ever have our guns trained on the rescue swimmer."

"Copy."

Passing abeam the bow of the *QM2,* Rosenbaum began a left turn and called the Hawkeye. "Ringleader, Salty Four-oh-six, we have a positive ID on the *Queen* and we're ready to dance."

"You're cleared in hot."

"Roger that."

Although he wasn't being shot at, Rosenbaum made an aggressive roll-in maneuver toward the stern of the ship and flipped his master armament switch on. "One's in hot."

He concentrated on placing the gun sight reticle squarely on the hull where it met the waterline. Squeezing the trigger for a short burst, Rosenbaum watched as the water appeared to boil. *Buuuurrrpp.*

Salty 406 pulled off hard, clearing the ship by 200 feet and disarming his master arm switch. "One's off, nose cold."

Petty Officer Red Bailey was stunned when the Hornet flight leader began firing at the ship. He sprawled on his belly and prayed that nothing would ricochet toward the bow. *God, I hope they don't start bombing before my ride gets back!* He kept his head down and his eyes closed while the second fighter strafed the stern of the *QM2. Buuuuuurrrrpp!* The sound of the cannon reminded Bailey of a long, deep belch.

After each jet made another strafing pass, Bailey's curiosity began to get the best of him. He rose to his knees and watched the fighters attack the doomed ship. On the last run, the wingman barely cleared the cruise liner after his pass. Bailey drew in his breath. *That was damn close.*

Lieutenant Worthington felt the adrenaline shot to his heart as he disarmed the Gatling gun. "Two's off, nose cold." His voice was an octave higher than normal.

"Salty Two, you okay?" Rosenbaum asked.

Worthington pulled the Hornet into a tight left turn. *Don't ever do that again.* "I'll be okay as soon as I catch my breath."

"Salty Four-oh-six, what's the status of the ship?" the Hawk-eye mission systems operator asked.

"We've made some progress; it's definitely taking on water."

"Are you making more strafing passes?"

"Negative, we're Winchester on ammo. Bombs are next."

"Copy."

"Salty Four-oh-six, coast guard Dolphin. We're five miles out."

"Roger."

Rosenbaum and Worthington circled the *Queen Mary 2* while Jeff Bergman picked up his PJ. Red Bailey was a happy man once he was in the basket and airborne.

Looking to the north, Rosenbaum could see the ship was due south of Jones Beach State Park. Although she was taking on water, the majestic liner was still traveling at a high rate of speed. "Ringleader, Salty Four-oh-six is ready for the heavy hardware."

"You're cleared in hot, expedite every chance you get."

"What about the air traffic around JFK?" Rosenbaum asked.

"They're diverting incoming flights and holding everything else on the ground. You have priority."

"Roger that."

Rosenbaum flirted with the idea of making a single pass and dropping all four bombs at once, then discarded the notion. If something went wrong and he missed the ship, it would be up to Worthington to stop the *QM2.* "Salty Two, we're going to drop one—repeat—one bomb at a time."

"Copy, one at a time."

Punching up the proper switches and buttons for bombing, Rosenbaum keyed the radio. "Jon, let's concentrate on hitting her amidships at the waterline. Keep the pattern tight, left-hand pattern."

"Amidships, left turns."

Rosenbaum selected the program to drop only one bomb at a time. Next, he chose auto-bombing mode and flipped the master armament switch on. "One's in hot."

Rolling in on the ship, Rosenbaum snapped the nose down and placed the pipper on the center of *QM2*'s hull at the waterline. He designated the aiming point, hit the pickle button, checked his altitude, started pulling up while following the displayed impact line, and checked his wings level. The Mark-84 2,000-pound bomb released a split second later.

"Salty One's off, switches safe." Rosenbaum flinched when something flashed past his canopy. "What the hell!"

"Two's aborting!" Worthington said, as he pulled up. "Skipper, we have a news helo over the ship."

"Say again?"

"A dumb-ass in a news helo almost mid-aired you."

Agitated by the close call, Rosenbaum keyed his radio. "Ringleader, get this clown out of here—now!"

"We don't show anything, but we're talking with the Feds."

After another trip around the pattern, Rosenbaum saw the helicopter depart toward New York City. "Okay, Jon, do your magic."

"Two's in hot." Worthington aimed slightly to the left of the gaping hole in the hull. A tremendous explosion blasted water over 200 feet into the air. The impact ripped open a section of the ship that joined the damage done by his skipper.

Rosenbaum's next Mark-84 penetrated the hull to the right of his first attack. The ship was beginning to list to port and had slowed a few knots.

"Okay, Jon, work your way aft, see if we can flood the lower decks."

"Goin' aft."

Worthington's bomb caused a secondary explosion. It produced a thick cloud of black smoke that trailed behind the badly damaged *QM2*.

On his next pass, Rosenbaum placed his third bomb in the center of the smoke billowing from the ship. A huge ball of fire accompanied the blast, and the mighty ship began to slow even more.

"Salty Two, try one near the bow."

"Copy."

Rolling in for his third pass, Worthington put his bomb through the hull sixty-five feet from the bow.

"Nice throw," Rosenbaum said.

Click-click.

Rosenbaum's last Mark-84 went high and exploded in the center of the shuffleboard-and-swimming-pool area on Deck 12. "Jon, I screwed up. You gotta finish her off."

"I'll give it my best." Worthington went for the same area where the fireball erupted from the ship. The ensuing explosion caused a powerful concussion that rocked Worthington's plane as he pulled out of his dive. "I must've hit the jackpot."

Banking so Worthington could join on his wing, Rosenbaum glanced at the other Hornet and did a double take. "Salty Two, you're smoking, trailing something from your belly."

"Yeah, things just got busy in here."

"Take it to JFK—now!"

"Roger that, skipper." Worthington turned directly toward John F. Kennedy International Airport.

"Ringleader, Salty Four-oh-six."

"Salty, we're talking to the tower at JFK—your playmate is cleared to land. What's the status of the ship?"

"It's badly listing and continuing to slow, but we need more hits, like in the next few minutes."

"We have bombers—ah, four minutes out and a Texaco standing by to give you a drink."

Rosenbaum checked his fuel and decided to play it safe. "I'm going to orbit overhead, then go in to JFK."

"Roger that, and—ah, hold overhead at eight thousand."

"Climbing to eight, Salty Four-oh-six."

Right on time, the other F/A-18 Hornets attacked the slow-moving ship. After the third aircraft simultaneously dropped two bombs, the grand ocean liner began to capsize southwest of Long Beach. With incredible precision and timing, the tactical jets continued their relentless assault on the *Queen Mary 2*.

The Winslow Estate

Hartwell Prost called from the VIP helicopter when he left the White House landing pad. Molly silently swung into action and began preparing a hearty breakfast for Mr. Prost and his guests. Zachary, Jackie, and Scott assisted Molly while all four kept a watchful eye on the news concerning the beleaguered luxury liner. Wire-service reports were now confirming the worst fears: the entire crew of the *QM2* and all the passengers had died from unknown causes.

A news helicopter was providing television coverage from a safe distance, but the enhanced images on the screen seemed much closer, especially when the bombs exploded. It was surprising how accurate and detailed the initial news reports were. The media professionals dedicated to monitoring the various radio scanners were doing a great job of separating fact from rumor. A few media sources were reporting that two people had been rescued from the ship, but the reports were unconfirmed.

The disaster was flashing around the world while international press sources began focusing on the appalling terrorist attack. Most of the commentators made comparisons to the horrific assault on the World Trade Center and the Pentagon.

The minute-by-minute updates on the tragic story were heart-wrenching. But watching fighter planes from the U.S. Navy and the marine corps strafe and bomb the battered ship were too much for many viewers. It was like watching the Twin Towers collapse in slow motion.

On a split screen, viewers could see additional helicopters taking off in the general direction of the *Queen Mary 2*. Another live broadcast showed dozens of rescue boats leaving foaming white wakes as they rushed to intercept the stricken ship. The crews were betting that some of the passengers might still be alive and would abandon ship.

Suddenly Fox News interrupted their broadcast with a devastating announcement. The anchor was just taking his chair when the camera began transmitting the live report. "This just in to Fox News. We have, as of this moment, received confirmation from senior members of the White House that Secretary of State

Brett Shannon perished onboard the stricken *Queen Mary 2*. Initial reports state that his staff was with him. There are conflicting accounts of a delegation of lawmakers in his party."

The anchor continued to update the astounding story while U.S. Navy and marines corps planes continued to bombard the ill-fated *QM2* on the split screen. For many viewers, the images were surreal. The eye transmitted the information to the brain, but processing it into reality was difficult at best.

Jackie, Scott, Molly, and Zachary stopped what they were doing when the mighty ship began rolling faster and then capsized. The turbulent waves were carrying scores of bodies away from the *QM2* as she slipped beneath the water. Only her four-pod propulsion system and the red bottom of her hull protruded from the water. For most viewers, it was a horrifying sight.

Jackie was the first to find her voice. "Another phase of the jihad has begun," she said bitterly. "There's going to be hell to pay again, and I mean *hell* to pay."

"You're right," Scott said. He heard the sound of an approaching helicopter. "Hartwell's back."

When the national security adviser walked in, Zachary and Molly were putting the finishing touches on a buffet-style breakfast. Hartwell looked emotionally drained. He thanked Molly and Zachary and they left the room. The threesome quietly filled their plates and sat down in the breakfast nook adjacent to the kitchen.

No one spoke while Hartwell spread his napkin across his lap and reached for the coffee urn. He poured coffee to the brim of his cup. "The Berlin Wall has fallen, the Cold War is over, Saddam is history, and now we've entered another phase of the war on terrorism." Hartwell's eyes were full of contempt. "The eradication of the barbarians on this planet—every damn last one of them."

He explained the known details of the *QM2* disaster to Jackie and Scott, followed by news of the tragedy aboard USS *Truman*.

Stunned by the magnitude of the two disasters, Jackie and Scott stopped eating and listened.

"And there's more." Hartwell leaned back in his chair.

"Zheng Yen-Tsung was not your bomber in Texas. The Fort Worth policeman, who, by the way, is reported to be in good condition, told the FBI the driver of the car looked Middle Eastern. He only saw the man for a brief moment, but he remembers him having dark, deep-set eyes. Definitely not Oriental."

"Farkas," Jackie said. "Khaliq Farkas."

Hartwell nodded. "That would be my first guess."

"Ditto," Scott said. "Farkas is one of Shayhidi's most experienced thugs. He'll be in the middle of the action."

"That's how we see it." Hartwell reached for the briefing folder he brought from the White House. "We believe he's been in hiding outside the United States and had orders to eliminate the two of you before their next reign of terror began."

Scott glanced out the bay window. "Well, they had to start without our dead bodies." He caught Hartwell's attention. "What does the president plan to do?"

Prost took a sip of coffee. "As you saw after the attacks on New York City and Washington, *assured response* is the paradigm in our deterrent posture. We don't know where a lot of the terrorist leaders are, which embarrasses me a great deal, but Shayhidi occasionally surfaces in various places around the world. We're just never fast enough to snatch him before he disappears again, but I'm convinced we'll get him now."

"Echelon Two?" Jackie asked.

"Perhaps. He has social and business dealings all over the planet. He spends most of his time taking care of legitimate enterprises: shipping, banking, oil trading, charities, and other interests. He meets with the senior leaders in his terrorist organization, including Farkas, three or four times a year and then goes back to running his legitimate businesses."

Hartwell paused as if he were savoring the bouquet of a vintage Bordeaux. "We've created a large dent in Shayhidi's armor. For the past month, we've been able to track his new plane sixty-eight percent of the time."

"I don't understand," Jackie said.

"We bugged it," Hartwell admitted.

"That's great, terrific." Scott gave Hartwell a thumbs-up gesture. "The Bug Man?"

"Yes. We had some help from the Agency while the plane was undergoing an interior completion at Lufthansa Technik in Hamburg."

Scott allowed a brief smile, remembering shared beers and great ideas with the legendary CIA agent known as the Bug Man.

"He managed to install listening devices in the plane's cabin. The cockpit, where we really wanted access, was tightly sealed and unreachable in the amount of time he had."

Scott had a question. "Shayhidi never showed up to inspect the work while the plane was there?"

"Not once, but we were waiting. His pilots and the four guards who watched over the plane twenty-four hours a day were the only people we encountered."

Hartwell paused a moment when Molly walked in to refill their coffee urn. He thanked her and waited until she left the room. "Between Echelon Two and the listening devices, we've been able to keep fairly close tabs on Shayhidi, but not all the time. On many occasions, from what we've been able to cobble, Shayhidi gets off the plane at a given location and the pilots fly it to another airport. It's a cloak-and-dagger thing, and Shayhidi plays the game extremely well."

A momentary look of satisfaction crossed Hartwell's face. "At any rate, Mr. Saeed Shayhidi's daily or nightly routine is about to be inextricably altered—*shattered* is a better word for what's in store for him."

Hartwell folded his napkin on the table. "The president has a wide menu of options at his disposal. SecDef, General Chalmers, and I believe—when exercised—they will have a *profound* effect on Shayhidi, as well as on other terrorists. I don't know which options President Macklin will decide to use, but keep an eye on the news for the next few days."

Unable to shake the image of Brett Shannon from his thoughts, Hartwell extracted a few sheets of paper from his folder. "On to our project in the northwest. Marines from Camp Pendleton, the First Special Forces Group from Fort Lewis, and national guard units are being deployed along selected areas of the U.S.–Canadian border."

"What about surveillance?" Scott asked.

"We're putting on a full-court press, everything we have available, including two innovations from *black* programs." Hartwell studied his briefing points. "Taking into account where the three terrorists were killed by the U.S. Border Patrol agent, we would like to have you start at that point and do a low-level airborne search for anything suspicious."

He unfolded a highly detailed Great Falls sectional aeronautical chart and placed it on the table.

"From what we know, FBI, and CIA, there is a pattern emerging. It runs from the west side of the Montana–Idaho border to Coeur d'Alene, to Boise, and then to the Twin Falls area."

Jackie surveyed the chart. "Are those the areas where the suspicious people have been congregating?"

"Middle Eastern?" Scott asked.

"For the most part, but there are a lot of Islamic extremists who don't share the indigenous characteristics of the Middle East. We've also been observing Orientals, Caucasians, blacks, Ethiopians, and so on."

"What about the nukes?" Jackie asked.

"We believe the other six bombs came in the same way, but where they are now is anyone's guess." Hartwell handed each of them a thin bound folder. "You'll meet the FBI special agent in charge at Coeur d'Alene. He's been there for several months and will brief you, share what they have, before you start an aerial search with the helicopter." He looked at Jackie. "We have a LongRanger ready."

"Sounds good to me, one of my favorites." She glanced at the sectional chart. "Where's the helo located?"

"It'll be at Spokane International day after tomorrow. Your plane—I'm assuming you'll fly your plane to Spokane—will be guarded around the clock at the FBO, Spokane Airways."

"Thanks," Scott said. "Appreciate it."

Hartwell handed the sectional chart to Jackie. "You're on your own. If you find anything or need anything, let me know."

"We'll do it," Jackie said, as she and Scott rose from their chairs.

They shook hands with all around, thanked Molly and Zachary

for breakfast, and walked to their rental car. Scott slipped behind the wheel but made no effort to start the car.

"Are you okay?" Jackie asked.

"I'm fine." Scott turned the ignition key. "I'll feel a lot better when we get our hands on those nukes."

8

Gulfstream N957GA

Jackie flew the Gulfstream 100 from Baltimore to Dulles International, where they turned their new jet over to the linemen at Signature Flight Support.

After leaving the airport, they stopped by their office. Mary Beth Collins, their well-organized office manager, was so emotionally drained by the *Queen Mary 2* disaster that Jackie and Scott insisted she take the rest of the day off.

With Mary Beth on her way home, Scott turned the sound up on the office television. He sorted through the snail mail while Jackie checked their e-mail. She paused and looked at Scott, her eyes reflecting her sadness. "The world's lone superpower and New York City just got another bloody beating. The president better go after Shayhidi and destroy him at any cost."

"You have my vote."

A Fox News flash caught their attention.

> This just in from Reuters. A London-based Arab satellite television station has reported that, although no group has claimed credit, they have information that the terrorist attack on the *Queen Mary 2* is the beginning of another major assault on the United States.

"What else can they do?" Jackie wondered. "Security is tight everywhere; everything is covered."

Scott looked up. "That's when terrorism is most dangerous: when you think you have a handle on the problem and find out you don't."

The frowning TV anchor continued.

> Corroborating evidence of the terrorist campaign came from a correspondent for Reuters. Moh'd Qudamah said he and his cameraman were taken by helicopter across the Iranian border into southwestern Afghanistan, near Pakistan. There they were thoroughly searched and then briefed about the *QM2* by an unknown spokesman.

The anchor was momentarily distracted by more breaking news from Reuters.

> After the shocking disclosure, Mr. Qudamah and his cameraman were detained in Afghanistan until after the attack on the *Queen Mary 2* commenced.

The anchorwoman slid a small stack of new information across her desk, as file footage of military ships suddenly filled the screen.

> This just in to Fox News. Senior White House officials have confirmed that American armed forces have been put on high alert. Warships in Bahrain, headquarters of the U.S. Fifth Fleet, were ordered to sea.
>
> In addition, two American amphibious vessels have left the Red Sea port of Aqaba, cutting short a major military exercise. Our Pentagon correspondent will have an update at the top of the hour. Please stay tuned to Fox News for more breaking news on the tragedy at sea.

Scott checked the phone recorder, making sure it was turned on. "I think it's time to call it a day."

Her eyes brightened. "Let's go fly the Great Lakes, ring ourselves out doing aerobatics."

"Good idea."

"You can fly first," she said, disregarding the fact that the biplane used for aerobatics belonged to Scott.

A slow smile crossed his face. "You're spoiling me."

The Boeing Business Jet

While his plane taxied to the runway at Madrid's Barajas International Airport, Saeed Shayhidi sat in his wide white leather chair at the head of the conference table. The meeting with the prime minister had gone well, and the new shipping contract was expected to be lucrative.

Shayhidi left money on the table, but the prime minister always treated him like royalty. This was important to Shayhidi; most of his close business contacts knew how to exploit that flaw in his negotiating skills.

It had sometimes taken Shayhidi months to negotiate a profitable deal, but recently things seemed to be happening on a daily basis. Business was booming for the shipping magnate. He attributed much of the success to his new business jet. It was a material statement that underscored Shayhidi's status in the world of global business interests.

Powerful people he had known for years seemed to be more respectful now that he owned a $57-million jet. No question about it, things were looking up for Shayhidi and his businesses. The money was flowing faster than he could spend it.

Shayhidi had a satisfying smile on his face, but his happiness was not related to business, the renewed contract, or his jetliner. The *Queen Mary 2* mission had been an unqualified success even though the "death ship" had been prevented from steaming into New York City at full speed. The billionaire was anxiously looking forward to the next steps in his jihad on America.

When the BBJ lined up on the runway and began its takeoff roll, the CIA agent tracking the airplane contacted the Global

Response Center, located on the sixth floor of CIA headquarters. A special team of analysts had been waiting for the priority event to begin. Working with the FBI, the information was sent to their Strategic Information and Operations Center.

The Madrid-based agent had confirmed the instrument flight plan earlier that morning. Now the time of takeoff had been verified. Shayhidi was going to Tripoli for a meeting expected to last at least two hours. The information was immediately sent to the White House and given to President Macklin.

After the big jet lifted off the runway, a recently hired male flight attendant approached Shayhidi. "May I take your order, sir?"

"V-Eight juice, cashews, and warmed marshmallows," Shayhidi demanded in a condescending voice.

A pained look formed on the man's face. "I'm sorry, Mr. Shayhidi, but we don't have any marshmallows."

"What do you mean, you're *sorry*?" Shayhidi's eyes squinted. "You imbecile, make sure you have them in the future. Do I make myself *clear*?"

"Yes, sir." The man's voice quivered.

"What?"

"Yes, sir, you made yourself clear."

"I can't *hear* you."

"You made yourself clear, *sir*!"

"Then get on with it. Don't just stand there looking like an idiot." Shayhidi waved his hand lazily as if he were shooing a fly. The humiliated attendant turned and retreated to the galley. He was back with the juice and cashews in less than a minute.

His aides at the conference table, and the stunning Brazilian model accompanying Shayhidi, would eat and drink exactly what he ordered. That was standard operating procedure for everyone in Shayhidi's upper echelon. While the three senior managers worked on the presentation to be given to the Libyan oil officials, the tall woman with the pouting lips watched a movie about beauty queens. Rachel Portinari was blessed with an incredibly beautiful face and a perfect figure, but she would never be mistaken for a member of the intelligentsia.

Finishing the juice, Shayhidi walked to his executive desk in the office just forward of his stateroom. He signed the papers neatly stacked in the basket and then jotted down a few ideas he wanted to convey to Khaliq Farkas. Using his latest inspiration, Shayhidi sent Farkas a coded e-mail, the first since Farkas reentered the United States.

Echelon Two intercepted Shayhidi's message. The NSA analysts were disappointed to see the indecipherable gibberish. However, they were able to confirm that the destination server placed Farkas in the Idaho–Utah area. They would have to regroup and again work overtime to outmaneuver the wily Shayhidi.

When his plane began descending near Libya, Shayhidi sent an uncoded message to his home office in Geneva. He then took a hot shower and changed into a fresh suit for the important meeting in Tripoli. If things worked in his favor, he planned to celebrate wildly with his trophy girlfriend on the way back to Geneva.

U.S. Air Force Global Hawk

Northrop Grumman's high-altitude long-endurance unmanned aerial vehicle became the first such UAV to cross the Pacific Ocean successfully. The surveillance craft flew from Edwards Air Force Base in California to a military base outside Adelaide, Australia, a distance of 8,550 statute miles. Global Hawk traversed the Pacific in approximately twenty-two hours. Preprogrammed by ground-station personnel for the long flight across the ocean, the UAV was constantly monitored but not controlled, even when it encountered severe turbulence and unpredictable weather.

With a wingspan of 116 feet, the single-engine reconnaissance UAV has a range of over 16,500 statute miles at altitudes up to 65,000 feet. Dispatched with a maximum takeoff weight of 25,600 pounds, the autonomously controlled aerial platform can remain airborne for forty-two hours. Equipped with infrared capability and optical cameras, a synthetic aperture radar, and a four-foot satellite dish, Global Hawk can provide responsive data from anywhere in the world, day or night, regardless of the weather conditions.

When the UAV is employed as a surrogate surveillance satellite, a controller can redirect the vehicle anywhere in the world without having to wait for the next orbit to change course. Global Hawks can carry out their missions in more than one theater of operations while a single controller oversees the entire operation.

Because the UAV operates at a significantly lower altitude than a spy satellite, its sensors produce higher-resolution images with less distortion. The downside to using the UAV is the constant worry about colliding with commercial or military aircraft while ascending or descending. Upgraded models would address the problem of collision avoidance.

Based in the United Arab Emirates, one of the stealthy Global Hawks was loitering high over Tripoli, Libya. Situated along the southern coastline of the Mediterranean Sea, Tripoli is Libya's capital, largest city, chief seaport, and a haven for terrorists of all stripes.

Operating at 63,000 feet and flying much slower than its cruise speed of 454 miles per hour, the Global Hawk detected Shayhidi's BBJ. When the corporate jet entered Libyan airspace, the undetected UAV monitored radio calls between the pilots and the controllers. After the Boeing Business Jet landed in Tripoli and parked on the ramp, Global Hawk sent near-real-time intelligence imagery to President Macklin via worldwide satellite communications links. The integrated sensor suite in the UAV provided the commander in chief and his decision makers unparalleled reconnaissance data.

The Boeing Business Jet

Normally, Saeed Shayhidi preferred holding meetings in the safety of his plane, but diplomatic precedence, formality, and etiquette had to be followed for each occasion. Over the years, Shayhidi had compiled a thick instruction manual that included rules and regulations, necessary customs, and dress codes for most of the countries in the world.

For each host, president, sovereign, monarch, emperor, chieftain, prime minister, or crowned head, certain strict guidelines had to be followed to the letter. Today, a pair of identical limousines would take Shayhidi and his managers to the meeting site, while a third limo would cater to the dark-haired beauty from Brasilia. Rachel Portinari would go sightseeing and shopping during the stopover. While the jet was being refueled for Shayhidi's flight to Geneva, he approached the first limousine in line. His underlings walked to the second limo.

Exhausted from being on duty round the clock for three days, the Syrian pilots went over the flight plan for the last segment of the trip and then took a nap in the jet. The disconcerted flight attendant tidied the BBJ and went to see if he could find marshmallows in Tripoli.

The White House

President Cord Macklin projected the image of the consummate Washington politician, though he still thought of himself as an aging air force fighter jock. The former F-105 Thunderchief pilot—Thud driver, in fighter parlance—had survived many close calls, including being shot down, during his two tours in Vietnam.

Tall and trim, with silver-gray hair and deep blue eyes, Macklin was always impeccably attired, be it in a business suit, evening wear, or a pair of denim jeans and a cable-stitch sweater. An avid golfer and trapshooting enthusiast, he possessed a great sense of humor and a self-deprecating personality that made people feel at ease. Although Macklin was a thoughtful, considerate man, he didn't suffer fools well.

The Oval Office was quiet while the president reviewed the latest reconnaissance information from Global Hawk and various space-based assets. Knowing the window of opportunity was rapidly closing, Pete Adair, Hartwell Prost, and General

Les Chalmers were impatiently waiting for their boss to make a decision.

Leaning back in his chair, Macklin removed his tortoiseshell spectacles and turned to Prost. "What do you recommend?"

"Not wasting another minute."

The president was pleasantly surprised by Prost's emphatic response. The *QM2* tragedy had everyone on edge.

"Pete?" Macklin asked.

"I agree, sir," he said urgently. "It's time to move out."

"Les, what say you?"

"I strongly recommend *immediate* action," Chalmers replied.

Macklin clasped his fingers together and leaned his elbows on the desk. "Gentlemen, let's do it—no mistakes."

Georgetown

Scott and Jackie were packing for their trip to Spokane when the satellite phone rang. She answered it and then covered the mouthpiece with her hand. "It's Hartwell."

Scott nodded and continued packing.

Jackie mostly listened during the brief conversation, thanked Prost for the latest information, and put the phone down. "Some unexpected news, good and not so good."

"And?"

"The bad news first. Shayhidi is using a homemade code to send Khaliq Farkas e-mail, so we don't know what they're doing or are about to do. We'd know a lot more if Shayhidi was using encrypted messages."

"The good news?"

"Farkas is in the Idaho–Utah area. That's where the e-mail went, but they can't be more specific."

"Well, it's a start, and it tracks with the migration of terrorists coming into the area from Canada." Scott zipped his luggage closed. "Locating Farkas is the first step."

"Oh, one other thing," Jackie said. "Hartwell reminded us to keep an eye on the television."

The Boeing Business Jet

Stretched out in the comfortable backseat of his limousine, Saeed Shayhidi adjusted the air-conditioning and paused to reflect on his good fortune. He was pleased with himself, pleased indeed. The expanded oil-shipping contract was more than he had counted on or bargained for. Now, after he assured the Libyans he had the capacity to deliver on the newly signed agreement, Shayhidi would have to locate two additional tanker ships or forfeit a $14.3-million bonus.

The vessels would have to be supertankers, behemoths capable of carrying over seventy million gallons of crude oil. This was not going to be an easy task, given the time frame. Since there are not many idle supertankers floating around, it would cost a fortune up front, but the long-term payout looked good.

Shayhidi felt confident that he could again bribe the man who supplied his last two tankers. In the maritime shipping business, Alexi Ogarkov was known as a truly venal man who was both revered and feared by his associates. For a seabag full of unmarked cash, Ogarkov would produce the two tankers.

The pair of matched limousines were just entering the Tripoli airport ramp when Shayhidi gazed at his sleek, gleaming new plane. The third limo was parked parallel to the leading edge of the left wing of the Boeing Business Jet. The driver was carrying several large shopping bags aboard the airplane while the slender supermodel waited in the coolness of the shiny limousine.

The immaculate BBJ was shimmering in the heat rising from the blistering pavement. Through the tinted glass of his limousine, Shayhidi took a moment to gaze at his latest symbol of wealth and power. A smile of satisfaction was beginning to form on Shayhidi's face when a GPS-guided Tomahawk cruise missile slammed into his airplane's fuselage directly over the right wing root.

The horrific, blinding explosion blew the refueled airplane in half, slinging flaming debris and burning fuel in every direction. A secondary explosion caused a brilliant fireball to rise straight up, turning into black smoke as it gained altitude.

Frozen in fear, Saeed Shayhidi was thrown forward violently into the empty seats when his startled chauffeur jammed the brake pedal to the floor. The second limousine driver braked hard and swerved in an attempt to avoid Shayhidi's automobile. A second too late, he plowed into the rear of Shayhidi's limo, sending both cars sliding out of control.

Waiting inside the airplane for Shayhidi to arrive, the two pilots, the flight attendant, and the limo driver perished in the initial explosion. A third, thunderous explosion completely enveloped the burning jet in reddish-orange flames and billowing clouds of black, oily smoke. More flaming debris rained down, hitting other airplanes and bouncing off the tops of the limousines.

A smaller corporate jet, about to taxi for takeoff, caught fire when its fuel tanks were punctured by large pieces of flaming shrapnel. The panicked passengers and flight crew immediately evacuated the Sabreliner 65 and raced for cover. Innocent victims on the ramp were running for their lives, some stumbling over others in their desperate attempt to escape the burning jet fuel.

Waiting in the limousine, Rachel Portinari survived the first two earth-shattering explosions, but the vibrant young woman succumbed to the third powerful detonation.

Shayhidi was shocked speechless. His most cherished possession had been destroyed right in front of his eyes. *They know. The Americans must know I was behind the* QM2*—but how?*

Without a thought for the condition of the model, his longtime pilots, and his flight attendant, Shayhidi climbed out of the limousine and ran toward the terminal building. His trio of senior managers and the astonished limo drivers fell in step behind him while pandemonium reigned at the airport.

When the men were safely inside the structure, Shayhidi could no longer contain his rage. He began ranting and raving at the top of his voice, cursing President Macklin and the U.S. military forces for destroying his new jet. After the better part of a minute, he assumed a more coherent manner and sat down.

"If we were twenty seconds earlier, I would have been killed," Shayhidi bitterly complained while he stared at the remains of his burning plane. Firefighters were working feverishly to quell the inferno. "I would have been in the plane."

The excruciating reality cascaded through his mind. *The Americans will hunt me down. What do I do? Where do I go?*

He turned to his senior managers. "Get a chartered jet in here and don't use my name—move!"

"Yes, sir," the threesome said in chorus. Like lemmings, the hollow-eyed men rushed off to comply with the order. The rumors about their boss's connections to terrorist groups enveloped them in a cloud of doubt. *Was Shayhidi involved in the ocean liner disaster? If so, would this attack mean the end of their lucrative jobs, their luxurious lifestyles?* Their boss was an unpredictable man when he was angry. Either way, they understood their future was suddenly at risk.

Still dumbfounded by the precision missile attack, Shayhidi forced himself to breathe slowly. Fear began to fade as feelings of utter hostility swept over him. Raising both hands to wipe his face, he became aware that his hands were shaking. He crossed his arms over his chest in an attempt to appear calm and collected.

A pattern of illogical thoughts began consuming him. *The American president is going to rue the day he did this to me. I will show him what it is like to provoke Saeed Shayhidi.*

SSN 768 *Hartford*

Operating in the depths of the eastern Mediterranean Sea, the Los Angeles–class attack submarine *Hartford* turned on course to the U.S. Naval Base at La Maddalena, a small Italian island located off the northern coast of the island of Sardinia. The submarine's actual destination was Santo Stefano, a rocky, uncultivated island that was the home port of the U.S. Navy submarine tender USS *Emory S. Land.*

La Maddalena was a tourist resort, and the crew of the *Hartford* was looking forward to a few days of liberty while their submarine was serviced and replenished. They had just completed a successful operation, one that greatly pleased their commander in chief. In a message to the crew, President Cord Macklin assured the submariners he would provide them with a replacement Tomahawk cruise missile.

9

Georgetown

Taking an afternoon walk through the Heights section of Georgetown, Jackie and Scott were discussing their flight to Spokane. They were nearing home when they became aware that something unusual was happening. Neighbors and friends were congregating in the narrow old-fashioned streets. A buzz was definitely afloat.

"Wonder what's going on?" Jackie asked.

"I don't know, but something's in the mill."

Scott heard a Georgetown University student exclaim, "Way to go, Prez. Kick butt big time!"

"Let's jog home," Scott suggested.

"Shayhidi, I'd guess," Jackie said, as they hit their stride. "Hartwell told us to watch for developments."

When they reached their residence, there was a phone message from Mary Beth. Jackie was listening to the secretary's recording when Scott turned on the television to see an image of a charred airplane and a picture of the owner.

Jackie turned to Scott. "Quick, turn up the sound. Have to hear this."

"Got it."

They sat in silence and watched the destruction of Shayhidi's aircraft. The video, which began after the initial explosion, was clear and well focused. The picture tilted sideways and jiggled when the second and third explosions rocked the ramp area. Shayhidi, his three employees, and the two drivers were clearly visible as they ran from the wrecked limousines toward the terminal building.

"I'll be damned," Scott said under his breath. "Hartwell was right on the money. Macklin didn't fool around."

Jackie was still staring at the television images. "Going for the jugular vein, no holding back."

Scott watched the replay of the second and third explosions. "I don't think anyone, especially Shayhidi, doubts Macklin's resolve now."

"They're fools if they do."

Scott shook his head. "I can't believe they missed him by a matter of seconds. Damn close."

She smiled with great satisfaction. "He clearly didn't expect the president to target him personally within two days of the *QM Two* disaster."

"Which means we're going to have a difficult time tracking him." Scott turned down the sound on the television. "He's going to vanish, but someone has to manage his empire on a daily basis. The recon people need to concentrate on his corporate headquarters, his various homes, and his toys."

"Doesn't he own a large yacht?" Jackie asked. "A megayacht?"

"Yes. That's going to be hard to hide."

"He should've bought a submarine," Jackie quipped.

"I'll bet he *wishes* he had a submersible about now." Scott's eyes kept darting to the television. "We can hit you anytime, anywhere."

"Look at this," she said, fascinated by the angry, twisted face on the television. With the burned-out hulk of the BBJ in the background, a dark-haired, mustachioed journalist was speaking with a shrill English accent and gesturing wildly with both arms.

Jackie watched the dramatic gestures for a few seconds. "They don't even know what hit Shayhidi's plane, but the local media is already claiming that President Macklin is actively trying to assassinate one of their highly respected businessmen."

Scott watched as the agitated journalist worked himself into a frenzy. "You have to give them credit," he said. "They have it right, and Shayhidi knows it." He changed channels for a fresh look at the breaking news. "From top dog on his flying carpet to sewer rat on the run, all in the flash of a Tomahawk."

"No kidding," Jackie said. "An unexpected ration of Tomahawk jurisprudence. Gotta love it."

Geneva, Switzerland

Rumpled, unshaven, and exhausted from a circuitous route home to Geneva, Saeed Shayhidi collapsed into his familiar king-sized bed for a few hours of precious rest. On his orders, every light in the residence was turned off and would remain that way.

The normal six-man home security detail had been increased to eleven. The two gates, one for the main entrance and the other for delivery service, were locked and guarded twenty-four hours a day. The home fortress was completely surrounded by electronic surveillance equipment and high-intensity motion-sensor lights. Two of the long-term security supervisors carried shoulder-fired surface-to-air missiles.

Shayhidi's changes of chartered jets in Rome and Paris allowed him cover for the moment, but he knew he could not remain inconspicuous for long. He would have to go into hiding. That would require a great deal of in-depth planning, but first he needed rest. When he awoke, he would contact his second in command, Ahmed Musashi, and turn daily operations over to him. A secure system for communicating would have to be developed and implemented as soon as possible.

Shayhidi would now devote his full time and attention to completing his primary mission: driving the infidels and their military out of the Middle East. He was convinced beyond any doubt that his terrorist actions would soon have the American people crouching in fear. The naïve citizens of the vaunted superpower were about to be tossed from their warm beds into the freezing blizzard of reality.

Shayhidi reasoned, based on four years of immersion in the culture of the United States, that it was only a matter of time before the undisciplined, self-pitying, immoral masses would be begging Macklin to remove the U.S. military from the Persian Gulf and the Middle East. From his experience in the hallowed halls of academia, Shayhidi was certain the elite governing class of intelligentsia in America would soon be demanding an end to the war on terrorism.

Shayhidi would triumph and the Middle Eastern dictators, constitutional monarchs, absolute monarchs, federations of monarchs, rulers, crowned heads, presidents-for-life, and other sponsors of terrorism would breathe a deep sigh of relief.

Democracy? Power exercised directly by the masses? No way, not in the Middle East. These "loyal" subjects could not be trusted to vote for their leaders and representatives. No, that would be disastrous for the Middle East. Western-style democracy would undermine thousands of years of tradition.

Spokane, Washington

When they landed their jet at Spokane International Airport, Jackie and Scott were warmly welcomed at Spokane Airways. Four uniformed security guards met them at the plane and vowed to take good care of their new Gulfstream 100.

As promised, the LongRanger IV helicopter was waiting, the weapons they had requested inside. They unloaded their bags from the G-100 and stowed them in the Bell 206L-4. In less than an hour they would rendezvous with the FBI special agent in Coeur d'Alene.

The helicopter was painted bright yellow with black lettering that advertised SKY TOURS, INC. on the sides and the belly. Equipped with dual controls, the LongRanger had a two-person survival pack and two international orange survival suits in the passenger cabin.

Dressed in Banana Republic–style hiking shorts, boots, and denim shirts with epaulets and four gold stripes, Jackie and

Scott gave the helicopter a thorough inspection and topped off the fuel. Minutes later, they were off to Coeur d'Alene Air Terminal for their noon meeting. Approaching the quaint town, they watched a de Havilland Beaver seaplane land on sparkling Coeur d'Alene Lake. Jackie radioed Resort Aviation Jet Center to order a taxi.

A line tech was refueling the LongRanger when their taxi arrived. When the fueling was completed, Scott took care of the bill and they climbed into the backseat of the taxi.

"Welcome to Coeur d'Alene," the driver said, turning to face his passengers. He showed them his FBI credentials. "I'm Special Agent Frank Wakefield." He extended his hand.

"It's a pleasure." Scott reached to shake Wakefield's hand. "I didn't realize you were working undercover."

Wakefield glanced in the rearview mirror. "It's the only way to stay on top of things around here. These folks don't trust anyone in a business suit."

When they arrived at the FBI's rustic headquarters, Jackie noted a man in bib overalls tending a small garden next to the run-down cabin. They followed Wakefield inside and sat down on a dusty, tattered couch.

The agent took a seat in an oil-stained rocking chair. "First of all, I don't know who you are or what you do. All I need to know is that we're all working on the terrorist situation, correct?"

"That's about it," Scott said.

Wakefield gently rocked the chair. "The majority of people think these terrorists are illiterate street people, but most of them are intelligent, well educated, highly trained, and shrewd—suicide bombers being the exception."

"We've had firsthand experience with some of the best," Scott said, in a flat voice.

"Okay, then you realize the need to appear to be who you aren't. Like I said, it's the only way to gather information."

"We've had some practice," Jackie said, making eye contact. "How are you differentiating between legal immigrants from the Middle East and the terrorists?"

"Our field agents are working with local law enforcement

agencies to establish identities, citizenship, work histories, et cetera, but it isn't easy, legally speaking."

"Racial profiling?" Scott asked.

"Yes, but we're catching quite a few with bogus credentials and a variety of weapons. We try to keep it low-key and get them out of the immediate area as quickly as possible."

Jackie glanced out the window at the agent working in the garden. "From what we understand, this invasion of terrorists extends all the way to the Twin Falls area."

"That's the official line, but we've seen activity and problems branch out in quite a few directions. The primary trail seems to go through Salt Lake City into southern Utah near Cedar City. But Salt Lake City is a dispersal point; from there they go in various directions, sometimes backtracking to head in a different direction."

"How tight is the border?" Scott asked.

A hard look crossed Wakefield's face. "The addition of the military units has helped, especially the elite forces and their stealth operations. But the heavy concentration of military equipment in some areas is like sending up a flare."

Jackie was becoming anxious to get airborne and begin their search before they ran out of daylight. "Anything else you can tell us?"

"No, not much else, but I have a packet for you." He rose and walked to a wooden desk, picked up a waterproof container, and handed it to Jackie. "You'll find phone numbers, radio frequencies, locations of our command posts and the joint operations center, plus other info you may need. We're big on communications and keeping one another in the loop."

"You can count on us," Jackie said, without expression.

Wakefield's curiosity needed to be satisfied. "You *are* with the government, right? Some extension of the CIA or DEA?"

She smiled and tilted her head. "Actually, we're *not* with the government. No connection."

He tried to conceal his surprise. "Well, my orders came from the top, so that's all I need to know. How can I get in touch with you?"

Jackie gave him the codes for their satellite phones. "The first one is our primary means of communicating."

"Great," he said, and pocketed the piece of paper.

Scott rose from the couch. "We appreciate your help. Thanks."

"Happy to do it." The hard look returned. "As I'm sure you know, a lot of these terrorists are ruthless zealots from many different countries. Some are certified nutcases who look forward to dying. Even the most harmless-looking person could be a mass murderer, so don't let your guard down for a second."

Scott extended his hand. "Your point is well taken."

Wakefield gave him a firm handshake. "I'll have my *gardener* drive you back to the airport."

"Appreciate it."

When Jackie lifted the LongRanger off the ramp, Scott noticed four marine corps AH-1W Super Cobra attack helicopters preparing to land.

He pointed to the gunships. "Looks like they're bringing in some heavy firepower."

Jackie answered a radio call from the control tower before turning to Scott. "After all that's happened, I'd say it's time to project power."

They flew at a leisurely pace while Scott used his binoculars to survey the terrain. The closer they came to the Canadian border, the more helicopters and airplanes they encountered.

Scott raised his binoculars and focused on an army UH-1H Huey helicopter hovering over a road. "We sure have a strange mix of civilian and military aircraft clustered in the same area."

Jackie checked to her right and banked the helo into a sweeping turn. "We'll try another route back."

She remained fifteen miles east of the Washington border until they were closer to Coeur d'Alene. Low on fuel, they landed and stretched their legs. After refueling, they headed north again and searched an area south of the Canadian border and west of the Montana line.

They made another fuel stop at the tourist town of Sandpoint and then flew over picturesque Lake Pend Oreille. Hundreds of blue herons were perched in the backwater reeds, and a bull moose meandered close to the placid lake. When they reached the Coeur d'Alene National Forest, Jackie made a minor course change to the east and began a gradual descent. They covered another twelve miles and decided it was becoming too dark to see much in the thick forest canopy.

Scott was about to stow his binoculars when he spotted a small campfire. "Make a three-sixty to the left." The glow suddenly disappeared. "Someone just put out his fire."

"Are you sure?"

"Positive." He glanced at the GPS coordinates and kept his binoculars on the same spot. "Bring it around into a hover about—coming up at your one o'clock, sixty to seventy yards."

"You're seeing things."

"I know what I saw—hey, there's movement down there!"

The LongRanger was slowing to a hover when two rifle rounds shattered the helicopter's chin bubble.

"Go—go—hit it!" Scott said, as Jackie lowered the nose and pulled maximum power.

"Seeing things?" Scott asked with a dash of sarcasm. He opened the plastic packet Wakefield had given them.

"Did you notice the GPS?" she asked.

"Yeah, got it nailed." Scott used the satellite phone to contact Wakefield. He explained what happened, gave him the coordinates of the campsite, and signed off. "They're on it as we speak."

"Well," Jackie said, with a wide-eyed look, "I think that's enough excitement for one day, at least for me."

"Yeah. Let's stay in Coeur d'Alene tonight."

Jackie surveyed the minor damage their helicopter sustained. "Almost seven hours, par for the course."

"What?"

She glanced at him and smiled. "We haven't had the helo for a full day and it's already damaged."

He shrugged and studied the ragged holes. "We'll get some duct tape and patch the holes, keep the breeze from blowing through."

Coeur d'Alene, Idaho

Returning to Coeur d'Alene's signature resort, Scott and Jackie walked around for a few minutes to cool down after their three-mile jog. He pulled a quarter out of a pocket in his hiking shorts and flipped it. "Your call."

"Tails."

He caught the coin and slapped it on the back of his hand. They peeked at the results.

"You get the shower first," Scott said, as they entered their luxurious room.

After they were refreshed, Jackie opened her flight bag and retrieved the GREAT FALLS and SALK LAKE CITY sectional charts. "I think we need to use a search grid."

"Makes sense to take a methodical approach. We know Farkas is out here somewhere; we just have to find him."

She nodded and moved the floor lamp closer to the table. "Yeah, we know what he can do with an airplane or a dozen aircraft radios." Jackie neatly folded the GREAT FALLS chart into a small manageable square. "I think we should be airborne as early as possible. Okay with you?"

"Absolutely."

The satellite phone rang. As Scott answered it, Jackie began working on the chart with a colored marker. She wanted to check every out-of-the-way airport along the route to southern Utah. She drew a straight line to Cedar City and began studying the remote airports along the way.

Scott finished his conversation and sprawled across the bed. "That was Wakefield. It wasn't Farkas or any other terrorist who shot at us."

"Oh, really?" she asked skeptically. "How can he be so sure?"

Scott rolled onto his back. "The terrorists aren't into Miller Beer, Red Man chewing tobacco, or brochures for the local militia."

"Okay, who was it?"

"Wakefield thinks they were local good ol' boys—some drunken moron got trigger happy."

"Great. Can't wait for tomorrow."

10

Albany, New York

Omar Abdul-Baasit, Servant of the Extender, Creator, and his Saudi Arabian copilot, Uthman ibn 'Abd al-Wahhab, had flown the Bombardier Challenger 601-1A into Albany International Airport the previous evening. Like other corporate pilots, Abdul-Baasit chatted with the line service technicians while the copilot installed the engine covers. After the aircraft was secured for the evening, al-Wahhab hailed a taxi to the bus station. He would return to his rented home in Pittsburgh, Pennsylvania, and remain in the sleeper cell until his next mission was assigned.

Abdul-Baasit, along with twenty-two other specially selected flight students from the Middle East, had spent eleven months at various flight schools in Arizona, Texas, North Dakota, and Florida. They collectively terminated their training on September 6, 2001, and went to work for Shayhidi-controlled charities and businesses in Florida, Pennsylvania, Massachusetts, New York, New Jersey, and Maryland.

More experienced and knowledgeable than the suicide pilots who destroyed the World Trade Center and damaged the Pentagon, Abdul-Baasit and his fellow sleepers would not have to rely on hijacking airplanes to complete their missions. Besides, the possibility of commandeering U.S. airliners after September 11 was substantially diminished, if not all but eliminated.

Shayhidi paid over $3.4 million for the in-depth aviation training, including housing, essentials, and generous periodic stipends to the flight students. To Shayhidi's great delight, the time had finally arrived to begin capitalizing on his considerable financial investment. Abdul-Baasit and others like him were ready to carry out their missions.

Following explicit instructions directly from Khaliq Farkas, Abdul-Baasit slept in the corporate jet. Minutes before sunrise, Abdul-Baasit would file his flight plan with the FBO and order all the jet fuel the airplane could hold.

This particular Challenger 601 (N301EP) was quite different from standard versions of the twin-engine jet. Like many large transports once used by U.S. airlines and later sold to Latin American airlines and cargo operators, used corporate jets found homes in South America. Aircraft sales south of the U.S. border, and the modifications made to those airplanes, received little or no scrutiny.

During the past seventy days, 301EP was transformed into a flying armored tank. The radical change was not noticeable from the exterior, but the interior was unlike any other Challenger in the world. The inside of the jet was gutted, and heavy steel braces were welded together in a strong latticework. A sturdy bulkhead at the entrance to the airplane disguised the contents of the large cabin.

Combined with the seven barrels of fuel oil and the array of explosives on board, the myriad beams were so heavy the jet weighed only slightly less than its maximum gross weight of 43,100 pounds. With full fuel, the Challenger would weigh approximately 57,700 pounds.

Abdul-Baasit, having never flown the reconfigured plane with a full fuel load, was going to be a test pilot in the next thirty minutes. Would he need every inch of the 7,200-foot runway to get airborne, or would he need a lot more room to take off?

Feeling supremely confident, he went into the FBO, filed his instrument flight plan to Philadelphia, and ordered full fuel for the Challenger. The suicide bomber removed the engine covers while he oversaw the fueling. When 1,800 gallons had been pumped into the aircraft, the tires and landing gear were beginning to show the strain.

Abdul-Baasit thought about stopping the fueling at 1,900

gallons, but Farkas had made it clear: The jet must carry every ounce of fuel that could be squeezed in and not a drop less. The Challenger was going to be a huge bomb with wings, the "wings of death," as Farkas stated so strongly on many occasions.

When the fueling was completed, Abdul-Baasit paid his bill, started the powerful engines, and listened to the ATIS. He called Clearance Delivery, received his instrument clearance to Philadelphia International Airport, called Ground Control, and taxied toward Runway 19.

No one noticed that he was flying the jet single pilot, a major violation of FAA mandates. Seven tons over maximum gross weight, the Challenger felt sluggish and required more power than usual to taxi.

He keyed the radio. "Albany Tower, Challenger Three Zero One Echo Papa, ready for takeoff."

"Challenger Three Zero One Echo Papa, taxi into position and hold."

"Position and hold, Zero One Echo Papa."

While he waited for a twin-engine Piper Navajo to clear the active runway, Abdul-Baasit aligned his jet with the runway centerline and came to an abrupt stop.

"Challenger Three Zero One Echo Papa cleared for takeoff."

Abdul-Baasit read back the clearance. He held the brakes and added 60 percent power, released the brakes, and shoved the throttles forward. The airplane slowly accelerated while the engines howled at full thrust. Abdul-Baasit knew an aborted takeoff would be disastrous, but the lack of acceleration was alarming.

He would have to make a critical decision in the next few seconds. Live or die? Succeed or fail? With only 3,000 feet of runway remaining, and the speed still creeping upward, he had a moment of doubt. *Can't fail—won't fail.* Committed to flight, Abdul-Baasit stopped looking at the airspeed indicator.

He waited until the last 300 feet of runway to rotate the nose to its normal takeoff attitude. The Challenger staggered into the air, touched down briefly, and then slowly climbed away from the ground. Abdul-Baasit snapped the landing gear up and coaxed the jet to ascend at 400 feet per minute, an anemic performance for an airplane of its caliber.

Watching the takeoff, the tower controller knew something was wrong. "Challenger Three Zero One Echo Papa, are you experiencing a problem?"

"Zero One Echo Papa is having a pressurization problem," Abdul-Baasit lied. "We'll have it corrected in a minute or two."

"Roger. Contact Departure Control on one-one-eight point zero-five."

"Eighteen point zero-five, One Echo Papa."

Abdul-Baasit contacted departure, let the airspeed build, and slowly increased the rate of climb. The departure controller soon handed off the Challenger to the en-route controller. Approaching 14,000 feet, Abdul-Baasit requested a level off to allow the airspeed to increase. He finally nursed the struggling airplane to 22,000 feet and requested to maintain that altitude. The controller granted his request.

A few minutes later, Abdul-Baasit reported smoke in the cockpit. Following his well-rehearsed plan, he turned the radio volume down, tuned his transponder to 7700 (Emergency) for one minute, and then changed the code to 7600 (Communication Failure).

Abdul-Baasit had flown this same route four times in light planes, and he was extremely familiar with the landmarks. He passed his final checkpoint and began a fairly steep descent, accelerating to Mach 0.85, the maximum Mach number for the airplane.

Flying the heavy Challenger by hand, Abdul-Baasit spotted his target dead ahead on the bank of the Hudson River. He continued to tweak the jet's nose lower and lower until the plane's attitude was 45 percent nose down. He ignored the chattering Mach "knocker" as the Challenger quickly accelerated to Mach 0.89.

His throat was dry, but he was in the zone now, focused on his final mission. Omar Abdul-Baasit never blinked as he bracketed his target twenty-nine miles north of New York City. Feeling a tingling sense of euphoria, the pitiless fool took in a deep breath and let out a piercing scream. Two seconds later the

Bombardier Challenger slammed into the Indian Point Unit 2 Nuclear Power Plant. The incredible kinetic energy created an explosion that registered between 3 and 4 on the Richter scale of several seismographs in the area.

The Pentagon

CNN Pentagon correspondent Christine DeSano was about to deliver an update on the condition of the aircraft carrier USS *Harry Truman* when a flurry of activity interrupted her. Someone offscreen was loudly forwarding breaking news, so Christine tossed the telecast back to the anchor in the studio.

Less than a minute later, the grim-faced DeSano was back live. "We're receiving initial reports that a nuclear power plant, the Indian Point Unit Two, twenty-some miles north of Manhattan, exploded only minutes ago."

She was reading from notes handed to her. "There are conflicting reports on what caused the blast. We understand there are casualties and a large number of injuries."

Another note was held up in her view. "We're . . . just a moment . . . okay: A fireman, apparently at the scene, believes a bomb may have done the damage. That has not been confirmed at this time, but an official believes a bomb, possibly a terrorist-made bomb, may have gone off."

DeSano's cameraman snagged an army lieutenant colonel briskly walking down the hallway. The colonel was discussing the power plant disaster with a junior officer.

"Colonel," DeSano said, thrusting the microphone toward him, "can you tell us what happened at the Indian Point nuclear plant?"

"From what we're hearing, and it's preliminary, an airplane may have struck the power plant. Sorry, have to run."

Frowning, DeSano faced the camera. "Jim, I've just been told by a senior officer that an airplane, possibly another hijacked airliner, struck the nuclear facility. We're looking at another possible series of airline hijackings or worse. Back to you, Jim."

Air Traffic Control System Command Center

Located at Herndon, Virginia, near Dulles International Airport, in an impressive 29,000-square-foot building, the Air Traffic Control Command Center serves as the nerve center for the busy U.S. air traffic control system. Alert for any possible threat or conflict, FAA specialists constantly monitor air traffic, departure delays, and weather conditions nationwide. Networked with the NORAD complex and the joint FAA/Defense Department Air Traffic Services Cell, the Herndon controllers work with the Air Route Traffic Control Centers to help keep the complex system in harmony and flowing smoothly and safely.

After the four airline hijackings on Black Tuesday altered the course of U.S. aviation history, FAA authorities implemented new operating procedures at the command center. The time from the discovery of suspicious actions to alerting NORAD, the North American Aerospace Defense Command, was minimized.

NORAD is a unified U.S. and Canadian command charged with the missions of aerospace warning and aerospace control for North America. Commanded by a senior four-star officer, NORAD is the front line of detection and defense against air and space threats to the United States and Canada. Buried deep inside Cheyenne Mountain near Colorado Springs, Colorado, the complex replaced NORAD's previous vulnerable aboveground facilities in a converted hospital at Ent Air Force Base, Colorado Springs.

This morning the air traffic controllers were frantically trying to confirm what kind of plane hit the Indian Point nuclear power plant. One report said a regional jet airliner crashed into the reactor. Other reports from en-route controllers indicated a Bombardier Challenger corporate jet hit the plant.

The controllers confirmed an emergency squawk from the Challenger but didn't know the nature of the problem. A controller heard a radio call about smoke in the cockpit, but there was no call sign to match against an airplane. The ATC tapes would have to be analyzed.

A quick check with the national Air Route Traffic Control

Centers offered the confirmation that no airline hijacking attempts had been made. From New York Center to Los Angeles Center and Seattle Center to Miami Center, everything seemed in order. The incident at the nuclear power plant appeared to be an isolated event caused by a dire emergency on board the Challenger.

From reports issued by the Albany Control Tower, the Albany departure controller, and the en-route controller, a general consensus soon formed within the FAA community. A pressurization problem or fire and smoke *probably* overcame the Challenger flight crew, but only an investigation by the National Transportation Safety Board (NTSB) could illuminate the real cause of the accident.

Once the crisis mode began to ebb and pulse rates receded, a collective sigh of relief filtered through the command center. The men and women began to relax and enjoy their morning coffee. The flow of air traffic was running smoothly and life was stable once more.

Twenty-one minutes later, another corporate jet deviated from its filed instrument flight plan. The transponder ceased operating and the pilot stopped communicating with the suspicious air traffic controller. Shortly after the break in communications, the fully fueled three-engine Dassault Falcon 50 smashed into the Waterford 3 Nuclear Power Plant in Taft, Louisiana, twenty-three miles west of the French Quarter.

Four minutes later, a Westwind II corporate jet full of fuel and explosives plowed through the Crystal River Nuclear Power Plant seventy miles north of St. Petersburg, Florida. The force of the horrendous impact and explosion instantly knocked out all power to the resort city adjacent to Tampa Bay.

Total chaos erupted in the Air Traffic Control Command Center. The same twisted combination of fear and anger that permeated the ARTCC system during the September 11 airline hijackings returned with a suddenness that thoroughly stunned everyone.

The FAA controllers quickly alerted the FBI and NORAD. The senior officers at NORAD became the focal point for increased military air protection over the United States and Canada. The

NORAD Battle Management Center told each air defense sector to generate sorties as fast as they could. They would direct the fighter pilots sitting alert duty and those flying combat air patrol over major cities in both countries. Some of the first fighters to assume battle stations and get airborne came from Langley AFB, Virginia; Tyndall AFB, Florida; Otis Air National Guard Base, Massachusetts; and Ellington AFB, Texas.

The Cheyenne Mountain Operations Center (CMOC), the core of NORAD operations, was humming with activity. Canadian Forces Brigadier Ian Thackerey, the vice commander of CMOC, rapidly responded to the suicide attacks and was directing the evolving operation.

Acting on a direct order from the four-star commander, NORAD, Thackerey ordered all aircraft, including airliners, corporate jets, general aviation airplanes, and military aircraft not being scrambled for combat air patrols, to land at the nearest suitable airport. The objective was to sanitize the airspace over the United States and Canada as quickly as possible.

President Macklin ordered the military to implement a Force Protection Condition Delta wartime posture. Barricades were quickly erected at gates to many military bases, and machine guns were at the ready. On the orders of the commanding general, the massive steel doors at NORAD were closed for only the second time in its history.

Off the coast of South Carolina, the USS *Enterprise* battle group was at general quarters. The carrier was launching F-14 Tomcats, F/A-18 Hornets, and an E-2C Hawkeye for combat air patrols over any assigned cities or high-risk structures. More aircraft on the flight deck were being armed with heat-seeking Sidewinder missiles and slammers—AMRAAMS—Advanced Medium Range Air-to-Air Missiles. The slammers have an active radar-guidance system and, at Mach 4.0, they are the fastest of the air-to-air weapons. Other ordnance personnel were loading 20mm rounds into the Hornets' and Tomcats' M61 Vulcan cannons.

Dozens of other fighter planes from Canada, the U.S. Air Force, the U.S. Navy, and the U.S. Marine Corps were airborne in a matter of minutes and assumed their combat air-patrol patterns over strategic positions and major metropolitan areas. Dozens of aerial tankers, including KC-135s, KC-130s, and KC-10s, were soon airborne to provide the thirsty fighters with fuel.

Two U.S. Air Force Boeing E-3 Airborne Warning and Control System (AWACS) aircraft from the 552d Air Control Wing at Tinker AFB, Oklahoma City, were providing long-range radar surveillance for the fighter planes. The AWACS mission specialists and the mission crew commanders were primed and ready to direct fighter intercepts against potential bogeys. After a reasonable amount of time to allow possible threats to land at a suitable airport, the fighter pilots received new orders from NORAD.

They were to intercept anything flying in their assigned areas and escort it to the nearest suitable airfield. If they encountered any aircraft that did not respond to radio communications or hand signals, the pilots had blanket permission to shoot it down, preferably over empty fields or sparsely populated areas.

NORAD would continue to direct air operations over Canada and the United States from three subordinate headquarters located at Tyndall AFB, Florida; Elmendorf AFB, Alaska; and Canadian Forces Base, Winnipeg, Manitoba.

New York City

Panic ensued in New York when tens of thousands of motorists, most of whom were unprepared for an evacuation, clogged the freeways and principal highways heading south and west. Fearing more attacks on high-profile targets, most of the drivers left with only what they were wearing. Many of them soon ran out of gas, causing massive traffic jams and short tempers. Lines at service stations stretched for half a mile to a mile before the stations began running out of fuel.

With the airlines grounded at Newark, La Guardia, and Kennedy, idle passenger trains were soon mobbed. Others crowded into New York City's subways to escape the dreaded radiation fallout.

Manhattan was in a state of gridlock, with the bridges and tunnels closed for security reasons. The National Guard was mobilized, and off-duty law enforcement officers were called to work. The mayor of New York City and the governor of New York were soon on television offering reassurance and calming words.

New Orleans, Louisiana

After the suicide attack at the Waterford 3 Nuclear Power Plant west of the Big Easy, the Vieux Carré was almost deserted in a matter of twenty-five minutes. Interstate 10 was bumper-to-bumper from the heart of New Orleans to Slidell. North of Slidell, motorists who still had fuel branched out on Interstate 59 north or Interstate 10 eastbound. Once they reached that point, fuel was readily available.

Unlike New York City, there was not the same degree of panic in the Crescent City, but thousands of people were rapidly moving away from the radiation fallout and likely targets, including the Superdome and high-rise buildings. Most individuals fleeing east and northeast simply wanted to get out to "flyover country" and find a motel or hotel until they were sure the situation was reasonably under control. The only person who could assure them was President Macklin.

St. Petersburg, Florida

With the Crystal River Nuclear Power Plant well north of the Tampa–St. Petersburg metropolitan complex, and the prevailing west-to-east wind, most people wanted to stay and protect their businesses and personal property. Several wealthy families left their domestic help to watch their mansions while they traveled south in their yachts.

A much larger percentage of the Tampa–St. Petersburg citizens packed their vehicles and drove south to Fort Myers; some went as far as the Fort Lauderdale–Miami area, and a few thousand descended on the Florida Keys and Key West. Hotel rooms quickly sold out, and many enterprising guests began subleasing their rooms for double the rate.

The folks who were in the most peril were the people of Crystal River, located on the coast of the Gulf of Mexico. To a person, they were fearful for their lives. Some headed north or south on Highway 19 to escape being contaminated with radiation. A few families gathered together in church, while others stayed home and prayed for the best.

11

The White House

When Hartwell Prost walked into the Situation Room, there was an underlying feeling of tension in the air. Not panic, but a growing sense of uneasiness at this early hour of the morning. To a person, they were asking themselves the same question: *What next?*

Flanking the stone-faced president were Pete Adair, secretary of defense; Les Chalmers, chairman of the Joint Chiefs of Staff; Jim Ebersole, FBI director; George Anderson, cabinet-level director of homeland security; Army General Jeremiah Jamison, commander, Homeland Security; the director of the Federal Emergency Management Agency (FEMA); and a representative of the National Domestic Preparedness Office.

"Have a seat," the president said quietly. "Gentlemen, before we begin, I should tell you that these civilian planes—business jets—that targeted our nuclear power plants were either stolen or purchased by the terrorists, we don't know which. Either way, this brings another dimension, another unknown into the equation, and more uncertainty for all Americans."

Macklin paused as his emotions began to seep to the surface. "We'll address this new threat in detail later. At the moment, George is going to bring us up to date on the damage." He loosened his tie and looked Anderson in the eye. "George, how many casualties so far?"

"At least twenty-one so far at the Indian Point plant, and it will be much higher before the day is over." Anderson was not his usual confident, effusive self. "It's going to take some time to sift through the rubble."

"What about the other plants?"

"We don't have any firm numbers from the other sites yet, but it's my understanding from our sources in the Tampa–St. Pete area that we can expect heavy casualties at the Crystal River location." Nervous and uneasy, Anderson took a sip of water. "The airplane that crashed into the Indian Point plant hit the turbine building and some adjacent structures. It's a real mess." He hesitated and then removed his glasses. "The explosion destroyed the equipment that is necessary to bring the plant to a safe and stable shutdown."

The room was quiet until Prost spoke. "Are you saying we have a Chernobyl-type situation, a meltdown in progress?"

Avoiding Prost's prying eyes, Anderson stared at his briefing notes for a long moment. "Yes, I'm afraid so."

"Oh, Jesus," Pete Adair said, under his breath. He cast a look at the director of homeland security. "How much radiation is leaking?"

Anderson glanced at the latest numbers from the scientists who studied the disaster at the Chernobyl nuclear power plant in the Ukraine. "The best estimate is roughly seven to ten percent into the atmosphere. That's just an educated guess from the resident experts at the International Atomic Energy Agency."

"Translate," Macklin demanded.

"Well, sir, there will be significant contamination at the site and in the area east of the plant. Beyond that, the radiation should be carried over the Atlantic by the prevailing winds."

The president's shoulders sagged in relief. *I hope he's right.* "What's the situation in New York City?"

"Not good, sir. The shelters were filled to capacity within thirty minutes of the attack; others are using the subway stations as shelters."

Macklin removed his glasses and looked at his FEMA director. "What are we doing to help those people?"

"Sir, the National Guard and the Red Cross are gearing up. They're going to set up medical facilities and food stations throughout the city. But their resources are going to need replenishing in the next twenty-four to thirty-six hours."

"Maybe we don't have to put so many people through this." The president turned his attention to George Anderson. "If the radiation is confined to the east side of Indian Point, let's get the word out to the people, encourage them to return to their homes."

"That's what we're getting ready to do: television, radio, and the emergency broadcast system." Anderson hesitated a moment. "Sir, there's so much conflicting information out there. It would help a lot if you would address the American people."

"I fully intend to do that as soon as we get organized." Macklin's neck muscles were beginning to telegraph his intensity. "What kind of visual aids do you have: mandatory evacuation areas and areas to be avoided, things like that?"

"They're being prepared—we should have them soon."

The president made eye contact with Anderson. "Okay, George, stay on top of this, and let me know if you need anything—*anything.*"

"Understood, sir."

Macklin rose from his chair, thanked Anderson and the others for arriving on such short notice, and walked them to the exit. The president asked Prost, Adair, and Chalmers to keep their seats.

Macklin returned and slumped into his chair. "Gentlemen," he said in a weary voice, "I want your input on Saeed Shayhidi; keep it short and to the point. Hartwell?"

"Mr. President, before I address the Shayhidi issue, I have to insist that you board the airborne operations center immediately. Even with the air defenses available here, there is no guarantee we could stop a suicide bomber from hitting the White House."

"Hartwell," the president interrupted. "I understa—"

"Sir, please allow me to finish. I'm amazed they didn't hit this place first. Now they've acquired other jets to attack us at will, you could be targeted at any—"

Macklin held his hands up in submission. "I've already had the lecture from Pete and Les. My bags are being packed and the first lady is en route to a secure shelter."

"Good. I'm relieved. The vice president and his staff are on their way from Chicago to Cheyenne Mountain and should be landing in Colorado Springs within the hour."

Prost rubbed his chin. "About Shayhidi: it's time to play hardball with these people, and I mean to put Shayhidi and his cronies out of business—permanently."

The president looked up. "Les and Pete have the same opinion, no argument from me, but what I need is a *specific* target. Any ideas?"

"Hartwell," Pete Adair said as he slid Prost a piece of paper. "Les and I have outlined some suggestions for striking Shayhidi. We think they'll have a devastating impact on his operation. We'd like you to review them, give us your opinion, or add anything you think will help."

Prost accepted the paper.

"The president has already seen the list," Adair continued. "We have to act now, can't afford to keep reacting to attacks."

"I couldn't agree more," Prost said, as he studied the recommendations. "The sooner we strike Shayhidi, the better."

The president frowned when he thought about missing the funerals of Brett Shannon and his colleagues. "Gentlemen, I want to expedite your plans for Shayhidi." Macklin paused to consider his priorities. "In regard to homeland security, I want air cover—helicopter gunships or fighter aircraft—for our nuclear power plants until this crisis is over. All of them, including the damaged ones."

Prost politely interrupted. "Sir, we need the same type of protection, if not more, for the Pantex plant in Amarillo. The materials from our dismantled nuclear warheads are stored on-site."

"Done."

Hartwell held up a hand. "One other consideration: the facilities at Arco, Idaho, where we reprocess nuclear fuel taken from ships and submarines that are being deactivated and disposed of."

"Make those priorities," Macklin said firmly. "Be sure we have troops with shoulder-fired SAMs at all the locations, twenty-four seven, until further notice."

"That's a lot of plants to protect," Prost reminded him. "It's going to take a while to implement this."

Macklin scribbled a note. "Whatever it takes is what we're going to do. Have the FAA issue a new emergency notice to airmen making every U.S. nuclear power plant a Prohibited Area until further notice. Fifteen-statute-mile radius up to infinity."

"Yes, sir."

Macklin balled his fist and gently tapped the palm of his other hand. "I want to get the airlines and general aviation back into the air as quickly as possible, but we're going to have to implement some restrictions."

Prost didn't look up. "Two of my people are working with the FAA. I'll get back to you later today with their recommendations."

"Excellent," the president said, and closed his eyes for a few seconds. "And, while I'm thinking about it, work out a plan, whatever you want to do, to cover our other power-generating facilities."

"Yes, sir." Prost paused a moment. "I strongly recommend that the FAA NOTAM include the fact that armed helicopter gunships and surface-to-air missiles are protecting those restricted areas."

"Sounds good. Send the message." Macklin felt an inner calm come over him, a sense of morality and duty. "We have the weapons and we have the manpower. We'll use active-duty military personnel and the reserves."

"I've already been working on it," Prost said, looking at the list he compiled during the helicopter flight from his estate.

"Ahead of the game, as always," the president said robustly. "I intend selectively to make life an absolute living hell for Shayhidi and his lieutenants, if we can find them."

"We need to take Shayhidi out," Adair said in an even voice. "Send a message throughout the Middle East and the entire world."

An aide quietly interrupted the discussion. It was time for President Macklin to fly to Andrews AFB and board the E-4B National Airborne Operations Center known as Night Watch.

At the behest of his national security adviser, the president had recently updated the Enduring Constitutional Government measures that dealt with the succession of political authority in the event of his death or incapacitation.

Successors to the president are tracked at all times to ensure each is always in a different place. During the State of the Union address, for example, at least one cabinet member is kept in a secret location in the event of a disaster on Capitol Hill.

If he died, Macklin had delegated individuals with authorization to launch nuclear weapons. The identities of those people, civilian and military, were being kept classified to prevent them from being targeted. In addition, senior commanders at the NORAD complex had been given nuclear-weapons-release authority.

Macklin turned to his close friend. "Les, I'm going to shuffle things around a bit. I want you and Pete with me, the other joint chiefs inside Cheyenne Mountain with the vice president."

"Yes, sir."

"Hartwell, I'd like you to accompany us."

"I'm packed and ready."

The president rose from his chair and turned to leave. He spoke over his shoulder to his aides. "I'm going to take a shower. I'll meet you at *Marine One* in twenty minutes and we'll go over the suggestions for targeting Shayhidi."

"What about addressing the nation?" Prost asked.

Macklin stopped and turned around. "Set it up for Andrews, before we take off."

"Yes, sir."

Manassas Regional Airport, Virginia

Located twenty-eight statute miles southwest of the heart of Washington, D.C., Manassas Regional Airport was a busy general-aviation destination for people with business inside the Beltway. Shortly before 7:30 A.M., a pristine Gulfstream G-IV landed to pre-position for an 8:30 A.M. charter flight to San Diego, California. The trip had been arranged by an engineering consulting firm based in Chula Vista, California.

The cocaptains, Bob Carpenter and Nick Jablonski, refueled the flagship of their growing charter operation. A fast, roomy, and comfortable jet, the plane was stocked with a wide variety of quality snacks and refreshments. Current magazines and newspapers were aboard, along with fresh coffee, assorted juices, breakfast meals, and a luncheon entrée. The only thing missing was their company flight attendant, who had called in sick at the last moment.

A few minutes before 8:30 A.M., a limousine approached the ramp near the spotless G-IV. A clean-cut young Filipino man in a well-tailored dark-blue suit emerged from the Lincoln with a wide smile and firmly shook hands with the pilots. His three associates remained inside the limousine.

"Are we set?" Emilio Zamora asked in a friendly voice. His English and diction were impeccable, as would be expected from the son of an English-born mother who was a professor of history at the prestigious University of Cambridge. Zamora's father, Benigno, met his mother when he was a visiting professor at Cambridge for three years.

Jablonski maintained his easy smile. "Well, we're set to go, but the FAA has instituted a ground stop, like they did on nine-eleven. They've grounded all flights until further notice."

Zamora's disappointment was visible, but he showed no irritation. "Do you know why or how long this will last?"

Carpenter shrugged. "We don't know how long the delay will be, but it has something to do with a couple of planes that crashed. We just heard about it a few minutes ago."

The agreeable smile remained on Zamora's face. "I hope the

problem can be resolved soon. We have an important meeting today."

"We'll hope for the best," Carpenter said.

The unexpected development jeopardized Zamora's plan, but he could deal with the sudden change. That's why he was the senior leader of the special-action cell.

Zamora studied the impressive Gulfstream for a moment. "Well, if we have to wait, do you mind if we take a look at the airplane?"

"No, not at all," Jablonski said, with open enthusiasm. "Come on aboard. We'll give you the grand tour."

"Okay, let me get my business partners."

"Sure."

Carpenter entered the roomy cockpit while Jablonski waited at the bottom of the air-stair door. After the FAA-mandated ground stop and the news of mysterious crashes, both pilots were having reservations about taking this trip. Neither showed any outward signs of concern, but the feeling was rooted in the backs of their minds. They exchanged glances while keeping their smiles as natural as possible.

Emilio Zamora proudly led his three smiling associates to the G-IV, greeted Nick Jablonski, and climbed the stairs. Zamora's clean-shaven colleagues were as well dressed as their leader, all in fashionable business suits and shined shoes. Like Zamora, two of the men were Filipino. The third man, Rajiv Mukherjee, was born and raised in Calcutta, India. While everyone gathered around the cockpit, Carpenter explained the workings of the different items in his "office."

"Would anyone care for coffee?" Jablonski asked, from the front of the passenger cabin. "It's fresh and hot."

"That sounds good," Zamora said, as he shoved a handgun with a silencer deep into Carpenter's side and fired twice. In one quick motion, the other three terrorists jumped out of the way and Zamora turned and fired three rounds into Jablonski. The pilot stumbled backward and then dropped to his knees before Zamora shot him again, this time in the head.

Emilio Zamora stepped aside to allow the other men to carry the bodies of the dead pilots to the back of the passenger cabin.

While Zamora and two of his fellow murderers returned to the limousine, Rajiv Mukherjee remained inside the airplane.

After the limousine drove away, Mukherjee casually walked down the air-stair door, quickly removed the chocks, and returned to the blood-soaked cabin. He closed the air-stair door and removed his coat and tie.

Having compiled the best overall grades of all the foreign students attending U.S.-based flight schools, Mukherjee had been chosen for the ultimate special operation. His dedication to Islamic extremism and his ability to speak English well were factored into the decision to allow him to be the "honored" pilot.

With eighteen hours of training time in the Gulfstream G-IV simulator and seven hours of intense instruction in the actual airplane, Mukherjee was supremely confident of his ability to accomplish his important mission. After settling into the left seat, Mukherjee started the engines and called Ground Control to request a high-speed taxi test to check a nose-wheel shimmy. Reluctant at first, the supervisor/ground controller finally gave him permission to taxi but expressly cautioned him about the recently invoked FAA ground stop.

Mukherjee calmly acknowledged the instructions and carefully taxied to Runway 34-right. With permission from the control tower, Mukherjee aligned the big Gulfstream with the runway centerline, checked to make sure the transponders were turned off, and smoothly moved the throttles forward. The powerful G-IV rapidly accelerated. When it was still gaining speed two-thirds of the way down the 5,700-foot runway, the tower controller almost had a fit.

"Gulfstream Three Three Kilo Tango, abort! Abort your takeoff! Abort—abort—abort!" He knew there was no way the airplane could stop in the remaining distance, but he had to try to prevent the takeoff. "Three Three Kilo Tango, you are in violation of an FAA NOTAM immediately grounding all civil flights in this country."

The stunned controller watched the corporate jet lift off and accelerate close to the ground. *There goes my career.*

After the G-IV was airborne, Mukherjee kept trimming the

nose down while he raised the landing gear and flaps. Barely 120 feet in the air, he banked the airplane steeply to the right and set his course straight for the White House, home of the infidel leader of the great superpower.

Mukherjee had memorized the heading, distance, and time to his target. He would be there in less than five minutes—four minutes and some odd seconds to eternal glory. His name would be forever treated with reverence in his adopted homeland of Iran, perhaps as well known as that of his hero, Osama bin Laden.

All hell broke loose when the controller at Manassas made contact with the FAA command center. Shocked by the unthinkable flaunting of the rules, the tower controller explained that the low-flying jet was on a straight course to Washington, D.C. Heads would roll all the way up the chain of command at the "Tombstone Agency."

The FAA instantly contacted NORAD headquarters near Colorado Springs. The vice commander of CMOC immediately scrambled more fighters on the East Coast. At the same time, a Boeing E-3 AWACS surveillance and control aircraft flying high above the Chesapeake Bay located the ground-hugging jet on its radar.

Two Air Force F-16s patrolling southeast of the University of Maryland were given a snap vector to intercept the intruder. Both fighters were armed with two AIM-9 Sidewinder infrared-homing air-to-air missiles, four AIM-120 AMRAAM active terminal radar missiles, and one multibarrel cannon with a full load of 20mm high-explosive ammunition.

Turning southwest, the fighter pilots from Langley AFB tapped their burners and quickly went through Mach 1, sending powerful sonic booms reverberating across D.C. and the surrounding terrain. The shocking noise sent many people running for cover.

As the Gulfstream continued to accelerate, Rajiv Mukherjee climbed another 100 feet to keep from scaring himself. He had never flown this low at such a fast speed. One sneeze or hiccup and the plane could hit the ground. Seconds later, Mukherjee eased the power back when the G-IV reached 405 knots. Trees, homes, golf courses, schools, and roads were flashing past in a frightening blur.

Air Force Major Alan Kenner and Captain Stacy D'Angelo were frantically searching for the low-flying bogey. With all the ground clutter, it was much more difficult to spot the low-flying aircraft.

"Sterno," the AWACS crew member excitedly radioed, "I have a primary target—repeat primary target—at your eleven o'clock—nine miles—on the deck, four-hundred-plus knots."

"We're cookin' and lookin'," Kenner replied in a tight voice. "Stacy, let's take it down, stand by to arm 'em up."

"Roger," she said tersely, as they began a steep descent. *We only have a few seconds, make it good.*

Mukherjee was gripping the control yoke with both hands when he blasted low over the highway interchange of Beltway 495 and Little River Turnpike.

Many cars and trucks pulled off the road after the jet thundered overhead, barely above the trees. Some of the motorists, fearful of another massive terrorist attack, began praying for divine intervention while they used their cell phones to call family members.

Reacting on visceral instinct, D'Angelo keyed her radio. "Sterno, you might want to start a left turn to intercept. I'll continue on for a couple of seconds."

"Concur—hang in." He began his turn and lowered the nose.

"Sterno," the AWACS air defense systems operator radioed, "bend it around hard, nine o'clock in the weeds!"

"Sterno is coming around," Kenner said with a low groan, as he pulled more Gs. "Say posit—target."

"Ten—low!"

"Copy."

Booming across the northern finger of Lake Barcroft and then over Jeb Stuart High School, the howling Gulfstream was setting off scores of car alarms. To make matters worse, the sonic booms from the screeching F-16s were shattering dozens of windows. The deafening noise added one more ingredient to the turmoil and fear that was gripping the city.

When the hijacked jet streaked over Arlington Boulevard,

Major Kenner caught a glimpse of the ground-hugging G-IV. "Sterno has a tally, have the Gulfstream in sight." He quickly reduced power and pulled heavy Gs to intercept the intruding aircraft.

"Sterno, you have permission to fire—bag him!" an excited voice said from the AWACS.

"Arm 'em up, Stacy," Kenner said crisply.

"Copy," D'Angelo replied, already pulling 7 Gs to align her fighter in trail of her flight leader. She was closing on Kenner at the speed of heat and eased the throttle back.

Sterno keyed his radio. "He's *really* in the weeds."

Sucking oxygen, Captain D'Angelo spotted the G-IV. "I have both of you in sight—get him."

"Have to."

D'Angelo rechecked her master arm switch and eased the throttle forward.

Freshly showered and shaved, Cord Macklin was tying his tie in the presidential living quarters when an aide and three Secret Service agents barged through the main entrance.

"This way, Mr. President!" the senior agent said, in the command voice of a marine corps drill instructor. "We have an imminent threat. Follow us *now*!"

"Lead the way," the startled president said, as he was pushed through the main door. Without asking a single question, Macklin ran between the men as they headed for the nearest shelter. He knew something big was about to happen and it was probably going to involve the White House. He was thankful the first lady was in a safe, secure place.

The Gulfstream was rapidly approaching Arlington National Cemetery when Major Kenner fired the first Sidewinder missile. It wavered a moment and then flew straight into the rear of the G-IVs left engine. The explosion almost ripped the engine from the side of the fuselage.

Rajiv Mukherjee felt the impact and panicked when the cockpit lit up with warning lights. The left engine was destroyed, but the airplane was still flying and controllable. *Need a few more seconds.* He gripped the yoke with all his strength and stared straight at the White House.

Kenner fired the second AIM-9 missile when the smoking G-IV reached the western perimeter of the historic national cemetery. He saw the missile undulate and then explode in the exhaust of the right engine. The concussive force of the detonation severely damaged the T-tail of the airplane.

Blocking everything from his mind, Mukherjee ignored the cockpit warnings and glanced at the Potomac River. *I'm going to make it, have to make it, won't fail.*

Switching to guns, Kenner had a malfunction that prevented him from firing the cannon. "Stacy, take him out!" he said as he pulled his F-16 straight into a vertical climb and continued pulling until he was on his back going the opposite direction from D'Angelo.

Without hesitation, she fired a Sidewinder missile that hit the Gulfstream in the heavily damaged right engine. The burning Rolls-Royce turbofan departed the G-IV, taking the tail of the airplane with it.

D'Angelo fired another 'winder at the same instant the corporate jet pitched down. She flinched when a shoulder-fired surface-to-air missile slashed past her fighter. *Time to exit.* She simultaneously stroked the burner and reefed the F-16 into a punishing vertical climb. *Hold your fire, guys—I'm on your side.*

Pulling back on the useless yoke with the strength of a man who knew he was going to meet Allah, Rajiv Mukherjee glimpsed the White House a split second before the Gulfstream slammed into the intersection of E and 17th Street. The deafening explosion blew out windows and rattled china in the executive mansion.

The Secret Service agents pulled the president down in a White House corridor and covered him with their bodies. Seconds later, they yanked him to his feet and continued running for safety.

* * *

The bulk of the G-IV fuselage crashed into the southwest gate of the White House grounds, and then careened across the South Lawn, hitting *Marine One* a glancing blow before smashing into the visitor entrance and the security fence. The crushed, burned aircraft and the remains of Rajiv Mukherjee and the two Gulfstream pilots came to rest on East Executive Avenue.

The marine flight crew of the VIP helicopter survived the collision with only minor injuries, but the Sikorsky VH-3D was heavily damaged. The exterior of the White House and the lawn sustained extensive damage. Flaming jet fuel sprayed the mansion, and flying chunks of the left engine and the fuselage carved deep furrows in the manicured lawn.

In a matter of seconds, the president was hustled off to Andrews AFB in a caravan of Secret Service vehicles. Pete Adair, General Chalmers, and Hartwell Prost followed a few minutes later in a separate convoy crammed with agents. Steely-eyed veterans, the Secret Service troops were spring-loaded to kill anyone who tried to interfere with their mission.

12

Coeur d'Alene, Idaho

Awakened at 6:15 A.M. Pacific Time Zone by a cheerful recorded voice, Jackie and Scott were overwhelmed when they turned on the television. In stunned silence, they assimilated the breaking news about the aerial attacks on the nuclear power plants and the White House. All civil air traffic had been grounded and combat air patrols were being flown over all major U.S. cities. Marine helicopter gunships were orbiting over the White House and the U.S. Capitol Building.

The three-hour time difference between Washington, D.C., and Coeur d'Alene left Scott and Jackie with a lot of information to absorb. They watched a series of videos from the first live reports near the power plants. The destruction at the nuclear facilities was immense, and the list of casualties was growing. Firefighters were still trying to contain the flames at the plant adjacent to St. Petersburg, Florida.

FAA officials, who followed the flight of the Challenger jet on radar, easily traced the airplane to the FBO in Albany, New York. The FBI was currently interviewing employees and had confirmed the pilot was of Middle Eastern lineage.

"Farkas?" Jackie asked.

"I don't think so." Scott turned the sound down a notch. "It's not his profile. Besides, he's much too valuable to Shayhidi."

She gazed at the screen for a few seconds. "You're right, most likely one of the zealots slated for a rendezvous with the vestal virgins."

"That would be my guess."

"Look at that," Jackie said, pointing to the television. A Fox News White House reporter appeared on the screen. Behind him on the South Lawn, *Marine One* lay heavily damaged, with myriad debris scattered across the scorched lawn. The Secret Service was out in force and two companies of heavily armed marines were taking up positions around the perimeter of the White House grounds.

The demolished G-IV was still smoldering while a group of NTSB investigators began exploring the wreckage. The animated reporter was trying his best to reassure the viewers that President Macklin was safe. However, it was obvious that he didn't have a clue as to where the commander in chief was.

Jackie reached for her watch. "I'll bet the president is headed for the flying command post or already on it."

"No doubt."

"Where Hartwell is concerned," Jackie said, and paused to catch a sound bite, "we're probably *really* on our own."

"True. He has bigger problems on his scope."

Jackie walked to the window and stared at the soft, diffused light from the early morning sky. "I don't know about other Americans, but I'm beginning to feel pretty damn vulnerable."

"We've seen it coming for years, ignored our own borders while we ran around the world trying to save everyone else from harm."

Jackie turned around and crossed her arms. "They're invading our country with low-tech weapons, and no one knows what's coming next or where. All we can do is react, fire-fight."

"We need to be aggressive, go after them on their own turf," Scott said, standing up to stretch. "Let's have breakfast and then concentrate on finding Farkas."

"Uh . . . you're forgetting something."

He gave her a blank look and then the synapse took place. "We're grounded. Terrific."

"The terrorists win in more ways than one," she conceded, with a dismissive shrug. "They paralyze our ability to track the perps."

"Then we have to get *ungrounded.*" Scott's voice was full of determination. "I say it's time to saddle up and hit the trail."

She shook her head. "You've been watching too many old Westerns."

"Take the initiative, be a self-starter."

"You need to double up on your medicine," Jackie said and then gave him a brief smile. "You shave, and I'll see if I can get in touch with Hartwell—like he needs another problem." She reached for the satellite phone. "Little Bighorn."

"What?"

"General Custer showed a lot of initiative, too."

Andrews Air Force Base, Maryland

Prestigious Andrews AFB is the port of entry for many foreign dignitaries and the home of the 89th Airlift Wing, the proud unit that operates the world's most famous plane, *Air Force One.*

President Macklin delayed his departure to address the American people. He spoke calmly and reassuringly for sixteen minutes. The president explained what the government, the military, and the law enforcement agencies were doing to protect the American people and the United States. He assured the nation that his administration would prevail in the fight against the terrorists.

After a short delay to repair a mechanical problem, the E-4B National Airborne Operations Center, a modified Boeing 747-200 airliner, taxied to the runway. The E-4B, based at Offutt AFB in Omaha, Nebraska, was one of four sister ships that operated from various bases around the world. At least one NAOC "doomsday plane" was always on fifteen-minute alert with a full battle staff.

With President Cord Macklin on board, the airplane was automatically designated *Air Force One.* However, under the current circumstances, the flight crew of the airplane would use a different call sign once they were airborne.

Security at the legendary base was always a priority, but it was extremely tight this morning. Most people who worked at Andrews, civilians and military personnel alike, were not smiling today. They were deeply concerned about the shocking events and fearful of what might follow.

Before the Boeing reached the end of the 9,700-foot runway, the plane was cleared for immediate takeoff. Once airborne and climbing through 12,000 feet, the E-4B was joined by four F-14D Tomcats flown by VF-102 Diamondbacks stationed at NAS Oceana, Virginia.

Other air force, navy, and marine corps fighter squadrons would rotate around the clock to provide blanket protection for the command post. The E-4B was capable of remaining aloft for seventy-two hours with aerial refueling. The seventy-two-hour limit was based on the length of time it takes for the engine oil to begin breaking down.

Depending on the threat assessment, the airplane's route of flight could be changed on a moment's notice. At any given time, the E-4B might be over the middle of the Atlantic or high above the wheat fields of Oklahoma and Kansas.

Hartwell Prost was discussing the target list with the president, Secretary of Defense Pete Adair, and General Chalmers when Jackie's call was received. He had anticipated the communication and quickly solved the problem. Their LongRanger was exempt from the grounding order.

Coeur d'Alene, Idaho

"What was the squawk again?" Scott asked, as he reached for the transponder. "Something-something-six-six?"

"Let's see," Jackie said, as she pulled a slip of paper from her pocket. "We—three-four-six-six and center is waiting for us."

He donned his sunglasses. "Okay, we're ready."

She started the engine and took her time completing the checklist. The sun was above the horizon when the LongRanger lifted off and turned south. Scott and Jackie were wearing their standard uniforms.

She checked in with Seattle Center and found the controller to be tense but friendly and helpful.

Scott had their grid chart on his lap, circling small out-of-the-way airstrips. "We'll stick to our basic search pattern, check anything that looks out of place."

He picked up the binoculars and studied the unsullied terrain. "I expect they'll use anything flyable . . . if it's big enough or fast enough."

She gave him a slight nod. "I'm going to use two thousand feet above the ground as a basic altitude."

"Sounds good."

As the sun rose higher, they carefully scanned the ground along their flight path. After twenty minutes, Scott held the chart in front of Jackie. "I'll take it for a while, give you a chance to pick out the places you think we should check."

"You'll take it?" She gave him a look laced with suspicion. "I thought you said you didn't fly helicopters."

He took the controls and glanced at her. "I said I didn't *fly* helicopters, didn't say I don't *know how.*"

"You flew jets; were you cross-trained?"

"No, I had a few rotary-wing lessons while I was still in college."

She grinned good-naturedly and smoothed the chart. "That was long before you had your head examined, right?"

"You said it, I didn't."

"Did you finish your training?"

"No, but I did solo before another student crashed the machine. He really trashed it, but walked away with only minor injuries."

"So, all this time you've been sandbagging me, huh?"

"Hey, you're the helo expert. I'm just an innocent victim along for the ride."

Monaco

The stately Principality of Monaco, one of the crown jewels of the lush Riviera, was the latest home port for *Evening Breeze,* a 242-foot megayacht owned by Saeed Shayhidi. Hoping to outflank the crafty Americans, Shayhidi secretly passed the word via his personal messenger to have his yacht stand out to sea as soon as practical. He planned to helicopter aboard the grand vessel and take an extended vacation while his jihad against the United States continued.

Having known Shayhidi for many years, the Greek captain of *Evening Breeze* was always prepared to get under way in two hours or less. Konstantinos Theotokas routinely had the chef replenish the perishable food every three days, dividing the "spoiled" groceries evenly among the crew of eight. The canned goods and the frozen supplies were replaced on a monthly basis. Topped with fuel and water, the freshly cleaned yacht sailed on the tide.

With a range of 3,800 nautical miles, the yacht provided the perfect way to tour the Mediterranean. A major retrofit had been completed, including engine room upgrades, exterior paint from bow to stern, and an interior with a distinctly Middle Eastern flair. Shayhidi had overseen every detail of the interior work himself.

Evening Breeze's large main salon offered intimate seating areas with panoramic views of the sea. Three full-width master staterooms boasted their own sitting rooms with bath and Jacuzzi. Four other staterooms with enclosed bathrooms offered passengers splendid living quarters.

A galley truly fit for a king and a Swedish chef who trained at the prestigious Culinary Institute of America ensured that the meals were on a par with the finest restaurants in the world.

Formal dining in a separate dining salon was complemented by imported china and crystal from Hong Kong and London. The shaded top deck was ideal for informal outdoor luncheons, while the aft deck on the main level was a charming alcove in which to have breakfast. *Evening Breeze* was truly a floating palace by anyone's standards.

Global Hawk

Loitering directly over Monte Carlo at 64,000 feet, a sister ship of the Global Hawk that had followed Saeed Shayhidi's Boeing Business Jet now stalked his prized yacht. *Evening Breeze*'s departure from Monaco was being monitored by the UAV while the stylish yacht sailed southwest, off the coast of the French Riviera. The reconnaissance data was updated on a regular basis and relayed to President Macklin on board the aerial command post somewhere over the Atlantic.

An hour after the sun had set over the Mediterranean, *Evening Breeze* was thirty-one miles due south of the resort city of Cannes. Flying low, an unlighted helicopter approached the yacht and landed on the helo pad. The owner was now on board. Global Hawk recorded the arrival and the departure of the helicopter and transmitted every detail to Washington.

Forty-five minutes later, the same helicopter delivered budding French movie starlet Danielle Pelletier to the yacht. It took five minutes to unload her stacks of luggage. An inch short of six feet tall, the dazzling blond actress was an occasional companion to Shayhidi. Global Hawk again recorded the event and transmitted the images to Washington.

National Airborne Operations Center

Four marine corps F-18C Hornets from the Thunderbolts of VMFA-251 had just relieved four air force F-16s. Based at MCAS Beaufort, South Carolina, the Hornets had recently refueled from an air force KC-135 and would continue to rotate to the tanker.

President Cord Macklin was receiving an up-to-the-minute brief on the nuclear power plant disasters when the information about Shayhidi's yacht reached him. He, Prost, Adair, and Chalmers retired to the privacy of the E-4B's conference room and took their seats. To a person, they were excited about the possibility of eliminating Shayhidi, although no one showed any outward signs of emotion.

The president remained quiet for a few moments while everyone read the most recent brief. "Gentlemen, we're going into uncharted waters, no pun intended."

Macklin slid his briefing folder to the side of the table. "I want to send a loud signal, a graphic example to Shayhidi, his lieutenants, and his followers."

It was imperceptible, but Prost frowned and nervously rubbed his earlobe. "Mr. President, if we sink the yacht with the wrong person on board . . . I don't have to tell you about the political consequences. They'll burn you at the stake."

Considering the consequences, both political and moral, President Macklin looked at Adair and then Chalmers. "Les, is it possible that Shayhidi *isn't* aboard?"

General Chalmers hesitated. "Anything is possible. There is no way to be absolutely certain who got off the helicopter. It *is* Shayhidi's yacht and there are passengers aboard."

"I think we have to assume Shayhidi is on board," the president said decisively. "Why else would a helicopter arrive and depart at night with no lights showing? It just makes sense. I think we *have* to take the shot."

"I would have to agree," Chalmers said. "*Toledo* has identified the target during daylight and is closely tracking it. We have a 99.99 percent chance of getting the job done with no witnesses and no foul-ups."

Pete Adair closed his briefing folder. “If we do this, the sub can’t surface for any reason, even if there are survivors in the water.”

“Agree,” Macklin said. “Any questions, suggestions?”

“Let’s do this at night,” Adair said. “This night.”

“*Toledo* is in position off the yacht’s stern,” Chalmers said, without any visible emotion. “Mr. President?”

Macklin reached for his pipe. “Give the order.”

USS *Toledo*

From the time they rendezvoused with *Evening Breeze,* Commander Allen Nettleton and his executive officer, Lieutenant Commander David Saddler, had had second thoughts. They didn’t normally stalk civilian yachts, even large ones, with their attack submarine. Although both officers felt some degree of trepidation about their mission, there was no doubt about their final order. It had come straight from the flying Oval Office.

They were in a perfect position to attack the brightly lighted yacht. The closest vessel to their position was nine miles away. The weapon was ready. Nettleton decided to use only one 3,400-pound Mark 48 Advanced Capability (ADCAP) torpedo, since the target was truly a sitting duck. No one would be firing back and they didn’t have to concern themselves with depth charges.

Nettleton stepped to the raised platform in the middle of the Control Room/Attack Center for one last look through the Mark 18 search periscope. The scope had a low-light operating mode and a 70mm camera. He snapped three more pictures.

The torpedo tube was flooded and the outer door was open. Looking through the periscope, Nettleton spoke in a firm, clear voice. “Firing point procedures.”

The skipper waited a few seconds. “Match bearings and shoot.” The weapons officer manning the BSY-1 (Busy One) launch control panel pressed the firing button. Trailing a guidance wire behind it, the Mark 48 ADCAP torpedo was on its way to the target at 60-plus knots. The torpedo's seeker head/computer instantly tracked the yacht, negating the use of the guidance wire.

Everyone in the Control Room silently counted the seconds before impact. Peering through the search scope, Commander Nettleton began snapping photos while he waited for the fireworks to begin.

The *Evening Breeze*

Saeed Shayhidi and Danielle Pelletier had finished a late meal in the dining salon and were preparing for bed in his aft master stateroom. When his valet left the suite, Shayhidi was adorned in silk pajamas he had purchased on a recent trip to Hong Kong. He never wore nightclothes more than once, so the valet kept at least three dozen new sets of pajamas on board the yacht at all times.

The doe-eyed actress was wearing a fetching negligee from one of her favorite Paris boutiques. Shayhidi poured champagne for them and they stretched out on his king-size bed, staring at their images in the mirror on the overhead. Shayhidi felt relaxed and safe.

He had successfully eluded the treacherous Americans. Now it was time to enjoy a serene cruise around the Mediterranean while his pursuers searched in vain. This was the good life, complete with a sultry movie star all to himself. Shayhidi would embark his wealthy friends at three ports of call over the next few days. He would make the cruise a vacation to be remembered.

He turned off the main lights and closed his eyes for a moment, smiling in the semidarkness. Enthralled by the scent of her perfume, Shayhidi reached for Danielle.

A few seconds later the Mark 48 torpedo penetrated *Evening Breeze*'s hull and exploded in the engine room amidships. The effects of the horrendous blast blew the stately yacht apart, sending fire and flaming debris hundreds of feet into the air.

The concussion knocked Shayhidi and Pelletier out of bed. In shock and panic, Shayhidi scrambled up the stairway leading to the main deck. *What happened? Did the Americans do this?*

"This way," an injured crewman yelled, and ran toward the life rafts on the outer deck. Barefoot and frightened, Shayhidi sidestepped shards of broken glass, fractured mirrors, and other sharp obstacles as he followed the young assistant chef. Left on her own, Danielle Pelletier trailed Shayhidi up to the main deck. The yacht was rapidly flooding and the sea was ablaze with burning diesel fuel.

Another crew member joined his friend in launching the eleven-man life raft. There was no time to launch the twenty-two-foot Boston Whaler attached to the transom. The older man pulled the exposed lanyard that automatically ejected the raft from its case. The raft quickly inflated and they lowered it over the side of the yacht, and then helped Shayhidi into it. After the owner scrambled to the aft section of the raft, the two men helped Danielle down and then jumped into the raft.

Using their hands, the crewmen frantically paddled the raft away from the rapidly spreading flames. In less than five minutes, *Evening Breeze* slipped beneath the sea as the flames slowly subsided. It was obvious the rest of the crew had perished in the powerful explosion.

An eerie quiet settled over the raft while the shivering men and Danielle tried to warm themselves. In the distance, a ship with a spotlight shining on them raced toward the raft.

Knowing help was on the way, Saeed Shayhidi calmed down enough to think rationally. *They're trying to kill me. Macklin's trying to assassinate me. How did they know I was on my yacht?*

Shivering uncontrollably, Danielle hit Shayhidi on the arm with her fist. "You are, without a doubt, the most despicable, cowardly person I've ever known. You're worthless!"

Incapable of being embarrassed, even in front of his employees, Shayhidi ignored the stinging rebuke.

Three hundred yards away, Commander Nettleton lowered the search scope. The USS *Toledo* quietly left the scene and set course for her operating area in the Eastern Mediterranean.

Twelve miles above the raft, Global Hawk captured the entire event, and the images were now in front of President Macklin. Clearly, there were four survivors in a life raft, but it was impossible to determine if one of them was Shayhidi.

13

Grangeville, Idaho

While the LongRanger was being refueled, Jackie and Scott used the fixed base operator's courtesy car to drive to Oskers Restaurant for a late-afternoon lunch. After filling the car with gas, they returned to the airport and learned the FAA was beginning to lift flight restrictions in most areas of the country. Large metropolitan areas, including Washington and New York, were still suffering from restraints and limitations, but general aviation planes were gradually returning to the skies.

Scott took his turn at the controls of the helicopter. Following Highway 95 south, they passed Gospel Peak on the left and Hell's Canyon on the right. The mountains and peaks made for magnificent viewing in the late-afternoon sunlight.

When they approached the Brundage Mountain Ski Area, Jackie took the controls of the LongRanger. A few minutes later, Scott trained his binoculars on an isolated grass airstrip. He could see a hangar and a dilapidated home beside it, but something wasn't computing.

"Jackie," he said, taking the controls, "I have it for a second. Take a look at that strip at twelve to one o'clock, about a mile or so."

She reached for the binoculars and focused on the primitive

airstrip. The valleys were in total shade, making it difficult to distinguish many details. "Yeah, I see it."

"You've got it," he said, relinquishing the controls. "Let's drop down and have a closer look."

She began a descent and slowed the helicopter. "The hangar looks nice, looks new."

Scott stowed the binoculars. "Too nice to be sitting next to a decaying cabin with an outhouse."

"The rusted Jeep Cherokee on blocks adds a nice touch," Jackie observed, leveling the helicopter 120 feet above the ground. "Want to land or make a low flyby?"

"Let's just continue on," he said, focusing his attention on the open hangar doors. "I'll be damned."

"What?"

"They have a B-25—they're closing the hangar doors."

"Want to land?" she asked again.

"Yes."

"Sure seems odd." She began her flare to land in front of the hangar. "Check out the new pickup."

"And the Harley Davidson motorcycles, expensive ones."

Jackie darted a look at the run-down residence. "Kind of incongruous to own a warbird and live in a shack like that."

"Uh-huh."

"Better leave our weapons in the helo," Jackie suggested.

"Probably should."

"What's our story?" she asked.

"We're delivering this to a tour company over at Sun Valley."

"And we're having a slight mechanical problem," she added. "Needed to make a precautionary landing."

"Spot on."

Jackie gently set the LongRanger on the ground and shut down the engine. "Are you sure it was a B-25?"

"I've seen *Thirty Seconds Over Tokyo* enough times to know how to *build* a B-25 Mitchell."

"Well," Jackie said with a raised eyebrow, "let's get ready for curtain call—see what we have."

They climbed out of the helicopter and walked innocently

toward the hangar. When they were about thirty feet away from the entrance door on the right side, a grim-faced woman rounded the corner of the building.

Dressed in faded, baggy denim jeans, scuffed lace-up boots, and a sleeveless black leather jacket, she was a real show-stopper. Tall and grossly overweight, the forty-something woman was missing a front tooth. She had an overbleached rat's-nest hairdo and sported a variety of tattoos on her flabby bare arms.

"Hello," Scott said with a friendly smile. "We—"

"You're trespassin' on my propertee," she interrupted, in a cigarette-hoarse voice. "This here's *private* propertee, *private* airfield."

"We don't mean to intrude," Scott said, noticing a slender middle-aged man and his bulldog walk out on the front porch. They took a seat on a weathered couch, and the man laid a sawed-off shotgun across his lap.

Scott maintained a pleasant persona. "We're having a minor mechanical problem and we were wondering if we could borrow a few tools, happy to pay you for your trouble."

She folded her arms across her ample breasts and frowned. "We ain't got no tools. You best git back in that thang and git on outa here."

Jackie spotted someone looking out the window of the cabin and had an immediate reaction. "Uh, I think we can make it to Boise if we take it easy," she said to Scott, with a new urgency in her voice. "Let's move on."

"Yeah, okay." He glanced at the man on the porch and then faced the woman. "Sorry to bother you, ma'am."

Jackie and Scott turned and walked toward their helicopter.

"Let's get the hell out of here," Jackie said, under her breath.

"What's the deal?"

"I'll tell you when we get airborne," she mumbled.

When the engine came on line, she quickly brought the LongRanger to a hover and accelerated down the grass strip. "Did you see the guy looking out the window?"

"No, what guy?"

"Farkas or his twin brother."

"You're serious?"

"Serious as a heart attack." She began a gradual climb, heading south. "I wonder why he didn't try to take us out?"

"Probably because he has bigger plans: the B-25. He didn't want to take a chance on having something go wrong."

Scott grabbed the satellite phone and called Frank Wakefield, told him what happened, and gave him the specific GPS coordinates for the grass airstrip. After consulting with someone on another phone, Wakefield confirmed that he would organize and direct an FBI raid in the wee hours of the morning.

Scott signed off and placed the satellite phone down. "Well, the ball is rolling. Frank is familiar with Khaliq Farkas. Whatever is going on in that hangar, they sure don't want any attention."

Jackie made a minor heading change to go directly to the Boise Air Terminal. "I think we should keep an eye on the place until the FBI gets there, refuel, and watch the place from a safe distance."

"That isn't a bad idea, except for two things."

"Farkas and the black of night," she guessed.

"Yup," he said, noting the grass airstrip was not on their chart. "If that *was* Farkas, we've already tipped our hand."

"I'm ninety-five percent sure it was Farkas."

"I don't doubt you," he said evenly. "Echelon Two tracked his e-mail to the Idaho–Utah area."

"Yes, and we know he has a penchant for warbirds." She leveled the LongRanger and adjusted the power. "Location, a door hurriedly shut on a B-25 bomber, the cold reception, and the face of Farkas or a lookalike." She turned to him and removed her sunglasses. "Seriously, what if it *is* Farkas and we allow him to get away?"

"Uh, let's see. I believe it was none other than the president's national security adviser who told us not to act unilaterally." He glanced at her and smiled. "Correct statement?"

"Yes, that's right."

Scott tuned the radio to Boise Approach Control. "The FBI has been notified. That's precisely what we're supposed to do."

"Follow orders," she said, with a chuckle. "That's a unique concept."

The New Hangar

Having recognized Jackie Sullivan and Scott Dalton, Khaliq Farkas was in a near panic. The realization that his mission might be compromised before he could carry it out was unthinkable. A lot of time and money had gone into setting up the operation.

Saeed Shayhidi was adamant about this particular aspect of the jihad against the United States. It was the centerpiece of his entire plan, the idea Shayhidi had so strongly endorsed. He could not fail in his mission, no matter what obstacles he might face.

"Hurry up!" Farkas said to the two mechanics. "Get the airplane out of the hangar. Move it!"

Farkas barked a succession of orders to the men and then hurriedly climbed aboard the bomber while they were positioning it on the small ramp. As soon as the tug was disconnected from the B-25, Farkas started the powerful Wright Cyclone radial engines. Each 14-cylinder air-cooled power plant started with a belch of grayish-white smoke and then settled into a rhythmic loud rumble.

Although he wanted to get airborne as quickly as possible, Farkas knew it was essential to warm the engines and stabilize the oil pressures and temperatures. Unlike turboprops or turbofans, which could be started and immediately shoved to full power, the old radials needed tender loving care and understanding. Farkas could not afford a blown engine, not this close to executing his plan.

Once he was satisfied the engines were ready, he taxied to the end of the grass strip. He carefully ran through the before-takeoff checklist, made sure the transponder was off, then came up on the power and released the brakes. Much earlier than he planned, Farkas was on his way to the forward operating airport.

Airborne, he raised the landing gear and retracted the flaps. He set the power at a conservative level and began a slow climb, preferring to keep his speed up. As the minutes ticked away, he began to breathe normally, though he was not completely relaxed. Farkas had never flown the Mitchell at night and he had never flown to this particular airport. *I have to get this right. My reputation—my life—is on the line.*

Lake Charles, Louisiana

Twenty minutes after the stroke of midnight, an unlighted helicopter dropped three high-powered explosives on the Citgo refinery six miles southwest of Lake Charles on Highway 108. A steady series of explosions rocked the countryside, and a firestorm quickly enveloped three-quarters of the 600-acre refinery.

Windows were blown out for miles around the complex, and huge plumes of dense smoke eclipsed the moon. Most people, still reeling from the deadly *Queen Mary 2* assault and the terrorist attacks on the nuclear power plants and the White House, did not doubt this was another massive assault by the terrorists.

The series of ground-shaking blasts and secondary explosions destroyed the plant's self-contained firefighting system. Chaos ruled at the refinery while firefighting units responded from Lake Charles, New Orleans, and Lafayette, Louisiana. Other teams were dispatched from as far away as Port Arthur and Beaumont, Texas.

In an ironic twist, the initial blast had been so powerful it literally knocked the low-flying helicopter out of the air, killing the Iranian pilot and his accomplice.

During the next eighteen minutes, similar attacks were carried out at Valero's Texas City refinery located on the Texas City Ship Channel and Chevron's refinery near El Segundo, California.

In all, U.S. petroleum production was instantly and violently reduced by approximately 950,000 barrels per day, a severe blow to the energy industry and to the American economy.

National Airborne Operations Center

The E-4B flying command post known as Night Watch was being refueled by a USAF KC-135 tanker when President Macklin received the disheartening news about the refineries. Angry and frustrated by having to react to events instead of attacking the enemy, the president had Hartwell Prost and Pete Adair awakened to join General Chalmers and himself.

Fresh coffee and juice were being served when the men gathered in the conference room. The mood was somber, with anger boiling just below the surface.

Chalmers gave his boss and Prost a thorough update on the refineries and the efforts being made to bring the fires under control. Then he sadly updated them on the situation at the Indian Point Nuclear Power Plant in New York. Thousands of people had been evacuated from the area. Reactor experts expected to be able to contain the leaking fission products in the next forty-eight to seventy-two hours.

The president was red-faced. "Gentlemen," he said impatiently, "we know they used helicopters to bomb the refineries. We have scores of eyewitnesses and a crashed helicopter containing the bodies of two foreign nationals. How in *hell* did this happen when we're in such a high state of readiness?"

No one had an answer.

"Where were the AWACS?" Macklin asked. He was growing more irritated by the minute. "How can we have so much air cover and these people aren't detected?"

Chalmers took the hot seat. "Sir, I believe the helicopters, transponders off, were moving slow and low to the ground. Unlighted, they could have followed the interstate, blending in with the traffic. They can mimic ground vehicles, make right-hand turns, and follow the roads instead of flying a straight line that would give them away."

The president was not convinced.

"He's right," Pete Adair interjected, aware they were being tested. "If you're flying a helo directly over heavy traffic in nighttime conditions, at the same speed, it's practically impossible to determine what's rolling and what's flying—unless you have eyes on it."

Macklin raised a hand, palm out, fingers spread. "I'm not going to debate whether it can be done or cannot be done. It happened, and I'm damn teed off about it." He slammed his fist on the table. "I'm tired of reacting!"

The president paused, took in a deep breath, and lowered his voice. "First on my list is immediate and complete protection for our refineries, same as with the nuclear power plants. I don't care if we have to double or triple the CAPs, have combat air patrols swarming over every priority."

The president glanced at Prost and Adair. "I know we have a helluva lot of operating refineries and this isn't going to be easy, but we have to use every resource available—redouble our efforts."

"We'll get it done," Prost said, as an aide brought him a briefing folder and quietly left the cabin. He skimmed over the contents and closed his eyes for a moment.

"What is it, Hartwell?" Macklin asked.

"Reliable sources in the French media saw Saeed Shayhidi being helped ashore after his yacht sank. They even have pictures of him in his wet pajamas. The growing speculation among European and Arab newshounds is that the U.S. military was directly involved."

"They're going to have a lot more to speculate about." The president tapped the end of his pen on the table. "I want recommendations. How do we get this asshole Shayhidi?"

As he usually did, Prost assumed the lead, thinking out loud. "He has a fleet of thirty-seven cargo ships and oil tankers. If he won't respond out of fear for his life, maybe he'll respond when we hit him in the wallet."

Macklin raised an approving eyebrow.

Prost handed the president a briefing folder. "Here is a list of all his ships: their names, classification as to cargo or tanker, and where most of them are located at the present time."

"Impressive. You've really been doing your homework."

"Actually, my staff has been doing it for me. The information just arrived about twenty minutes ago."

Prost waited until Macklin thoroughly perused the data. "Sir, I recommend we immediately begin reducing his ship inventory and keep reducing it until he caves in and calls off his terrorists."

"Or," Chalmers said dryly, "until Shayhidi has no assets to continue funding the attacks: terrorism in general."

Adair nodded his consent. "I would also add freezing his accounts at the financial institutions on our list. And while we're at it, let's go after his vacation homes, his primary residence in Geneva, and his office building there."

Prost looked at the president. "We have the coordinates of his residences, all of them."

"How current is your data?" Macklin asked, remembering the Chinese embassy blunder.

"Less than six hours old. But Shayhidi isn't at any of them at the moment. I think we should accomplish these goals from the ground. We don't want to risk a Tomahawk or two going off course and hitting a nursing home or elementary school."

"Les?" the president asked.

"I agree with Secretary Adair, and Mr. Prost is right on target. But we don't want to peck away at Shayhidi. This has to be a concerted, organized effort to bring him to his knees *quickly*—or kill him—before we have massive casualties in our country."

Prost gave a nod of approval.

Chalmers reached for his coffee cup. "We have to use every available asset we have, including our special ops forces: Army Rangers, Green Berets, Pathfinders, Delta Force, and Navy SEALS. They did an *outstanding* job in Afghanistan and Iraq."

Macklin saw Prost cock his head. "You have a question?"

"No, sir," Prost said. "I just want to underscore what General Chalmers has suggested. We must conduct these operations as covertly as humanly possible. Keep them under the radarscopes, especially the scopes on Capitol Hill."

Pete Adair piped up. "Jesus, Hartwell, our homeland is under siege. We can't be worried about what other people think. We didn't throw the first punch, but we can damn sure throw the last one."

"What I'm saying"—Prost went on calmly—"is that we don't have to overcompensate and use a sledgehammer on a gnat. We're going to be deep-sixing unarmed civilian ships. Let's do it in a surgical way to save as many lives as possible. Nor can we afford to sink oil tankers and pollute the oceans. We'll have to sabotage them in port so they can't get under way—SEAL teams, gentlemen."

"Hartwell is right," Macklin said, contemplating the titillating aspects of destroying Shayhidi's assets. "We have to be smart, we have to be quick, and we have to do it right the first time."

Prost removed his glasses. "Sir, can you give us a couple of hours to put together a specific target list and decide how to best carry out the operations?"

"You have it," the president said. "Operation Stopgap. Get back to me when you're ready."

"Yes, sir."

14

Boise, Idaho

Luggage in hand, Scott and Jackie were about to leave their room at the Grove Hotel when the satellite phone rang. Scott picked it up and stared out the window while he talked.

Jackie sat on the edge of the bed and listened to the short but lively conversation. Scott was clearly agitated when he signed off.

"What's wrong?" she asked.

"When Wakefield's team went in early this morning, there

was no trace of the B-25, zip-point-nothing. The hangar was empty, and no one was around except Ma and Pa Kettle."

"Well, we shouldn't be surprised," she declared. "Farkas offered the charming couple a pot of cash to erect a hangar and set up shop to continue his assault on our country."

"Then we showed up and he bolted," Scott said in frustration. "I should've stressed the immediacy of the situation to Wakefield."

"Look, we did what we were supposed to do." She rose from the bed and walked over to him, taking his face in her hands. "Remember, you're the one who gave me the lecture about following Hartwell's instructions."

"Yes, and Farkas got away." Scott buttoned his shirt. "This will come back to haunt us. I have a gut feeling."

"Next time, we act swiftly," she reassured him.

"If there is a next time."

Jackie reached for her luggage. "Somehow, I'm sure there *will* be a next time. There always is when we're dealing with Farkas."

They checked out of the hotel and drove their rental car to the Boise Air Terminal/Gowen Field. Passing through the Western Aircraft FBO, Jackie loaded their luggage and completed a preflight on the LongRanger while Scott turned in their rental car. He soon joined Jackie in the helicopter.

After the engine was started, she checked with Clearance Delivery and received a new transponder code. Things were getting back to normal in the world of general aviation.

She called the control tower and received permission to take off from the joint-use civilian/military airfield.

"You ready?" Jackie asked.

Scott tightly cinched his straps. "All set."

She added power and pulled up on the collective. The main rotor lift overcame their weight and the LongRanger slowly rose from the ramp. Seconds later, at a height of nine feet, the helicopter went violently out of control.

Jackie aggressively fought the controls, but it was too late to salvage the landing. "Hang on—we're going in!"

The helicopter rotated horizontally and tipped over at the same time, ripping the two main rotor blades to shreds. The LongRanger crashed on the ramp and beat itself to pieces while Jackie frantically worked to shut down the engine.

Finally, after what seemed an eternity, the loud scraping and grinding sounds ceased and the machine came to a quiet halt. Stunned by the sudden teeth-rattling crash, Scott unstrapped from his seat and helped Jackie out of the twisted wreckage.

Both had minor scrapes and bruises, but the helicopter had taken the brunt of the crash. It was strike damage, totally destroyed except for a few components. From all directions, people were running toward the crumpled LongRanger. In the distance a crash truck was heard barreling down the taxiway toward the downed helicopter.

Scott looked at the crumpled wreckage and stepped away from the growing pool of jet fuel flowing across the ramp. "What went wrong?"

Before she could answer, the senior line service technician from the FBO rushed up to them. "Are you okay?"

Jackie and Scott assured him they were fine.

The young man stared at the crushed and mangled helicopter. "I guess your mechanics must've made a mistake."

"Mechanics?" Scott looked confused. "What mechanics?"

The technician was taken aback. "Them two guys who drove in late last night and worked on your chopper."

Scott and Jackie darted a look at each other.

"Fred, the night manager, told me 'bout the guys before he left this mornin'. Said they was kinda strange."

"Did Fred know the men?" Jackie asked.

"Naw. He said they was drivin' a small Ford pickup. Parked it right next to your chopper."

Scott stopped to address the onlookers. "Folks, we don't want to disturb the accident site until the NTSB people get here." The small crowd disbursed and Scott turned to the technician. "I didn't catch your name."

"Jimmy Parker."

"Jimmy, did Fred ask the men what they were doing?"

"I dunno, maybe you should talk to Fred." The young man

grew hesitant, sensing something was wrong. "Fred said they was gone in 'bout fifteen minutes, maybe less."

"Okay, thanks."

Jackie and Scott exchanged another look before the crash crew arrived. They talked with the senior crew member while the other men hosed down the ramp to disperse the jet fuel.

When the crash crew left, Jackie caught sight of Jimmy Parker standing a few feet away. "Let's continue chatting with our new friend."

"You bet, just getting to the good part."

When Parker saw the couple approaching him, he turned and walked in their direction.

Jackie greeted him with a friendly smile. "Jimmy, you said the people who worked on our two-oh-six were strange?"

Parker lowered his voice and cast his eyes down. "Well, Fred said they was foreigners, A-rabs, but they spoke English pretty good."

"Two Middle Eastern men?" Scott asked.

"That's what Fred said."

"Did Fred tell you anything else?"

"Nope, that's 'bout it."

Realizing there was nothing else to be learned from Parker, Scott surveyed the crash site. "Jimmy, do you have anything we can rope off the wreckage with?"

"You mean like that yellow crime scene tape?"

"Sure, whatever you have," Scott said with a smile. "Oh, by the way, have you heard anything about a B-25 bomber being flown around here?"

Parker's eyes opened wide. "Yeah, what's goin' on with that deal?"

"What have you heard?" Scott asked.

"An instructor, Pam Bowers, and her student saw a B-25 flyin' real low and fast near Payette 'bout sundown last night." He raised his baseball cap up and firmly clamped it over his mussed hair. "We don't see that kind of thing often, old warbirds flyin' around."

"Did they say in which direction it was headed?" Scott asked.

"Southeast toward Twin Falls. That's what everyone was talkin' 'bout this mornin' when I come in from breakfast."

"Thanks, Jimmy, we appreciate it," Scott said, and shook his hand. "Do you have a business card?"

"Yes, sir," he said with pride, and gave Scott his card. "If you need anything, let me know."

"We'll do it. You've been helpful."

Parker was confused and it showed in his eyes. "Is there somethin' goin' on, somethin' wrong we should know about?"

"No, nothing wrong," Scott assured him. "I heard the same rumor about the B-25. Just curious."

While Parker made arrangements to secure the helicopter, Jackie and Scott removed their personal belongings from the wreckage. They were careful to make sure their weapons were safely zipped in canvas bags and not visible to the bystanders.

After they piled everything a safe distance from the helicopter, she closely inspected the flight control system. It was evident that the actuators on the main rotor had been tampered with, but it would not have been noticeable from the ground. The tail rotor was so badly damaged that it was impossible to tell if it had been sabotaged.

Jackie picked up a piece of the shattered main rotor blade and curiously studied it. "In retrospect, telling Ma and Pa Kettle we were going to Boise was a bonehead move."

"Well, it's too late for hindsight. We've managed to live through another 'character-building' experience." He put his hands on her shoulders and looked her straight in the eye. "Are you okay, really okay?"

"I feel great. I'm still alive . . . what more could I ask?"

"It wasn't your fault." He glanced at the wreckage. "I'm just glad we weren't three hundred feet in the air."

"Yeah, that wouldn't have been a pretty sight." She dropped the piece of shredded wreckage on the ramp.

Scott noticed Jimmy Parker was in the process of isolating the LongRanger from the onlookers. "Most likely, Farkas flew the B-25 south to another airfield and a couple of his partners did this job."

"What he plans to do with a B-25 is the big question," Jackie said. "The obvious thing that comes to mind is *what* or *who* is he going to bomb?"

"That's the question," Scott mused. "It *is* a bomber, and we have six missing nukes."

"That's a cheerful thought. I better go initiate the dog-and-pony show with the Feds."

"If there's any static from the Gestapo, call Hartwell and have him take care of the Feds."

"I can handle it," she said firmly. "I've dealt with the FAA before."

Scott glanced at a Cessna Caravan amphibian floatplane sitting on the edge of the ramp. "As soon as you finish your rug dance with the Feds, we need to hit the road."

She looked exasperated. "Hit the road in what?"

"A new flying machine." He pointed in the direction of the big single-engine turboprop. "The Cessna Caravan sitting over there. It belongs to the FBO."

"How do you know?"

"I asked last night when I was getting our car. They use it for sightseeing and hauling fishing parties."

"And?"

"It's not making any money at the moment," he said, with an air of certitude. "I'll see if they'll rent it to us."

"Right, you can bet on it." Jackie's smile made a short appearance. "I'm sure they'll be jumping with joy after we just crashed on their ramp." She paused, placing her hands on her hips. "Say, Mr. FBO manager, could we try again with one of *your* flying machines?" She lowered her voice. "Sure thing, folks. Are you two just learning to fly . . . or are you just naturally uncoordinated?"

"Hey, I have my seaplane rating," Scott said with confidence. "If they won't rent it, we'll buy it."

"Better get in touch with Hartwell first. I don't need to remind you, this is not a good time to bother him."

"Well." Scott paused and again glanced at the Caravan. "He said we're on our own, have to improvise every now and then."

"This should be good."

"You can laugh, but look at my track record."

"*Whatever* you do, don't dare mention your track record," she deadpanned. "Otherwise, we'll be walking."

Scott smiled and started toward the FBO.

The *Alyssa Langford*

One of the newest containerships owned by Saeed Shayhidi, the 1,024-foot *Alyssa Langford,* was 170 miles southeast of her destination, Charleston, South Carolina, one of the chief ports on the Atlantic Coast. Carrying a full load of twenty-foot containers, and powered by a single twelve-cylinder 75,000-horsepower diesel engine, the merchant ship was making a steady 21.4 knots.

The crew of fifteen had finished lunch, and many of them were preparing for their visit to the historic city. They were looking forward to a dose of Southern hospitality, lots of cold beer, and plenty of fried chicken with all the trimmings. Charleston, a major center of southern culture, was a favorite port for many seafarers, foreign and domestic.

The master was in his quarters taking a nap when a loud explosion awakened him. The ship shuddered from stem to stern. The captain, fully awake in an instant, ran to the bridge. He ordered ALL STOP on the engine while he stared at the heavily damaged bow.

His mind raced, but nothing made sense. It was difficult to comprehend that someone had deliberately torpedoed them. But there was no denying the fact unless they had hit a mine or something inside the ship exploded. *Not a mine,* he argued with himself.

No matter what the cause, the master knew *Alyssa Langford* was in serious trouble. He began broadcasting a Mayday signal, which included their GPS position. The ship was taking on water at an alarming rate and was beginning to list.

When the first tongue of flames began appearing in the gaping hole in the bow, the captain knew it was time to act. They could not afford to wait until *Alyssa Langford* was actually going under to abandon the vessel. The master gave the order and the crew scrambled to their assigned lifeboat stations.

USS *Montpelier*

"All ahead slow," Commander Art Schweitzer ordered while he peered through the search periscope.

"Aye, aye, all ahead slow," the Officer of the Deck repeated.

Schweitzer watched quietly as the crew members of the containership *Alyssa Langford* abandoned the craft in an orderly fashion and connected their boats together.

Schweitzer then swept the horizon in a slow, deliberate 360-degree circle, noting a ship's bridge coming into view many miles away. Feeling confident the crew he torpedoed would be rescued quickly, he folded the handles. "Down scope." Schweitzer stepped away from the retreating periscope. "All ahead one third, level at four hundred feet."

"Aye, aye, Captain, all ahead one third, level at four hundred feet." The Officer of the Deck watched the sailors as they responded to the skipper's commands.

Schweitzer had orders to loiter eighty nautical miles southwest of Bermuda and wait for further instructions. Another Shayhidi-owned cargo ship was preparing to sail from the port of Miami bound for Amsterdam. Under constant surveillance, *Stephanie Eaton* would be tracked to her rendezvous with USS *Montpelier.*

Other U.S. attack submarines were being positioned to intercept cargo vessels owned by Shayhidi. The Los Angeles–class boats were spreading out in the Atlantic, Pacific, and Indian oceans, and in the Mediterranean Sea. They had orders to positively identify their target in daylight before attacking.

As the president ordered, Shayhidi oil tankers were off limits to the attack submarines. They would be dealt with in port by another elite branch of the U.S. Navy.

National Airborne Operations Center

When President Macklin's E-4B touched down at Barksdale AFB near Shreveport, Louisiana, another gleaming Night Watch aircraft was standing by with two engines running. Four USAF

F-15 Eagles were taxiing for takeoff. They would rendezvous with the NAOC shortly after the president was airborne.

Macklin and his entourage changed planes and settled into their quarters while the fresh flying command post prepared for takeoff. Once airborne and climbing, the E-4B picked up an escort consisting of one KC-135 refueling tanker and four fighters from Mountain Home AFB, Idaho.

The F-15s were responsible for shepherding the Boeing southeast over Florida and the Atlantic. Three hours later, a quartet of marine corps F/A-18C Hornets from the Crusaders of VMFA-122 would rendezvous with the flying command post.

With two of their own KC-130 tankers in position along the route, the marines would provide protection for the journey to a holding pattern near the Grand Banks southeast of Newfoundland. Later, with a navy escort of F/A-18s, the Boeing would head toward the Seattle area before landing at Dyess AFB near Abilene, Texas.

Everyone was in the conference room when Hartwell Prost walked in. He wasn't smiling, but his demeanor reflected a sense of satisfaction. "Gentlemen, Saeed Shayhidi is missing another asset. The *Alyssa Langford* is en route to the bottom of the Atlantic," he announced. "All hands were safely picked up by another ship."

"Great news," the president said, and looked at Pete Adair. "How are we doing on the refineries and power plants?"

"We're about sixty percent covered, but I expect full coverage in the next six to eight hours."

"What about the NOTAM?" Macklin asked.

Prost glanced at his wristwatch. "It was issued forty-five minutes ago. The word is also being passed from approach, departure, and en-route controllers, saturating the airborne pipeline."

The president removed his glasses and looked at General Chalmers. "Les, any of Shayhidi's tankers in our sights?"

"Not at the moment. We're making good progress, but safety has to be our first priority," Chalmers said, in a tired voice. "We have to be deliberate, and we have to be extremely cautious."

After listening to the conversation, Pete Adair was growing more and more uncomfortable with the plan to sink Shayhidi's ships. "If we're exposed, using our attack submarines to sink civilian ships, even if they *are* owned by a terrorist who is funding attacks on us, there's going to be a political firestorm the likes of which we've never seen."

Unusual for Prost, he instinctively made a decision to remain silent. *Secretary Adair, sometimes you have to do whatever it takes to survive and win. We can put out the fires later.*

"Pete," Macklin began, "let me worry about the political fallout. I'll take the heat if there is any. This country and the safety of its citizens mean more to me than hanging on to the White House for another term."

Surprised by the president's statement, Adair nodded his head. "Sir, if I don't speak my mind, I'm no good to you."

"Your candor is always appreciated." Macklin turned his attention to Prost, whose face was placid. "How are we coming on the State Department replacements?"

"Jim has completed the vetting process, and the list has gone to the majority leader in the Senate."

"We're in the middle of a war," the president said angrily. "I need someone *now* to help me with the international responsibilities and foreign relations."

"Well, sir," Prost said diplomatically, "as you know, Congress is in special recess because of the attacks. No word yet on when they'll be back in session."

"They're always in session when you don't need them," Macklin grumbled, "and never there when you *do*."

Prost looked at the vetting list. "Word on the Hill is they're going to stall your nomination when they return, payback for not keeping them in the loop."

Sensing the president's foul mood, no one ventured a response.

"Hartwell," Macklin said bitterly, "get Brad Austin on the phone."

"Yes, sir."

"Let's see if he'll consider an emergency recess appointment as acting secretary of state."

Prost smiled broadly. "I'm sure he would be honored, sir."

Boise, Idaho

It had almost taken an act of Congress, and it did require a special insurance endorsement and a $15,000 refundable damage deposit, but Scott was checked out in the Cessna Caravan amphibian.

After two hours of intense instruction, including numerous water landings on a nearby reservoir, Scott was cleared to fly as pilot in command. Dalton purchased twenty hours of block flying time, not to exceed ten days. With a phone call to the manager of the FBO, the flying hours and number of days could be extended.

One of the largest single-engine aircraft on floats, the roomy, reliable turboprop was often called the ultimate amphibian. Considered by many pilots to be one of the toughest airplanes in its class, the rugged eight- to fourteen-passenger Caravan could operate safely from most water or land destinations anywhere in the world. From its introduction in 1985, the airplane had been a consistent hands-down favorite of operators from Federal Express to bush pilots in Third World countries.

"How'd it go, or should I ask?" Scott said, when Jackie casually walked up to the big plane.

Although she tried to conceal her irritation, the animus was close to the surface. "Just have to make an appointment for a one-way gab fest with an FAA chief yakker."

Scott gave her a thin smile. "Yeah, you probably need a little pep talk about being more careful around terrorists."

Not in a humorous mood, she ignored his comment. "I made arrangements to have the wreckage removed by the Feds."

His surprise was evident. "The same Feds we're supposed to be staying away from?"

"Same ones," she said, with a straight face. "I called Hartwell and he's taking care of the problem."

"So everything's tied up nice and neat and we're free to mosey on down the road?"

"We sure are," she said, and glanced at the sun. "But there's only about three hours of daylight left."

Scott glanced around the ramp. "That's better than sitting here twiddling our thumbs. Been trapped here most of the day."

Jackie climbed up the struts on the Wipline amphibious floats and looked inside the spacious cabin. Scott had loaded their luggage and survival gear, and they were firmly secured by a cargo net. The gray leather seats looked comfortable, and there was even a potty seat in the back.

She stepped down, nonchalantly put her arm on one of the chest-high floats, and donned her traditional aviator-style sunglasses. "Light the fire and let's mosey."

"Hop aboard."

Jackie looked at the small tires protruding from the giant-sized floats. The main gear on each side had two wheels, while the bow of each float had one caster landing gear. "I can see where this could lead to major problems."

"You just have to remember to raise the rollers to land on water and put them down to land on a runway—not that cerebral."

She grinned and climbed into the cockpit. "I guess not—if a *marine* aviator can *remember* to do it."

He glanced casually over the rims of his sunglasses.

"Start the motor," she said, with a demure expression.

Scott settled into his seat, turned the battery and fuel boost on, engaged the start switch, and eased the fuel-condition lever into low idle when the gas generator (NG) speed passed through 15 percent.

The big 675-shaft-horsepower Pratt & Whitney turboprop smoothly came to life. Scott checked ATIS and called Ground Control. He taxied to the beginning of Runway 10-Right, contacted the tower, and took off, heading southeast toward Twin Falls. As the fully fueled Caravan gained altitude, he moved the large gear lever up to stow the wheels inside the floats and then raised the flaps.

The huge floats brought the normal cruise speed down from 186 knots at 10,000 feet to 162 knots at the same altitude. With the flaps extended, the plane could loaf along at 75 to 80 knots for optimum viewing.

"This is a really great airplane," Jackie said, as she began exploring the wide well-engineered cockpit.

Scott leveled at 800 feet. "It's a simple, rugged, reliable, go-anywhere-and-haul-a-crowd airplane."

"I'm convinced." She was especially impressed with the straightforward systems, the redundancy of a twin-engine plane, and the same avionics and four-color radar found in the Cessna Citation Jet.

"What do we have here?" she asked, noticing a small box lying on the floor next to her right foot.

"That's a handheld VHF marine radio."

Jackie reached down for the box.

"Go ahead, open it. The guy who checked me out strongly recommended having one on board."

"To communicate with boaters?" she guessed.

"Right. Let them know our intentions before we land or take off."

"Makes sense." She examined the radio.

"The guy said this was a top-of-the-line totally submersible model that does it all."

"Okay, we're set for air and water," she said, reading the instructions for the Raytheon 106 radio. "This is an interesting toy."

"See if it works."

She turned it on. "What channel do we monitor?"

"The common marine channel is sixteen."

Jackie selected 16 and turned up the volume.

Scott adjusted the rudder trim. "You call other operators on sixteen and ask them to join you on another channel, to keep sixteen free for emergencies."

"Got it," she said, listening to a distant conversation between a marina operator and a boater who was having engine trouble. They switched channels and Jackie followed, monitoring the call. "I can see how this could come in handy out in the middle of nowhere."

"A lifesaver, like our sat phones." Scott eased the power back for long-range cruising. "We have to have a call sign for the radio, like the name of a boat or something."

Jackie thought for a few seconds. "How about Water Bird?"

"What?" Scott said with a slow grin.

"Water Bird, like Sky King's Song Bird."

"That'll do."

They surveyed several airfields, searching for the B-25 or anything else that looked suspicious. After passing Burley, Scott flew northeast to Idaho Falls and Rexburg. With the sun dipping well below the mountains, he removed his sunglasses. "Have you had enough for today?"

"Actually," she admitted, "I'd had enough when we crawled out of the LongRanger."

"I'd have to agree." He turned south and landed at the Pocatello Regional Airport. "It's been quite a day, one for the books."

"That it has." She sighed. "Are you as sore as I am?"

"At least. Feels like I took a ride in a clothes dryer."

After they secured the Caravan for the night and rented a Chevy, Scott started the car's engine and turned to Jackie. "What's for dinner?"

She smiled and rested her head on the seat back. "I *always* like to celebrate my crash landings with a thick, juicy filet mignon, baked potato swimming in butter, crisp, cold salad, and a good Merlot—lots of Merlot."

"I believe we can handle that."

15

Valero Refinery, Houston, Texas

Located directly on the Houston ship channel, the massive 250-acre refinery had deepwater access for off-loading heavy, sweet crude oils. Extra security personnel were in place inside the busy facility, while members of the Texas National Guard patrolled the perimeter of the refinery.

Moored in forty feet of water alongside the ship channel frontage, the 1,112-foot *Gulf Courier* was in the process of off-loading her crude oil. Owned by Saeed Shayhidi, the behemoth supertanker carried 74 million gallons of oil.

Rain was coming down in sheets at 9:17 P.M. when six hand-picked members of SEAL Team Four approached the *Gulf Courier*. Wearing the LAR V rebreathing apparatus that allows them to swim underwater without leaving surface air bubbles, the divers carried satchels of high explosives. Only the team leader raised his eyes above water to take a final bearing on the ship before the six submerged to a deeper depth. Minutes later, they reached the stern of their target.

The men attached most of their specially prepared explosives to the rudder of the tanker. Working in total darkness, they hooked the other explosives to one of the massive propeller blades. The charges were designed to destroy the rudder and propeller without penetrating the ship's hull. They set a timer that was connected to both packages. It would allow them thirty-five minutes to return to their entry point, board their innocent-looking thirty-two-foot fishing boat, and be miles away when the charges detonated.

Two U.S. Army AH-64 Apache Longbow multimission combat helicopters were circling the Houston refinery, one at 900 feet and the other at 1,500 feet. The two-man crews from the 1-227th Attack Battalion stationed at Fort Hood, Texas, were responsible for protecting the facility from ground or air attacks.

The veteran aviators had been secretly briefed about the SEAL operation. Along with the members of the Texas National Guard, the flight crews knew the approximate time the "event" would happen.

Gulf Courier was finished off-loading when the quiet evening was shattered by a huge blast of water shooting straight into the air. Small waves rippled across the ship channel while security personnel hurried toward the tanker.

In the water before 10:30 P.M., scuba divers with powerful underwater lights discovered the extensive damage done to the *Gulf Courier*. The huge rudder was almost twisted from the shaft connecting it to the ship, and one propeller blade was lying on the bottom of the channel.

The supertanker would have to be towed to a dry dock large enough to accommodate a ship of her size. Unfortunately for Shayhidi, there was not an abundance of those facilities available. In addition, shipyard work of this magnitude generally needed to be scheduled well in advance. Another of Shayhidi's revenue spigots was now turned off. The money-draining liability would be idle for an extended period of time.

Pocatello, Idaho

After a great dinner and a relaxing drive to Idaho Falls and back, Scott and Jackie were turning into the Best Western motel when the satellite phone rang. Jackie answered the call. From the sound of the conversation, Scott could tell it was Frank Wakefield. She told the special agent about the sabotaged helicopter, the subsequent crash landing, and the Cessna Caravan floatplane.

When she hung up, Scott reached for the door handle. "Farkas?"

"Yes. He *was* in the shack next to the hangar," she said, and opened her car door. "Let's go inside and I'll fill you in on the details."

"Sounds good." Scott picked up the fresh bottle of Merlot on the seat and followed her to their room. He shut the door and headed toward the bathroom. "I'll get the wineglasses."

They kicked off their shoes, pulled two straight-back chairs up to the bed, and propped their feet on the bedspread.

Jackie reached for a pillow and shoved it behind her back. "Following the raid on the hangar compound, Wakefield conducted an interview with the charming couple. When they began hedging their answers, he showed them a picture of

Farkas. The couple identified him as the person who negotiated the hangar deal and ran the show."

"Did Wakefield tell them who Farkas is?"

"Yes, and after they came out of shock they were singing their hearts out. They thought Farkas was just an eccentric, wealthy recluse who restored old warbirds."

Jackie glanced at Scott. "Farkas and his crew, the two who *worked* on our LongRanger, had one heck of an operation going and two unwitting stooges for cover."

"Did they acknowledge the presence of a B-25 bomber?"

She smiled and stretched her long, shapely legs like a contented cat. "Oh, yes. And Farkas was flying the plane by himself."

"I don't suppose they knew where he was going?"

"No, but they did mention the two mechanics and their Ford pickup and the fact that they disappeared shortly after Farkas departed."

Scott rolled his head toward Jackie. "Any chance they remembered anything about the bomber, paint scheme, numbers, et cetera?"

She smiled serenely. "What do you think?"

"I know, a stupid question."

"At any rate, the good news is we know who we're dealing with *and* we flushed Farkas out of his base of operation."

Scott looked at her from the corner of his eye. "Ah, we just happened to stumble over it, not like we solved some age-old mystery."

"Hey, I'll take a win any way we can get it."

Scott reached for the remote and turned on the television. "What's Wakefield going to do about Farkas?"

"He said the FBI and local law-enforcement agencies are going to search every airport west of a line from Chicago to New Orleans. He said the Washington brass—read Jim Ebersole—put a major priority on finding the bomber and Farkas, like right now."

"Did he have any advice for us?"

"No, but he wants an update if we discover anything else of interest."

"Well," Scott said, "I think we follow our instincts, see what happens."

"I'm with you."

He thought for a moment. "I don't think Farkas went very far. The bomber would attract too much interest, especially when so many people are looking for it."

"Yeah, he has to have a hangar not too far from here."

"Or the bomber could be camouflaged," Scott replied.

Their conversation came to a halt when a breaking-news logo appeared on the television screen. Seconds later, a tired Pentagon correspondent faced the camera.

The anchor welcomed her.

Christine.

Bob, senior Pentagon officials and a spokesperson for the ATF have confirmed new intelligence that indicates Islamic terrorists have smuggled surface-to-air missiles into the United States. The weapons have been identified as shoulder-fired antiaircraft missiles. They are believed to be Russian-made SA-7s with a range of approximately three miles. Our experts tell us they can hit aircraft flying as high as thirteen thousand five hundred feet.

The other missiles are reported to be U.S.-made Stingers with a range of five miles and the ability to destroy aircraft up to ten thousand feet. The missiles, approximately four hundred of them, were obtained covertly in Afghanistan and Pakistan, said a senior Pentagon official, who spoke on condition of anonymity.

She glanced at her notes.

The missiles, which I'm told are fairly lightweight, are easy to obtain on what the official called the gray market. According to our source, a senior al-Qaeda commander has admitted the missiles were sent to the United States in shipping containers from Hong Kong and Shanghai. As of now, the port or ports of arrival are still classified and the hunt for the missiles continues. Bob.

Thank you, Christine. In related news, U.S. customs inspectors found three Iranian and two Saudi Arabian stowaways inside a shipping container at the port of Charleston, South Carolina, today. The stowaways had thin foam-rubber mats to sleep on, food, water, a makeshift toilet, counterfeit documentation, and seven AK-47 assault rifles. They have been taken into custody for questioning.

Scott hit the mute button. "That's comforting news. Hundreds of portable surface-to-air missiles inside our country, and we don't have a clue where they are."

Jackie's gaze was fixed on the silent television. "Well, if we don't find the missing nukes, we're gonna have bigger problems than the SAMS."

Ramstein Air Base, West Germany

Two hours before sunrise, a Lockheed C-5B Galaxy slowly descended out of low gloomy clouds on an instrument approach. With the glaring landing lights on, the U.S. Air Force strategic airlift transport looked like a huge prehistoric archaeopteryx, a flying reptile from the Jurassic period. The "aluminum overcast" came to earth in a surprisingly soft touchdown on its sturdy twenty-eight-wheel landing gear. The aircraft rolled most of the way down the runway while the aircraft commander spared the brakes and tires.

After the Galaxy taxied to a remote area at the home of Headquarters, U.S. Air Forces in Europe, members of the 1st Special Forces Operational Detachment Delta, or Delta Force, met the transport plane. The Delta Force contingent had arrived on a C-17A Globemaster only minutes before the Galaxy landed.

Stationed in a secluded site at Fort Bragg, North Carolina, the 1st SFOD-Delta is made up of recruits from the U.S. Army's Special Forces Green Berets and Rangers. Delta Force is one of the Federal Government's CT, or counterterrorist, groups and performs a wide variety of covert missions, including hostage rescue, seizure and retrieval of hostile personnel, and direct action.

When the C-5B's huge nose was fully open, the soldiers from Delta Force greeted the helicopter pilots and support personnel from the army's 160th Special Operations Aviation Regiment (SOAR). Along with the helicopters inside the Galaxy, additional helicopters from the 160th Nightstalkers had arrived earlier that morning.

Based at Fort Campbell, Kentucky, and Hunter Army Airfield, Savannah, Georgia, the 160th uses specially modified helicopters and skilled pilots to fly special warfare teams to the mission through inclement weather or hostile environments, day or night.

The Nightstalkers fly the versatile MH-60K/L Blackhawk, the AH-6 Little Bird, and the MH-47D/E Chinook tailored for clandestine operations. Classified as medium transport helicopters, the big Chinooks are configured for in-flight refueling, thermal/night imaging, and crew armor, and they are equipped with 7.62mm Gatling miniguns.

For the upcoming classified operations in Switzerland, the SOAR unit was using six handpicked pilots from its "black" battalion. Other select teams of special operations forces and Nightstalker aviators were working together in France and Spain.

USS *Montpelier*

Commander Art Schweitzer and his executive officer had officially identified the cargo ship *Stephanie Eaton* shortly after sunrise. They tracked the civilian vessel for fifty minutes before reaching a spot where there were no other ships on the horizon. The CO gave the order, and the Mark 48 was soon en route to its target.

After Schweitzer fired the torpedo, he watched the *Stephanie Eaton* and photographed the horrific detonation. Blackish-red smoke and water shot skyward, and the stricken ship immediately began slowing. Schweitzer snapped several more photographs.

Less than three minutes later, the crew of fourteen began

abandoning their ship. When the lifeboats were clear of *Stephanie Eaton,* the attack submarine descended to 200 feet to wait for the cargo carrier to sink and break up.

Nearly an hour later, after sonar detected other ships in the vicinity, Schweitzer became impatient and gave the order to come to periscope depth. Two ships, one a large containership and the other a small freighter, had come to the aid of the torpedoed crew.

Stephanie Eaton was still afloat. Schweitzer was sorry he had not fired a second Mark 48 after the crew cleared the vessel. As he was silently cursing his situation, a secondary explosion blew a gaping hole in the side of the ship. Schweitzer ordered *Montpelier* to again level at 200 feet.

A few minutes later, the sonar operator detected the sounds of a ship breaking apart. Another Saeed Shayhidi asset was descending to the bottom of the Atlantic.

Montpelier turned on course to her home port at Norfolk Naval Base, Virginia, the largest naval installation in the world. The mood aboard the submarine was unusually subdued. The men were not proud of sinking unarmed civilian ships, but they carried out their orders without question.

Gstaad, Switzerland

Overlooking the Bernese Alps, the magnificent Grand Hotel Park stands alone on a quiet hill only moments away from world-class alpine skiing and a charming village center. The Swiss Forest–style resort hotel has an interior dominated by natural stone, solid wood, and ceramic tiles.

The Grand was playing host to a large group of Hollywood celebrities, including movie stars, well-known producers and directors, and a handful of top-tier agents. In addition to its glitzy guests, the world-famous resort had another celebrity in residence. However, Saeed Shayhidi was not seen at Le Grand Restaurant or Le Salon Montgomery hobnobbing with the elites from the American film industry.

Sitting morosely in his two-bedroom suite with a trusted aide and two heavily armed bodyguards, Shayhidi was riding an emotional roller coaster. One moment he was hostile and illogical, the next moment paranoid, sullen, and withdrawn. He would go through a calm period for an hour or so and then repeat the cycle.

The loss of his prestigious Boeing corporate jet and the sinking of his yacht had had an adverse effect on Shayhidi. He had become extremely nervous and sometimes paced the floor, no longer the confident, assured international businessman.

The terrorist leader was clearly the person now being terrorized. The feeling was one of agonizing fear and total hopelessness. With no avenue to buy his way out of his predicament, the hefty fortune he inherited and continued to build was useless to him. He was trapped by his own arrogant cleverness and his feeling of intellectual superiority.

Both mentally and financially, Shayhidi was relentlessly and methodically being destroyed by the United States. His assets were being used against him and his freedom had been taken away. He was a hunted man; his life was in ruins. The irony did not escape him. It was a maddening, horrible feeling to have to live like a caged animal.

The familiar Fox logo suddenly flashed on his TV with more breaking news about the jihad against America, accompanied by a recent photo of Shayhidi.

Shayhidi stared intensely at the screen; an attractive, unsmiling woman looked up from her notes.

> Fox has learned that financier and reputed terrorist leader Saeed Shayhidi, believed to be the mastermind behind the deadly attacks on the United States, has himself become a target.

Shayhidi froze in his chair, starring at video footage of one of his containerships sinking in the Pacific. An uncontrollable, panicky feeling swept over him, and he shuddered momentarily.

> State Department officials have confirmed that Shayhidi's ship, shown here in this amateur video taken from another

> cargo ship, was destroyed by an unknown source. The entire crew was safely rescued and the accident is under invcstigation.

"It wasn't an accident!" Shayhidi blurted through clenched teeth. "Macklin had it blown up—He's trying to destroy me!"

> In addition, Shayhidi's yacht reportedly sunk in the Mediterranean Sea off the coast of southern France after an onboard explosion.

"Liars, liars!" Shayhidi shouted at the television. "You filthy bastards are going to pay for this! Macklin is going to pay! The American people are going to pay!"

> We're receiving initial reports of other Shayhidi-related news from our White House correspondent, Wesley Herman. Wes.

> Sharon, senior White House sources have told Fox that two of Shayhidi's cargo ships have mysteriously disappeared, believed to have sunk in the Atlantic during the last day or two. A senior administration spokesman denied the U.S. military had any involvement in the incidents. He pointed out that Mr. Shayhidi has made dozens of enemies all over the world.

Shayhidi's eyes bugged out, and he hurled an empty ashtray at the television, barely missing the screen and impacting the wall. "Macklin, you're dead! As good as dead!"

His aide and the two bodyguards exchanged concerned glances. How long would it be before their boss snapped?

"They will pay—*he* will pay!" Shayhidi yelled at the top of his lungs. "Macklin has underestimated me!"

The seasoned correspondent continued in his clipped manner.

> Mysteriously, two other vessels belonging to the shipping magnate, both believed to be petroleum tankers, suffered serious mechanical failures while in port. They are reported to

be inoperable, one at a Houston refinery and the other at the port of Valdez, Alaska. Sharon.

Shayhidi leaped out of his chair and kicked the television screen in, cutting his leg in the process.

"They are going to pay," he bellowed. "Send an e-mail to Farkas. I'm changing the plans. Macklin has to pay for this! The American military has to pay for this. The American people have to pay!"

The aide attempted to reason with him. "Mr. Shayhidi, I don't think you should jeopardize your—"

"Get in touch with Farkas or get out of my sight, forever!"

The adviser cast his dark eyes down. "Yes, sir, I'll contact him."

"Now!"

"Yes, sir."

Ashen-faced and shaking, Shayhidi turned to his two bodyguards. "We're leaving—going to Saint Moritz."

They nodded silently.

"Macklin is going to pay!"

National Airborne Operations Center

The E-4B was humming at 4:35 A.M. Pacific Coast Time when Hartwell Prost received the CIA briefing from Langley, Virginia. The president and his advisers had retired early in the evening during a lull in the events. Refreshed and relaxed after a light breakfast, Prost checked his wristwatch and closed his leather folder. It was time to bring President Macklin and his closest advisers up to date on world events.

Prost entered the E-4B's conference room, chatted with an aide, and turned to greet Macklin. "Good morning, Mr. President."

"Morning, Hartwell."

Prost hesitated when Pete Adair and General Chalmers walked in and sat down. After exchanging pleasantries, Prost began his summary. "We have disabled two more of Shayhidi's tankers, the *Gulf Trader* in the Corpus Christi ship channel and the *Gulf Patriot* at a California terminal. Don't have the details yet."

"Great," Macklin said energetically. "Who gets the credit?"

"SEAL Teams Three and Five. We're just now getting confirmation and a situation report on the Corpus Christi mission."

"How about those guys." The president smiled. "As we expected, a professional job." He looked at Chalmers. "See to it that they receive my personal thanks for a job well done."

"Will do," Chalmers said, with a slight nod.

A senior military aide entered the room and spoke quietly to the national security adviser. Prost thanked the army colonel and faced the group. "More good news, gentlemen. Shayhidi can chalk up another containership loss. The *Cape Moundville* had a fender bender with a torpedo from *Charlotte* about fifteen minutes ago. Her crew is safe, but the ship is on her way to the bottom of the South Pacific."

Macklin methodically added the latest information to his growing list of Shayhidi's assets that had been destroyed. "Let's keep the pressure on him—even intensify it, if we can do so safely."

"Yes, sir," Prost said, with a feeling of satisfaction. "We have a number of things in the planning stage."

"Good," the president declared. "No matter where he's hiding, Shayhidi has to know by now what's happening to his fleet."

"And to his fortune," Prost quietly added, slipping his briefing page under a synopsis from U.S. Central Command headquarters at MacDill AFB, Florida. "On a different but familiar topic: the Middle East."

"What now?" Macklin said, half question, half recognition.

Prost cleared his throat. "Since we're immersed in stabilizing Iraq, other factions have decided to take some unusually aggressive stabs at us."

The president's eyes hardened. "Let's have it."

"During the past nine hours, multiple surface-to-air missiles and antiaircraft artillery have downed two drones over the Middle East. Both were Predators conducting surveillance."

"Where, exactly?"

"One was over Iran; the other was over western Afghanistan. During the last few days they've taken dozens of shots at us from a variety of locations throughout the region. It's as if they're taunting us, daring us to engage them."

"Have we lost any manned aircraft?"

"No, sir, but an F-16 was damaged over northern Iran two hours ago. That SAM site no longer exists." Hartwell reached for his coffee cup. "One of the pockets of resistance in Afghanistan damaged a British jet, but the pilot, who was seriously injured, nursed it back to base."

Macklin turned to Adair. "Pete, I don't care where these antiaircraft sites are located. I want random retaliatory strikes at all sites that fire, or have fired, on coalition aircraft. If the site is near a military airfield, destroy the runways and hangars. Flatten the place."

"Yes, sir."

"Stagger the raids round the clock. Keep them on guard day and night and hit them hard; really do it big."

"Will do." Adair glanced at General Chalmers and then looked the president in the eye. "We'll start by pounding their air defense sites with Tomahawks and fighters, including carrier-based assets. If the sites are close to a military airfield, we'll use B-52s and B-1s to carpet-bomb the bases."

"That should be a good start."

Chalmers spoke up. "I recommend we use a combination of manned and unmanned aircraft to keep the pressure on, potential strike packages and recon assets constantly overhead."

"That's up to you," Macklin said evenly. "Just make sure each manned strike package has more than adequate support aircraft and SAR helos to retrieve any crew members who might get shot down."

"You can count on it," Adair said firmly. "We can't afford to have anyone captured."

The president frowned. "Yeah, we've been damn lucky."

Adair turned to Chalmers. "I'd like to coordinate all our mission planning with the British."

"I'll see to it," Chalmers said to Adair and Macklin. "We need to concentrate on air defense sites from all quadrants. *Washington* just arrived in the Gulf this afternoon. We'll take advantage of her air wing plus their combat rescue capability."

"Les, handle it any way you and Pete want to, but keep the pressure on. Don't give anyone time even to use the latrine."

"Yes, sir," Chalmers said, anxious to set his plans in motion. "We'll keep them at the ready day and night."

Macklin leaned back in his chair and faced Prost. "The word is out on Shayhidi's assets going south. Every leader in the Gulf region wants to talk to us. They know we're behind this operation; we can't hold them off much longer."

"I'm aware of that, sir."

"Where are we on the Brad Austin situation?"

"He has accepted the position."

"Outstanding, glad to hear it."

"Sir, I took the liberty of asking him to meet us at Dyess so we can brief him. All you have to do now is sign the order."

"Consider it done."

"Yes, sir." Prost paused for a moment. "Austin will be a strong addition to your team."

"I have every confidence—want him headed to the Persian Gulf as soon as practical."

"New subject?" Prost asked.

"Sure, what's up?"

"Speaking of the British, we could sure use their help if you approve of my suggestion."

A faint smile creased the president's face. "At this stage, I'm open to almost anything, *almost* anything."

Prost's voice was emotionless. "Consider it a diplomatic gesture to a true and trusted ally."

16

HMS *Trafalgar*

The nuclear-powered British attack submarine submerged into the depths of the Gulf of Mexico after launching a U.S.-built Tomahawk cruise missile on a test flight. Closely followed by U.S. Air Force chase planes, the unarmed missile made a perfect flight across a section of the Florida Panhandle. Arriving precisely over its target coordinates, the upgraded weapon made an uneventful parachute landing on the spacious grounds of Eglin AFB.

The Royal Navy submarine crew was working closely with the U.S. Navy on a joint U.S./U.K. version of the Advanced Tomahawk Weapon Control System software. The ongoing classified tests in the Gulf of Mexico were designed to promote commonality and interoperability between the two navies. Today was the last day of testing for *Trafalgar,* and all hands were extremely pleased with the final results. In the near future, the submarine's sister, HMS *Torbay,* was scheduled to continue the testing.

Late in the morning, with the eighty-seven-foot coast guard cutter USCG *Bonito* providing security, *Trafalgar* neared the surface of the tranquil gulf to receive routine satellite communications. The first message, routed through several high commands, including the U.S. E-4B National Airborne Operations Center and No. 10 Downing Street, was a shocker for the submarine's skipper.

Clearly taken by surprise when he read the communiqué, Commander Douglas Thornton-Williams, the captain of *Trafal-*

gar, was puzzled and requested a verification of his highly unusual orders. He promptly received confirmation directly from the British prime minister. Still, Thornton-Williams and his second in command were uncomfortable.

The cargo carrier *Savanna Lorenzo,* one of Saeed Shayhidi's newest vessels, was departing the deepwater port of Pascagoula, Mississippi, at 2:43 P.M. Central Time. The specialized ship had taken on a wide variety of perishable items from the cold storage warehousing. Bound for the port of Boston, the spotless cargo ship was only ten miles from the blue waters of the gulf shipping lanes.

The highly experienced master of *Savanna Lorenzo,* along with everyone else in the maritime shipping business, had heard what was happening to the dwindling fleet owned by suspected terrorist Saeed Shayhidi. Speculation was running wild, and many of Shayhidi's ships were hurriedly making their way to the nearest port.

Reports from their corporate headquarters confirmed that three of Shayhidi's masters and their crews had abandoned their cargo ships, one at Grays Harbor, Washington, another in Singapore, and the third in New Bedford, Massachusetts. Their employer was offering huge salary bonuses to captains and crew members who stayed with their ships.

The captain of the *Savanna Lorenzo,* Enrico Antonellia, a crusty Italian with thirty-eight years of command-at-sea experience, was not the least bit worried about the cruise. The old sea dog calmly assured his faithful crew that nothing could happen to them in the benign Gulf of Mexico.

As a final assurance to any doubters, the master explained that he was going to remain in close proximity to the East Coast of the United States. No one in a submarine, American or otherwise, would dare risk coming that close to land.

Unfortunately, the skipper was wrong, but not dead wrong. While the crew of the cargo ship *Savanna Lorenzo* was being rescued by a U.S. Navy frigate, the fragmented vessel and most of its cargo was settling to the bottom of the gulf. A few tons of the floating perishable goods were providing a feeding frenzy for thousands of fish.

Twenty minutes after the picturesque sunset faded from the Gulf of Mexico, the officers and crew of HMS *Trafalgar* were beginning their long voyage home to the United Kingdom. All hands agreed they would certainly have one hell of a sea story to tell their grandchildren.

South of Lancaster, Pennsylvania

Sam Bertorini, founder and CEO of Bertorini Development Corporation, was flying his company Raytheon Beech C-90B King Air from State College, Pennsylvania, to Millville, New Jersey. He had stopped to pick up a close friend, Pennsylvania State University business professor Arnold Pezzella. Whenever Bertorini's company was considering a new construction project, in this case an upscale apartment complex, Pezzella acted as a trusted consultant and sounding board.

Flying VFR at 15,500 feet on a star-studded night, Bertorini requested flight following from the New York Air Route Traffic Control Center. Although the controller was busy with IFR traffic, he accommodated Bertorini's request.

A self-made multimillionaire, Sam Bertorini was accustomed to bending the rules and getting away with it. A multiengine-rated private pilot with no instrument rating, Bertorini flew with a professional pilot whenever the weather was questionable. If the forecast looked reasonably good, he took pride in flying his twin-engine turboprop himself.

His aircraft insurance clearly stated that a professional, instrument-rated C-90 simulator-trained pilot had to be on board every time King Air N44SB left the ground, but as his former flight instructors could attest, minor details like rules and regulations never slowed Sam the Man Bertorini.

Pezzella, who had been in the passenger cabin studying a pro forma balance sheet, joined Bertorini in the cockpit.

"Sam, I want to go over these numbers with you, make a few suggestions I think will help."

"Sure. Think we're going in too light?"

"Want to wait and discuss this over dinner?" Pezzella asked, buckling his restraining harnesses.

Bertorini glanced at him in the soft light of the cockpit. "No, always open to fresh ideas."

"Well, it's not the retroactive effect of the financing that concerns me." Pezzella opened his spiral binder. "It's the unknown quantity of renters available at these prices."

"What do you mean?" Bertorini turned down the volume on the aircraft radio and pushed back the headset over his right ear. "There are masses of renters in that area."

Pezzella studied the numbers. "You're on the borderline between renters who can afford this kind of apartment complex and people who can afford to get into a new home, a starter home."

"You think we're overpriced for the amenities?"

"I won't really know until I check the demographics and some other data. Being that close to Delaware Bay could be a problem."

The men continued their conversation while the King Air approached the dividing line between New York Center airspace and Washington Center's area of responsibility.

Sitting at his radarscope in the faintly lighted room at New York Center, Dwight Moffitt was getting more nervous by the minute. "King Air Four-Four Sierra Bravo, New York Center."

A new father of less than three hours, Moffitt was trying to concentrate on the task at hand. He waited a few seconds and spoke slowly and deliberately. "King Air November Four-Four Sierra Bravo, New York Center, do you read?"

Moffitt swore to himself. He tried again and then waited a few seconds. "King Air Four-Four Sierra Bravo, do you copy?"

Silence.

Becoming more concerned, Moffitt called one more time. "Four-Four Sierra Bravo: If you read Center, ident."

There was no return from the King Air's transponder.

"King Air Four-Four Sierra Bravo," Moffitt said, in a tight

voice. "You are about to enter restricted—prohibited—airspace! Turn left to zero-two-zero now—left zero-two-zero!"

No reply.

God, don't let this happen to me, not tonight! Moffitt contacted Washington Center on the landline and quickly explained the situation. The Washington controller frantically tried to establish contact with the King Air. Time was running out and there was nothing he could do. The distraught controller continued to call the wayward aircraft until a supervisor relieved him.

"Thumper Zero-Eight," the controller radioed to a marine corps AH-1W Super Cobra attack helicopter, "we have a situation. Traffic at your nine o'clock, passing left to right, about to penetrate prohibited airspace! No radio, no comm!"

"Thumper has the target," Captain Humberto Chavez said, as he armed his weapons. "How far, how soon, will he break the cone?"

"Approximately twenty seconds."

"Confirm traffic at my ten o'clock is the target?"

"That's correct—that's the target. Now at your eleven o'clock!"

"Zero-Eight."

Immersed in his conversation with Pezzella, Sam Bertorini suddenly realized he needed to begin his descent. He programmed the autopilot to commence descending at 500 feet a minute. Feeling pressured to get down as expeditiously as possible, Bertorini looked at the en-route Low Altitude Chart his professional pilot used for instrument flying.

He changed radio frequencies and tried to call Washington Center. They could hear him, but he couldn't hear the controller. Bertorini finally realized the volume on his radio was turned down, but it was too late.

Captain Chavez had no other choice. Orders were orders and they were unambiguous. He rolled in behind the civilian King Air. *God, I hope this isn't a mistake!* After the Sidewinder locked onto the target, Chavez steeled himself and took the shot. The air-to-air missile streaked straight for the turboprop.

Sam Bertorini reached for the control knob at the same instant the King Air penetrated the fifteen-statute-mile Prohibited

Area around the Salem Units 1 and 2 nuclear power plants near Salem, New Jersey.

"Washington Center," Bertorini radioed, "King Air Four—"

The Sidewinder slammed into the left engine and exploded. The left wing promptly separated between the engine and the fuselage. Pinned into their seats by heavy G forces, Bertorini and Pezzella knew they were going to die in the next few seconds. They also knew there was absolutely nothing they could do to prevent it.

Chavez and his copilot in the front seat of the Super Cobra gunship watched the blazing King Air roll over to the left and spin downward out of control. The C-90B plunged nose first into the ground near Interstate 95 and the New Castle County Airport, Wilmington, Delaware.

The tragic event was monitored on VHF radios by a number of individuals, including other pilots and a television news crew. The horrifying story, complete with accompanying video of the crash scene, was soon breaking news on all cable news networks. The message was clear. General aviation pilots needed to be extremely cautious about flight planning and orientation. Even a small error in navigation or a momentary lapse in communications could be fatal.

Dyess Air Force Base

Located in the wide-open spaces of west Texas, the colorful city of Abilene conjures an image of weather-beaten cowhands, dusty cattle drives, rowdy saloons, and gunfights at high noon. The ancestors of Abilene's current residents would be shocked to see their west Texas town now. It was home to the supersonic Rockwell B-1B strategic bomber. After showcasing its capability in Operation Iraqi Freedom, the sharklike Mach 1.5 bomber continued to be a linchpin in the war on terrorism.

The early morning arrival of the E-4B was not a surprise to the flight line workers at the air base. One of the other airborne command centers had landed at 4:20 A.M. and was standing at the ready when the president's plane arrived. Routine by now, the debarkation and embarkation evolution went smoothly. The 747 would remain on the ramp while the president held a short meeting.

When Macklin and his senior aides entered the waiting E-4B, they found Brad Austin aboard.

A former F-4 "Phantom Phlyer" fighter pilot in Vietnam, Bradley Carlyle Austin was a trim 166 pounds and stood five feet ten. The streaks of silver-gray hair at his temples accented his twinkling hazel eyes. A distinguished graduate of the U.S. Naval Academy, Austin had opted for a commission as a second lieutenant in the U.S. Marine Corps.

Upon completion of flight training at Kingsville, Texas, he was assigned to a marine F-4 squadron. He later became an exchange pilot with a carrier-based navy F-4 fighter squadron. His performance—some would say exploits—during the Vietnam era were legendary throughout the naval aviation community.

To a person, his fellow naval aviators knew that Captain Austin had flown a captured Mig-17 behind enemy lines. Less well known was the fact that he almost faced a court-martial during his first carrier tour for breaking the restrictive rules of engagement.

After his active duty obligation, Austin remained in the marine corps reserve. He later earned his graduate degree in international studies at Georgetown University.

Cord Macklin and Colonel Brad Austin, USMCR (Retired), had met on several occasions during their years inside the Beltway. The president was aware that Brett Shannon thought highly of Austin. Shannon had relied on Austin's judgment and experience, especially in situations requiring a military or global perspective.

"Brad, welcome aboard," President Macklin said, as he enthusiastically extended his hand.

"It's an honor to be here, sir."

Macklin gestured for everyone to take a seat at the conference table. He sat down and turned to Austin. "I trust you've been thoroughly briefed on our current situation."

"Yes, sir." Austin glanced at Prost and the secretary of defense. "Mr. Prost and Secretary Adair had their staffs bring me up to speed."

"Then you know we have an international diplomatic powder keg on our hands that could blow wide open at any moment."

Secretary Austin nodded solemnly. "Yes, sir. Brought my flak jacket and helmet with me."

The president smiled. "I'm not so concerned about our close allies; I'll deal with them. But when word gets out that our submarines have been sinking Shayhidi's ships, that we've been destroying his private property, there's going to be some heat generated."

"I understand," Brad said. "Our greatest exposure is with our pseudo-allies in Europe, the Far East, Russia, and the Middle East. Shayhidi is an icon to many people in the Middle East, and it's going to require some hand-holding sessions."

"The bottom line?" Macklin said, looking Austin squarely in the eye. "People are going to cry *foul* to the U.N. and to the international press. Count on it."

"Sir, they already are."

The president slipped out of his windbreaker. "Well, I hope you'll be able to minimize the impact and smooth their ruffled feathers."

"I'm going to need some bargaining chips."

"Whatever you need, it's your show." Macklin was impressed with Austin's straightforward no-nonsense approach.

Brad didn't hesitate. "Leverage—foreign aid. I've talked with Commerce about expediting lucrative construction projects in the region, military aid packages, et cetera." Austin glanced at Prost. "It would be helpful if I had a noose to hang over Shayhidi's head."

Macklin turned to Prost. "Hartwell, anything we can release without compromising sources or methods?"

"Everything we've gathered on Shayhidi at this point is highly classified. If we find him, have him in our custody, that would dramatically change the picture."

"Or if we get our hands on Farkas," Adair added.

"That's another story," the president said.

"Farkas is still around?" Austin asked.

"He sure is, and we're trying to close the deal," Macklin said, darting a look at his watch. "Gentlemen, if there's nothing else, I suggest we let Secretary Austin get under way."

Brad rose from his chair on cue. "I'm going to be on the move a lot, but I'll keep you fully informed."

"Just don't start any wars," the president said, tongue in cheek.

Austin smiled, knowing the president was fully aware of his escapades during the unpleasantness in Vietnam.

"Thanks, Brad," Macklin added, as he shook Austin's hand firmly. "Again, welcome aboard. Sorry we have to throw you into the lion's den your first day on the job."

"I wouldn't know how to respond if it were any other way."

"Good luck," Prost said, shaking Austin's hand.

"Thank you, sir."

As soon as Austin left the 747, it began taxiing to the active runway. Escorted by four air force F-15s, President Macklin and his staff were soon airborne and on course to a patch of sterile sky above Lake Michigan near Green Bay, Wisconsin.

Granby, Colorado

The Amtrak California Zephyr, train number 5, was precisely on time as it passed near Rocky Mountain National Park. Originating in Chicago, many experienced travelers considered the California Zephyr the most comfortable and safest way to travel to San Francisco. The relaxing train trip was certainly one of the best ways to see the towering peaks of the Rockies, follow the winding Colorado River, and ascend the famous mile-high Donner Pass in the heart of the Sierra Nevada.

The passengers aboard the California Zephyr were beginning to see the effects of the bad weather plaguing the northwestern states. By the time the train began its leg to Glenwood Springs, Colorado, many of the contented diners were having dessert and coffee. Most conversations quietly shifted from terrorism to the myriad pleasures of San Francisco, the romantic city by the bay.

From his vantage point high on a ridge above the train, Waleed Majed waited until the second passenger car passed over the marker he had placed beside the tracks. Gleefully, he triggered the twin sets of dynamite explosives. In what appeared to be a movie in slow motion, the California Zephyr derailed in jumbled sections, its cars, piled into each other, ripping open like bags of potato chips and spilling their contents.

Laughing aloud, Majed turned and raced to the idling helicopter perched on a narrow slope behind him. He and his accomplice would be many miles away before the first news helicopters, emergency medical technicians, and law enforcement officers arrived at the scene of devastation.

17

Pocatello, Idaho

"What do you think?" Jackie asked, looking out the car window at the low clouds and steady drizzle. "Go or no go?"

"We've been stuck here an extra day." Scott stared at their Caravan for a moment and then looked down the regional airport runway. "I don't know about you, but I'm ready to continue the search. Need to find Farkas and the nukes."

She pondered the situation for a few seconds. "This low is a big system, part of three low-pressure areas mingled together."

"I know, saw it on the Weather Channel."

"And it's not going away anytime in the near future," she added, in a slightly guarded voice.

Scott didn't respond.

"You're the chief," she conceded. "You make the call on this one."

"As long as we have reasonable visibility, we can motor along at seventy-five to eighty knots and take our sweet time."

Without hesitation, she popped the car door open. "Then let's load our gear and get on with the program."

He reached for the door handle, sensing Jackie's uneasiness. "If it gets too bad, we'll pick up a clearance and go to Salt Lake City."

"Sounds good to me."

Once their luggage, coffee, and doughnuts were aboard the airplane, Jackie turned in their rental car. Scott oversaw the refueling of the Caravan and completed a thorough walk-around while Jackie climbed into the airplane.

Scott slipped into the left seat, ran the checklist, and started the turboprop. "We barely have minimums for VFR."

Her finely drawn brow arched. "I'd say that's an honest assessment. We haven't filed a flight plan either."

"That's because we don't know where we're going to land or how many times we're going to stop," he said, before calling Ground Control for permission to taxi. Once they were airborne, Scott raised the landing gear and leveled the Caravan below the dark clouds.

With pen in hand, Jackie closely studied the sectional chart. "It looks like we could check Logan and then start our grid search, providing we have the visibility."

"Okay." He glanced at the GPS, lowered the flaps, and began slowing the Caravan. At 80 knots indicated airspeed, a computer-generated voice announced a warning. "Gear down for runway landing."

"Ah, yes indeed, you have a backup," Jackie said, noticing the flashing annunciator light on the panel. "Marine proof."

When they were a few miles west of Preston, Idaho, the sky to the south and west began to get darker, much darker. Scott turned eastbound while Jackie called the Boise Flight Service Station for a weather update.

"Logan has gone below minimums," she announced. "Pocatello is going down too. Our options are shrinking."

Scott added power and raised the flaps. "Well, this isn't going to work VFR, not in the direction we need to go." He studied the chart for a moment. "We're only a few miles from Bear Lake." He checked to make sure the landing gear was up. "We'll put down there, throw out the anchor, and have our breakfast."

Jackie was dubious about landing on a lake in this kind of weather, but she kept her feelings to herself. They flew low over the Cache National Forest and began their approach to the lake.

Scott keyed the marine radio. "Bear Lake traffic, Caravan amphibian on a right base for a landing to the west."

There was no response.

"Probably no one out on a day like this," he said, needing to hear the reassurance of his own voice.

Jackie remained quiet. *Let's go to Salt Lake.*

The drizzle had turned to steady rain and the visibility was rapidly deteriorating. Scott selected full flaps and began reducing power. Because he was barely able to see the surface of the lake, he began slowing his rate of descent when the radar altimeter hit 200 feet. A few seconds later the aural warning sounded, prompting him to quickly recheck the landing gear.

"Scott, I think we should climb out of here and pick up a clearance to Salt Lake—anywhere." She was straining to see through the rain-soaked windshield.

"Hang on, we're almost there."

He was totally concentrating on setting up for the landing flare when the satellite phone rang. At the same instant, a pair of stunned fishermen in a small fishing boat appeared in the Caravan's wide windshield. While the panicked, wide-eyed anglers dove to the floor of their boat, Scott simultaneously pulled on the yoke and shoved the thrust lever forward. Violently rocking the small craft with prop wash, the amphibian skimmed over the top of the boat and began climbing.

Scott milked the flaps up. "I think that's a great idea."

"What?"

"A clearance to somewhere—anywhere."

"No *kidding,*" Jackie said, as she answered the satellite phone. She asked Frank Wakefield to hold for a moment.

Scott banked into a spiraling ascent. "We'll take direct to Salt Lake."

She nodded and checked in with the controller. With an instrument clearance in hand, and the plane climbing to altitude under radar contact, Jackie spoke with Wakefield and wrote a few notes on the aeronautical chart. She signed off and placed the satellite phone down.

Scott's adrenaline was returning to normal. "What's up?"

"Well, things are beginning to get hot. There's been a flurry of activity here in the Northwest."

"What kind of activity?"

"The National Security Agency has been intercepting phone calls and messages from Europe and the Middle East to a number of individuals in the northwestern states."

"Anything on Farkas?"

"He didn't mention anything. The intercepts indicate that the cells are being activated. They are beginning to assemble in groups. Wakefield's people are investigating a number of reports. He wants us to check out a situation that popped up early this morning."

"Where?"

"Just a second." She paused to answer a radio call from Salt Lake Center and then turned to Scott. "The FBI received a tip from some guy who overheard a drunk in a bar late last night, actually at one o'clock this morning."

Scott shook his head. "A tip from a guy in a bar after midnight?"

"That's right. The guy was apparently bragging about getting a thousand dollars in cash for renting a houseboat, in his name, for two men."

"The significance?"

"According to the informant, who has been thoroughly checked out, the drunk claimed the men were Middle Easterners."

"Where, what lake?"

"Lake Mead."

"Has there been anything strange, anything out of the ordinary, going on in the Lake Mead area?"

"There have been reports of Middle Eastern types around the lake. The men, assumed to be the two who paid the guy to rent the houseboat, have been seen before at different areas on the lake."

Scott carefully adjusted the power and trimmed the airplane. "Wakefield wants us to see if we can locate them?"

"He doesn't want us to spook them." Jackie's expression reflected her concern. "Wakefield says they want us to isolate them."

"Do we know their last location?" Scott glanced at the ominous clouds.

"They're somewhere in the southwest section of the lake. Wakefield's people don't want to move in until they've gleaned all the information they can get."

"Do you have a description?"

"There's a number, thirty-one, painted in bold black on the roof. The boat is one of the largest houseboats on the lake, so we don't have to dink with the small fries."

"Okay, we're on our way." He looked at the en-route chart. "Let's stay over in Salt Lake. We'll buy some fishing equipment, check the weather in the Boulder area, and get an early start in the morning."

"So, what's our plan?"

"Sit on the floats and fish, look natural and relaxed like we know what we're doing. We'll observe the houseboaters and stay in touch with Wakefield."

She folded the VFR chart. "Well-heeled anglers without a care in the world."

"Right. Need a couple of those Australian bush hats and some khaki vests adorned with fishing lures."

"Do you even know how to fish?" she asked skeptically.

Scott chuckled. "You underestimate me."

Bryce Canyon Airport, Utah

Outside the maintenance hangar, Khaliq Farkas and eight other men in the terrorist cell were putting the finishing touches on the last of the handmade camouflage nettings. Viewed from the air, the specially crafted nylon material blended almost perfectly with the surrounding terrain and completely hid two World War II B-25 Mitchell bombers.

Farkas's bombers, one purchased in Colombia and the other in Ecuador, were mechanically sound. They had recently been restored to good flying condition, not excellent, but sound enough to carry out the mission Saeed Shayhidi planned.

One of the Mitchells was painted in brown and dark gray colors while the other one was dull silver. Powered by 1,700-horsepower engines, the sturdy warbirds had a maximum speed of 275 mph. They could carry 3,000 pounds of bombs 1,350 statute miles.

Farkas had just received another coded e-mail from Shayhidi. The hot-tempered and impetuous financier was pressuring him to expedite the operation, but the precious weapons were still being attached inside their containers.

Saint Moritz, Switzerland

Located in southeastern Switzerland in the Oberengadin, or Upper Inn Valley, surrounded by breathtaking Alpine peaks and deep valleys, Saint Moritz—Sankt Moritz in German—is one of the world's most famous winter-sport centers. Known for its classical elegance and extensive variety of facilities, it was the majestic scene of the Winter Olympic Games in 1928 and 1948.

After visiting this magnificent village for the first time, Saeed Shayhidi had decided to build one of his vacation homes there. Perched high on a steep hillside, the 7,800-square-foot chalet had wide eaves imported from Italy. Everything about it was custom made. The rooms, hallways, bathrooms, stairs, windows, spa, and doors were all oversized. It had taken an international team of twenty-seven architects, construction specialists, and interior designers the better part of a year to build and decorate the grandiose chalet.

Shayhidi and his entourage arrived shortly after 11 P.M. He promptly ordered the butler and the maid to extinguish all lights and remain inside. The two bodyguards and the butler were posted to stand watch until daybreak. Exhausted and depressed,

Shayhidi retired to the master bedroom on the second floor and promptly fell asleep.

The two CIA operatives watching the chalet reported Shayhidi's arrival to the Agency, noting that the home was completely blacked out. They estimated five or six people were in the residence. One of the agents, posing as a writer for an architectural digest, had duped Shayhidi's butler into giving him a tour of the home the previous day. The agent's copious notes and detailed sketches of the imposing chalet were helpful to the special operations forces.

Less than seventy minutes after the analysts at Langley were informed about Shayhidi's arrival, the elite soldiers of Delta Force were boarding their four MH-47D Chinook helicopters at Ramstein Air Base, Germany. Two highly classified missions had been thoroughly planned and practiced. Now it was time to put the arduous training to good use. The powerful twin-rotor helicopters lifted off in the dead of night. Two headed in one direction while the other pair flew toward a second secret destination. Each mission was assigned a primary Chinook and a backup.

Other special operations forces and SOAR flight crews were launching to conduct other clandestine missions. By order of the commander in chief, the Chinooks were being escorted by helicopter gunships.

Saeed Shayhidi was rudely awakened from a deep sleep by deafening explosions and horrific submachine gunfire. Panicked, he knew who the intruders were. *How did they know I was here? Have to get away or they'll kill me.*

This home, like all of Shayhidi's residences, had a built-in escape route. He opened the faux laundry chute and climbed in feet first, closed the outside cover, and dropped into a small room next to a tunnel. He grabbed the prepared stash of clothes, shoes, and money and quickly slipped the shoes on his bare feet.

He could hear more explosions and the staccato sound of

submachine gunfire intertwined with yelling and pounding. It sounded like the chalet was being destroyed from within. He heard glass breaking, followed by a huge thud.

Entering the narrow, dimly lighted tunnel, Shayhidi rapidly covered the thirty-five yards to an opening under a small storage shed near the back of his property line.

After crawling out of the tunnel and replacing the wooden hatch, Shayhidi watched through a small window as his home was being demolished. He yanked his clothes on in the darkened shed and returned to the window. Catching his breath, he watched in shock as the soldiers of Delta Force withdrew from his badly damaged chalet.

When the darkened Chinook helicopter levitated into the black sky, Shayhidi saw lights coming on inside his home. He could see smoke pouring from the oversized windows. Most of the glass panels had been blown out. The interior of his marvelous chalet had been virtually destroyed, including the custom-made furniture, the ornate bric-a-brac, and his expensive paintings.

Soon after the departure of the Delta Force soldiers, fire trucks, police cars, ambulances, and assorted media vehicles began converging on the badly damaged residence. His neighbors joined other stunned bystanders as firemen quickly extinguished a small blaze in the kitchen.

A few minutes later, Shayhidi watched while rescue workers and medical attendants carried out the bullet-riddled bodies of the two men sworn to protect him. Unhurt, but still shaking with fear, the butler and maid were led to a police van and driven away.

Shayhidi decided to wait until things calmed down before leaving his hiding place. A half hour after the firemen and police officials left his home he slipped quietly out of the shed and walked several blocks to the Suvretta House. He checked into the mansionlike hotel under a different name and made arrangements to travel incognito to a safe haven. His identity would be closely guarded in his permanently leased suite in France at the La Reserve de Beaulieu.

Auburn, Washington

Pauline Garretson sat in the dark hushed room in the Seattle Air Route Traffic Control Center and concentrated on her radarscope. The screen was growing more congested as the afternoon push was getting under way. Like many other air traffic controllers, she was still on edge after the devastating aerial attacks of recent days. In the recesses of her subconscious, the King Air tragedy in Delaware was Pauline's worst nightmare come true.

Garretson, aware she was responsible for hundreds of lives, felt she was working much harder than usual. The notice to airmen (NOTAM) prohibiting flight operations around all nuclear power plants and refineries added another layer of stress to the already demanding job. She was trying to balance her patience with her desire to keep pilots on course and away from potential hazards.

Working a Convair 580 cargo flight originating in Kalispell, Montana, bound for Bowerman Airport adjacent to Hoquiam, Washington, Garretson was surprised by a female voice with a Middle Eastern accent, but quickly discounted her concern. In growing numbers, women were continuing to join the ranks of commercial pilots, aviation technicians, air traffic controllers, and flight attendants, and a small percentage of the newcomers had not mastered the English language. Garretson cleared the Convair to descend and handed the aircraft off to the Terminal Radar Approach Control, or TRACON, in Seattle.

Jared Matus, comfortably ensconced in his chair on the fourth floor of the main terminal building at the Seattle-Tacoma international airport, gave the Convair 580 a vector to avoid other aircraft. "Direct Express Three-Twelve, fly heading two-one-zero for traffic."

"Two-hun-zeeraw, Diweck Express Thee-Hun-Two."

Hearing the voice, Matus had an unsettling feeling in the pit of his stomach. It slowly faded when the pilot complied. After the Convair was clear of conflicting traffic, Matus cleared the flight direct to Bowerman Airport. Shortly thereafter, the pilot canceled her instrument flight plan. She was instructed to squawk 1200, the code for visual flight rules. With other traffic to manage, Matus did not follow the flight of the Convair.

Hameeda Nashashibi, a Saudi-born dissident and fervent follower of Saeed Shayhidi, guided the 56,000-pound cargo version of the twin turboprop toward Runway 24 at Bowerman, an airport with no control tower. The veteran airliner-cum-cargo-tramp was loaded with jet fuel, high explosives, steel beams, and nineteen drums of fuel oil. Having accumulated a total of 29,968 flying hours, the rugged Convair was making its farewell flight. Nashashibi lowered the flaps and landing gear and then said a prayer for guidance and focus.

Nashashibi had been the second woman to attend the Salman Pak terrorist training camp near Baghdad. Along with eight male members of Saeed Shayhidi's terrorist network, she had trained to be a pilot at the secluded Sabzehar School of Aviation in Syria. After her initial training, Khaliq Farkas personally made arrangements for Nashashibi to receive intensive Convair 580 training in South Africa. Now the young woman who despised America was at the controls of a powerful weapon.

Near the approach end of Runway 24, she added power, turned off the transponder, and raised the landing gear and flaps. Remaining low and gaining speed, the 580 flew over the uncontrolled airport and made a gentle right turn to fly north along the scenic Washington coastline. She worked diligently to set maximum power so she could concentrate on flying the tired cargo airplane.

The Convair 580 thundered over Copalis Beach, Pacific Beach, and Cape Elizabeth and then continued to hug the coast to Elephant Rock. Nashashibi made another easy right turn to skirt up the west side of the Olympic Mountains. She cleared the top of Mount Olympus by thirty feet, banked to the right again, and eased the nose down. With the big Allison turboprops screaming at full power, Nashashibi fixated on her target and continued to trim the airplane as it rapidly accelerated.

Bangor Naval Submarine Base

Located on the east bank of the Hood Canal thirteen miles north of Bremerton, Washington, Bangor Naval Submarine Base is the home port for a squadron of Trident submarines. The base is 155 nautical miles from the Pacific Ocean, which requires a slow and potentially hazardous trip through the Strait of Juan de Fuca to reach open water. The 560-foot Ohio-class boomers are an extremely important part of the nation's nuclear deterrent triad—land, sea, and air.

Petty Officer Second Class Carlos Navarro was kneeling on the broad hull of the USS *Nevada* SSBN 733 repairing a connection that provided shore-to-submarine electrical power. In the picturesque background west of the strategic base, the Olympic Mountains rose high above the calm water and lush trees.

On the aft section of the mighty hull, close to the waterline, a bevy of sea lions nonchalantly sunned themselves on the deck. Over the many years, the playful sea lions and their plentiful offspring had learned that the U.S. Navy was a kind and benevolent innkeeper. A good share of the large-eared seals even had their favorite submarine and reluctantly migrated to other boomers when their boat went to sea.

Carlos Navarro did not so much hear the deep-throated sound as sense something strange. He looked around, but nothing seemed out of the ordinary; no obvious threat loomed. When some of the lounging sea lions began skittering into the water, Navarro stopped and concentrated again, this time on the sound.

He glanced behind him at the Olympic Mountains and froze. Practically scraping the trees on the gently sloping hills, a Convair 580 was roaring at full power and descending at an unbelievable speed. Navarro could see the airplane was headed straight for the USS *Nevada*. Astonished, he stared at the Convair for a moment before his mind reacted.

Navarro jumped into the cold water on the side of the hull away from the oncoming airplane and began thrashing through the water in an attempt to evade the aircraft. The remaining sea lions made a hasty departure and dove beneath the surface.

To the startled bystanders on the pier, the Convair looked like it was going to plunge into the water 200 yards away. When the plane's nose abruptly snapped up to a level position, the paralyzed sailors turned and ran for their lives. The 580's huge propellers were kicking up spray as it bull's-eyed *Nevada*'s sail, known on prenuclear submarines as the conning tower, and exploded in dramatic fashion.

Flaming wreckage and thousands of parts showered USS *Alaska* SSBN 732 and its many crew members. The damage was catastrophic. The USS *Nevada* was destroyed, sinking in only eight minutes. Carlos Navarro and eleven other sailors died in the initial explosion.

18

National Airborne Operations Center

Aboard the E-4B Night Watch, President Macklin's primary physician had just completed a mini physical on the commander in chief. U.S. Navy Captain Royal Fortenberry was jotting a note in Macklin's medical chart while the president dressed. Dr. Fortenberry, who had earned the reputation of being a worrier, placed his pen down and turned to Macklin.

"Mr. President, may I speak frankly?"

"Certainly, R.F. Find something wrong?"

Fortenberry closed the medical jacket. "No, you're in great shape, but I'm concerned about the effects of being encapsulated in a pressurized environment for an extended period of time." He explained the possible effects of deep vein leg thrombosis.

The president thought it over for a moment. "I don't see that I have much choice at present, all things considered."

"What about Cheyenne Mountain?"

"You're really concerned, aren't you?"

"Yes." Fortenberry removed his glasses. "Lack of proper exercise, poor sleeping pattern, and being inside this pressurized environment are not good. The mountain would be better for your health, not to mention the well-being of your staff."

"I'll think about it." Macklin slipped into his lightweight jacket. "Thanks, Doc."

"You bet."

When Macklin entered the conference room he knew something was wrong when he saw the look on Pete Adair's face. Hartwell Prost's and Les Chalmers's expressions mirrored the SecDef.

"What now?" the president asked, taking his chair.

Adair spoke first. "We just received the news a few minutes ago." He explained the disastrous circumstances surrounding the terrorist attack at the Bangor naval base.

Macklin was incredulous. "It doesn't make sense. How could this have happened at a Trident submarine base?"

Adair was on the defensive. "Sir, we don't know yet. The plane came in undetected until the last few seconds. It happened before anyone could react."

"Dammit!" Macklin exclaimed. "We have to get a handle on this. It's beyond ridiculous."

"Yes, sir," Adair said. He turned to General Chalmers.

While they were conferring, Prost gained the president's attention. "Sir," he said in soft voice, "we have an update, good news, on the destruction of Shayhidi's assets."

Macklin's features remained impassive. "Let's have it."

"Another two tankers have been disabled, including his new supertanker *Cape Bender*. They'll be out of commission for the better part of a year."

"Great news."

"There's more, much more. The cargo ships *Emily Martelli* and *Isabella Estrada* have gone to the bottom. The *Martelli* crew suffered three casualties and four seriously injured."

"We knew that could eventually happen." The president leaned back. "Sinking ships with innocent civilians on board is not something any of us are proud of."

"Least of all the sub crews," Prost said.

Macklin glanced at the detailed physical world chart on the wall. "What about the rest of Shayhidi's fleet?"

"Most of his remaining ships have docked at their nearest port. Some of the facilities, for security reasons, have refused entrance to any of Shayhidi's ships."

The president nodded. "We'll take all the help we can get."

"From what we understand, one freighter captain and his entire crew abandoned ship in the middle of the Arabian Sea. They were taken aboard another freighter."

The president's eyes reflected his pleasure. "Where's the ship now?"

"It's adrift approximately two hundred miles southwest of Bombay. We have a sub, *Connecticut,* closing in as we speak."

"Our new Seawolf-class boat?"

"Yes, sir. The skipper is an old friend, a good man."

"Well, it would seem to me the Shayhidi ship is a hazard to navigation, can't have that."

"You're absolutely right," Prost said, a twinkle in his eye.

"Let's give your friend some work to do: Sink the ship."

"Yes, sir." Prost turned to Adair and Chalmers, quietly conveyed Macklin's order, and again faced his boss. "The downside to our progress is that Shayhidi got away, vanished into thin air."

"The CIA had a positive ID on him, didn't they?"

"Yes, sir." It was evident that Prost was off stride. "They swear it's true—had him tagged. Two agents identified him with night-vision binoculars, and no one left the premises before the special ops people stormed the place."

The president flexed his jaw muscles. "I'm sorry, Hartwell, but that just doesn't make sense. It doesn't compute."

"I know, but the Agency swears he was in the chalet."

"What *exactly* did Delta Force find?"

"Two armed guards, who were quickly dispatched, and Shayhidi's domestic help. Nothing else."

"Did they check the attic and basement?"

"Yes, sir—thoroughly—in the short time they were there. Shayhidi's bed in the master bedroom had been slept in, but he'd simply disappeared into the night."

Macklin glanced away for a moment and then cast his eyes toward Prost. "Something's missing here. I want the CIA, whatever resources it takes, to inspect that house inch by inch."

"Yes, sir."

"Tell them to take it apart board by board to find the answer, if they have to."

"I'll take care of it."

The president reached for a cigar and offered Prost a smoke. "What about the other homes, his primary residence in Geneva?"

"The house in Geneva has been gutted, but we had two people wounded, one seriously." Hartwell paused when an aide stepped in to deliver a message to the secretary of defense. "It could have been much worse if the Army Pathfinders had not done such a superb job of scouting the Shayhidi compound."

"How so?"

"They worked a local stool pigeon for intelligence about the house, the grounds, and the security measures. The guy delivered groceries. The place was guarded like a fortress, including shoulder-fired SAMs and an unknown number of land mines."

"Land mines? You're kidding."

"No, sir," Prost answered, lighting his cigar. "The stoolie told them he thought there were probably ten to fifteen people guarding the place. Some were new hires from a local security firm. He possibly—probably—saved some lives on our side."

The president caught Adair's imploring look. "Hold on a second, Pete."

SecDef nodded.

"What about the other homes?" Macklin asked.

"The château in the south of France and the villa near Cartagena will undoubtedly be listed in the fixer-upper section of the real estate brochures."

"Excellent," Macklin said, and turned to Adair. "From the look on your face, I guess I'd better prepare myself for more bad news."

SecDef's voice betrayed his tension. "Two more passenger trains have been attacked—blown off their rails like Matchbox toys."

"Where?"

"The Amtrak Cascades near Portland and the Empire Builder near Libby, Montana. There are a number of casualties at both sites."

The president glanced at General Chalmers and then Prost. "Any suggestions?"

Hartwell swore to himself. "Attack helicopters, army and marine gunships, from the Rocky Mountains throughout the entire Northwest."

"I like it," the president said. "Let's have them on site ASAP."

Prost continued with a sense of urgency. "We could use Civil Air Patrol units to help watch the tracks."

"Good idea!" Chalmers exclaimed. "The more eyeballs we have in the air, the better our chances of catching them in the act. We can use our A-10 Warthogs and F-15 Strike Eagles to supplement the attack helicopters."

The president finally lit his cigar. "Let's get on it, coordinate this well so everyone knows where the other players are. We don't want any midair collisions while we're trying to save lives on the ground."

"Constant communications," Prost said firmly. "And mandatory radio calls at designated checkpoints to keep things orderly."

General Chalmers looked first at Prost and then at the president. "I'll have it operational by early morning. We'll use night-vision equipment, keep the bad guys honest day and night."

"Go to it," Macklin said, and then paused. "By the way, how are our ordnance stockpiles coming along at our bases in the Middle East?"

Chalmers had the numbers memorized. "We have an almost continuous stream of aircraft arriving at al-Udeid and our bases adjacent to the Red Sea. In addition, we have eighteen cargo ships shuttling weapons. We have enough on hand now to sustain operations for twelve to fourteen months."

"Excellent." The president looked at Pete Adair. "With the air strikes we're planning in Iran and Afghanistan, what's the status of our munitions production rate?"

"We have more than doubled the production rate of laser-guided bombs and boosted production at three ammunition factories to their highest levels in seventeen years. They've increased the output of precision-guided bombs from one thousand a month to over three thousand. These increases have tripled the lethality of our carrier battle groups."

"Well," Macklin conceded, with a trace of a smile, "at least something is going well. What about Tomahawks?"

"They've added a third shift and production has nearly doubled. We believe the Tomahawks, supplemented with the precision-guided bombs, can last for at least six to seven months."

A pleased look spread across the president's face. "On that note, I think I'll rest before dinner."

Salt Lake City International Airport

After a delay caused by inclement weather, Scott and Jackie checked out of the Airport Hilton and had breakfast at a local Denny's, having dispensed with their wings and epaulets in favor of denim shirts and fishing vests. They drove their rental car to the Million Air FBO, loaded their supplies and fishing gear into the Caravan, and departed for beautiful Lake Mead.

With CAVU weather—clear and visibility unlimited—Scott leveled off at 1,000 feet. "While we're going in the general direction of the lake, let's check all airports with runways longer than four thousand feet. See if we find anything interesting."

"Okay, I'll circle them."

Scott engaged the autopilot and poured each of them a cup of coffee. Following Interstate 15, they proceeded southwest over the Fishlake National Forest. Scott descended into valleys to check the airports and then climbed over the mountains to the next valley. They found nothing suspicious.

The low-flying Caravan was burning a lot of jet fuel, and by the time they reached the Dixie National Forest, Jackie was ready to land and stretch her legs. "Let's check the Bryce Canyon airport and then land at Cedar City for fuel."

"Sounds good."

Taking in the view of the scenic national park, they circled high above Bryce Canyon Airport. Jackie raised her binoculars and surveyed the airfield and the parked aircraft while they made two wide 360-degree turns. "I don't see anything interesting, except the canyons."

"Then we're off to Cedar City."

She placed the binoculars down and folded the chart. "Step on the accelerator every chance you get."

Standing in the shade of the camouflage nettings, Khaliq Farkas watched the big Cessna amphibian circle the airport and head west. His antennae were on full alert. It was unusual to see a plane loiter over an airport and then simply fly away.

Farkas could feel it in his gut: Someone was looking for the B-25. He couldn't wait much longer. The noose was tightening on the terrorist cells and he had to make his move soon—that or abandon the project and go back into sleep mode. The satellite phone rang, signaling another tirade from Saeed Shayhidi.

Leaving Cedar City, Jackie and Scott again followed Interstate 15 while they checked more airports. When they reached Mesquite, Nevada, they began banking to fly over the Lake Mead National Recreation Area, and Jackie took in the spectacular vista of the setting sun and cobalt-blue sky.

"It's going to be dark soon," she observed, stretching her legs. "Let's go to Boulder City and get a fresh start early in the morning."

"Yeah, we're ready for a break."

Minutes later, they landed at Boulder City Municipal Airport. After topping the fuel tanks and securing the Caravan at the Air Excel facilities, they hailed a taxi and headed to the Railroad Pass Hotel Casino.

National Airborne Operations Center

Orbiting in a racetrack pattern high above Mobile, Alabama, the E-4B Night Watch was flying under a bright, silvery moon.

President Macklin and Hartwell Prost were visiting in the conference room when SecDef and General Chalmers entered with a CIA update on the hunt for Saeed Shayhidi.

Pete Adair was upbeat for the first time this evening. "Between the CIA and our special ops people, we're steadily gaining on Shayhidi."

"Don't keep us in suspense," Macklin prompted.

"The four penthouses he leases, one each in Hong Kong, London, Paris, and Sydney, are empty and under constant surveillance by the Agency."

"Where does that leave us?" Hartwell asked.

"Delta Force is preparing to visit Shayhidi's home in Aspen. We don't expect him to be there, but we're ready."

"Unbelievable," Chalmers said, with undisguised irritation. "The guy buys a palatial multimillion-dollar home—six bedrooms, no less—in an artsy mountain town and then secretively backs a terrorist organization in a holy war against the United States."

"You know," Adair said, quickly formulating a plan, "like his bank accounts, we should seize Shayhidi's home in Aspen, sell it, and use the funds to help offset the cost of the war."

SecDef looked at the president. "What do you think, sir?"

"I think it's a great idea—the taxpayers will love it. Get in touch with Delta Force and tell them not to destroy the place."

"We'll take care of it." Pete Adair nodded to Chalmers, who immediately went to the communications center.

Adair continued. "The CIA is getting ready to check a hotel in Beaulieu-sur-Mer, France. Shayhidi maintains a suite at the hotel and is known to spend a lot of time there."

"Where in France?" Macklin asked.

"Beaulieu-sur-Mer. It's on the Mediterranean coast fairly close to Nice. They're watching the airport too, the one Shayhidi uses when he stays at the hotel."

"Sounds good," Macklin said, his gaze narrowing. "Maybe we'll get lucky and snatch him at the airport."

"I certainly hope so," Adair replied. "The Agency is also checking a suite in the Hotel Seiyo Ginza in Tokyo, another city he is known to frequent. He has to turn up somewhere. He can't stay hidden forever."

Macklin nodded, disguising his frustration. "Stay on it until we find him. The longer he's out there, the higher the risk of more major tragedies."

"We'll find him," Adair said, in a convincing voice. "We've frozen a number of his assets, including charity funds in the Philippines, the Sudan, Egypt, India, Pakistan, and the States. Huge bank accounts have been frozen in Germany, France, and the Sudan. The same with his primary businesses in Germany, Uganda, Switzerland, Pakistan, and Sudan."

Adair couldn't resist a smile. "It has to *really* be hurting him financially, hemorrhaging money all over the planet."

"To say the least," Prost quietly chimed in. "Like others who have attacked the United States, Shayhidi grossly miscalculated the resolve of our country."

"And the reach of our influence," the president added.

General Chalmers walked back into the room. "A message just came in a few minutes ago. The Agency found out how Shayhidi slipped through our fingers in Saint Moritz."

"Let's have it," the president said, in a voice that was becoming raspy.

"He had a built-in escape route, a tunnel that surfaced in a storage shed in his backyard. Delta Force didn't consider the small storage shed when they planned the raid. He probably has something similar in his other homes."

"You can bet on it," Prost said. "He's been working on this jihad for many years."

"Let's keep that in mind," Macklin said, absently rubbing his right shoulder. "No more egg on our face."

Silence prevailed.

"Well, gentlemen, I believe I'll turn in for the evening. See you bright and early in the morning."

"Yes, sir," the men said, rising with the president.

Macklin paused at the open door. "By the way, Doc Fortenberry thinks—healthwise—that it would be better for us to go to Cheyenne Mountain than stay airborne for extended periods in this pressurized cabin."

Eyebrows raised around the table.

"Just think about it. We'll discuss it tomorrow."

19

Beaulieu-sur-Mer, France

Feeling more confident and secure, having arrived at La Reserve de Beaulieu, Saeed Shayhidi was having breakfast in his splendid Florentine suite when the phone rang. Hotel manager Jacques Debroux, Shayhidi's only close friend from their days at Princeton, was in a full-blown panic. His chief of security had just reported that several men were canvassing the hotel and its grounds. The frightened manager assumed the clean-cut men had to be members of the famous U.S. CIA.

Shayhidi froze for a moment before responding. "We have to put our plan in motion," he said excitedly. "I have to get out of here!"

"I'll be there shortly," Debroux said, in a hushed voice.

"Is everything in place?" Shayhidi asked.

"Yes." Debroux glanced around the lobby. "There are two agents here already—inside," he urgently whispered.

"I'm counting on you," Shayhidi growled. "Don't lose your nerve, don't let me down."

Debroux cupped the phone while he kept his eyes on the suspected agents. "I won't. I promise."

Shayhidi hung up and quickly dressed in black slacks and a white polo shirt. *How are they doing this? How are they finding me?* He grabbed his wallet, jewelry, and attaché case and then ventured a peek out the window overlooking the tranquil Mediterranean Sea. Three unsmiling men in business suits were standing by the pool. *They must surely be guarding against an escape attempt along the coast. I have to do something . . . unpredictable. I have to disappear—now!*

Less than three minutes later, the hotel bell captain arrived with a large trunk on his luggage cart. Debroux quickly followed him into the suite. Shayhidi scrambled into the trunk and his friend closed and latched it. The two men strained to lift the container onto the luggage cart. Debroux placed a suitcase on the cart while the bell captain hung most of Shayhidi's wardrobe on the overhead rack.

Accompanied by the nervous manager, who acted the part of a guest checking out of the hotel, the bell captain wheeled the cart through the lobby to a waiting limousine. Debroux went through the motions of clearing his account while the bell captain and his assistant loaded the heavy container into the trunk of the limousine.

The two CIA agents sitting in the elegant lobby watched as Shayhidi's friend picked up his faux copy of the hotel charges, walked to the limousine, and calmly and deliberately stepped into the back of the car. The chauffeur shut the door and slid behind the steering wheel as three more agents entered the hotel lobby.

After the limousine drove away from the entrance, Debroux's nerves failed him and he almost became physically ill. Ten minutes later, the driver pulled into a secluded section of a village and stopped the car. Debroux jumped out and freed Shayhidi from the steamer trunk.

When the limousine again entered the road, Shayhidi picked up the car phone and called a Paris-based jet charter company. He used his corporate account to secure a jet but gave a different name for the passenger list. While Debroux fretted and drummed his fingers, Shayhidi made other business and travel arrangements as they continued the long drive to the Aéroport de Lyon Bron, France.

When the limousine arrived at the Transair FBO, a Falcon 900EX corporate jet was waiting on the ramp. While Shayhidi's luggage was being loaded into the Falcon, he brushed past the pilots and boarded the plane. He gave the attractive young flight attendant a sardonic smile and took a seat in the back of the luxurious jet.

He did not bother to pay for the leased limousine or to thank his friend from Princeton. For Shayhidi, life was all about himself. Nothing and no one else mattered, especially the expendable people who stood in obedient readiness, awaiting his command or wish.

Boulder City Municipal Airport

Promptly at 6:30 A.M., Jackie and Scott took a taxi to the airport. They loaded their things in the Caravan and took off for nearby Lake Mead. The day was clear and the morning sun rising high above the mountains provided a breathtaking view.

The Lake Mead National Recreation Area, twice the size of Rhode Island, is where three of America's four desert ecosystems meet. The Great Basin, the Sonoran, and the Mojave come together where one of the West's most powerful rivers, the mighty Colorado, was stopped by one of the largest dams ever built.

Completed in 1936, Hoover Dam is a national historic landmark that can hold back 9.2 trillion gallons of water. The 727-foot dam is a concrete arch-gravity type, in which the water load is carried by both horizontal arch action and gravity. Located an hour's drive southeast of the Las Vegas strip, the dam straddles the Arizona-Nevada border.

Its mission is to control floods, improve navigation on the Colorado River, store and deliver water for reclamation of public lands, and provide hydroelectric power. Hoover Dam also contains 28.5-million-acre-foot Lake Mead, the largest man-made lake in the United States.

Since September 11, 2001, security at Hoover Dam had consisted of roadblocks and vehicle searches of all automobiles, boats, motor homes, and trucks. Except for open-bedded trucks, big rigs and buses were banned from the dam's narrow Highway 93. They were detoured to a bridge near Bullhead City, Arizona.

The heightened alert status also brought a change to Hoover's previously modest police force. Park rangers and personnel from other federal agencies were brought in to augment the force. Metal detectors were installed at the visitor center, camouflaged machine-gun posts dotted the hilltops, marksmen were stationed in concealed areas, and individuals with shoulder-fired surface-to-air missiles guarded the supplier of water and electricity for the vast Southwest.

Flying at 1,200 feet above Lake Mead, Scott slowly eased the power back for a relaxed cruise speed to save fuel. "Can you believe the constantly changing blues of the water?"

"I've never seen anything like it."

Scott stared off into the distance. "This is a spectacular setting, rugged mountains in the background and sheer cliffs jutting out of the water."

"What a beautiful place." Jackie shaded her eyes. "Since the glare is so bad at this time of the morning, maybe we should fly up to the neck of the lake, make a one-eighty, and have the sun at our backs."

"That would make it easier."

They flew straight to the Temple Bar Marina in Arizona, made a descending turn, lowered the flaps, and cruised at 90 knots 600 feet above the pristine lake.

Jackie glanced at Scott. "It's nice to be this close to the water and not have to worry about losing the only engine you have."

"I know what you mean."

She raised the binoculars and scanned a wide array of boats. "Lots of people out here today."

"It's Saturday."

"And the weather's perfect," she added. "No wind and no waves."

They checked dozens of large houseboats, some in secluded coves, others in open waters. Many of the boaters waved, including a few who radioed the Caravan in the blind. Jackie chatted with a couple of the friendly people. One elderly gentleman even offered a refreshing Bloody Mary if they wanted to land. Soon, the Water Bird moniker became familiar to the boating crowd.

At half past noon, they circled Callville Bay Marina. Boasting over 600 slips, Callville Bay is one of the largest inland marinas in the United States. Scores of houseboats were carefully lined up in neat rows, beckoning their owners or renters to step aboard.

"See anything?" Scott asked.

"No, not a sign of number thirty-one."

"Want to go around again?"

"Sure, one more wide turn will do it."

They circled again and headed toward the western end of the huge lake. Another thirty minutes, now over the southern area of the lake, and Jackie figured it was time for a stretch, physiological relief, fuel, and food.

She placed the binoculars in the carrying case and removed her sunglasses. "How about a break for a juicy cowburger, some nutritional onion rings, and a big thick malted milk?"

Scott loudly groaned in disbelief. "How do you manage to stay so trim and thin?"

"Excellent genes. Step on it."

He smiled to himself and then added power and raised the flaps. "Cellulite City, here we come."

They were turning toward the airport when Jackie spotted a large houseboat about four miles northwest of Hoover Dam. There weren't any other houseboats in the vicinity and the craft was cruising toward the basin leading to the dam.

Jackie reached for the binoculars. "Keep the turn coming another twenty degrees or so—okay, hold what you have." She studied the top of the houseboat and saw the number 31 in bold black paint. "That's it! That's the one we've been looking for!"

"Are you positive?"

"Absolutely! The number and the deck color match the description Wakefield gave me."

"Okay, we'll hold our heading until we're a few miles away, and then go straight to Boulder City."

"Can you believe it? We actually found them!"

"Well," Scott said with a grin, "they won't be hard to find again."

"That's for sure. Let's make this fuel stop a quick turn. Forget the burger."

"You bet. Save the cholesterol overdose for later."

"We better contact Wakefield," Jackie suggested. "Let him know we found the houseboat and see if there's anything new we need to know."

"Give him a call."

Frank Wakefield was extremely pleased. He requested that Jackie and Scott keep number 31 under surveillance until he could mount a raid at dawn. Over Wakefield's protests, Jackie explained that a houseboat stakeout was not the focus of their mission. She would have to check with her superiors and get back to him as soon as she could.

Jackie attempted to call Hartwell Prost but could not make contact. She gave up as they turned on final approach to the Boulder City Municipal Airport.

South of Kennewick, Washington

Flying air force A-10 close-air-support jets, Captain Lex Ingraham and his wingman, Captain Corky Kamansky, were patrolling the train track used by Amtrak's popular Empire Builder. On temporary assignment from the 47th Fighter Squadron at Barksdale AFB, the two aviators were experienced Warthog instructor pilots and veterans of Operation Iraqi Freedom. Flying low above the Columbia River south of the junction of the Snake and Columbia rivers, they were looking for any sign of sabotage or terrorist activity.

Other twin-engine A-10 "tank killers" from the 47th and from Davis-Monthan AFB, Arizona, were patrolling tracks and monitoring trains in the Northwest. Each jet was equipped with a single 30mm seven-barrel rotary cannon that fires milk-bottle-size rounds at a blistering pace. Many pilots who have flown the Warthog in combat claim the plane can lose one engine, half a tail, one third of a wing, and parts of the fuselage and still remain airborne.

Approaching a bend in the scenic river, Ingraham spotted a

helicopter sitting directly on the tracks. The Eurocopter's rotors were turning and there were two men working beside the railroad. When the men heard the sound of the jet engines drowning the sound of the rotor blades, they glanced up at the A-10s and froze.

Ingraham keyed his radio. "Corky, see the helo on the tracks?"

"Roger, could be trouble."

"I'm going to check it out."

"Gotcha covered."

While Kamansky orbited overhead, Ingraham flew low over the men and then racked the A-10 into a steep turn around the suspicious helicopter. The men immediately dropped their tools and raced for the Eurocopter.

"We have a bite—let's go hot," Ingraham said, before he contacted the AWACS. The reply was nearly instantaneous.

"I'm rolling in hot," the flight leader said, in a calm, even voice. "Our customer looks like he needs a little off the top."

"A light trim."

The helicopter was about to lift off when Ingraham's Gatling gun ripped its tail to shreds. The beefy cannon made aluminum foil out of the enclosed tail rotor. The Eurocopter turned 90 degrees, jamming the twisted landing gear inside the railroad tracks.

"End of the line," Ingraham radioed.

Leaving the heavily damaged helicopter with the engines still running, three men emerged and sprinted for cover under the nearby fir trees.

"Boys, you shouldn't try to escape," Ingraham said under his breath. "You aren't going to like this, believe me." He rolled in again and gently squeezed the trigger. The huge cannon shells carved a wide swath in the trees about thirty feet in front of the trio. They skidded to a halt and changed directions, dodging and weaving through the fir trees.

"Corky, you have them in sight?"

"Got 'em."

"Your turn," Ingraham said, and then asked the AWACS controller to contact the nearest law enforcement agency.

Kamansky walked his rounds so close to the men that pieces of shredded bark and tree limbs were pummeling them. They stopped in their tracks and put their arms up, stretching them high above their heads.

With a few well-placed bursts of cannon fire, Kamansky herded them back into the open and continued to circle. A few minutes later a patrol cruiser came racing down the highway, followed shortly thereafter by a sheriff's deputy.

"Looks like this is a wrap," Kamansky radioed.

"Not exactly. Amtrak is headed this way."

Kamansky glanced up the tracks. "Perfect timing."

"I hope I didn't screw up the track," Ingraham said, as he rolled out of his orbit and shoved the throttles forward. "Cover the bad guys."

"Roger."

Approaching the train head-on, Ingraham rapidly slowed the A-10 and extended the landing gear. *Okay, guys, pay close attention. Haven't got a lot of time.*

The shocked engineer, along with the bug-eyed passengers in the Sightseer Lounge, weren't sure what was going on when the mean-looking Warthog roared low overhead with the landing lights glaring.

Come on! Ingraham wrapped the plane around in a tight circle, rolling wings level just before he had to pull up to miss the engine.

That did the trick. The lightbulb came on and the Empire Builder began slowing, but it was going to be close.

Ingraham cleaned up the A-10 and climbed to 800 feet above the ground. The authorities had the terrorists in custody and Kamansky was circling leisurely at 1,500 feet. The train was almost stopped when it pulverized the Eurocopter, grinding it into twisted pieces of jagged metal.

National Airborne Operations Center

The decision was made to transfer President Macklin and his staff from the E-4B to the safety of Cheyenne Mountain. However, they would delay the arrival of the 747 in Colorado Springs until more security personnel were in place. The vice president's entourage and the joint chiefs were on their way back to Washington.

Fresh from a late-afternoon nap, President Macklin was sitting alone in his quarters when Hartwell Prost gently knocked on the door.

"Come in."

Prost entered the compartment and wearily sat down. "Well," he began haltingly, "my good friends at the Agency are completely, *totally* embarrassed—again."

Macklin turned and stared out the window. "More bad news?"

"Shayhidi apparently slipped right by them when they had him cornered. They didn't know it at the time."

"Where?"

"At his hotel suite in Beaulieu-sur-Mer, France."

"What happened, what went wrong?"

"Our folks had local intelligence about his suite, but we weren't sure he was there."

"I assume he was."

"Yes, his breakfast was half eaten."

Macklin frowned and massaged the bridge of his nose. "Hartwell, I don't understand how these things keep happening, I really don't."

Chagrined, Prost remained silent.

"It makes us look really incompetent," the president said impatiently. "Like we have a collective case of somnambulism."

"I'm fully aware of that, sir."

The president calmed himself. "The media is going to have me for lunch and then have the Agency for dessert."

"Sir, I'm sorry."

"Hartwell, it's okay," Macklin said, and then softened his tone. "What happened? Give me the details."

"While we were getting our people in place, Shayhidi was whisked out of the hotel in disguise . . . right in front of our agents sitting in the lobby."

"How do we know that?" the president asked.

"The hotel's assistant manager admitted Shayhidi was there

but swore on his mother's grave that he didn't know how Shayhidi managed to disappear."

Macklin remained quiet.

"Now," Prost said with a tortured look, "after all this effort, he's disappeared and we have no leads—no idea which way he went."

"What about our people at the airport?"

"He didn't use the airport he normally frequents." Prost concealed his anger. "I apologize for this unmitigated mess."

"It's not your fault." The president tapped his friend on the forearm. "You're not working at the Agency anymore."

Prost gently shook his head. "I know, but I don't handle things like this well. Neither do you."

"Look at it this way. The guy's running for his life." Macklin shrugged. "We're nipping at his heels and he's desperate, making mistakes and looking over his shoulder."

"True, he's definitely in a state of duress. Knows we're tracking him like a pack of hounds. But I can't handle any more screwups at Langley."

"Don't be so hard on yourself. His homes are partially destroyed," Macklin observed. "His corporate jet no longer exists, his yacht is on the bottom of the Mediterranean, his shipping empire is kaput, his entire world is in shambles, and he's being hunted like a serial killer. I doubt if he has much time to think about anything other than his personal survival."

"You're right, but I want him at the end of a rope."

"Actually," the president said lightly, "this is much worse for someone like Saeed Shayhidi, a twisted narcissist who craves the limelight. Shayhidi, who thought he was so clever, knows he has made a tragic blunder of galactic proportions." Macklin lowered his voice and clearly enunciated each word. "Shayhidi knows he made the dumbest move of his life, and he can never make it go away—ever."

"Well, that's one consolation." A faint smile touched Hartwell's mouth. "There *is* one piece of good news to report this afternoon."

"Good news," Macklin said with a soft chuckle. "Better get the doctor in here before you tell me any *good* news."

Prost explained about the A-10 pilots and the dynamite being buried under the railroad tracks.

"That *is* good news," the president said energetically. "We finally nailed them first. Have they been turned over to the FBI?"

"Not yet. Probably in the next hour or so."

"Good." Macklin stretched his arms and stifled a yawn. "What's our ETA in Colorado Springs?"

"Three-twenty A.M."

"What's the status of our strikes in Iran and Afghanistan?"

"The final briefing is in progress, the weather looks good, and the combined air operations center has reported that the mission is on schedule."

"Excellent. Keep me informed."

"Yes, sir."

USS *Stennis*

The first strike on significant Middle Eastern air defenses was launching from the carrier. The E-2C Hawkeye was airborne and the F-14s and F/A-18s were being catapulted at a rapid rate. A second strike package was preparing to take to the skies when the first wave of aircraft were inbound to the carrier. A third strike would take off five hours later.

Many of the military's older unmanned aerial vehicles were being sacrificed to stimulate air defenses so they could be tagged and engaged. The Hunters, Pioneers, Gnat 750s, and the first generation of Predators were serving as decoys in high-risk areas. The disposable UAVs would remain on station until they were shot down or ran out of fuel.

Al-Udeid Air Base, Qatar

F-15E Strike Eagles, A-10 Warthogs, and F-16 Vipers were tasked to hit primary targets between the strikes from *Stennis*. The schedule would alternate, with some strikes following on the heels of others while intervals went by with little activity at certain locations. The missions would be flexible, but never more than two hours would pass without a harassment flight of a two-plane section or a division of four aircraft. Search-and-rescue aircraft and helicopters would be on station for every attack.

20

Phnom Penh, Cambodia

After an extended fuel stop in Riyadh, Saudi Arabia, Saeed Shayhidi's chartered Falcon 900EX touched down at the Pochentong International Airport. The capital of Cambodia, Phnom Penh, lies at the junction of the Basak, Sab, and Mekong river systems in the south-central region of the country.

Jumpy and tired from his many close calls with the Great Satan, Shayhidi ignored the flight crew and walked straight to his waiting limousine. He sat in the air-conditioned comfort of the stretched Cadillac while his luggage was loaded into the trunk.

The twenty-minute ride to his hotel gave Shayhidi ample time to reflect on the decisions he had made after his narrow escape from the CIA agents in France. The communications center in the long-range Falcon had been put to good use. Of course, Shayhidi had no idea that Echelon Two was listening to his conversations.

First on his agenda: cosmetic surgery, changing the color of his hair, assuming a different identity, and opening new bank accounts. He would have to trust his most senior executive, Ahmed Musashi, the man he had put in charge of his vast empire. In addition, Shayhidi would have to alter his style of dress and his arrogant demeanor.

Impulsively, Shayhidi opened the limousine's well-stocked bar. He filled a crystal glass with ice cubes and poured three fingers of Chivas Regal scotch. He swirled the amber liquid and then tossed it back in one swift motion.

Lost in his misery and despair, Shayhidi stared blankly out the window at the maze of traffic. Every time he began to feel the least shred of confidence returning, the gnawing reality of what he had done resurfaced. He fixed another stiff drink and ruminated about his predicament, how rapidly everything had unraveled. The swift descent from having his life and businesses well-organized and running smoothly to utter chaos was unfathomable. As hard as he tried, he could not face the simple fact that he had made some very poor decisions.

When the limousine arrived at the Hotel Le Royal, Shayhidi was pleased with the accommodations. Located in the heart of Phnom Penh, the elegant hotel occupied an entire city block and was situated amid fragrant tropical gardens. Opened in 1929 in a structure that was a blend of Art Deco, Khmer, and French architecture, the hotel offered eight restaurants and bars featuring a wide variety of cuisines.

Checking in under an assumed name, Shayhidi paid cash in advance for a three-week stay in their best suite. That would provide enough time to have his newly leased luxury villa refurbished and furnished. He had not seen the home, but the description he had been given while aboard the Falcon sold him on the residence.

In his suite and alone, Shayhidi's alcohol-induced confidence completely dissolved. Traces of paranoia were beginning to surface. *What if the crew on the Falcon were informers for the Americans? What if someone in the lobby recognized me?* The thoughts were flooding his mind so fast he could barely cope. Since leaving Princeton, Shayhidi had been constantly surrounded by bodyguards and his entourage of self-seeking male and female flatterers.

It was unnerving to be suddenly alone, totally alone. There was no one around to flatter him, no one stepping and fetching at his command. For Shayhidi, the sensation was like solitary confinement, albeit in a first-class prison. No bodyguards who had been vetted, no companions to party with, no servants to abuse, no attention from his followers, nothing but emptiness, loneliness, and paranoia. *I have all this money, but I have to hide from the world. What have I done?*

He called room service and demanded more Chivas Regal and a wide array of food, making it clear that he wanted his order delivered as quickly as possible. After three waiters hustled the spread to his suite, he ate and drank voraciously until he felt mellow and comfortable. He wanted a female companion, a beautiful young Asian woman, to keep him entertained, but he was too tired at the moment.

Mentally and physically, he was exhausted. After another double scotch, Shayhidi collapsed on the bed and fell into a deep, tranquil sleep. When he awakened with a savage hangover, he returned to the dark side of his existence.

He drank more Chivas and then called his contact in Geneva. This trusted friend was his link to Ahmed Musashi. After conversing with Musashi, the friend would get back to him. Shayhidi had no idea how *really* difficult life was going to get in the near future.

Boulder City Municipal Airport, Nevada

After they landed at Boulder City, Jackie again tried to contact Hartwell Prost while Scott refueled the Caravan from the self-service pump. The call to Prost would not go through. She waited a few minutes and tried again with the same results.

"You look frazzled," Scott said, while he cleaned the Caravan's windshield.

"I've been trying to get in touch with Hartwell—see what his priority is—but I can't get through."

"Let's take off," Scott suggested. "Gain some altitude in a different location and try again."

Minutes later, they were climbing through 3,000 feet and

Jackie again called Prost. He answered on the third ring. After an unusually lengthy conversation, Jackie signed off.

"What's the plan?"

"Hartwell wants us to work with Wakefield on the houseboat watch and then continue our search for Farkas. He said Farkas knows where the six nukes are and the Feds want to get their hands on him."

Scott engaged the autopilot. "Have I missed something?"

"He said they have solid intel suggesting that a nuke *may* be on the houseboat."

"Selective amnesia. Wakefield didn't tell you that little detail."

"Right, no need for us to be concerned. Hartwell believes the terrorists may take the houseboat up to the dam and detonate the nuke."

Scott banked the Caravan toward the lake. "So we're supposed to baby-sit a possible nuclear bomb until the Feds get there?"

"That's the way I read it. I better call Wakefield and tell him we're on board—watchdogs for the evening."

When she signed off, Scott descended to 2,000 feet and soon located the houseboat. It was anchored a mile north of the entrance to the waterway leading to Hoover Dam. Other boats of various types were scattered around the area; some were under way, but most were anchored for the evening cocktail hour. Scott removed his sunglasses, placed them on the glare shield, and began a steeper descent.

"What do you think?" Jackie innocently asked. "What's our strategy going to be?"

"We'll land in the open space between number thirty-one and the shoreline, and then drop anchor for the night."

"Do you think that's too close, too obvious?"

"No," he said, setting up for the approach. "Floatplanes, most airplanes that operate from water, would go to shore or anchor close to it."

"I'm not so sure."

"We're supposed to be gathering information for our forthright pal, Wakefield. Can't do it well from a mile away."

"It's your call," she said, and tightened her straps.

He reduced power, checked to be sure the landing gear was retracted, lowered the first 10 degrees of flaps and then another 10 degrees, slowing through 150 knots, and the final 10 degrees at 125 knots. Maintaining a shallow descent rate, Scott continued to slow the big amphibian. He waited for the floats to make contact with the water and hauled back on the yoke as the Caravan settled onto the lake. He raised the flaps and deployed the water rudders. "Voilà! We're a boat."

"Nicely done, I must admit."

"Got lucky."

He taxied to a position about 100 yards from shore and shut down the turboprop. He jumped out on the left float, opened the anchor locker, and then tossed the anchor into the water. Back inside the airplane, Scott went into the passenger cabin to observe the houseboat.

He began opening their large canvas bags. "Let's get the radio scanners going," he said, while Jackie retrieved the binoculars from the cockpit.

She took a seat in the cabin and began studying the suspicious houseboat. "I have a question."

"Shoot."

"You know more about boats than I do, but these people have three antennas and a satellite dish on the top deck." She handed him the binoculars. "Take a look."

He surveyed the houseboat from stem to stern, noting the antennas. "It does seem odd."

She activated the radio scanners, one for civilian aircraft VHF frequencies and the other for military aircraft UHF frequencies. They also monitored the VHF marine radio.

Scott observed a man who appeared to be preparing dinner in the galley. A second man walked out on the bow deck. He was wearing casual Western-style clothes and had a thick dark beard. The last of the sunlight was directly on his face.

"Confirmed," Scott said.

"What?"

Scott moved the binoculars slowly, inspecting every inch of

the houseboat. "At least one of them is Middle Eastern. Bet the other one is too."

"Can you see through the windows?"

"Not very well." He studied the man in the galley. "We may have better luck when it gets dark."

Carrying large round trays of food, the two men gathered on the forward deck to eat dinner. Occasionally smiling, they chatted quietly and constantly shifted their eyes. The sunlight glinted off something by the hatch leading to the galley area.

Scott focused on the entrance for a moment and then looked at Jackie. "Let's break out our weapons," he said matter-of-factly.

Her eyes grew large. "Our weapons?"

"Yes, they have at least one AK-47."

"We better get in touch with Wakefield," Jackie said, as she reached for the satellite phone. "I don't like this."

"We've been in tougher situations," Scott said, as he scrutinized the men.

"Yes," she said firmly, "but we weren't sitting ducks in an aluminum Spam can."

Scott forced a smile and stuffed his personal 9mm Sig Sauer into a flap pocket on his hiking shorts. "You call Wakefield while I go outside to do a little fishing."

She stared at him for a moment. "Fishing! Are you crazy?"

He grabbed a fishing rod and paused by the cockpit door. "Tell Wakefield we need heavily armed law-enforcement types, lots of them, in boats at first light."

Jackie initiated the call.

Scott stuck his head back in the cabin. "How about joining me as soon as you're off the phone?"

She nodded and glanced at their weapons.

Scott eased his way down the strut and made himself comfortable on the big float. Using a spinner, he repeatedly cast and slowly reeled in the line. He never looked directly at the men on the houseboat, catching a glimpse of them only when he cocked his arm to cast.

Carrying her fishing rod, Jackie soon joined him on the wide

Wipline float. She sat down and spoke in a whisper. "Wakefield is concerned, afraid they're going to take the houseboat up to the dam tonight."

"Is he rallying the troops?"

"He's working on it. He'll get back to us as soon as he can."

"You gave him our location?"

"*Exact* location—GPS and direct relation to the dam." She cast her line and absently let it sink. "He wants us to monitor these guys, let him know if they do anything strange, like prepare to get under way."

While they discussed their options, an arched pinkish band of twilight settled over the lake. The warm air was absolutely still and the water was like glass.

Scott propped his fishing rod against the struts and got to his feet. "I have to attach our all-around light pole."

"Need any help?"

"Thanks, but I've got it."

He retrieved the battery-operated antiglare recognition light from the cabin, stood in the cockpit door, and clamped it to one of the radio antennas. Scott glanced at the houseboat and saw the men cleaning the table on the forward deck. He turned on the bright light, climbed down, and sat next to Jackie. A few minutes later the men went inside their boat.

Jackie reeled her line in and set the rod next to her. "Maybe we should think about getting out of here, let Wakefield and his crowd deal with this situation."

"Well," he began in a hushed voice, "that would be my preference too."

She leaned close to him. "But it's too dark, right?"

"You got it." He reeled his line in for the last time. "We're not going to take a chance on hitting some idiot, anchored in the middle of the lake, who has his radio and lights turned off for the night."

"That makes sense," she said, and rose from the float. "I'll fix us a nice cold dinner if you'll open some of that *vintage* wine we picked up in Boulder City."

"With pleasure."

To save the aircraft electrical power, Scott positioned three flashlights in the cabin. He rigged a plastic screen made from large trash bags to separate the cockpit from the cabin. Periodically, he would enter the darkened cockpit, let his eyes adjust to the darkness, and then watch the houseboat. A few lights were on inside, but the mysterious men were nowhere in sight.

After dinner, Jackie and Scott sat on the port float. Shortly before ten o'clock, Wakefield called. Scott went into the cabin. The conversation was over in less than two minutes. He returned to the float and plopped down.

"What's the news?"

"They're going to be here in force in the morning."

"At daybreak?"

"Probably a little later, logistical problems."

"It figures." Jackie stared at the stars for a moment. "Do you think we should take off as soon as it gets light, give us an opportunity to get out of the line of fire?"

"That's certainly an attractive option." He put his arm around her shoulder. "We'll see what Wakefield's timetable is."

Long Beach, California

A major gateway to the global market for tens of millions of manufacturers and consumers across the United States, the busy port of Long Beach has had over $105 billion in trade move across its wharves in one year. The 3,000-acre facility provides excellent service for its numerous customers, who represent some of the largest and most prestigious shipping lines. No doubt about it, the Long Beach facility was considered one of the most efficient ports in the world. It had the ability to move large amounts of goods across the land-sea interface.

The port also was extremely critical to the base infrastructure of California. The state depended on a single pier for offloading 45 percent of all maritime crude shipments to California each day. This amounted to approximately 25 to 30 percent of the crude oil consumed by the state during each twenty-four-hour cycle.

Farooq al-Zawahri, a trusted employee who had worked on the piers for over three years, was getting worried. His shift was about to come to an end, and his long-awaited mission had not been completed. He worked rapidly, filling out forms to accompany cargo that had arrived from Honolulu. Glancing at the wall clock every minute or so, he kept an ear tuned to the marine radio.

Al-Zawahri's supervisor, Mariano Aguinaldo, a retired U.S. Navy chief petty officer, had not noticed that his protégé had become more restless in the past few days. But tonight he saw a clear difference in al-Zawahri's behavior. The younger man, who normally worked at a leisurely pace, was constantly in motion and unusually quiet.

"Farooquie." Aguinaldo affectionately called him this. "Are you feeling okay? Stomach bothering you?"

"No, I'm fine."

Aguinaldo had reservations. "Why don't you go ahead and take off. Go get some sleep."

"No, I'm okay."

"Sure?"

"Uh-huh."

"Suit yourself."

The *Lucille Garrett,* one of the largest containerships in the world, was fifteen minutes from sailing through the Queens Gate entrance to the port of Long Beach. The 1,124-foot vessel was carrying the equivalent of 5,200 maritime shipping containers. The behemoth ship, which drew 46.5 feet of water, was loaded with many varieties of cargo from various ports in Southeast Asia.

Only a tiny fraction of the thousands of containers aboard the *Lucille Garrett* would be opened by the Customs Service inspectors. There was not enough time or manpower to check even 10 percent of each arrival. Otherwise, ships would start backing up ad infinitum.

Under a moonless sky, a lightly armed U.S. Coast Guard patrol boat pulled alongside the *Lucille Garrett.* An armed team boarded the ship, half the men going to the bridge, the other half remaining in the engine room until the vessel docked. Thc patrol boat's men would accompany the big containership, as they did with cruise ships, supertankers, bulk cargo ships, vessels from Middle Eastern ports, and other high-interest ships.

Overhead, a coast guard HH-65A Dolphin helicopter slowly circled the *Lucille Garrett.* The helicopter's powerful searchlight constantly scanned the dark waters, looking for anyone who might attempt to commandeer the vessel and ram it into another large ship or petroleum storage tank.

The *Lucille Garrett* was running late and al-Zawahri was becoming more nervous by the minute. There was no way to know its exact location unless he tried to raise it on the radio. That would be too risky, with his boss sitting nearby. The minutes seemed to pass more quickly than usual, and al-Zawahri's shift was about to end.

"Hey, time to go," Aguinaldo said to al-Zawahri as their replacements arrived. "Want to get some breakfast?"

"Thanks, but I have a few things to do," al-Zawahri said mechanically. "I'll see you tomorrow."

"Okay, take care."

"You, too," al-Zawahri said, as his boss greeted the newcomers and then left the building. He chatted amiably with the two men and then heard the radio announce the news he had been waiting for. The *Lucille Garrett* was about to enter port.

He excused himself and went to his locker to retrieve his oversized lunch pail. Saying good-bye to his co-workers, al-Zawahri left the office and walked to his car. Instead of leaving the port, he drove to an area where he could watch the *Lucille Garrett* enter the harbor's narrow entrance.

Opening his lunch bucket, he attached two wires from a battery pack to his transmitter. Farooq al-Zawahri was about to create some major headlines around the world. Patiently, he waited for the huge ship as the helicopter slowly circled the vessel. Al-Zawahri was beginning to feel ebullient when a security guard stopped his vehicle nearby and shined a spotlight at him.

This can't be happening. He reached under his seat, pulled out a 9mm Beretta, and placed it in his lap.

The guard drove up next to al-Zawahri's well-used Ford Escort and stopped. "Everything okay?"

"Yes, sir." Al-Zawahri smiled and showed the man his credentials. "Just passing time, watching the stars and the ships."

"Yeah, it's kinda relaxin', ain't it?"

"It sure is, especially on a clear night like this."

The young security guard continued a steady stream of banal blather as al-Zawahri's nervous system went on edge. *Go away, before I have to blow your head off.*

Time was rapidly running out. The bow of the *Lucille Garrett* was about to enter the crowded port. In desperation, al-Zawahri triggered the powerful bomb on board the containership. Twice as potent as the Khobar Towers bomb, the thundering explosion blew the ship's massive hull wide open on both sides.

With his mouth agape, the dumbfounded guard became hollow-eyed. "Holysonofabitch! Gotta go!" He roared off as total chaos erupted in the port.

The *Lucille Garrett*'s bow and a long section of the keel were already dragging on the bottom. She sank with her stern thirty yards inside the harbor's narrow opening. Many of the maritime shipping containers and the twisted superstructure of the ship jutted out of the water like a macabre sculpture.

Although the shock wave from the mind-numbing explosion severely rocked the coast guard helicopter, the pilot maintained control of the craft. The Dolphin worked with the damaged patrol boat to rescue eleven of the fifteen crewmen and all the coast guard team. The other members of the crew either perished in the explosion or drowned after they panicked and jumped overboard without their life jackets.

Smiling with great satisfaction, Farooq al-Zawahri drove to the edge of a remote pier and tossed the incriminating evidence into deep water. He did not want to be seen leaving the port after the calamitous event. He would wait until midmorning when things settled down. Al-Zawahri had been instructed to remain on his job and wait for further orders.

Trying to temper his feelings of elation and accomplishment, he drove back to the familiar parking lot to sleep in his car. However, he soon discovered that it was impossible to sleep with all the commotion caused by the deadly assault.

The terrorist attack would close the port of Long Beach for

many long weeks. Because California's refineries were operating at full capacity, only a small supply of petroleum was stored in the state. The crushing disaster would seriously erode California's gasoline supply, causing great damage to the economy of the western United States.

21

Peterson Air Force Base, Colorado Springs

Located in the shadow of the Rocky Mountains and the famous 14,110-foot Pikes Peak, Peterson AFB was one of the finest military installations in the world. The clear atmosphere, idyllic blue skies, and wide variety of recreational activities beckoned nature lovers to the facility. Usually quiet at this time of morning, the base was buzzing as officers and enlisted personnel waited for the president of the United States to arrive.

Dressed in their finest uniforms, the men and women represented the North American Aerospace Defense Command (NORAD), the U.S. Air Force Academy, the 50th Space Wing, the 21st Space Wing, the U.S. Space Command, the Army and Air Force Space Commands, Cheyenne Mountain Air Force Base, and Fort Carson, the army's "mountain post."

National Airborne Operations Center

Ten minutes before the Night Watch landed at Peterson AFB, the president was receiving a last-minute briefing from Hartwell Prost.

"Mr. President," Prost said, as he spread his papers on the conference table. "We've received the latest reports."

"Iran and Afghanistan?"

"Yes, sir."

Macklin sipped his coffee. "I'm listening."

"The air strikes are continuing as we speak." Prost donned his glasses. "Coalition aircraft have hit over three dozen air-defense assets in Iran and western Afghanistan, including a number of new SAM batteries—advanced SA-6 sites."

The president placed his cup down. "Any casualties yet?"

"No sir, but a Navy F/A-18 was heavily damaged and the pilot had to eject before he could reach *Stennis.*"

"Is he okay?"

"He's a bit banged up, but he'll be fine. Ejected one mile from the ship and the helicopter had him out of the water in no time."

"Hats off to those helo guys." Macklin looked at Prost. "Anything on Shayhidi?" There was a hint of rawness in his voice.

"I'm afraid not. We're monitoring his home office in Geneva."

Pete Adair stepped into the room and apologized for interrupting. "Sir, we've had another event, a big one."

The president's shoulders sagged.

"A large containership just exploded and sank in the entrance to the port of Long Beach." SecDef gave President Macklin the latest information while the E-4B made its approach to Runway 35-Right at Colorado Springs.

"How did they do it?" the president asked.

"Nobody knows for sure, but it would be easy to smuggle a huge bomb in a shipping container. Divers will conduct a preliminary investigation before they begin removing the wreckage."

Macklin closed his eyes for a moment. "What the *hell* else is going to happen?"

Adair wavered. "It's impossible to second-guess this kind of thing."

Prost was disgusted. "We're going to have to inflict real pain."

SecDef nodded. "Sir, we need to find Shayhidi."

"What do you suggest?" The president let his sarcasm show.

They were interrupted when an aide entered, handed Prost a message, and left promptly.

Hartwell smiled and looked at the president. "The Echelon Two analysts just detected Shayhidi."

"Where?"

"Phnom Penh. Made reservations at the Hotel Le Royal."

"Get someone on this, now!"

"I'll take care of it," Prost said. "We're about to land."

The three men fastened their seat belts. A minute later the 747 touched down while the president was discussing widening the war. Macklin confronted Adair. "We're the only superpower, and if we don't start demonstrating that fact to our enemies, no one else is going to respect us. Turn up the heat!"

Dover Air Force Base

Located three miles east of the Delaware state capital, Dover AFB is an aerial port that provides timely movement of passengers, cargo, and mail to locations worldwide. The base is home to the 436th Airlift Wing and the 512th Airlift Wing and their scores of huge C-5 Galaxies. The 436th is the only combat-ready Galaxy wing capable of employing airdrop and special operations tactics in support of global airlifts.

The C-5, with a maximum gross weight in excess of 830,000 pounds, is the largest cargo aircraft in the U.S. Air Force inventory. A typical long-haul mission would carry a flight crew of fourteen, including a minimum of two pilots, two engineers, two loadmasters, outsized cargo, and 250 to 270 passengers.

Major Blaine Holden, who was about to trade in his gold rank insignia for the silver insignia of a lieutenant colonel, awakened at 3:30 A.M. for his 5:30 A.M. flight from Dover to the al-Udeid Air Base at Qatar. With increased activity over the Middle East, the sprawling desert base was being resupplied on a daily basis.

As the aircraft commander, Holden had the responsibility of transporting 243 support personnel, including technicians, engineers, and their equipment and supplies, to al-Udeid.

With the aircraft near its maximum takeoff weight, Holden taxied to the runway while he went through the challenge-and-response of the pre-takeoff checklist. When the tower cleared them for takeoff, Holden maneuvered the lumbering Galaxy onto the centerline of the runway. A meticulous pilot, Holden handled the flight controls like a gifted concert pianist.

The power came up on the four engines, and the aircraft began accelerating. To the people watching the takeoff, it seemed like an eternity before the nose slowly rose into the air and the heavily laden Galaxy lifted into the morning sky. Next came the landing gear, retracting into the belly of the huge bird. With the speed increasing, the flaps followed as the copilot switched from the tower to Departure Control.

The aircraft was still accelerating and climbing when they crossed the western shoreline of Delaware Bay. The water was smooth as a millpond, and the air was so still Holden felt like he was sitting in his living room.

Abd-al-Azim al-Makki sat patiently inside the cabin of his newly purchased Barr-Craft walk-around fishing boat. The rig was truly a sportsman's dream come true. In addition to the fishing gear, the boat carried two portable Stinger surface-to-air missiles with launchers.

As soon as al-Makki spotted the big Galaxy, he stepped into the cabin and brought both missiles up to the deck. Al-Makki waited for the aircraft to get closer. The morning stillness allowed him to hear the throaty whine of the four engines. He looked around and saw a few boats in the distance. No matter, his mission was at hand and he would carry it out. He stood up, braced himself, and fired the first missile. He tossed the launcher into the bay and grabbed the second Stinger.

He braced again and raised the missile launcher at the same instant his first SAM hit the right outboard engine. Al-Makki fired the second missile, tossed the launcher overboard, and started the twin outboards. It was time to disappear and prepare for his next assignment.

* * *

The second missile went ballistic and flew over the plane. The outboard engine was still attached, but the uncontrolled blaze was burning through the wing structure.

Major Holden and his flight deck crew were working feverishly to extinguish the fire. The copilot, Captain Sean Kowlinski, was making a Mayday radio call while Holden tried to nurse the heavy lifter back to Dover. There was a debate about dumping fuel, but the flight crew agreed it could be fatal with fire trailing the length of the plane.

Holden kept the nose slightly below the horizon to keep his airspeed up. He was going to have to make a fast approach or risk pulling the power back on the left outboard engine. They could see the crash trucks racing to the runway. There was absolute fear in the passenger compartment, and the crew was trying to calm everyone.

Major Holden waited as long as he could and then called for the flaps. Next came the landing gear. They were getting close to turning final. Holden was cutting the pattern as close as he dared. Rolling out on short final, he began easing power on the left outboard engine. He kept sliding the throttle back as they slowed.

Carrying extra speed, Holden made a smooth landing while the crash trucks raced after the burning plane. The heavy lifter was quickly evacuated and the engine fire was extinguished. The emergency was a close call, but Holden had lived up to his reputation.

Lake Mead

The star-sprinkled Nevada sky was still jet-black when Scott awakened Jackie at 4:45 A.M.

"What is it?" she whispered, turning on the flashlight next to her.

"There's activity on the houseboat."

She propped herself up on one elbow. "Are they getting ready to leave?"

"I don't know, but I have an idea. The galley light came on about five minutes ago, but I haven't seen anyone—wait, I see one of the men in the galley. Just walked in."

Jackie poured bottled water on a kitchen towel and wiped her face. "I'll fix some hot tea."

"We don't have time. I need you to cover me."

She looked at him suspiciously. "What are you talking about?"

Scott pointed to the neatly coiled nylon dock line. "I'm going to foul their props so the boat can't go anywhere."

Jackie was incredulous. "Have you *lost* your mind?"

"Listen, just listen for a second." He picked up the end of the braided line. "These two lines—I've tied them together—are used to secure the airplane to docks. I have sixty feet of five-eighths-inch nylon line with a tensile strength of fifteen thousand pounds—same kind I have on my sailboat."

She raised her hand. "Stop. Not another word; don't say anything, period. In fact, I have one *hell* of a plan. We raise the anchor, start the engine, turn on the landing light, and ease out of here—gone. Adios."

"Jackie, do you know what will happen if these people *do* have a nuke and it goes off next to the dam?"

"Do you know what will happen if they detonate a nuke next to us?"

"That's why we're going to do my plan first—immobilize their houseboat—and then we're going to implement your plan—get out of Dodge."

"Immobilize the houseboat?" Her eyes quizzed him. "Won't the props cut through the nylon line?"

"That's the point. The props won't be able to turn."

"Unbelievable." Jackie reached for one of the Heckler & Koch compact submachine guns. "We could have been in Hawaii doing something totally normal, like watching the sun set."

Scott removed his boots, and then slipped out of his shirt, socks, and hiking shorts. "Just cover me. If things go south, make every shot count. Take them both out."

He grabbed the nylon line, climbed out on the float, and slipped quietly into the calm water. The water temperature was comfortable and Scott was a strong swimmer. With the line looped around his left shoulder, he did a modified breaststroke toward the houseboat.

Jackie switched off the flashlight and sat in the cockpit with the door open. She held the submachine gun in her lap, ready to fire at the first sign of trouble.

Closing on the boat, Scott swam in slow motion as he approached the stern. When he was next to the stern drives, he eased beneath the surface and fastened the line around one prop. *I hope they don't start the engines now.*

Looping the line in a figure eight from one prop to the other and around the lower units, Scott surfaced four times to take a deep breath. Finally, he wrapped the last ten feet of line around the middle of the figure eight and tied a tight knot. The three-blade props were securely lashed port and starboard and fore and aft. The houseboat was not going anywhere under its own power until the braided line was removed.

When Scott surfaced, he heard voices nearby. The two men on the houseboat were outside talking in hushed voices. Scott could not risk swimming directly to the Caravan. He treaded water for a few minutes and then decided to go the long way back. That would mean making a wide arc from the houseboat to the Caravan.

Jackie, straining to see any movement in the water, was becoming more anxious as the minutes passed. The sky was hinting at turning light. *If they see him in the water and then realize something is wrong with their boat? Not a good place to be.*

Swimming slowly and quietly, Scott kept his nose an inch out of the water. *If they catch me in a spotlight, I'm in serious trouble.* After traveling about fifty yards behind the houseboat, Scott began a wide arc to reach the Caravan on the unexposed side.

Halfway to the airplane, he realized dawn was beginning to break. *Going to have to move faster and shorten my route.*

Bryce Canyon Airport, Utah

The high-altitude airfield was practically deserted so early in the morning. The sky was clear and the sun was still below the horizon. It was a perfect morning for flying: no wind to speak of, and no turbulence close to the ground.

Securely strapped into the left seat of the former Tokyo Express, Khaliq Farkas was pleased with the satellite phone connections to the lookouts at both targets. He followed his checklist and started the B-25's big radial engines. They sputtered a few times, coughed up clouds of thick oily smoke, and then rumbled to life.

His wingman, Tohir Makkawi, also started his bomber's fourteen-cylinder engines. Makkawi, an Iranian who was in the United States on an expired student visa, had acquired only ninety-three hours of total flying time, but Farkas had found him to be a quick study.

Each pilot had a crewman with an AK-47 for last-ditch defense against an adversary in the air or on the ground. They could shoot from the large openings on each side of the fuselage behind the wings, formerly the waist gunner's position.

If everything worked as planned, one of these two reconditioned survivors of World War II would be flying its last mission this morning. While the Mitchell's engines warmed sufficiently, the ground crew checked for leaks and other anomalies on the warbirds. Everything appeared normal on the exterior, while the engine gauges in the cockpits reflected the same status. It was time to fulfill Saeed Shayhidi's grand plan, the mastermind's most elaborate scheme yet.

The senior mechanic gave both pilots the signal to taxi. Once the airplanes were off the ground, the mechanic and his fellow terrorists would make their way to a secluded cabin in the backwoods of Canada. They would remain there in sleep mode until activated to strike again.

Flying the brown and dark gray bomber, Farkas led Makkawi in the silver B-25 to Runway 21. The Bryce Canyon Airport is classified as an uncontrolled airport. All pilots, whether inbound, outbound, or flying in the traffic pattern performing touch-and-goes, are expected to communicate on a common frequency.

After each pilot ran up his engines, checking that all systems were functioning properly, Makkawi keyed the radio and told his flight leader that he was ready for takeoff. Partially lowering his flaps, Farkas made the necessary radio call to take the active runway and taxied into position. He slowly added power and then released the brakes.

Once Farkas was rolling down the 7,400-foot runway, Makkawi lowered his flaps, made the mandatory radio call, and taxied onto the airstrip. Carrying an extra 300 gallons of fuel in his plane, Makkawi walked the throttles forward and released the brakes. A few seconds later, he knew he was in trouble. The bomber began drifting to the left side of the seventy-five-foot-wide runway.

With his heart stuck in his throat, he shoved in the right rudder and overcorrected, sending the B-25 careening toward the right side of the runway. Clutching a handhold, the crewman in the back was praying he would live through the takeoff.

With alternate jabs at the brakes and the rudders, Makkawi finally managed to get the bomber off the runway and climbing. His heart was pounding so fast that he froze on the controls. He had come close to losing control of the Mitchell and jeopardizing the mission.

Passing near the Best Western Ruby's Inn, Farkas was in the process of adjusting the engine controls. Waiting for Makkawi to join him in loose formation on his left wing, Farkas began a gentle left turn. He didn't want to use the radios unless it was absolutely necessary. After a minute, he began to bank more steeply to the left. *Where is he?* Farkas rolled wings level on course to the initial point for their first target.

"One, slow down." The voice was tinged with anxiety.

Slow down? Something is wrong. Rolling into a tight bank to the left, Farkas was approaching 180 degrees of turn when he saw the problem. He keyed the radio. "Two, raise your landing gear and check your flaps up."

The wheels disappeared.

"Fly our course heading," Farkas ordered. "I'll rendezvous on you."

"Okay—sorry."

"Settle down. I'll lead you in."

"Okay."

Farkas pulled up on the right side of Makkawi and slightly ahead of him. Flying at less than 600 feet above the ground, they continued toward their objective.

Makkawi noticed a thin trail of gray smoke coming from his leader's right engine, but he didn't mention it. There was too much at stake to worry his flight leader and mentor unnecessarily. Besides, Farkas had made it clear at the preflight briefing: Once they were under way, there would be no turning back.

With everything under control, Farkas used his satellite phone to once again contact the lookouts at each target. If there were fighter planes in the area, the cell members on watch would fire flares into the air in an attempt to distract the U.S. pilots. If the jets were low enough, the terrorists had shoulder-fired surface-to-air missiles available. The men on the boats had only one task to accomplish: Make sure Farkas and his wingman hit their targets even if it resulted in all of them sacrificing their lives.

Phnom Penh, Cambodia

Pacing the floor in his suite at the Hotel Le Royal, Saeed Shayhidi was becoming extremely frustrated and angry. After four attempts to use his intermediary, trusted friend Hafiz al-Yamani, to communicate with Ahmed Musashi in Geneva, no one had called back. Now, for some inexplicable reason, al-Yamani refused to take any further calls, and he was ignoring Shayhidi's e-mail.

With his bellicosity increasing by the minute, the mogul-turned-fugitive checked his diamond-encrusted wristwatch. Given the time in Switzerland, Musashi would be getting ready to go to lunch at the Atrium Bar in the Beau-Rivage Geneva.

Shayhidi called him at his office and the secretary, surprised to hear from *the* man himself, quickly patched him through to Musashi. When the acting president of Shayhidi's vast empire answered the phone there were no pleasantries.

"You better have an explanation," Shayhidi threatened, his face twisted in anger, "and it better be a damn good one."

Shocked to hear directly from Shayhidi, Musashi paused a moment. "I don't think this is a good idea."

"I don't care what you think!"

"Listen to me," Musashi said harshly. "The Americans are monitoring our communications, e-mail, phone calls, faxes, everything."

Ignoring Musashi's warning, Shayhidi was clenching and unclenching his left fist. "Why hasn't al-Yamani returned my phone calls or answered my e-mail? What is going on?"

"He works for me now," Musashi snapped. "We have to stay as far away from you as possible. The Americans are using eavesdropping technology to track you. They're probably using voice recognition and encryption."

Shayhidi was taken aback. "How would you know that?"

"It's only common sense. You know it's true and you better be careful, for the sake of everyone."

Calm was returning to Shayhidi's voice. "I want you to set up an account in Hong Kong that I can access under a different name."

"I'm afraid I can't do that," Musashi declared, in a defiant voice. "We've been suffering too many loses."

"What do you mean you can't do that?" Shayhidi snarled. "You make it a priority to get it done today or clean out your desk."

"Well," Musashi began slowly, "things have changed around here." He hcsitated, gaining the courage to say what he had wanted to put in words for years. "You've become too much of a liability to our company."

Speechless at first, Shayhidi went ballistic. "*Our* company? What the hell are you talking about, *our* company?" His face was beet-red and the veins protruded from his neck.

"I can't allow your mistakes to adversely effect the reputation and performance of the company."

Stunned, Shayhidi's mind reeled. "Are you threatening me—trying to oust me from the company *I built*?"

"Unfortunately, we've had to terminate you." Musashi found pleasure in saying the words.

"I'll sue you and take every dollar you ever make," Shayhidi yelled in outrage. "I'll see you a pauper, you ungrateful bastard!"

"I don't think so," Musashi said, with a touch of pure venom "You're an international fugitive, a terrorist. You don't have any money, can't get to any money, don't have any power, and I doubt if there's a single lawyer out there who wants to be associated with a hunted international terrorist."

Trembling with rage, Shayhidi slammed the phone down. He'd been a fool to give Ahmed Musashi power of attorney to control the entire corporation. *That deceitful bastard—I'll kill him!* Then panic consumed him. *The infidels know where I am. I have to find someone else to communicate for me.*

Quickly, he packed two small leather bags, locked the door to his suite, and left the hotel without checking out. He personally flagged a limousine and threw his luggage in the backseat.

Six minutes later, two CIA agents and five local law-enforcement officers arrived at the hotel to take Saeed Shayhidi into custody.

The drive to Siem Reap, Cambodia, gave Shayhidi time to calm down and think through the unthinkable. Using a phony name, he checked into the Grand Hotel, a historic landmark resort located in the heart of the city. One of Asia's finest hotels, the Grand was only eight kilometers from the famed Angkor complex.

Focused on taking his company back and seeing Ahmed Musashi and Hafiz al-Yamani dead, Shayhidi began thinking more clearly and methodically. He had the hotel concierge call Tang Cheng-hsi, a close friend who owned a hotel and a prestigious Hong Kong–based jet charter operation. They had done business together for many years. A long-range Gulfstream V was soon on its way to the Siem Reap Airport.

22

Lake Mead

Keeping a wary eye on the houseboat, Scott began swimming faster as the sky turned lighter. One of the men stepped outside on the forward deck and raised his binoculars. Scott plunged underwater and swam as fast as he could until he had to come up for air. He tossed a glance at the houseboat. The other man was now outside talking on a phone and his pal had his binoculars squarely on Scott. Rolling on his back to begin a strong, smooth backstroke, Scott looked searchingly at the Caravan and spoke in a loud voice. "The water's great—you should take a dip."

Jackie immediately answered. "Maybe later, I'm working on breakfast."

"Suit yourself."

"Your eggs are almost ready," she said in a commanding voice.

"Be there in a second."

When Scott pulled himself aboard the float facing the houseboat, Jackie handed him a towel. He calmly dried his legs and made his way into the cabin. Unconcerned about Scott, the men went inside their boat.

"Any trouble?" she asked quietly.

"They aren't going anywhere."

The darkness was rapidly disappearing when the men again walked out on the forward deck.

"Jackie," Scott said as he steadied the binoculars. "We have some action here. One of the guys studies the surroundings while the other one talks on the phone. Something strange here."

She accepted the binoculars and took a seat.

"I don't have a good feeling about this," Scott said. "Something is in the works and these guys are part of it."

"I think we should contact Wakefield," Jackie said, as she reached for the satellite phone. "We can keep an eye on the houseboat from high in the sky, out of small-arms range."

"Or a nuke's range." He glanced at the houseboat. "Getting out of here, that's a plan I can work with." Scott picked up the other H&K compact submachine gun and placed it on a seat next to the cargo door.

She called Wakefield twice without any result. "No luck, probably busy with organizing the operation to capture these guys."

"We'll try again in a little while," Scott said, concerned that the houseboat crew might try to start their engines.

She cast a look around the cabin. "I'll start stowing everything. I don't know how you feel, but the sooner we get out of here the better."

"Same here. I have that uneasy feeling in the pit of my stomach."

Scott was keeping an eye on the houseboat while the sun rose higher into the clear blue sky. Boaters were gathering on the decks of their various floating dwellings to have breakfast or a cup of coffee. The anglers had been enjoying themselves since the first sign of twilight. Scott glanced around the interior of the Caravan. Everything in the cabin had been stowed and tied down for takeoff.

Jackie again tried to contact Frank Wakefield. "I'm not having any luck—not even ringing."

"Well, we can't stay here forever," Scott said, and then handed her the binoculars. "Something is going on, but I don't know what. Wakefield will have to figure it out."

She watched the two men on the bow deck. They were checking the sky, and one was talking on a phone. "There's definitely something in the wind—something coming down."

"Let's try Wakefield one more time and then pack it out of here."

"The sooner, the better," Jackie said, and picked up the satellite phone. She waited a few seconds and shook her head. "No answer. We need info, and all we have is silence."

"Give it ten minutes," Scott suggested.

"Five," Jackie countered.

"Sounds about right."

The minutes passed slowly.

"Forget Wakefield," Scott said. "We've seen enough to know that we're in a precarious position."

"I'm with you."

"Listen to that," Scott said, aware of the sudden increase in radio traffic on the marine VHF.

"This can't be good," Jackie declared. "There's been some kind of accident. Maybe a tour boat, a paddle-wheeler going down."

"I don't have a clue, but it makes my hair stand up."

Channel 16 was becoming so cluttered and distorted it was impossible to make out what was being said. Scott switched to another channel and found it clobbered too. He kept trying other channels until he heard a clear but excited female voice broadcasting the bad news. There was a lot of background noise, but she talked over it.

It had been over forty minutes since confusion in Page, Arizona, had cleared enough to figure out what had happened. Shock had caused another delay before cooler heads prevailed. Finally, after the local authorities took control, the word had begun to hopscotch down the Colorado River and through the Grand Canyon.

Jackie and Scott stared at each other in disbelief as the gruesome facts emerged over the airwaves. There had been a tremendous disaster at Lake Powell, some type of huge explosion, and then a report that the Glen Canyon Dam had been breached.

Momentarily stunned, Scott looked at Jackie. "Breached—or did the whole dam collapse?"

"I don't know," she snapped. "But it's time to get airborne."

"Past time."

In a matter of seconds, the marine channels became swamped as the horrific news was being relayed down the river to Lake Mead. The warnings continued to race south toward Lake Mohave, Laughlin, Needles, Lake Havasu, Parker, and across the Mexican border. It was clear that a major tragedy had taken place at Lake Powell and the people on Lake Mead were in great jeopardy.

More troubling than the delay in getting the warning out, there was great concern about the physical integrity of Hoover Dam. Would it withstand the strain of the additional pressure? Would the intake towers survive the crush of water as billions of gallons flowed over the crest of the dam?

In order to save Hoover Dam, would officials be forced to release water from Lake Mead and flood the Colorado River all the way through Mexico's delta to the Gulf of California? If so, the Davis Dam, Parker Dam, Imperial Dam, and Laguna Dam would have to begin releasing water to protect *their* integrity. Time was running out for the people downriver from Lake Powell.

Panicked boaters were hauling up their anchors, starting their engines, and heading for the nearest marina. Others, Jet Skiers and kayakers who saw the unexpected stampede of boats, were initially confused. After hearing the frightening messages shouted from the fleeing boaters, they promptly set course for the closest place to beach their watercraft and climb to higher ground.

"Let's get airborne," Scott said as their satellite phone rang.

Jackie snatched the phone from the glare shield. After a few seconds, she frowned. "Why didn't you let us know sooner?" she said angrily and signed off moments later. "Wakefield. His sat phone was turned off because he was too busy *unorganizing* the houseboat operation."

"He obviously knew about the dam."

"Oh, yes," she said, with a rare look of disgust. "Quite some time ago. Because of all the confusion, he just now remembered us."

"Great, thanks for the heads up."

He hopped on the left float. "Shut the doors."

"Got 'em."

Scott stopped when he heard the unmistakable sound of big radial engines in harmonious sync. He looked up to see two B-25 Mitchell warbirds approaching their position from the northeast. Spellbound, Scott stared at the twin-engine medium bombers as the silver-colored plane broke away and turned west. *I'll be damned. The dark one is the same plane I saw in the hangar.*

"Jackie, check—"

"I see them."

The darkly camouflaged airplane was trailing thick grayish-black smoke from the right engine nacelle. Flying low over the water, the distinctive-looking airplane took on a new appearance when the bomb bay doors swung open.

Scott experienced a strange dichotomy of sensory overloads. "Jackie, we're in *big* trouble."

She hurried to the pilot's door and heard the deep roar of the radial engines. *This isn't good.*

"The B-25's bomb bay doors just opened and it looks like—" Scott fell silent when the airplane entered a gentle bank to the left. "He's headed straight for the inlet, the channel leading to the dam!"

"Farkas?" she asked, shocked by the abrupt turn of events.

"That'd be my bet." Scott stared at the bomber while he hauled in the anchor. "It's the same plane I saw in the hangar."

"You're sure?"

"Ninety-nine percent, not that many B-25s around with the same camouflage paint scheme."

She glanced at the silver B-25. "The other plane must have bombed the Glen Canyon Dam."

"No doubt."

They noticed their mysterious neighbors on the houseboat had their engines running, but there was a lot of confusion about why they weren't moving. Their job to provide information about airborne threats to Farkas was complete, but they could not escape. Scott watched the larger man working the engine controls while the younger man headed aft to check the engine compartments.

Scott stowed the anchor. The big picture suddenly came into focus for him. "*The Dam Busters* from World War Two," he said, as he swung into the cockpit and began starting the engine. "They made a movie about them in 1954."

"What are you talking about?"

"Those round steel bands, four of them, that were designed to encompass the suitcase nuke found on the Canadian border."

"Yes, what's your point?"

The Pratt & Whitney turbine came on speed and Scott began adding power to taxi clear of the numerous boats. "The Royal Air Force used round bombs to skip across the water—over torpedo nets—to hit dams, sink to the bottom, and then explode."

"Skip across the water?"

"Yeah, they flew four-engine Lancasters. The pilots came in low at night and skipped the bombs into strategic dams. They blew the hell out of them and sent thousands of tons of water down valleys in the heartland of the German industrial complex."

Jackie's eyes opened wide. "And you think that's what the other plane did at Lake Powell?"

"What else?"

"Using a nuke?"

"Think about it," he said, taxiing the Caravan into an open space of navigable water. "A single B-25 bomber, even two, can't hold enough conventional tonnage to drop a dam like the Glen Canyon."

He worked the water rudders to avoid a speeding cabin cruiser and a wallowing deck boat. "Using old-fashioned iron bombs, you'd have to drop a lot of tonnage to get the job done."

He donned his sunglasses and glanced at her. "Suitcase nuke, that's a different story."

It was difficult to compute the devastation that a nuclear bomb would cause at Lake Powell's Glen Canyon Dam. It had taken over seventeen years to fill the lake to the planned level or "full pool." Now it would be drained in a matter of hours. Even harder to assess would be the incomparable damage to the dams and towns downstream to San Luis Río Colorado, Mexico.

Bobbing and rolling in the colliding wakes of several boats, Scott maneuvered around a large pontoon boat and then stowed the water rudders. "Here we go."

He simultaneously pulled the yoke into his lap and eased the engine thrust lever forward.

"You have traffic at ten o'clock—closing fast," Jackie cautioned.

He swore as he pulled the power back to avoid a collision. After the high-powered ski boat flashed past, Scott again shoved the thrust lever forward. As the Caravan climbed onto the step like a boat skimming across the surface of the water, he eased the yoke forward to accelerate before lifting off.

Jackie and Scott saw the problem at the same time.

"Hang on!" he said, as they rapidly approached a large swell. Appearing out of nowhere, it had been caused by the catastrophic force of thousands of tons of water pouring into the lake. Smooth and rounded, the long swell looked like a small tsunami approximately eight to ten feet in height. There was no way to avoid the growing wave.

Using both hands, Scott hauled back on the yoke before the airplane was ready to fly. "Gonna take a hit!"

Glen Canyon Dam, Arizona

Few people who had closely observed the two B-25s were still alive. The mental picture indelibly imprinted in the minds of the survivors was crystal clear. The vintage bombers, one low over Lake Powell and the other flying at about 500 feet, approached the dam from the north-northeast. Traveling at high speed, the lower bomber waited until the last second to drop a round object out of its belly.

Astonished by the dangerous stunt, the early morning anglers stared in disbelief as the object skipped across the water a couple of times and impacted the dam almost dead center. It immediately sank as the bomber sharply pulled up, missing the top of the dam by only a few feet. Both airplanes turned west-southwest and soon disappeared at low level.

After a few seconds of stunned silence, the fishermen began to speculate about the reason for a simulated bomb run. Most concluded that it must have been carried out by some group of eccentric environmentalists. The Glen Canyon Dam was a prime target of national environmental movements. They wanted to empty the 187-mile-long lake and restore the ecosystem.

Three minutes after the B-25 bomber cleared the dam, all the questions were answered. A colossal geyser of water and silt erupted near the middle of the dam. Like a super-powerful depth charge, it exploded outward and upward for thousands of feet. Water, mud, and fish remnants rained on everything within a half mile of the nuclear detonation. A misty mushroom cloud rose into the clear sky, climbing over 11,000 feet in the still morning air.

The nuclear bomb encased in the round steel jacket had indeed survived the severe impact with the concrete. The gigantic explosion had blown the Glen Canyon Dam completely apart, sending millions of tons of water cascading down the narrow Colorado River.

The boats near the dam were ripped to shreds, while those farther away were sucked through the jagged opening. Another minute and twenty seconds passed before the sandstone spillways began to give out. Soon after the spillways failed, two-thirds of the dam collapsed, opening a gaping hole.

Eight-point-five trillion gallons of water from the second largest man-made lake in the United States was headed for Lake Mead, the largest such U.S. lake. In a relatively short period of time, millions of tons of water would be descending over 2,475 feet during its deadly race through the Grand Canyon.

Since the dawn of man, no one on earth had ever seen water do what it was doing: rising to unbelievable heights, smashing into the sides of Glen Canyon, plunging backward and sideways and spinning into huge whirlpools before accelerating again.

The sheer volume and weight of the liquid, combined with the incredible drop in elevation, accelerated the raging water to a velocity that was heretofore unimaginable. The loud roar could be heard for more than a mile down Glen Canyon, sparing a few lives.

Thirty people beginning a rafting adventure at Lee's Ferry, the official beginning of the Grand Canyon, were saved when word reached them just as they were shoving off. Panicked, they scrambled to higher ground seconds before the awesome fury viciously consumed their rafts, supplies, personal gear, the dock, the campground, and the ranger station, tearing everything into shredded pieces. It was almost like an explosion. Nothing was left but multitudes of particles, minuscule in size as they rushed down the turbulent river.

Alternate Highway 89's Navajo Bridge spanning Marble Canyon collapsed in a twisted maze as the canyon walls gave way. A vacationing family in a new minivan was almost across the famous bridge when it dropped out from under them.

After cascading through Marble Canyon into the core of the Grand Canyon, a wall of water reaching 120 feet slammed into ridges of limestone, sandstone, and volcanic rock. The water ripped huge chunks of rock loose and cut furrows in the riverbed at each bend. Boulders were tossed around like Ping-Pong balls as the churning water scoured everything like a giant fire hose. The thunderous noise and complete destruction were incomprehensible.

Others farther south in the Grand Canyon, including scores of uninformed hikers, rafters, canyoneers, backpackers, a film crew completing a documentary about the canyon, and a team of three archaeologists, were not so lucky. Many of them were over 4,500 feet below the rim of the canyon. Even if they had received a warning, it would have been virtually impossible to escape the riverbed in the short period of time between the dam break and the arrival of the towering flood of water, bodies, animals, boats, and other debris.

To a person, they knew death was imminent when they heard the faint sound of distant thunder steadily and rapidly growing into a ferocious pounding and crashing sound, a chilling sound unlike anything they had ever experienced. It was not the sound of a flash flood, especially with clear blue skies overhead. It was the sound of death, sudden, ferocious death. Still, the utter shock was mind-boggling when the 120-foot wall of water and debris rounded the bend.

Lake Mead

"Come on," Scott said through clenched teeth, as the Caravan staggered into the air in a nose-high attitude. Gripping the yoke tightly, he braced himself for the impact while Jackie ducked.

The bottom of the wide floats slammed into the top half of the huge swell, forcing the airplane to go almost straight up. Scott shoved the yoke forward to keep the Caravan from stalling, but he couldn't keep it from impacting the water.

"Made it," he sighed, as the airplane accelerated and rose gently from the lake. He allowed the Caravan to gain speed before raising the nose. "Close—very close."

"But we made it." Jackie slowly let out her breath and craned her head to the right. "Turn back toward the dam, keep it tight."

Scott banked steeply to the right.

Seeing the approaching B-25 bomber flying up the channel leading to Hoover Dam, an army sergeant major used his portable radio to send an urgent warning to his men and then paused. *I can't let this happen again.* They had been on edge since the news about the Glen Canyon Dam reached them.

"Come on, you goddamn sonsabitches," he said out loud. "Step up to the plate. Come and get it." He again activated his radio. "Stand by."

The low-flying bomber was rapidly approaching the heavily protected dam. The sergeant major knew they were up against terrorist saboteurs when he saw the open bomb bay doors. The grizzled army veteran did not hesitate to give the command to open fire.

Following the machine-gunners, the snipers opened up and the two soldiers with portable surface-to-air missiles aimed and fired at the aircraft. The water in the channel was being pelted as the rounds bracketed the B-25. The sergeant major swore when the missiles, one going low under the right wing, the other corkscrewing high over the left wing, hit the water and disintegrated.

The other shooters were getting hits, but not enough to bring down the airplane. Everyone but the fleeing civilians saw the round object drop from the bomber. It skipped across the smooth water as the B-25 eased up just enough to clear the dam. Rounds were still hitting the aircraft, but it continued to thunder down the Colorado River.

The stunned sergeant major had his men immediately reload in the event of another sneak attack. He watched as panicked drivers and pedestrians jockeyed to get off the dam.

"What the hell," he said to himself and lit a cigarette. *It's way too late to run now.*

Scott saw the smoking B-25 in the distance. It was low, heading south, and then it began a shallow turn to the southeast followed by a heading change to the east.

Jackie and Scott were unprepared for what was about to happen. When the nuclear bomb detonated, it sent a shock wave radiating from the plume of water and mist.

Jackie gripped Scott's lower arm and stared in disbelief. "That was a *nuke,* no mistaking that."

"Yeah, up close and in your face."

"Oh, my *God,*" Jackie said, as the plane was buffeted by the shock wave. "Those people on the dam . . ." She trailed off.

"They're not with us anymore."

Appalled, she watched the rising mushroom cloud. "All those innocent people gone—vaporized."

For a moment, Scott was speechless. "Incredibly twisted people—sick."

Jackie was too shocked to respond.

Scott searched for the B-25. "Farkas has four more nukes. We have to nail him and find them."

It was a replay of the Glen Canyon disaster, but the damage to the Hoover Dam wasn't as severe. The center and a portion of the east side of the structure had been shattered, but the dam was still standing. However, hundreds of thousands of gallons were pouring through unchecked. The question was on everyone's mind: How would the dam react when the water from Lake Powell was added to Lake Mead?

Scott strained to see the departing B-25 and caught sight of it low to the ground. "We have to go after Farkas."

"We can't catch him in this plane, don't even see him."

"He's at our eleven-thirty, extremely low and trailing smoke." Scott banked to the left to intercept the bomber at an angle. "See it?"

"Not yet . . . okay, got him."

Scott glanced at the instruments to make sure the Pratt & Whitney turboprop was producing maximum power. "His right engine is trailing smoke. If it fails we'll have a good chance of catching him, or at least keeping him in sight."

"Let's call center and get some fighters on him," she suggested.

"Go ahead."

Jackie called the controller and tried to coordinate an intercept. With both dams being overrun by airplanes and news helicopters, the controller was busy sorting out traffic. A constant stream of radio calls blocked other transmissions while everyone tried to talk at the same time.

She shook her head. "Looks like we'll have to take a number."

"We'll stay on him," Scott said, as they slowly gained on the B-25.

They remained silent while the distance between the two planes continued to decrease.

"There it goes," she said as they watched clouds of black smoke pour out of the right nacelle. "The engine just cratered."

"Did it ever."

In less than twenty-five seconds, the propeller was feathered and the engine was shut down.

"No more smoke," Scott said as they slowly closed in on the limping bomber. "I want to fall in trail about a thousand yards behind him and come up his six."

"You might want to stay slightly below him. Better chance that no one sees us coming."

"We'll give it a try."

They watched for other traffic while the Caravan gained on the bomber. Scott eased the power back as they grew closer.

"They're on to us," Jackie said quietly, watching through the binoculars.

"What?"

She handed him the binoculars. "Someone is eyeballing us from the tail gunner's position. You look; I have the airplane."

"You have it." Scott relinquished the flight controls and surveyed the tail of the crippled bomber. "Damn."

"New plan?" she calmly asked.

"Yeah, new plan." He took the controls again, maneuvered the Caravan to the left side of the B-25, and slowly added power. "It looks like someone has put a number of rounds through the wings and fuselage."

"Maybe that's what happened to the engine."

"Who knows? Just glad it slowed him down."

"We *have* to have some fighters," Jackie said, and again keyed the radio. "Los Angeles Center, Caravan November Three-Two-Three Fox Lima."

The wooden-voiced controller was going nonstop. When he paused for a fraction of a second, she tried again. No reply. He kept stepping on her radio transmissions. "Well, I'll try someone who isn't so busy, see if we can relay our message and position."

"Have at it."

She called Las Vegas Approach Control and explained their situation. Shaken by what had happened at Hoover Dam, the controller promised to send the message immediately.

Jackie placed the binoculars on the floor. "The guy just left the tail gunner's hangout."

A few seconds later, the man reappeared at the waist gunner's opening in the left side of the fuselage.

"Well," Jackie said hesitantly, "let's see if Farkas is at the wheel, what do you think?"

"Why not?" Scott said, as he carefully eased the big Cessna even with the cockpit of the B-25.

Khaliq Farkas turned and looked at the Caravan for a long moment, staring at the cockpit.

"That's him," Scott announced. "No doubt about it!"

"Let's ease back," Jackie suggested. "We need some maneuvering room in case he tries to ram us."

Scott inched the throttles aft at the same moment the crewman in the bomber opened fire with his AK-47. The high-powered rounds ripped through the Caravan's right float and passenger windows, shattering the interior of the cabin.

23

East of Las Vegas

Hugging the terrain, Tohir Makkawi carefully advanced the throttles as the silver B-25 flew southwest of the Muddy Mountains. His potential targets were easy to distinguish with the morning sun at his back. During their briefing before takeoff, Khaliq Farkas had left the final decision to Makkawi. He could choose any of the hotel casinos to crash his bomber into, but Farkas suggested one of the larger complexes in the heart of the famous gambling strip.

From a distance, Makkawi studied the Aladdin, Bellagio, Mandalay Bay, and a few other well-known landmarks. He particularly liked the tempting hotel casino known as Caesar's Palace. Makkawi had heard fascinating stories about Caesar's Palace from Saudi princes who vacationed at the hotel during their frequent visits to the United States. As he gazed at his choice of targets, a smile creased Makkawi's face. The rich and arrogant scions of wealth would have to evaluate new lodging accommodations.

Spying two F-16s flying 1,000 feet above the Las Vegas strip, Makkawi decided to make a wide circle to avoid the fighters.

The crewman/gunner sitting in the back of the plane was wistfully smoking a cigarette and looking forward to getting back on the ground. *Why are we going around in circles?* After the scary moments during the takeoff run, he was anxious to get through the landing phase of the mission. He had "enjoyed" all the flying he cared to experience for the rest of his life, especially with novice pilots.

Due to a hydraulic pump failure in the scheduled AWACS, an Airborne Warning and Control System aircraft was not yet covering the airspace over Lake Powell and Lake Mead. Air force fighters had been scrambled when the news about the Glen Canyon Dam reached Nellis AFB. Along with four F-16s from the New Mexico Air National Guard, the four Nellis-based F-16s proceeded to Lake Powell. They rendezvoused over Page, Arizona, with a KC-135 tanker and then split up in four sections to hunt for the illusive B-25s.

With the help of controllers who occasionally picked up a primary radar return from the bombers, the ANG fighter pilots from Kirtland AFB, Albuquerque, were first on the prowl. Continuing reports from eyewitnesses in the air and on the ground matched what the controllers were observing.

Three other F-16s were now patrolling the skies over Nellis AFB and the nearby city of Las Vegas. The fighter pilots cast occasional glances at the jammed highways and streets, where panicked vacationers and gamblers scurried to get out of town. Dozens of emergency vehicles and law enforcement cruisers were racing to various accident scenes.

A large number of sport utility vehicles had gone off-road to get around the growing traffic jams. McCarran International Airport was in total gridlock, with nothing moving on the ground or in the air. Local law-enforcement agencies were providing the front line of security for the airport and its support facilities.

* * *

Although he didn't know it, Tohir Makkawi had been discovered. His bomber was being pursued by two New Mexico Air National Guard F-16s in afterburner—full blower and supersonic. Known as the Tacos, the ANG squadron was blessed with an abundance of talented aviators. The pilots chasing the B-25 were airline captains who had many years of experience in fighters.

Makkawi, in his quest for more speed, intentionally overboosted the radial engines. The heavily vibrating Wright Cyclones weren't going to last much longer, but Makkawi was not concerned. He only needed two more minutes of maximum power and his mission would be accomplished. The infidels remaining in Caesar's Palace were in for the shock of their lives. The majority of the decadent sinners did not have long to live. Makkawi would soon be with Allah, and Khaliq Farkas would be proud of his successful trainee.

The crewman in the rear of the plane was wondering why they were flying so low and why the engine noise had increased so much. He guessed it was an evasive maneuver and lit another cigarette. They would soon be on the ground. He was looking forward to going back into sleep mode.

Makkawi's B-25 was making a heading change when Lieutenant Colonel Clay Yeatts, leader of the ANG section, screeched into position at the bomber's six o'clock. Taco One used his M61 20mm Vulcan cannon to blast the right rudder completely off the bomber's horizontal stabilizer.

Another barrage of shells ripped the right engine cowling to pieces, sending a thick stream of black oil flowing from the wing. The engine caught fire as Yeatts swung smoothly over to the left side of the plane and worked the left engine over. It lasted only a few seconds before a blazing streak of fire erupted from the cowling.

The right landing gear dropped out of its wheel well as the B-25 began a steep bank to the right. Yeatts continued to pour cannon fire into the burning plane as it slow-rolled onto its back and crashed nose first near the southern boundary of the Desert Rose Golf Course.

A foursome that heard the three planes approaching ran for

cover and spread-eagled with their hands over their heads. They were only slightly injured by the flying debris that hurtled over them. They unanimously decided to adjourn to the nineteenth hole and have a round of Bloody Marys.

The fiercely burning wreckage of the bomber was lying in a crater seven miles from Caesar's Palace. The Tacos had come through with a grand slam, saving the lives of many unsuspecting tourists and hotel workers.

The news about the B-25 crash on the outskirts of the Las Vegas strip flashed through the city in a matter of minutes. With black smoke still rising into the sky, a second wave of visitors scrambled to check out of their hotels and leave the city. Only the hard-core gamblers remained. Most of the city's 128,000 motel and hotel rooms were now vacant.

North American Aerospace Defense Command

The massive command center was a beehive of activity as hundreds of military aircraft filled the skies. General-aviation airplanes and airliners were again ordered to land at the nearest suitable airport. Sanitizing the airspace was a major priority for NORAD and the FAA.

With the surprising efficiency gained after September 11, there were soon hundreds of fighters, tankers, and surveillance aircraft airborne to protect the U.S. heartland from other deadly terrorist attacks. The tankers were quickly assigned to predetermined refueling tracks at strategic locations around the United States. No one had any idea where or when the next assault would take place. The frontline military aircraft were given whatever priority they needed to be in a position to protect the nation.

Navy E-2C Hawkeyes, air force E-3 AWACS, and U.S. Customs P-3 Orions were pressed into the surveillance role to detect, monitor, and assess anything airborne that might constitute a threat. They also helped to streamline the around-the-clock combat air patrols over major cities. The fighters were constantly cycling off and on the tankers until they returned to their bases to switch crews. Many other fighter aircraft at strategic locations were on ground alert.

Fifteen military transport planes were assigned to fly to various civilian airports to collect stranded airline pilots and return them to their military air guard units. During the interim, many guard pilots were flying double shifts or volunteering for duty at the nearest base. A host of retired military personnel of all ranks began showing up at bases to help in any way possible.

President Macklin was receiving the latest brief on the twin disasters in the Southwest. The U.S. director of homeland security, the head of FEMA, and many other directors of federal and state organizations were swinging into action. Macklin gathered his top advisers in a private conference room at NORAD. The mood was somber.

"Have a seat, gentlemen," the president said. That he was outraged was clearly evident by the set of his jaw. "Pete, you and Les plan for multiple strikes on our primary terrorist targets, military targets first. Suppress enemy air defenses, airfields, tactical aircraft, triple-A sites, SAMs, weapons storage and assembly facilities, and command-and-control centers. Thoroughly neutralize them with cruise missiles first."

Hartwell Prost caught Macklin's attention. "We should use carpet bombing to flatten every terrorist training camp on our list, including the new ones under construction and the ones they're currently rebuilding. The message for the terrorists and the leaders of the countries that support them has to be stunning—paralyzing."

"I agree," the president said. "The next phase needs to include the states' infrastructure—power plants, major dams, bridges, petroleum storage facilities, and main highways and roads. We are literally going to bomb them into submission. No peace talks, no compromises, no settlements, no *bullshit*—period!" The president turned to General Chalmers. "Les, which carrier do we have in the North Arabian Sea?"

"*Stennis,* sir."

"How soon can we have a second carrier in place?"

"Four days, maybe five. *Washington* has left Singapore, probably in the Strait of Malacca as we speak."

"Good. Start hitting them with air force and carrier assets as soon as possible. We'll step it up when the second carrier is on station. We'll use whatever we need to get a handle on this problem. Everything is on the table—theater nukes if we have to go that far."

Approaching Red Lake

Khaliq Farkas remembered seeing the rare float-equipped Caravan circle the Bryce Canyon airport. He was certain it was the two American operatives. They were like a plague, continuing to torment him. While Farkas tried to think of a way to escape his pursuers, he coaxed the bomber to climb at 150 feet per minute. With only one engine operating, he didn't want to get too slow and lose control of the airplane.

Farkas pressed the intercom button to talk to his crewman in the back. "Where's the plane, can you see it?"

"It's directly above and behind us."

"Can you get another shot at it?"

"I can't lean out far enough to take a shot. The wind blast is too strong to aim precisely."

Farkas knew his time was limited. "If they try to pull alongside again, shoot at their engine."

"I'll try my best."

"You *better* do your best," Farkas growled. "These people will kill us."

Knowing Farkas's explosive personality, the crewman remained silent.

They were nearing Red Lake, an isolated dry lake, when Farkas made radio contact with the helicopter pilot waiting to fly them to safety. They quickly decided on a course of action. The helicopter would land next to the B-25 and if the people in the Caravan attempted to interfere, the gunner in the helo would shoot them down. That seemed like a reasonable solution, but Farkas had another plan. The timing had to be right, but he knew the risky idea could work.

"He turned the float into a sieve," Jackie said, and looked into the passenger cabin. Two windows were shattered, and the interior was riddled with rounds from the AK-47. "That definitely eliminates a water landing."

"That's why we have wheels too—options, lots of options."

"If they aren't damaged," she countered.

"Remember the word *optimistic*?"

"That's not *exactly* the word that comes to mind at the moment."

Scott glanced at the bomber. "I believe we need some firepower, take out the guy in the back."

"The MP-5?"

"Yeah, that should do it."

She handed him the compact submachine gun.

"You have the airplane."

"I've got it," she said.

He lowered his seat to make himself more comfortable.

"Don't shoot through the prop," she warned.

"Not a chance."

"Right."

Scott opened the small triangle-shaped vent window in the forward section of the pilot's door window. "If you come up on his right side, say about a forty-five-degree angle, I'll have a clear field of fire if he shows himself."

She smoothly added power.

"Easy, looking good." Scott checked to make sure the weapon was in the full automatic position and then stuck the short muzzle through the vent. He braced the submachine gun against the back of the small window.

Jackie moved into position and stabilized the Caravan close to the bomber. She kept one hand on the yoke and the other on the thrust lever, constantly making small corrections.

After a few seconds, the unwitting man appeared with his

AK-47 braced against his shoulder. Before the terrorist could take aim, Scott squeezed the trigger and the man staggered backward and fell over. He tried to get up, but only managed to get to his hands and knees before he collapsed next to his assault rifle. Jackie maintained position for another minute, but no one else appeared at the opening.

"Okay, let's move back," Scott said as he kept the submachine gun trained on the B-25.

Jackie eased the power. "Nice work, neat and clean."

"I have an idea," Scott said, as he raised his seat and placed the submachine gun on the floor. "I'll take the airplane."

"You have it."

"Now stay with me," Scott said, as he stabilized in position behind the bomber. "I think we can stop him right now."

"You think we can shoot up his other engine?"

"No, not with what we have."

She rolled her eyes. "I'm not liking this idea."

"Jackie, these floats—"

"No, we're *not* going to stick a float into the prop arc, not even going to think about it: absolutely *stupid.*"

"You have to trust me on this," he said, moving forward over the bomber. "This will work. We have to force him down."

She caught his eye. "This is over-the-edge *stupidity.*"

"That's why I thought of it. Keep the faith."

Still leery, she stared at him for a moment. "Have you noticed the twin tails, the two obstacles sticking up at the back of the fuselage?"

Scott concentrated on positioning the Caravan directly over the bomber. "Our plane is about twelve to fourteen feet shorter. The Blues fly with three feet of wing overlap."

"We're *not* the Blue Angels," she protested.

"Relax."

Jackie cinched her seat restraints. "If we live through this, I'm going to find some professional help—for *you.*"

"Hey, we've flown tighter formation than this."

"Not with someone who has a fervent desire to kill us."

Scott had to move fast before Farkas figured out what was

happening. When the forward third of the huge left float was even with the B-25's propeller arc, he eased the Caravan down a few feet. *Steady, keep it coming.* Another foot down, and only inches separated the float and the spinning propeller. Scott deftly eased the yoke forward. *I'm close, hang on, be smooth.*

The violent collision produced an anguishing combination of screeching and thudding. Metal flew in every direction, puncturing the fuselage of the bomber and the belly of the Caravan.

At the moment of contact, Scott snatched the yoke back. The moderately damaged Caravan shot straight up, rolling away from the bomber. After clearing the B-25, Scott rolled the airplane wings level and moved toward the mortally wounded warbird.

"Farkas has a B-25 glider," Scott exclaimed, as the bomber's smoking left engine came to an abrupt stop. Three twenty-inch stubs protruded from the propeller hub. "He's finished. We got him!" Then Scott looked at Jackie. "Are you okay?" he asked, noting her ashen complexion and wide eyes. "You can start breathing now."

"I need a double martini. It's an emergency."

Scott turned to watch the bomber gradually nose over and begin a steep, spiraling descent. After several revolutions, the doomed B-25 Mitchell crashed two miles from the isolated dry lake. Having taken off with a light load of fuel, when the bomber slammed into terra firma, there was a bright flash from the explosion but little fire.

"Farkas is finished—history!" Jackie was jubilant. She looked at the twisted wreckage. "We finally nailed him!"

"That we did," Scott said, as he banked the Caravan. "His luck finally ran out—maybe ours too."

"The loose nukes?" she asked.

"Yes. But Shayhidi knows where the other four bombs are located."

Flying in a wide circle around the wreckage, Scott was surveying the crash site when two ANG F-16s from the Tacos pulled alongside. The pilots, Major JoEllen Janssen and Captain Ernie Underwood, had seen the bomber crash.

When they were abreast of the Caravan, both were amazed at the damage it had suffered. Along with a multitude of holes in the fuselage, the forward third of the left float was gone. What was left of the big float was open to the wind and had jagged edges all around the opening.

Adjusting the trim due to the yaw caused by the open float, Scott was startled when he glanced out and saw the F-16s. "We have company, and I don't think they're too happy."

"Where were they five minutes ago?" Jackie asked, switching the aircraft radio to 121.5 VHF, the civilian emergency frequency monitored by military aircraft. Jackie recognized the F-16's tail logo. "Tacos, Caravan November Three-Twenty-Three Fox Lima on guard."

The other female voice was surprised. "Three Fox Lima, how do you know the Tacos?"

"I'm a former F-16 pilot, and the guy next to me is a former marine aviator—Harriers."

There was an uneasy pause.

"Did you have a midair with the bomber?" Janssen asked.

"Uh . . . I'm going to toss that question to the attack pilot."

Scott keyed the radio. "Tacos, it's a long story. That was the B-25 that dropped the nuke on Hoover Dam. We saw him do it and chased him down after his right engine failed; couldn't let him get away."

"I see," Major Janssen said, a trace of suspicion in her voice.

With the tension ebbing, Scott and Jackie glanced at each other before Scott keyed the radio. "We would sure like to buy you and your wingman an adult beverage if you'll escort us to Nellis."

"Why Nellis?"

"I need to put this thing down on grass, and Nellis has a nice golf course."

"Okay," Janssen radioed, "let's go to Nellis."

"Roger that." Scott turned to Jackie. "You might want to call Wakefield, explain the houseboat situation."

She favored Scott with a thin smile. "I'd like to give him a piece of my mind."

Nellis Air Force Base, Nevada

Running low on fuel, the Taco F-16s left the plodding Caravan behind and raced toward Nellis AFB. After explaining the unusual situation to the senior tower controller, Major JoEllen Janssen made arrangements to have the crash crew standing by at the golf course. The links were being cleared while the damaged Cessna limped to the base.

Jackie was flying the Cessna while Scott was on the satellite phone with their secretary. He had been unable to reach Hartwell Prost. After many holds for Mary Beth to use another phone to communicate with Hartwell's office, Scott finally signed off. "We're all set."

"How's that?"

"Mary Beth contacted Tim Covington in Prost's office. Another Two-oh-six LongRanger will be available for us, and a *new* float-equipped Caravan will be ordered for the FBO at Boise."

"Sounds good," Jackie said. "First, we have to survive this landing."

He stowed the satellite phone in the back of Jackie's seat and reached for the flight controls. "I'll take it."

"You have it."

Los Angeles Center handed the Caravan to Approach Control, who in turn handed it off to Nellis Tower.

Scott called the tower, completed the landing checklist, and lowered the flaps. "Do you want to move to the back?"

Jackie considered the option. "No, I'm fine."

"Nellis Tower," Scott radioed, "Caravan Three-Two-Three Fox Lima would like to circle the golf course, see what we have."

"Two-Three Fox Lima, that's approved. The course has been cleared, winds are calm, and you're cleared to land on any freeway—fairway."

"Three Fox Lima, appreciate the assistance."

"No problem."

Scott circled the course twice and decided on a long fairway with few hazards. "Cinch up tight."

"I can barely breathe."

He extended his approach and turned on final. Coming in low, slow, and flat, Scott was hanging on the prop at 67 knots. When he knew he had the fairway made, he shut down the engine and turned everything off, including both of the fuel tanks. "Brace yourself."

"I am," she said tight-lipped. "Don't catch a sand trap."

Holding the nose up as the airspeed rapidly dwindled, Scott allowed the Caravan to gently touch down on the aft section of the floats. "Come on, we're almost home."

He held the yoke back, trying to nurse the nose down as slowly as possible. "Easy, nice and smooth."

The next few seconds became a blur as the floats settled on the fairway and began sliding over the grass.

"We're down," Scott said, as he let his breath out.

Without warning, the jagged bottom of the left float dug in like a shovel, violently yawing the Caravan to the left. The right wingtip hit the ground with enough force to bend the outboard section upward two feet. The plane rocked up on its nose, teetered a brief moment, and then smashed down with a resounding thud.

"Let's get out of here," Scott said, as they exited from their respective doors and moved away from the battered plane. They glanced at the idle air force crash trucks.

Jackie gave Scott a stern look. "Well, that was exciting—enough for today."

After gathering their luggage and weapons from the Caravan, Jackie and Scott gladly accepted a ride to Las Vegas. The young first lieutenant, familiar with the Las Vegas strip, recommended a hotel. They thanked him, checked in, dumped their belongings in their suite, and went straight to the cocktail lounge.

The bar was practically empty, as were the streets and casinos. The normally crowded city had become a ghost town. Although the prevailing winds were west to east, a majority of visitors deserted the city in a panic. They were afraid of the fallout from the nuclear bomb dropped at Hoover Dam, thirty-seven miles east-southeast.

Enjoying a refreshingly cold draft beer, Jackie and Scott sat quietly, mesmerized by the live television coverage from Lake Powell and Lake Mead. Scott leaned his elbows on the bar. "Can you believe this is actually happening?"

"After September eleventh, I can believe anything."

They watched as news helicopters showed the devastation at Lake Powell. From the northern tip of the lake at Dirty Devil River to the collapsed Glen Canyon Dam, the scenes were astonishing and surreal. The attack turned a pristine lake into a sea of mud in a matter of hours. The marinas, including Bullfrog, Hall's Crossing, Wahweap, and Dangling Rope, were like scenes from a war movie.

Houseboats, fishing boats, sailboats, and expensive cabin cruisers were resting on the bottom of the muddy lake, some hanging from their mooring lines. Dangling Rope Marina, only accessible by boat before the dam was destroyed, was now indistinguishable from the landmass that surrounded it.

The footage and narration continued as the story moved to the shattered dam and then down the Colorado River to the Grand Canyon. The aerial tour above the canyon rim was graphic enough to know that the disaster was far from over.

The live shots of the debris-strewn Grand Canyon revealed the awesome destruction the powerful flood generated. Nothing in the sea of debris and mud was moving. The stories of the scenes of horror and the unselfish acts of heroism were both heartbreaking and heartwarming.

"Let's go to our room and unwind," Jackie suggested. "We need to get organized and find out about our helicopter."

As they entered their suite, the sat phone rang. Scott answered it and mainly listened while Jackie turned on the television. He walked to the window, stared at the lifeless main strip, and then sadly signed off.

Jackie glanced at Scott. The usual twinkle in his eye was gone. "We can't catch a break—too much to ask."

"What's wrong?"

"That was Tim Covington."

"How'd he get our number?" she asked.

"Mary Beth."

Jackie felt a knot in her stomach. "Out with it."

"There was only one body in the B-25."

She shook her head. "No, there were two people," Jackie insisted. "Farkas and the guy in the back."

"Jackie, there was only *one* body in the wreckage, and it *wasn't* Farkas."

Unblinking, she stared at him for a few seconds. "He bailed out?" she rationalized.

"Must have. No one survives when a plane goes straight in at that speed—impossible to survive."

"I'll be damned," she said, in disbelief. "How did we miss seeing him?"

"Just one of those days," he said, in a tight voice. "Ready for that martini?"

"Yes, let's call room service. Make mine a double."

24

Lake Mead

The sun was low in the afternoon sky when the lake began filling faster than the water pouring through the dam could compensate. Hoover Dam officials, the ones who had been fortunate enough to be off work at the time of the explosion, were afraid to release more water because of the flooding that would occur at the other dams downstream.

They were in a real quandary. No one, including senior officials, was willing to make a decision that would be seen as controversial and possibly deadly. The paralysis of indecision led the officials to a consensus to wait and watch.

To further complicate matters, employees who had the training and experience to open the floodgates did not want to go anywhere near the dam. Authorities could only guess at the amount of radiation in the vicinity.

At 3:57 P.M., the pressure on the dam was beginning to show. A small section in the middle of the structure caved in and fell on top of the power plant. Minutes later, the unthinkable began to happen. Shortly after 4:02 P.M., Hoover Dam began snapping and popping as cracks started appearing in the center and edges of the rim.

Telltale puffs of concrete powder indicated where the greatest amount of damage was occurring. News helicopters reporting from a distance were using their long-range lenses to focus on the fractured dam. It was evident to the flight crews and to their viewers that something unprecedented was about to happen. The biggest dam break in the history of the United States was only moments away.

Eleven minutes later, while Americans watched on television, the dam imploded, crushing the main turbines and the hydroelectric generators. The main structure ripped away from the intake towers and crashed into the Colorado River. One section after another followed. In seconds, the full fury of the overflowing lake was turned loose in a 430-foot wall of water in the narrow canyon.

Jackie and Scott were relaxing in their suite when the breaking news logo flashed on the screen. Spellbound, they watched as a news helicopter followed the gargantuan wave down Glen Canyon, capturing sights that made even desensitized viewers squirm or avert their eyes.

Electrical power was lost in Las Vegas, Phoenix, Tucson, San Diego, Los Angeles, and many other cities and towns in Nevada, Arizona, and California. Scott and Jackie noticed their room's lights flicker when the hotel's generators came on line.

Like the power problem, domestic water needs would be drastically affected in the same areas. Lack of irrigation for over a million acres of rich croplands would wipe out a wide variety of vegetables, wheat, cotton, fruits, sugar beets, alfalfa, hay, and other crops, costing local economies billions of dollars in lost revenue and thousands of lost jobs.

The unimaginable failure of the Hoover Dam would forever change the character of southern California, from the Los Angeles megalopolis down the coast to San Diego. Combined with the terrible tragedy at the port of Long Beach, southern California was going to see tough times for an extended period. State taxes and utility costs, already some of the highest in the country, were about to go through the roof.

Fourteen miles south of the destroyed Hoover Dam was the Willow Beach Harbor Marina, on the Arizona side of the Colorado River. The popular establishment was almost deserted. The nervous manager and a few die-hard fishermen were drinking beer and watching television when the dam collapsed.

Leaving the front door wide open and the cash in the register, they went racing south down Highway 93 as fast as their vehicles could go. The exodus from the entire area was like a huge cattle stampede. Raw panic was being shared by thousands of people along the river as they sought to escape with their lives. Many simply could not comprehend what had just happened, but their survival instincts told them to mash the accelerator and not look back.

The normally smooth and glassy Colorado River was about to undergo a colossal change in the next twenty seconds. The news helicopter was abeam the unstoppable wall of water as it roared over Willow Beach, sweeping away the convenience store, the marine fueling facilities, the launch ramp, and all the rental boats. There was nothing left. In a split second the marina ceased to exist.

Transfixed, Scott and Jackie stared at the television screen. Scott leaned back and stared at the ceiling. "Can you imagine being down there and not knowing it was coming—this mountain of water?"

"Don't even want to *think* about it," Jackie said. "It's mind-numbing."

Scott darted a look at her. "At least the people downriver had a couple of hours of advance notice."

"True," she said with a sigh. "What a blessing for them."

Scott turned his attention back to the screen. "Imagine being asleep in your tent or peacefully floating down the river in your canoe and have this come down out of nowhere."

The helicopter was traveling at a fast pace to stay up with the wall of liquid death. Giving a blow-by-blow description of the carnage, the helicopter pilot was becoming emotional.

"The guy is about to lose it," Scott said.

"Can't blame him."

"This is . . ." Scott was speechless. *God have mercy.*

Absorbed by the magnitude of the man-made disaster, Jackie and Scott remained silent while they thought about the consequences. The ramifications of the terrorist attack were impossible to calculate. One thing was for certain: The terrorist network was going to pay the price.

The fast-moving ultra-powerful wall of water continued to churn straight through hurriedly abandoned campgrounds and recreational facilities, destroying everything in its path. Trees, assorted boats, trailers, camping tents, cars, coolers, fishing gear, picnic tables, deck chairs, sleeping bags, beer and soft drink cans, charcoal stoves, propane tanks, fish, and a host of other items became weapons as they tossed and turned in the maelstrom.

Soon, the water reached Lake Mohave, which was formed by Davis Dam, and then swept through Pyramid Canyon, taking out Davis Dam like a cardboard box. The raging water then pummeled Laughlin, Nevada's third-largest gaming center. Everything bordering the river was tumbled over and over in the tumultuous flood.

Next, the water destroyed bridges near Bullhead City and smashed through the evacuated town as it continued its march toward Needles, California. The community had turned into a virtual ghost town when Hoover Dam collapsed. Once again a bridge was ripped apart and swept downstream with all the other debris. South of Needles, the raging flood weakened the Interstate 40 span until the erosion caused the roadway to collapse in two sections.

Another news helicopter joined the chase when the original pilot had to depart for fuel. The new reporter was a well-known and respected journalist from the Las Vegas area. Her helicopter was soon joined in formation by two more news helicopters.

Scott went to the window and cast his gaze east-southeast where the Hoover Dam had held back Lake Mead for over half a century. Turning to Jackie, he spoke in a quiet voice. "This is like watching the events of September eleventh in slow motion . . . over and over until you're numb."

"I know, but I can't take my eyes away."

The helicopter reporter was reporting that Lake Havasu City was still being evacuated. Some ill-informed members of the community had been under the impression that Davis Dam would protect them.

Late evening was approaching when the millions of tons of water and debris swept through Lake Havasu, which was created by Parker Dam, and continued the sweep down the violently raging river. With twilight fading, the huge torrent of water crushed Parker Dam, knocking out power to many more communities in Arizona and southern California.

The helicopter pilots tried using bright spotlights, but it was difficult to tell what was happening in the swirling, twisting waters. What surprised many viewers were the enormous whirlpools, some large enough to suck under a twenty-five-to-thirty-foot boat.

Jackie sank back on the couch and closed her eyes. "This disaster will take years to overcome."

Scott switched to another cable channel. "Think about the time needed to rebuild the dams and the time to refill the lakes. Where's the water going to come from for the entire southwestern section of the country?"

"Who knows? It's beyond comprehension."

"We don't even know the half of it," he mused. "One thing we *do* know: We have to find Farkas and the four nukes."

They continued to watch the water invasion of Interstate 10 near Blythe, California. The powerful torrents of water finally weakened the highway to the point that chunks of concrete began falling into the raging Colorado River. Minutes later the span sagged a couple of feet and then broke into three pieces.

With the two major southwestern east-west interstates closed, commerce ceased to flow across southern California. Gridlock became the norm as thousands of trucks and other vehicles had to be rerouted north or south. Soon a detour was implemented west of Tucson to swing Interstate 10 traffic to Interstate 8 through Yuma, Arizona.

Next came the destruction of the Imperial Dam and the Laguna Dam. The television coverage of the events was excellent, both from the air and the ground. News crews, most of whom had powerful floodlights trained on the water, had been stationed in advance along the river.

Shortly after the Laguna Dam was destroyed, the flooded river wreaked havoc in Yuma before surging into Mexico. Although Interstate 8 suffered some minor damage, the highway survived the pounding waters. A few of the news helicopters flew into Mexico to follow the flood, but most stopped at the border.

Continuing south, the waters spread out far and wide as the flood surged into San Luis, Guadalupe Victoria, Estacion Coahuila, Riito, and Oviedo Mota, before reaching Mexico's Colorado River delta and finally spilling into the Golfo de California.

NORAD

With the entire southwestern section of the United States now declared a disaster area, President Macklin made the decision to return to the White House. In his judgment, he could not successfully lead the country from the confines of the NORAD complex.

NORAD provided the safety and communication capabilities the commander in chief needed to pursue the war on terror, but it did not look right for the president of the world's only superpower to lead the country from the bowels of a cave. The citizens needed to see him, know he was okay and in good health, and hear his comforting, reassuring words.

Minutes after the Hoover Dam was bombed, Macklin gave the order to send the USS *Nimitz* battle group to the North Arabian Sea to join the USS *Stennis* and the USS *Washington* and their escorts. Now, before he left for the White House, the president ordered the USS *Constellation* battle group to sail into harm's way. En route to her home port of San Diego, California, the aircraft carrier and her support ships reversed course for the North Arabian Sea. The homecoming parties would have to be delayed for now.

The USS *Enterprise* and her battle group assumed station on the East Coast of the United States, while the *Abraham Lincoln* covered the West Coast. Ships from the coast guard were also on station to help defend all waterways and air routes close to the country.

Shortly after 10 P.M. the president and his staff left Cheyenne Mountain for the E-4B waiting at Peterson AFB. Macklin was looking forward to having breakfast with the first lady. Maria Eden-Macklin would be arriving at the White House only minutes after *Marine One* delivered her husband to the residence.

Security was tight at the White House. The marines were out in force, and fighter planes circled the mansion around the clock. Construction crews were working twenty-four hours a day to repair the damage caused by the crash of the hijacked Gulfstream G-IV.

En route to Peterson AFB, Hartwell Prost used a satellite phone to call Scott and Jackie. Farkas had been sighted far from the location of his crashed B-25, and their Bell 206 L4 Long-Ranger would be in Las Vegas early in the morning. The FAA had granted a discreet code for their transponder, and agent Frank Wakefield requested they contact him early in the morning.

Yuma, Arizona

Military search-and-rescue helicopters, including units and squadrons from the marines, coast guard, navy, air force, army, air national guard, and army national guard, were tasked to hunt for stranded survivors along the entire Colorado River. Some of the units were coming from as far away as the East Coast. Other units were volunteering but being held in abeyance until the situation could be assessed in the light of day.

The U.S. Border Patrol was galvanized into an organization to assist in rescue efforts on both sides of the river to Page, Arizona. Like most law enforcement agencies along the river, every available Border Patrol agent had been called to duty. Military transport planes and helicopters from active duty squadrons and air guard squadrons were flying the agents to critical areas along the river.

The FAA authorized civilian law enforcement and EMS helicopters to assist with the efforts to rescue people. The Feds restricted the number of news helicopters and forced the media to use pool reporters along the river.

Everyone was operating under intense emotional and physical stress. The civilian and military helicopter pilots were flying in dangerous conditions, sometimes having to hover under live power lines, close to trees, and near telephone poles and other obstacles.

Most of the victims were along the riverbank. Others, who were far from the river, had believed nothing could happen to them. Unfortunately, hundreds of them paid the ultimate price for underestimating the power of the raging water.

Overhead, a navy E-2C Hawkeye early warning aircraft was helping to coordinate the efforts of helicopters from Naval Air Station North Island, California, helicopters from Marine Corps Air Stations Miramar and Camp Pendleton, California. It was a difficult task, especially at night, to keep the massive rescue operation as safe as possible.

Due to the chaos along the river, innovation become the rule. Certain helicopters flew at higher altitudes than others, using searchlights to look for survivors. Other helicopters went in low to rescue stranded people and take them to medical facilities.

The rescue operation was proceeding at a reasonable pace until half past midnight, when a totally unexpected phenomenon began to occur. Beginning in the flooded areas of Mexico between Yuma, Arizona, and El Centro, California, and spreading southeast toward Sonoyta, Nogales, and Agua Prieta, first hundreds and then thousands of illegal aliens began storming the U.S. border.

In Mexico, the word had spread like a wind-driven forest fire. The destroyed dams and unprecedented flooding presented a chance for a brighter future for many Mexican citizens. If illegal immigrants wanted to enter the United States and not get caught, now was the time to go.

Like the famous California gold rush of 1848, every precious minute lost could be an opportunity gone forever. The encouraging message was being broadcast from radio stations in Tijuana, Matamoros, Nuevo Laredo, Chihuahua, Guadalajara, Mexico City, and Monterrey.

The same theme prevailed throughout Mexico. "Let's take back the land the Americans stole from us! Don't worry, the Americans aren't going to shoot tens of thousands of Mexicans. Take advantage of this once-in-a-lifetime opportunity! Follow your dreams! Go to America and prosper!"

The first large concentration of migrants began crossing the All American Canal in the El Centro border sector near Calexico, California. The irrigation waterway follows the Mexico–U.S. border for eighty-two miles, and 11,000-plus farm workers were hoping to find employment in the Imperial and Coachella valleys.

In their haste to enter the United States, 271 laborers drowned in the water of the canal during the first twenty minutes. Seeing their friends and family members being swept away, hundreds of illegal migrants frantically passed the word down the line at the canal. Most of the second wave of laborers decided to cross the border in the desert.

In certain areas of narrow passage through the border, many hopeful immigrants found themselves in the midst of mob rule. Mexican gangs set up checkpoints where everyone had to pay their last peso to cross the border. There were no exceptions, unless you wanted to trade the favors of your wife or daughters.

The sections of the border patrolled by horse units were particularly active. Inaccessible to standard all-terrain vehicles, the trails were saturated with thousands of fleeing Mexicans. Many wept as they ran across the border and stood on U.S. soil.

Texas was the first state to close their fourteen commercial crossing points into Mexico. El Paso, Pharr, Laredo, Eagle Pass, and Brownsville were overrun by 1:20 A.M. Seven illegal aliens were trampled to death on the Mexican side of the Zaragoza-Ysleta Bridge south of El Paso. Local law enforcement officials and highway patrol officers were called to help secure the crossings. California, New Mexico, and Arizona quickly followed suit.

The Mexican stampede was on, and the numbers were growing by the minute. Desperate people slapped together whatever they could carry and joined the frenzied rush of illegal aliens heading for isolated sections of the border. From battered pickup trucks carrying twenty riders to small caravans of pack mules, these people were willing to overcome any hardship, face any ordeal, to escape their miserable, poverty-ridden lives.

The image of a prosperous and happy life in America was addictive. With the United States dealing with a huge disaster, and 72 percent of the Border Patrol agents detailed to the Colorado River, the timing could not have been better.

The White House

Sixteen antiaircraft missiles were now deployed around the official residence of the president, to provide a multilayered air defense. In addition, hundreds of man-portable heat-seeking Stinger missiles were part of Operation Safe Skies. Supported by tankers, fighter aircraft patrolled Washington, D.C., twenty-four hours a day.

President Cord Macklin, continuously updated on the border situation, went straight from *Marine One* to the Oval Office. Vice President David Timkey was conferring with General Jeremiah Jamison when Macklin, Prost, Adair, and General Chalmers walked in and sat down.

Dave Timkey, a former governor of Tennessee, was Macklin's point man with members of Congress.

"Where do we stand?" the president asked the commander of homeland security.

Shoulders squared, General Jamison responded without looking at his briefing notes. "Mr. President, the invasion is growing by the hour. CIA agents in Tuxtla Gutiérrez, Chiapas, have reported that illegal immigrants are pouring into Mexico from Guatemala, Honduras, and Nicaragua. Some of the immigrants from Colombia and Ecuador have been waiting months to enter Mexico on their way to the United States."

Back from attending a funeral in Norway, Dave Timkey spoke up. "Chiapas is the Mexican state that borders Guatemala. This invasion from Ecuador through Chiapas, a main crossing point for undocumented immigrants entering Mexico, began about two years ago. They've been gathering in Guatemala."

Macklin was bone-tired and his patience was running low. "Dave, I appreciate the information, but I need to know what's happening on *our* border."

Timkey, a tough lawyer-turned-politician, stood his ground. "Sir, ninety to one hundred thousand immigrants from south of Mexico have passed through Chiapas in the last three months to enter the United States illegally. At least one third of them are militant Muslims who openly encourage a jihad against America. Along with the Mexicans, they are now coming across *our* border."

Jamison had one more piece of bad news. "In the last fourteen months, an estimated twenty-five thousand Ecuadorians have traveled on the high seas to get to Mexico. Their goal, too, is to enter our country. Mr. President, we have to take control of our border at any cost, and then round up the illegal immigrants."

Macklin slumped in his chair, and then looked at his national security adviser. "Hartwell?"

"General Jamison is right. We have two major dams destroyed, there's a devastating flood, and thousands of Mexicans are storming our southern border. Everyone knows the Mexican army and the federal police have been helping illegal aliens cross the border for years. I say we warn President Cárdenas of dire consequences if he doesn't stop this invasion within twenty-four hours."

"And if he doesn't?" Pete Adair asked.

"That's why we have a military," Prost said, without hesitation. "To protect our borders."

The president leaned on his desk. "I agree with Hartwell. We'll send an urgent message to President Cárdenas, but I want Secretary Austin to speak face-to-face with him before we resort to a military option, if it comes to that."

"Mr. President," Prost said firmly, "I know you're tired, but I recommend that you go on television this morning after the Cabinet meeting. The American people need your reassurance that we can handle the war on terrorism *and* the border problems at the same time."

Macklin sat in quiet contemplation for a moment. "Ten o'clock Eastern, Oval Office."

"Yes, sir."

The president slid his chair back. "Cabinet meeting at eight sharp?"

25

On the Mexican Border

By 3:50 A.M., illegal immigrants were scurrying across the border from Baja California to Brownsville, Texas. In many isolated areas, trampled fences, toppled signposts, abandoned personal items, and trails of litter presented clear evidence of the frantic rush to seize the opportunities waiting in the United States.

Along the West Texas border, Mexican citizens were crossing the Rio Grande in anything and everything that would float. One enterprising group even had a small Zodiac inflatable boat with an electric trolling motor. In addition to the cramped adults in the ten-foot boat, they were towing another inflatable brimming with children.

For the militant Muslims who had been waiting in Mexico and in South America for their opportunity to infiltrate the United States, the time had finally arrived. The Syrian, Saudi Arabian, and Iranian regimes, along with factions still in Iraq, secretly backed the "volunteers for martyrdom." Leadership elites in this oil-rich region planned to destabilize the United States and wear out Washington's resolve to have a presence in the Middle East.

Deming, New Mexico

The first signs of daylight were only minutes away when a section of F-16s assigned to the 20th Fighter Wing at Shaw AFB, South Carolina, were vectored to intercept an unknown bogey southwest of Deming. The low-flying fast-moving aircraft had crossed the border from Mexico and was westbound eighteen miles inside U.S. territory.

The young pilot of the Fuerza Aérea Mexicana F-5E Tiger II was disoriented and thought he was still inside his homeland. Captain Jorge de Jesús Martino had crossed the boot heel of New Mexico and was about to enter Arizona. Aside from being lost, his other problems included faulty radios and a missing wingman. His friend had aborted his takeoff because of a malfunction in one of his engines.

Martino's air defense fighter was armed with two 20mm guns and two AIM-9 Sidewinder air-to-air missiles. With the sudden flurry of activity along the border, and growing tensions between Mexico City and Washington, the Santa Lucía–based fighter squadron had been ordered to patrol the border.

When the F-16s intercepted the F-5E, Martino was startled. He could not believe the Americans were violating Mexican airspace. He maintained his current speed and course while the F-16 flight leader tried several times to communicate via radio.

After talking with a mission specialist in the E-3B AWACS, Major Tanner Axelson tried to use visual signals. No luck.

Captain Martino believed the Americans were trying to force him north into U.S. airspace. That could create an international incident and end his air force career.

As the seconds ticked away, he rapidly considered his options. With two armed F-16s flying next to him, they were limited at best. Martino, a cocky pilot with a "grandstander" reputation, made a hasty decision to roll the dice. He would make a move to lure the Americans farther into Mexico. Surely they would not chance shooting him down over his own country.

He yanked the throttles back and snapped into a knife-edge turn to the left. He was heading directly south when he slammed into the tail of the American flight leader.

Both aircraft exploded in a bright reddish-yellow fireball, instantly killing the pilots. The remains of the fighters impacted the ground twenty miles west of the New Mexico–Arizona border.

The horrified wingman, Captain Daryl Milner, contacted the AWACS and then circled the crash sites until he was forced to depart because of low fuel. He dreaded having to face his friend's bride of one month.

Las Vegas

Unable to stop watching the news updates about the tragic disasters and the border incursions, Jackie and Scott had slept a little over two hours when they awakened at 6:10 A.M. The horrible, sickening assault on America had not been a bad dream.

The destroyed dams, the unthinkable flood, and the border disasters were real. The numbers of the dead or injured far exceeded that of September eleventh. Many Americans were numb with shock; many more were deeply angry. There was talk about using nuclear weapons on the foreign countries that sponsored terrorists.

The same conversations that were taking place at local cafés in Wyoming and Montana were taking place in Manhattan and in the District of Columbia. Many of those who had previously been concerned about the treatment and rights of combatant detainees at Guantanamo Bay were now strangely silent.

The issue of using national guard troops to act in a law enforcement role on the border was still unsettled. Some politicians suggested the guardsmen simply detain the illegal immigrants for law enforcement officers, but that idea had set off alarms throughout the Beltway.

At this early hour, accusations of racial profiling were being made on Capitol Hill and the morning television shows. The politicians were tight-faced and in full screech.

Although the American markets were temporarily closed, tempers were flaring on the network's financial news programs. The bears were predicting a global collapse of financial markets. The bulls in the debate were calling for calm, rational thinking.

The search for victims was still under way and growing as more military and civilian helicopters arrived in the Southwest. Makeshift morgues were hastily set up in every square foot of available warehouse space, and most were filled to capacity. Those who survived the flood were either injured or had been exposed to low levels of radiation.

With the horrible events in the southwestern states, many Americans were just beginning to focus on the sudden tension between the United States and Mexico. The uncontained breach of the U.S.–Mexico border had resulted in President Macklin's activating army national guard units from Texas, New Mexico, California, and Nevada. They would augment Arizona's national guard, already on duty, to assist border inspectors and reduce traffic delays at key crossings.

The national guard's new orders were clear: Police the entire border and detain all illegal aliens trying to enter the United States. *Clamp down hard* was the word, straight from the White House.

President Macklin had made his position on terrorism crystal clear in a televised press conference following his Cabinet meeting.

"I *will not* sit idly by while additional thousands of Americans are murdered in the next terrorist attack. You can forget the term *politically correct* and all other such catchphrases. On my watch, common sense and a strong backbone will carry the day."

He paused, staring straight into the camera. "If you're a Middle Eastern male between the ages of sixteen and sixty, you're going to be profiled, no doubt about it. If you're Latin American or Hispanic, plan on being stopped and checked for proper documentation."

His features softened and his voice sounded upbeat. "On the other hand, if you're a white-haired eighty-seven-year-old widow from Topeka, Kansas, you're not likely to be questioned."

He went on to explain to the assembled reporters that after the disastrous midair collision between the air force F-16 and the Mexican F-5, a second strong warning had been sent to the government of Mexico and its military leaders. Any foreign aircraft straying into U.S. airspace would be intercepted and forced to land. If the pilot did not comply, the plane or helicopter would be shot down without hesitation.

Macklin explained that Secretary of State Bradley Austin was en route from Saudi Arabia to Mexico City for an emergency meeting with his counterpart and the Mexican president.

Scott finished shaving and splashed water on his face. "Things are getting warm down south."

Jackie closed her luggage. "I'd say President Macklin is running short on patience this morning."

"You can hear it in his voice." Scott paused and looked at Jackie. "This would be a good time to correct some of the problems we have with Mexico."

She started to grin and then realized he was not joking. "What do you mean, problems with Mexico?"

He dried his face. "Corruption in the Ejército Mexicano—the Mexican army—and the culture of corruption in the police forces. The drug lords will spend more than seven hundred million dollars this year in bribes and payoffs to Mafia-like Mexican generals and police officials."

"Yeah, it's a mess down there," she said, reaching for Scott's luggage. "The system is corrupt from the top down, always has been."

"It's time for our government to help correct the problem, for the sake of both our countries." He turned off the television. "Let's head for the airport—lots to do."

"Yeah, we'll tackle the Mexican problem on our lunch break."

Geneva, Switzerland

Since his return to Geneva, Saeed Shayhidi had not communicated with anyone. He would keep the Americans guessing. He had spent the entire time planning how he was going to regain control of his far-reaching conglomerate. The betrayal by Ahmed Musashi and Hafiz al-Yamani had been devastating, but the resolve that arose from the gut-wrenching incident was rock solid.

Everything was planned down to the most minute of details, including a new identity. Recovering from cosmetic surgery, Saeed Shayhidi was pleased with the early results. His face had been transformed without having to do radical surgery. With his hair now salt and pepper, he looked twenty years older. An inexpensive ill-fitting suit and scuffed shoes added another dimension to the makeover. Topping it off was a scruffy pale-yellow straw hat and tiny round wire-rim glasses without any correction.

No one but his one lifelong friend knew Shayhidi was in Geneva. Essam Afzal, a rich and powerful man in his own right, was using his contacts to construct an entirely new identity for Shayhidi. Bank accounts, credit cards—everything a person needs to start over—were in the works.

Afzal walked into the enormous game room, followed by his butler, who fixed them drinks at the bar. The butler, a heavyset Syrian, brought the libations to the sunken seating area and then left the room.

Also educated in the Ivy League, Essam Afzal raised his glass in a toast. "Well, you certainly won't be recognizable."

Shayhidi smiled and sipped his scotch and soda. "That's *good* because I want to see the looks on Ahmed Musashi and Hafiz al-Yamani just before I kill them."

Afzal frowned and stroked his neatly trimmed beard. "That's too risky. Have someone else take care of them."

"Don't worry, I have a solid plan."

"If you're caught, the authorities will discover who you are. That, my friend, is not good. Trust me."

Shayhidi took a deep gulp from his drink. "The authorities can always be bought."

"That may be true, but the people who have worked hard to arrange a new identity for you can't be bought."

A deep frown formed on Shayhidi's forehead. "What are you talking about? What are you suggesting?" he asked, tossing back the last of his scotch and soda.

"Their business, their cover, and their reputation will be harmed if you don't play by their rules. Simply stated, they will kill you, and it will take a long time for you to die, my friend."

Shayhidi discounted the threat, ever certain of his ability to get away with anything he planned. "Good advice. I'll keep it in mind."

Mexico

After landing at Benito Juárez International Airport, U.S. Secretary of State Brad Austin's gleaming C-32A, a Boeing 757, was directed to the VIP parking area at the Presidential Transport Squadron. After deplaning, Secretary Austin and his entourage were greeted with assumed earnestness by Antonio Ferreira, the Mexican secretary of foreign affairs, a foppish, impertinent fellow with an oily shine to his coal-black hair.

A band played several tunes, including the U.S. National Anthem. Young girls formed a line and handed Austin homemade gifts, cards, and an assortment of colorful flowers.

After the pleasant ceremony, Austin and Ferreira entered a shiny limousine and headed for Los Pinos, Mexico's stately presidential palace.

Las Vegas

Waiting for their helicopter to arrive, Jackie called Frank Wakefield while Scott remained in the taxi with their luggage and their weapons. Because of the tight security at airports since the dams were destroyed, he would take their weapons out of town to a rendezvous point. They had agreed on a location where Jackie could land and pick him up.

With special permission provided by the FAA, and a select transponder code, the Bell 206L-4 LongRanger landed a few minutes early. Other than military aircraft, law enforcement helicopters, and news helicopters, few aircraft were flying.

The ferry pilot was an FAA employee who was curious about his special flight. Jackie was pleasant to him but apologized for the rush. She thanked the pilot and walked outside to signal Scott. Minutes later, she took off and headed for their rendezvous with Scott. He would be waiting south of the point where Interstate 15 merges with Highway 93.

After she landed, Scott stowed their luggage and their weapons in the back of the LongRanger. Airborne, they headed southeast.

Adjusting his Bose headset, Scott keyed the intercom. "What did Wakefield have to offer?"

"An update on Farkas."

"Any idea where he might be?"

"Let me start from the beginning," she said, glancing at the helicopters near the Colorado River. "A group of people cavorting around in dune buggies saw the bomber crash and also saw Farkas descending in a parachute. They went to see if they could help, but a helicopter landed nearby and Farkas limped to the helo and climbed in."

"Limped?"

"That's right." Jackie paused to answer the controller's question. "He apparently injured himself when he bailed out—which I still can't believe we didn't see—or when he hit the ground."

"Which way did they go?"

She checked her notes. "Southeast—a blue-and-white MD 500 with wheels."

"How do they know what kind of helicopter it was?"

"There was a helo pilot in the dune buggy group. He swore it was an MD 500. Said he had about two hundred hours in that particular model—unimpeachable eyewitness."

"Anything else?"

"Yes, here's the strange part. According to Wakefield, an MD 500 matching the description of the one at the B-25 crash site landed in Flagstaff to refuel. From the time it left the dune buggy group to the time it arrived in Flagstaff matches the flying speed of the MD 500. The manager of the FBO became suspicious when he saw the two men, both definitely of Middle Eastern origin. He contacted the FBI immediately after the helo took off."

"Did he see anyone limping?"

"No." Jackie paused to switch radio frequencies. "Only one person got out of the helicopter, and he didn't match Farkas's description. The guy was bigger than Farkas and had thin hair—paid in cash, too."

"Still headed southeast?"

"South, straight south."

"Any advice from Wakefield?"

"Yes, but let me finish. About forty to fifty minutes after the MD 500 left Flagstaff, two hikers in the Coconino National Forest saw a blue-and-white helicopter land near an abandoned fishing lodge. After the pilot shut down the engine, two Middle Eastern men got out—one was limping—and went inside the old lodge. The hikers were concerned and contacted the FBI field office in Phoenix. The special agent there called Wakefield."

"Is Wakefield sending his people up?"

"Yes, as soon as they can get everyone to a staging area." Jackie paused to check in with the next controller. "He wants us to reconnoiter the area and see if we can locate the helo."

"Sounds good. You want to top off in Flagstaff?"

"Yes. Then I want to go high and be as unobtrusive as possible."

USS *Stennis*

Steaming in the North Arabian Sea south of Gwadar, Pakistan, the carrier *Stennis*'s battle group and Carrier Air Wing Nine (CVW-9) were preparing to launch a night strike. The targets were in western Afghanistan and remote sections of Iran and Syria. Many of the aircraft actually delivering weapons were armed with the SLAM-ER (standoff land-attack-missile expanded response) or the JSOW bomb (joint standoff weapon). Others would be armed with Saddam Specials, 2,000-pound GPS-guided JDAMs (joint-direct attack munitions).

Tomahawk cruise missiles from surface combatants and submarines were already raining destruction on various terrorist training camps and weapons storage and assembly facilities. Two of the missiles had leveled a headquarters building near the Iranian–Afghanistan border, killing a senior al-Qaeda leader, his son, and six members of his staff.

In eastern Iran a terrorist stronghold was about to be targeted by a B-2 stealth bomber. U.S. intelligence sources were convinced a meeting of senior al-Qaeda operatives was about to begin at the underground bunker.

The bomber was carrying the new ten-ton Massive Ordnance Air Blast Weapon. The 21,500-pound, all-weather, precision-guided bomb, known as the mother of all bombs, would collapse the fortification. The detonation from the Big One would be heard and felt for thirty-two miles in every direction.

The U.S. Navy carrier air wing would be supplemented by a contingent of British Royal Air Force GR-1 Tornados and U.S. Air Force F-15E Strike Eagles based at Kuwait's Al Jaber Air Base. USAF tankers based in Qatar, along with British RAF VC-10 tankers, would provide fuel for the large strike package.

The launch would be a "pinkie" evolution in the fading rays of daylight. Although many of America's so-called allies continued to deny the United States permission to use their runways and facilities, the floating sovereignty of *Stennis* provided a perfect platform from which to fight terrorism.

Partway through the launch cycle, a marine corps F/A-18 from the Black Knights of VMFA-314 taxied to the starboard bow catapult. The pilot, Captain Kurt Turcotte, gave a thumbs-up to the crewman holding the weight board. The yellow-shirt signaled the pilot to keep his feet off the brakes and gave the tension signal. After the Hornet was in tension, the director signaled Turcotte to retract the launch bar.

The pilot completed a thorough wipeout, carefully checking the flight controls, and then concentrated on his engine instruments. Satisfied that everything was normal, Turcotte checked to make sure he wasn't sitting on the ejection handle. Feeling on top of the world, he snapped a sharp salute and grabbed the towel rack to brace for the exhilarating E-Ticket ride down the short cat track.

A few seconds later the catapult fired and Turcotte staged both blowers—full afterburner. Expecting to accelerate from 0 to 157 miles per hour in a hair over two seconds, he had a sudden sinking feeling when the aircraft stopped accelerating halfway down the track. It felt as if he had plowed through a tar pit. *The launch bar broke or came out!*

Suffering from denial, Turcotte still had full afterburner on both engines, knowing the plane was not going fast enough to fly. *The brakes aren't going to stop me!*

The denial was still there, causing a moment of paralysis. *This can't be happening!*

The end of the flight deck was almost under him when the synapse finally shot through his mind. *I'm outa here!*

Seeing only dark oily-looking water, Turcotte aggressively pulled the loud handle and ejected from the doomed aircraft. He tumbled a couple of times before the parachute began to open, followed by a severe snap that stunned him. He caught a glimpse of his Hornet as it crashed into the water and blew apart with a muffled explosion.

Still hanging from his chute, a moment of panic seized him when he saw the huge carrier coming straight at him. *The ship is going to hit me while I'm still in the air!*

He reached for his Koch fittings and frantically detached himself from the parachute, dropping fifteen feet into the dark water. A strong swimmer, his arms and legs were already in motion when he splashed down. Quickly surfacing, Captain Turcotte swam as hard and fast as he could to clear his parachute and the starboard side of the ship. *I'm going to make it—don't stop—go-go-go!*

The ship was almost past him when he stopped swimming and looked up. There was a sizable crowd staring at him from the starboard side of the flight deck. *Thank God, I'm still alive.*

He was suddenly tumbled again, over and over, in the turbulence of the wake from the powerful ship. It was like going through the wash cycle in a gigantic 400-horsepower Maytag.

Mere seconds later the plane guard, an H-60 Seahawk search-and-rescue helicopter, was overhead and creating a mini-hurricane around Turcotte. He turned away from the helicopter rotor wash and waited for the swimmer to reach him.

"Are you okay, sir?" the petty officer asked.

"Yeah, I think so."

"Okay, we'll have you aboard in just a few seconds."

The swimmer quickly clamped the D-ring attached to Turcotte's torso harness to the hoist. A minute later the drenched but thankful pilot was safely aboard the Seahawk. After the swimmer had been retrieved, the helicopter turned to chase the carrier. *Stennis* was still launching aircraft at a rapid rate. Captain Turcotte was going to be sitting out this strike with some medicinal brandy in hand.

26

Coconino National Forest

Jackie and Scott had flown over Lake Mary and then searched the area around Mormon Lake. There was no trace of a helicopter. They continued flying in a southeasterly direction and reconnoitered Blue Ridge Reservoir and the surrounding area.

"I don't see anything," Scott said, as he lowered the binoculars.

Jackie gently banked the helicopter. "Let's go back and check the shoreline of the second lake."

"Okay."

Making a gradual descent, Jackie leveled off 100 feet over the lake and slowed the LongRanger. They flew along the shoreline looking for any sign of a lodge or a helicopter.

"Very few people around here," Jackie observed.

"That's why Farkas may be here, stay camouflaged, and let the hunt go in other directions."

They continued the search for another fifteen minutes.

Jackie descended to fifty feet and glanced at Scott. "We need a better description of the area where the hikers saw the—"

"There!" Scott exclaimed. "Two o'clock, a lodge in the trees."

"I see it—got it."

Jackie maneuvered the helicopter into a hover over the grassy shoreline thirty yards from the once-exotic retreat. She turned the LongRanger 90 degrees and gently set it down. "I don't see any activity or any sign of a helo. Want to continue down the lake?"

"Let me check the place, and then we'll move on."

"Be careful."

Scott nodded as he touched his 9mm Sig Sauer and reached for an H&K compact submachine gun. He started to get out of the helicopter and then hesitated, reaching for three full magazines for the H&K. "Back in a minute."

He climbed out of the helicopter and cautiously approached the deteriorated lodge. The oversized front door was gone. Behind the main dwelling were two small log cabins, one of which was partially collapsed. Scott walked up three steps to the uneven front porch and entered the dusty main building. He checked the rooms on the ground floor and then went up the short flight of stairs to the loft. A ragged sleeping bag and three crushed beer cans were the only items on the dirty floor.

Turning to go back down the stairs, Scott felt a cold chill when he saw crushed cigarette butts on the downstairs floor. He descended for a closer look. They were freshly smoked cigarettes, the same U.S. brand Khaliq Farkas was known to use.

With his adrenaline surging, Scott began scrutinizing the rooms again and noticed something strange in one of the bedrooms. In the corner of the inside wall he noticed a lot of footprints on the dusty floor. *Why would there be dust tracks from the door to an empty corner? Why all the activity in the corner and no tracks across the room?*

He paused a moment and then started walking toward the corner. Five feet from the junction of the walls, he stepped on the end of a floorboard and almost tripped when the other end of the board popped up. He gently pushed on his end of the board and grabbed the other end when it came up. Setting the loose board aside, Scott looked into the space beneath the floor and froze. *Oh, shit—the nukes!*

At the same instant he heard something familiar. He paused a moment and then rushed into the living/dining area and turned toward the open front door. Jackie could not hear the sound because of the noise her helicopter was making.

Scott had started to bolt for the LongRanger when a blue-and-white MD 500 rose above the nearby trees.

Khaliq Farkas aimed an M79 grenade launcher at the Bell 206 and fired. The 40mm grenade exploded under the tail rotor blades, twisting and snapping the tail rotor drive.

Opening fire with the submachine gun, Scott did not count on getting many hits from his position. He fired a few more rounds while Jackie scrambled out of the helicopter. With the engine winding down, she raced for the lodge with the other submachine gun.

Farkas smiled, amused by his strange turn of luck. He finally had the two Americans trapped like rodents in a cage. He and his pilot, Omar Musa, had planned to lie low in the abandoned lodge for a few days. Too many people had seen their helicopter at the B-25 crash site and at the Flagstaff airport.

Farkas had correctly figured that the description of their helicopter would have been sent to all the airports and law enforcement agencies in this part of the country. With a stash of food and water from the helicopter, they planned to wait a day or two and then fly at night to a rendezvous point with their driver. Farkas was going to move the four nuclear bombs to a safer location, but first he had to dispose of the two Americans.

Farkas and Musa had rolled their light MD 500 under a thick stand of trees and then carefully camouflaged it with branches from other trees. They had not counted on the hikers who watched them land and get out of the helicopter.

When the LongRanger suddenly came into view, Farkas and Musa were caught completely off guard. Fearing the FBI might be rapidly closing in, they grabbed all of their gear and raced out the back door. After an eighty-yard run, they yanked the camouflage off the MD 500, tossed their belongings inside, moved the helicopter out into the small clearing, fired up the engine, and immediately took off.

Although he only had three more grenades, Farkas was stubbornly determined to use the grenade launcher to eliminate his tormentors. The opportunity was too inviting to throw away. He knew it might take some time, and it would attract a lot of attention, but now was the moment he had been waiting for.

On the other hand, Omar Musa wanted to get as far away as possible in short order. However, like many others in the terrorist community, Musa knew it was a bad idea to question Khaliq Farkas.

"Are you okay?" Scott asked, as Jackie flew through the open door.

"Yeah, but the helo's trashed—we're stranded."

"The nukes are here, all four of them!"

Jackie's eyes opened wide. "Oh, my God."

"The sat phone?" Scott asked.

"I was in a bit of a hurry—left it in the helo," she said with a shrug. "But I have my cell phone."

"Now might be a good time to use it."

Jackie called Frank Wakefield and explained their dire situation. She gave him their basic position and quickly signed off.

Scott heard the MD 500 slowly circling over the lodge, waiting for the right opening to hit them again. When the helicopter slowed with the left side to the lodge, Scott looked at Jackie. "They're going to try putting a grenade through the front door. Follow me!"

They went into the large kitchen, putting a wall between them and the open front door.

"Get on the floor," he said as a grenade blasted through the wide door and hit the stone fireplace. It shattered the fireplace and blew out the only window remaining in the main room.

Jackie looked up. "I think they're directly over us."

"Into the bathroom!"

They slammed the door as another grenade ripped through the decaying roof and exploded in the main room. It blew debris out the door and the windows.

Scott opened the door a few inches. "I don't know how many grenades he has, but they're going to take us out if we don't do something."

"Let's get some rounds into them, do some damage."

He listened to the sound of the turbine helicopter. "They're directly behind the lodge; I'm going out the front. Let me know which side they're coming up."

"Okay."

Rushing out the front door, Scott's instincts told him to go to his right. Helicopter pilots traditionally fly from the right seat and Farkas would be on the left side of the MD 500. He heard the helicopter approaching. "Which side?" he yelled.

"I can't tell!"

Counting off three seconds, Scott jumped off the porch and started firing head-on at the helicopter.

Omar Musa yanked the cyclic back and the MD 500 shot skyward. Some of the rounds had penetrated the cockpit, slightly wounding Musa. Most of Scott's rounds had hit the belly and tail.

He quickly ducked inside the shattered lodge. "Well, they know we're still here. Don't know how long they can stand off and pick away at us."

Jackie took a deep breath, and then exhaled. "We know they

topped off their fuel in Flagstaff, so I'd say at least another hour or more."

He looked out the window as the MD 500 passed over the lodge. "They'll eventually get us if we don't do something. We have to split up."

"Are you nuts?"

"No."

Another grenade blew a large hole in the roof over the kitchen, stunning Jackie. Ears ringing and bleeding from a minor wound on her neck, she stumbled into the main room. "They're going to level this place if we don't do something."

"After they make another pass," Scott said, as he darted a look at the circling helicopter, "you take off out the back door and run straight into the woods. Once you're twenty yards inside the tree line, cut a right forty-five and go about a hundred yards in and camouflage yourself."

"What are you going to do?"

"I'm going out the front door and run ninety degrees to your right. Do the same thing you do, but to the left. You stay in your position, and I'll come to you."

"Okay," she said, and wiped the layer of dust off her face. "How are you on clips?"

"I have two full ones left."

The MD 500 had climbed and picked up speed. It circled the lodge three times and then made a high-speed pass low over the roof. Farkas raked the structure with an AK-47 while the helicopter climbed steeply and turned back toward the lodge.

"Let's hit it!" Scott said.

Farkas and Musa saw the Americans run into the dense woods and disappear. They swore and Musa slowed the MD 500. He was against flying directly over the area where the two people had vanished, but Farkas insisted on it.

They discussed the idea of landing so Farkas could get out and track the Americans with Musa orbiting over them. They collectively ruled out the idea as too risky. When Farkas finally caught a glimpse of Jackie, he ordered Musa to turn around.

"Slow down," Farkas ordered.

"It isn't safe."

"I *said* slow down."

Musa quietly complied. *We're going to be a perfect target.*

"Get lower."

When the tail of the helicopter was finally pointing at him, Scott fired three short bursts and continued running toward Jackie. He did not want them to see any muzzle flashes and give away his position. When he had another chance, Scott fired two short bursts. It was difficult shooting up through the trees, but at least he had some cover. He was confident that he was getting hits, but it seemed to have little if any effect.

After taking a circuitous route, Scott finally found Jackie.

"Any idea how much longer on fuel?" he asked, breathing hard.

"I really don't know, but it can't be much longer or they won't have enough to reach an airport."

Scott schooled himself to breathe slower. "If we can keep them guessing, they either have to depart for fuel or Wakefield's boys will show up."

Jackie was about to speak when a high volume of automatic weapons fire ripped through the trees, spraying rounds in every direction. The indiscriminate rain of fire was unnerving.

Scott grimaced as he shoved another magazine into the submachine gun. "They're going to get us if we don't respond now."

"Let's open fire at the same time," Jackie asserted. "Pour it to them."

"Give me a few seconds to get about thirty, forty yards away." Scott closely watched the helicopter. "Catch 'em in a cross fire."

"Go!"

The MD 500 again picked up speed, but it was flying much lower than it was before. Another long burst from the helicopter shredded everything in a large area twenty feet from Scott. When the weapon went silent, Scott rose and began firing. Jackie commenced firing a split second later. They ceased firing when the MD 500 made a tight climbing turn to reposition for another firing run.

"Concentrate your fire on the engine," Scott yelled above the sound of the helicopter.

Jackie yelled back. "These are designed for close-quarters combat, lucky to hit anything!"

Scott was waiting until the last second when Jackie began firing. He immediately responded, trying to bracket the engine area. Whether he or Jackie had connected, there was an instant effect. Smoke poured from the MD 500 as the pilot tried to make an emergency landing.

As an experienced helicopter pilot, Jackie could discern the attempt to auto-rotate into the small clearing by the lodge. "He's going in hard!"

"Let's go—get on 'em!"

Scott and Jackie were almost to the edge of the tree line when the MD 500 slammed into the ground, shedding its skids and wheels.

"Hit the deck!" Jackie ordered, seeing what was coming.

They sprawled on their bellies and covered their heads.

The helicopter bounced high into the air and rolled as the main rotor blades made contact with the ground. The shattered blades came off and became deadly shrapnel, flung in every direction. The MD 500 hit the ground again and violently tumbled into the tall trees on the other side of the clearing.

With their weapons in hand, Jackie and Scott rose to their feet and raced toward the smoldering wreckage. Approaching the destroyed helicopter, they had their submachine guns pointed at the hulk.

Scott motioned for Jackie to hold her ground while he inspected the totally demolished aircraft. He carefully approached the crushed cockpit and peered inside.

He stepped back and lowered his weapon. "Clear, no threat."

When Jackie viewed the remains of the cockpit, she could see that the pilot had died from head injuries. Khaliq Farkas was still alive but rapidly losing blood. He was semiconscious but able to move his legs and arms. They needed to get him to a hospital if there was going to be any chance for the FBI and the CIA to interrogate him about other terrorist activities.

While Jackie was on the phone requesting a Life Flight helicopter, Scott retrieved all their gear from the damaged Bell LongRanger. He used one of the satellite phones to contact Hartwell Prost and gave him a situation report. Prost was more than pleased; he was elated by the double dose of good news.

Shortly after the medical helicopter landed in the clearing, another helicopter arrived carrying five members of Frank Wakefield's FBI team. They orbited overhead until the medical helicopter left and then landed in their spot.

The agent in charge had been briefed by Wakefield about the two covert operators and the nuclear weapons at the lodge. Questions about Scott and Jackie were off-limits. FBI agents would guard the suitcase nukes until the bombs could be removed.

The bureau's pilot gave Jackie and Scott a lift to Phoenix Sky Harbor International Airport. Once they were airborne, Jackie turned to Scott. "What did Hartwell have to say?"

"It was a brief conversation. He was ecstatic about Farkas and the nukes, but we may have a new assignment."

Jackie's usual pleasant smile and easygoing personality had gone missing. "*New* assignment?"

"I'm just reporting what he said. Prost is sending a military transport to pick us up in Phoenix and fly us to Spokane to retrieve our plane. He wants us to meet him at his home tomorrow night at seven."

"What do you think is up?"

Scott shrugged his shoulders in a noncommittal gesture. "I really don't know, but there was something in his voice."

"Like what: sorrow, elation?"

"Excitement comes to mind, a sense of enthusiasm."

USS *Stennis*

The tension was palpable on the bridge and throughout the ship. The nighttime raid from the North Arabian Sea deep into Afghanistan and Iran was about to enter the next phase. The strike aircraft had refueled en route to their various targets. Tomahawk missiles had damaged or destroyed key military airfield runways, tactical aircraft, enemy air defense sites, and weapons storage and assembly centers. Additional Tomahawks were striking terrorists' headquarters, supply centers, and training camps.

After the carrier aircraft struck their targets, B-2 stealth bombers would continue to pound specific terrorist targets and enemy air defenses. On the heels of the B-2 Spirits, B-1Bs and B-52s would carpet-bomb military and civilian airfields used by terrorists.

The Joint Chiefs had deployed eleven B-1B bombers to the tiny gulf state of Bahrain. A second detachment of B-1B bombers was en route to the island of Diego Garcia, a coral atoll in the Southern Indian Ocean. F-117 Night Hawk stealth tactical strike fighters were being deployed to Kuwait's Al Jaber Air Base. Other fighter planes, bombers, tankers, and support aircraft were landing at the al-Udeid Air Base in Qatar and the new base north of Assab, Eritrea.

The British were sending the Royal Navy aircraft carrior HMS *Ark Royal* to sail in harm's way for their dependable ally. Accompanied by several vessels, the British STOVL (short takeoff, vertical landing) ship would be carrying Harriers and Sea King helicopters. A trio of U.S. carriers, *George Washington, Nimitz,* and *Constellation,* would soon join *Stennis* in the ongoing war on terrorism.

The White House

Sitting at his desk in the Oval Office, President Macklin was relaxed when he directed his attention to the television camera. "My fellow Americans, as a nation we have suffered yet another brutal attack by terrorists. We will continue to assert our leadership in the war on terror. The time for fainthearted diplomacy has long passed. We will systematically destroy every known terrorist compound and the military capability of the host country.

"If the terrorist attacks continue, we will destroy the entire infrastructure of the host countries. We will keep relentless pressure on all our adversaries, al-Qaeda, Hamas, Islamic Jihad, Hezbollah, the PLO, and other terrorist groups. One by one, we will hunt down and bring the terrorist leaders to justice. The nations that are involved in terrorism, and that includes Syria, Iran, Saudi Arabia, Sudan, Lebanon, Algeria, Yemen, and Libya, will pay a tremendous penalty.

"From this day forward, while I'm president of the United States of America, we will answer terrorism with an *assured response.* If you host terrorists, support terrorists, or allow terrorism to thrive by ignoring it, your country will pay the ultimate price." His intense stare was locked on the camera. "You have my word."

Macklin allowed a moment for the message to be absorbed. *Prepare them for the skirmish with Mexico.*

"As we fight the terrorists overseas, we cannot overlook our battle against terrorism right here on our soil. Secretary of State Austin has conferred with the president of Mexico, and President Cárdenas has agreed to do everything in his power to regain control of the situation in his country.

"We applaud President Cárdenas for his efforts in this matter, but we must also look at our responsibility, both short-term and in the future. My administration is going to take immediate steps to seal our border with Mexico. We will restore law and order on the border.

"As a good neighbor to Mexico, it is incumbent on us to work with President Cárdenas to help improve their economy and living conditions. However, we *will not tolerate* blatant disregard for our sovereignty by drug smugglers, illegal aliens, or a corrupt military.

"These are grave and uncertain times for Americans everywhere. As your president, I ask only three things of you: patience, resolve, and your prayers. We must have the patience and resolve to see this war on terrorism to its conclusion. With your prayers, we will prevail."

The president paused. "Thank you, and God Bless America, the world's beacon of freedom."

* * *

After the president addressed the nation, Maria Eden-Macklin joined him for a few moments alone in the family living quarters. Ten years younger than her husband, the intelligent and gracious first lady was a retired foreign correspondent. Well traveled during her childhood, Maria had lived with her father in British East Africa until she returned to the United States to attend Wellesley College.

On a daily basis, Cord Macklin relied on Maria's instincts and her ability to bring common sense to bear on any situation. His White House aides were excellent, but Maria never hesitated to tell him the unvarnished truth. She was his sounding board. She offered rock-solid logic and opinions that made sense. There was never any willy-nilly Beltway-speak or elite-speak, parsing of words, or any of the other silliness of Washington politics.

She took a seat across from Macklin and folded her ankles together. "Good speech."

"Thanks." Macklin rubbed his temples.

Maria searched his face, worried because the strain and pressure were taking a toll. "I'm curious about one thing."

"What's that?"

"How do you plan to seal the southern border?"

He picked up his glass of fresh iced tea. "Les Chalmers has active-duty army units converging on the border as we speak. Marines from Camp Pendleton and Camp Lejeune are en route. The Border Patrol agents along the Colorado River have been recalled, and we have continuous aerial surveillance along the length of the border."

"Cord," she began slowly, "isn't it true, historically, that relations between the military establishments of the United States and Mexico have been contentious at best?"

"That's true: different cultures and values. Why do you ask?"

"What if something goes wrong? How far are you willing to go to take control of the border?"

"Whatever it takes. It has to be done."

"Are you prepared to engage the Mexican military in combat?"

"Absolutely."

"Over border incursions?" she challenged.

"Border incursions, drug smuggling, and two murdered Border Patrol agents in the past week."

Maria dropped her gaze. "It seems to me that we're setting ourselves up to look like the world's biggest bully. Isn't there going to be an image problem?"

"Perhaps, but here's the bottom line. We can't have a trail of illegal immigrants, some of whom are dedicated terrorists, pouring into our country through Mexico from as far away as South America and the Middle East. Many of these people want to destroy this country. It simply isn't going to happen as long as I'm in office."

The far-reaching implications unfurled in his mind. "It may mean a fence system from the Pacific Ocean to the Gulf of Mexico and triple the number of Border Patrol agents, heavily armed with assault weapons. It may mean our military will have a permanent role to play along the border. Makes sense; our military are guarding borders and protecting the sovereignty of other nations around the world. What about here on our own soil where we're wide open to terrorism and other criminal activity?"

She looked at him thoughtfully. "What about the Posse Comitatus Act? Isn't that going to cause some heartburn?"

"Not really. We can use military vehicles, aircraft, technical aid, surveillance, facilities, intelligence, et cetera, as long as there is no direct participation of Department of Defense personnel in law enforcement."

Maria reached for her tea. "How is this going to affect our war on terrorism overseas?"

"I don't expect it to have much of an effect. The latest strike on the terrorists is under way, and we're going to keep the heat turned up."

"I just hope we aren't taking on too many tasks at the same time."

Macklin gave her a reassuring smile. "We're not overextended. Everything is going to be fine."

27

Kashan, Iran

A quarter moon highlighted the clear star-studded night. On the ground around Kashan, Iran, the temperature was still 104 degrees Fahrenheit at 2:10 A.M. Everything was quiet, eerily quiet.

Lieutenant Commander Landon "Bulldog" Gaines, the flight leader of two F/A-18Cs from the VFA-147 Argonauts, was 30,000 feet over Iran and twenty-nine miles west of the Kashan command and control center when his SLAM-ER missile put the center and its unsuspecting crew out of business. Within seconds, other explosions began shattering the quiet morning in western Afghanistan and in central and eastern Iran. The coalition reveille was in progress.

Stennis-based navy and marine corps aviators were dropping 2,000-pound GPS-guided JDAMs on radar-guided antiaircraft (AAA) gun sites and surface-to-air (SAM) missile sites. Other aircraft were dropping bombs on selected terrorist camps and storage areas.

Many of the aircraft selected to hit the same target separated and then converged minutes later, dropping their ordnance at forty-five-second intervals. The timing was critical because their external aircraft lights were off. No one on the ground could track them without radar.

If the bad guys turned on their radar to "paint" the strike aircraft, the coalition pilots could use the AGM-88 HARM (High-speed Anti-Radiation Missile) to home in on the hostile radar and destroy the enemy complex.

Maintaining radio silence, Gaines and his wingman turned toward their secondary target, a particularly nasty antiaircraft gun site southwest of Tehran. The Iranian gunners had been alerted and were at their posts.

Gaines was caught off guard by the intensity and variety of the ordnance being thrown up. He had seen tracers on many missions but not in the quantity that was flowing skyward in steady streams.

Long chains of red, yellow, and white tracers were spraying back and forth like a loose fire hose. Large red balls like Roman candles were tracking the two Hornets. The web of tracers appeared to be a solid, impenetrable mass.

Gaines was breathing rapidly. *We're going to go through a wall of lead.* He forced himself to breathe slowly and concentrate on the mission at hand. *This is a bag of worms.*

Warning equipment lit up, indicating enemy radar was "illuminating" their planes. Bright tracer rounds flashed under the Hornets, followed by tracers ripping past the canopies. Going ballistic, two SAMs broke through the F/A-18's altitude, peaked, and then fell back to earth. They exploded near the SAM site, causing one death and a lot of collateral damage.

Gaines couldn't resist a smile. *The Iranian missile troops must be cursing the Russians.*

Seconds before he was going to drop his ordnance, Gaines felt a solid thump that violently shook the airplane. Warning lights and warning sounds immediately filled the cramped cockpit. Bitchin' Betty (the F/A-18 Hornet voice-alert system) announced in a calm voice, "Engine right. Engine right."

"Bulldog One, you're on fire!" Lieutenant Warren Smith radioed. "Fire—fire coming from your starboard engine!"

"Yeah—got big problems—let's check out! Comin' hard port, going for the deck! Switch backup."

They switched to a different radio frequency.

"Two's up," Smith said.

Click-click.

Gaines pulled into a left bank, nose low turn and rolled wings level when he was headed toward the North Arabian Sea. He began the steps to shut down the right engine and realized it was not running. Gaines eased the right throttle back and went through the engine fire checklist. *I'm on government time now, single-engine night carrier landing with battle damage and extremely high temperatures at the boat—can't beat it.*

He keyed his radio and inched the left throttle forward. "Dog Two—still hangin' with me?"

"Like a frog on a lily pad."

"Any fire?" Gaines asked.

"Uh-huh, small residual fire."

"How about checking me out."

"Okay, hold it steady."

Smith eased down and moved under his flight leader. Up close he could see the damage. "It looks like . . . uh, you must have taken a hundred-millimeter through the starboard engine. It's totally destroyed."

"Anything else?"

"Your tailhook is skewed to the left, and you have several punctures in the belly. Your hydraulics okay?"

"Holding so far."

"You're not going to have enough fuel to make the carrier."

"Then again," Gaines said, checking his fuel, "I'm only using one engine. Might make it if I'm lucky."

"It's a toss-up."

Click-click.

Gaines leveled off at 500 feet above the ground and 330 knots. The exceedingly high temperatures caused a large reduction in available engine thrust. As the Hornet decelerated, he had to use military power on the port engine to maintain level flight. Gaines checked to make sure the speed brakes were retracted. The coast was only four minutes away.

"You have some fluid streaming along the belly, but I can't see the color in the dark. Probably hydraulic fluid."

"Copy—thanks."

Smith clicked his radio twice and moved down and eased to the side of the flight leader.

Gaines was about to relax for a few moments when Betty screamed, "Pull up! Pull up!"

He yanked the stick back and shot skyward, barely clearing

the rapidly rising terrain. The bright flash in his canopy mirrors made him flinch. *Oh, God . . . no.*

Gaines's heart was in his throat when he keyed his radio. "Bulldog Two, Dog One, you copy?"

Silence.

"Dog Two—copy?"

Nothing.

Filled with anguish and guilt, Gaines banked into a steep right turn and orbited the crash site. He was praying for a miracle, hoping Smith had ejected in the last split second. It was too dark to see a parachute. At their low altitude, if his friend had ejected, he would already be on the ground. The residual fire was spread over 200 yards along the rising slope.

Continuing to circle the crash, Gaines waited for Smith to use his handheld emergency radio. The veteran aviator knew in his heart that Smith was not going to come up on guard frequency. Emotionally exhausted, Gaines finally radioed the air force AWACS to report his wingman down. He gave the mission specialist the coordinates and requested a search-and-rescue helicopter be sent to the site.

Gaines rolled out on course to the carrier and radioed the AWACS when he was "feet wet." Unable to make it to the ship without tanking, Gaines was given a vector to a nearby KC-135. After taking on 5,000 pounds of fuel, Gaines turned toward Mom. His mind was not on flying. He wasn't ready to tell anyone that he had killed his trusting wingman. That confession would have to be made in private to his commanding officer.

Climbing in minimum afterburner to 23,000 feet, he reduced the power to military and replayed the accident over and over. After a few minutes, he noticed the rapidly dwindling fuel supply. *That liquid streaming off the fuselage has to be fuel.*

Gaines checked in with the carrier and told them about the battle damage and the low fuel state. He was given priority to land. He jettisoned all of his external stores and both drop tanks. In order to conserve fuel, he waited as long as he could and then began an idle descent to 1,500 feet.

Nearing the carrier, he lowered the tailhook, dropped the

landing gear, and set the flaps to one half for the single-engine approach. In order to maintain his altitude and airspeed, Gaines had to use minimum burner. He waited until he was abeam the landing signal officer (LSO) platform.

"Four Oh Two's abeam, gear."

Click-click.

"Four Oh Two's single engine."

Click-click.

Afraid of flaming out, Gaines flew a tight approach. Rolling out on final, he had the meatball centered and an amber donut on the angle-of-attack (AOA). *Good start—keep it going.*

"Four Oh Two, Hornet ball, single engine, one-point-oh." *Approximately seven, maybe eight minutes of fuel—don't blow the landing.*

The LSO was shocked. "Say fuel again."

"One-point-zero."

"Roger ball." *This could be interesting.*

Gaines was drifting below the optimum glide slope, and he could see it on the ball. *Come on . . . ease some power on—save it.* He inched the left throttle forward to mid-range burner, but the heat-induced loss of thrust was too much for the damaged aircraft. Slow and dirty with the landing gear hanging in the breeze made it even more difficult.

Glancing at the flames from the afterburner, the LSO was becoming more concerned. "Power, a little more power."

Gaines was still settling as he approached the carrier's round-down. *I can't take it around—have to make a play for the deck!*

"Power-power-*power*!"

Gaines tapped the blower and shoved in a bootful of left rudder. The application of full afterburner was too late to salvage the approach. It also ignited the streaming jet fuel, leaving a sixty-foot trail of jagged orange-white flames. The onlookers standing on Vulture's Row were about to view a spectacular sight.

The LSO pickled the bright red wave-off lights. *"Wave off, wave off! Power, power, power!"*

With full left rudder, the jet was yawing to the right and still settling with maximum afterburner. Panicked, Gaines pulled the nose up and ejected. The blazing Hornet staggered across the flight deck while dancing on its tail and then plowed into a parked F/A-18 on the aft starboard elevator. Both aircraft exploded and went over the side of the flight deck.

Gaines landed safely in the water and was picked up by the plane-guard helicopter. After a trip to sick bay to have a thorough medical checkup, Lieutenant Commander Gaines took a quick shower and donned a fresh khaki uniform.

He waited until the other strike aircraft landed safely and then met in private with his squadron CO. With the entire story on the line, Gaines calmly removed his coveted wings of gold and placed them on the CO's desk. His promising career as a TopGun-trained navy fighter pilot was over. Gaines spent the rest of the night writing a letter to the family of Lieutenant Warren Smith.

Sasabe, Arizona

U.S. Army and U.S. Marine Corps units had been deploying along the southwestern border for a number of hours. Other army forces—from Fort Campbell, Kentucky; Fort Bragg, North Carolina; Fort Benning, Georgia; and Fort Stewart, Georgia—were deploying along the southeastern border. National Guard units were also patrolling the border at selected sites.

While the arriving military units spread out to their assigned grid coordinates, more cargo and troop transports were landing at airports along the border. The military personnel were to stop the illegal immigrants at the border and detain any who managed to cross over.

Marine corps helicopters and Harriers patrolled the western end of the dividing line at El Paso, Texas, while mostly army helicopter gunships and air force close-air-support (CAS) A-10 Warthogs patrolled the eastern section of the border. Working with forward air controllers (FACs) on the ground and in the air, the CAS assets could be over any hot spot in a matter of minutes.

Orbiting thirty-five miles south of Alpine, Texas, an AWACS E-3C Sentry watched as four Mexican F-5E Tiger II fighter aircraft lifted off from the Santa Lucia air base and headed northwest in sections flying a mile apart. Located in the southern central state of Mexico, Santa Lucia is the Mexican Air Force's principal base.

Other Mexican aircraft had been taking off, including armed Pilatus PC-7 turboprop counterinsurgency planes from Zapopan air base, La Paz air base, and the Santa Gertrudis air base. Bell 205, 206, and 212 armed counterinsurgency helicopters had been repositioned to Santa Gertrudis air base to patrol the border.

At the urgent request of the Mexican Army, three of the Mexican Navy's armed MD Combat Explorer helicopters were approaching the U.S. border near Sasabe in the late afternoon. Equipped with 70mm rocket pods and GAU .50-caliber Gatling guns, six of the helicopters had been purchased ostensibly to halt the flow of illegal drugs being smuggled on the high seas. The twin-engine gunships were able to outrun the drug traffickers and had the firepower to disable speeding drug boats.

The pilots of a marine corps UH-1N Twin Huey helicopter operating as a FAC spotted the three combat-capable helicopters. They confirmed the MD Combat Explorers had Mexican markings and radioed the fast movers orbiting high above.

The two Harriers from the famous Black Sheep of VMA-214 were six minutes away from the Mexican helicopters. The MD Combat Explorers turned eastbound to parallel the border on the Mexican side. Unable to keep pace with the much faster MDs, the Twin Huey was falling farther behind.

Inexplicably, one of the three MDs sharply banked to the left and flew north into the United States. The marine pilots were surprised and radioed the Harrier flight leader.

"Smoke Zero Two, Festus Ten."

"Smoke."

"You aren't going to believe this. One of our pigeons just turned north, headed for Tucson at about two hundred feet."

"Duffy," the Harrier flight leader radioed to his wingman, "I'll take the intruder. Stick with the others."

"Copy."

"Smoke—Festus. Another one turned north at two hundred feet."

"Okay, Duffy, you take the second idiot."

"Roger that."

"Festus, can you keep the other one in sight?"

"Maybe for a couple of minutes; they have at least thirty-five to forty knots on us."

"Okay, hang in."

"Copy."

Major Duncan Ventana, the Harrier flight leader, paused. He radioed the air force AWACS and requested to speak with the mission crew commander. He had the AWACS commander confirm that he was cleared to shoot down the intruder if the pilot did not comply with radio or hand signals. The confirmation was immediate and firm.

The Harrier flight leader keyed his radio. "Duffy, let's go jump them."

"This should be a good cocktail story."

Click-click.

They stayed in loose formation while the AWACS gave them vectors toward the first MD Explorer. Ventana detached his wingman and began slowing when he had a visual on the Mexican helicopter. The MD was west of Carmen, Arizona, twelve miles inside the U.S.–Mexican border.

Closing on the right side of the MD, Ventana continued to slow the Harrier to make eye contact with the pilot and copilot. The Mexicans made an abrupt, steep turn to the left and continued turning for 270 degrees, rolling level heading for Interstate 19.

Ventana swung around in trail. *Very clever, pal—can't risk shooting anything toward the interstate. Well, let's see about this.* He made a pass low and directly over the MD with the Harrier's nozzle deflected. The 23,000-plus pounds of extremely hot vectored-thrust had an upsetting effect on the small helicopter. The shaken pilots had their hands full for a few seconds before they regained control.

The MD Combat Explorer pirouetted toward the Harrier and

opened fire with the .50-caliber Gatling guns. Ventana's Harrier was taking hits as he accelerated away and armed his weapons. *Sonofabitch!*

"Duffy—Smoke. This guy just took a shot at me, hit me in the wing! Watch your step!"

"Yeah, this clown is all over the sky."

"Smoke—Festus Ten. The third helo just turned north."

"Okay, help is on the way," Ventana radioed, as he allowed the Harrier to accelerate to 300 knots. Keeping his eyes on the MD, he tightened his turn. The helicopter was flying southbound at 200 feet directly over the interstate.

"Smoke," Ventana's wingman radioed, "he fired—just fired at me!"

"Put him on the ground."

"Roger."

Ventana waited until there was an opening in the flow of interstate traffic and timed his pass perfectly. He opened fire with his 25mm cannon and chewed the MD Combat Explorer to shreds. It crashed in a ball of flames on the side of the interstate. Traffic from both directions began slowing when the drivers saw the flames and rising cloud of black smoke.

Without hesitating, Ventana went after the third helicopter.

"Smoke—Duffy. This guy is down."

"Roger, you're at my one o'clock low, passin' close to your port side. Don't do anything until you have me in sight."

"Copy."

Ventana searched the sky for a few seconds. "Duffy, do you have a visual on the third helo?"

"Negative."

Easing the power back, Ventana was frustrated. He could not locate the intruder. A call to the AWACS confirmed that they had lost contact with the gunship about two miles behind Ventana's Harrier. He snapped the airplane into a high-G turn. *I'll be damned.*

Sure enough, he found the helicopter, minus the crew, on the ground near a road leading to the Tubac Presidio State Historical Park. The terrified pilots, who had witnessed their CO and another squadron helicopter being blown out of the sky, had departed for another zip code.

The White House

President Cord Macklin was meeting in the Oval Office with his closest advisers about the next step to take with Mexico. The expanded war on terrorism was progressing reasonably well in the Middle East. Senior military officers were managing the well-planned campaign in a very professional manner.

Hartwell Prost caught Macklin's eye. "Mr. President, the events of the last few days underscore the need to limit the Mexican military before more people are killed on both sides."

Uncharacteristically, Pete Adair interrupted brusquely. "We can't just barge in and start a war with Mexico."

"I'm not talking about starting a war," Prost shot back acrimoniously. "I'm talking about preventing a war, *saving lives,* saving Mexican lives by not allowing them to get into a position to *be* killed."

Nerves were drawn tight and tempers were beginning to flare.

SecDef started to respond. "I'm telling you—"

"Pete, let him finish," the president said firmly.

Prost glanced at Chalmers, Austin, and Dave Timkey. "The Mexicans only have a handful of obsolete F-5 fighters—nine or ten, I believe. They're all stationed at Santa Lucia, the primary air base. If we bomb the runways and taxiways, they can't get off the ground to put themselves in harm's way."

"What if their planes have been dispersed to other air bases?" Timkey asked, in his soft southern drawl.

"We can get aerial and space-based reconnaissance fairly quickly." Prost turned to the president. "They also have sixty or seventy armed PC-7 counterinsurgency (COIN) aircraft, high performance turboprops. They operate the COIN aircraft primarily from the La Paz, Santa Gertrudis, and Zapopan air bases.

"If we destroy those runways and taxiways, and the runways closest to our border where they could operate, they're out of business. We don't have to worry about the air bases in southern Mexico because they don't have any refueling aircraft. No tankers, limited range, end of the Mexican Air Force problem."

Brad Austin voiced his thoughts. "Your idea has merit, but I would like to contact President Cárdenas and tell him why we think it's necessary to ground his air force. As we know, he has little if any control over the military, and he seems anxious to work with us."

All eyes turned to Macklin. "I can't disagree; anything to keep this situation under control. Let's see if we can contact President Cárdenas. Brad, you and I will talk with him."

"Yes, sir."

"Gentlemen," the president said, "let's take a break."

President Macklin was pleased with the conversation he and Austin had with President Cárdenas. When Prost, Timkey, and Chalmers returned to the Oval Office, Macklin turned to Austin. "Brad, would you bring everyone up to date?"

"Happy to, sir. Although President Cárdenas was initially surprised by our suggestion, he endorsed what we feel is in the best interest of both countries. His primary concern is for the safety of everyone involved, not the infrastructure." A hint of a smile crossed Austin's face. "He even went so far as to tell President Macklin that he wouldn't mind if we put the fear of God in his generals and admirals. He's a man reaching for a life ring, and he trusts our integrity and professionalism. He knows we aren't a threat to him or to Mexico's sovereignty."

Macklin picked up. "The most striking aspect of the conversation is a renewed feeling of trust. The more time we invest with President Cárdenas, the more visibility at the top, the stronger his base will become. Bottom line, he has given us his blessing on whatever we have to do to protect our country and our citizens."

Austin cleared his throat. "President Cárdenas requested a conference as soon as possible. We're in the process of making arrangements to meet him, hopefully in the next day or two."

The president placed his hands on his desk. "It's time to call it a day. Let's plan on meeting here tomorrow at eight A.M."

28

Crete, Greece

Elounda Beach Hotel & Villas is a distinguished luxury resort situated on the island of Crete between two quaint bays. The spectacular vacation destination caters to the rich and famous who demand the ultimate in tactile pleasure. Services include limousines, helicopters, yachts for hire, and Learjet charters.

Saeed Shayhidi reclined on an oversized settee in the roomy Imperial Penthouse Suite at the hotel complex. The suite included a well-equipped gym, personal fitness trainer, private pool, movie theater, masseuse, butler, pianist, and chef.

Ignoring the sage advice of his longtime friend Essam Afzal, Shayhidi contemplated his meticulous planning thus far. His new executive assistant, Gamaa al-Harith, had booked the suite under a fictitious name and paid cash. At this level of opulence, no one asked questions about cash or required a credit card on file.

Al-Harith had also leased a small out-of-the-way villa near Elounda Beach under an assumed name, again paying cash for the thirty-day rental. Gamaa al-Harith had no idea about Shayhidi's background or his real identity. But the important-sounding title, along with the generous salary and benefits Shayhidi offered, were better than anything he had ever dreamed of.

Shayhidi had instructed al-Harith to invite two business associates to an early morning breakfast meeting. When the guests arrived, al-Harith was to explain that for privacy and security reasons the venue had been changed to a villa near the hotel complex.

Shayhidi left his suite and took a limousine to the remote villa while al-Harith waited for the businessmen. When the men arrived at the lavish suite, they were disappointed that the prosperous shipping mogul was not waiting for them. Al-Harith apologized effusively for the inconvenience and explained that Mr. Oscar Palante was anxious to introduce them to his other important guests at the villa.

They went to the villa in transportation supplied by the hotel. When they arrived at the restored home, the well-dressed men stepped out of the van and approached the villa. As he was instructed to do, Gamaa al-Harith ushered the businessmen inside. Then, as ordered, he returned to the hotel suite and waited for further instructions.

Saeed Shayhidi was sitting in a large leather wingback chair in the corner of the living room. He smiled to himself when he heard the front door open and then gently close.

After the men walked down the short hallway, they found their host sitting alone. They were surprised and slightly uncomfortable, but they tried to conceal their feelings. A large divan sat in the middle of the room, facing the host.

The strange man made no effort to get to his feet or even offer a handshake to his guests. He was not anything like they had expected. Inexpensive rumpled suit, scuffed black work shoes, a strange-looking straw hat, and a large pillow on his lap. The shipping tycoon was certainly eccentric.

"Have a seat," Shayhidi said, in a deep, scratchy voice. "We have a lot to discuss and not much time to *kill*."

Both men eyed him curiously.

The shorter one spoke first. "Aren't we supposed to be having breakfast? Where's everyone else?"

Shayhidi spoke again in the deep voice. "I don't think you're going to have much of an appetite. Sit down."

There was some concern in their eyes, but they sat down on the wide divan. Both men felt a growing sense of uneasiness.

"How's my business doing?" Shayhidi asked, in his normal voice.

There was a moment of stunned silence, followed by an eye-bugging, mind-numbing panic.

"Speak up. How's my business coming along?"

Their shocked looks turned to raw fear as Ahmed Musashi and Hafiz al-Yamani tried to come to grips with reality. This funny-looking man was, in fact, Saeed Shayhidi, completely transformed.

Smelling the visceral fear, Musashi started to get up and flee.

Shayhidi pulled his 9mm handgun from under the pillow and fired at Musashi's feet, hoping to scare him. Shayhidi's aim was off slightly, and Musashi howled in pain as he collapsed on the divan. The round had gone through the center of his left foot. He took off his shoe awkwardly and held his bleeding foot.

"Excellent idea," Shayhidi said, with a smile of pleasure. "Take off your shoes, both of you."

Musashi quickly removed his other shoe while al-Yamani, trembling with fear, did the same.

Al-Yamani twitched and squirmed when Shayhidi waved the weapon toward him. Then he closed his eyes and balled his fists.

"Getting jumpy, weasel?"

Shaking uncontrollably, al-Yamani was afraid to say anything. Ahmed Musashi had categorically told him that Saeed Shayhidi was finished. The Americans had him under tight wraps and he would not be seen again. He would be in prison or, more likely, he would be put to death. Saeed Shayhidi would never rise again. He would never have any power again.

Al-Yamani gritted his teeth and mumbled.

"Speak up, *weasel*!"

"He—Ahmed—told me you were dead."

Writhing in searing pain, Musashi snapped his head around. "I never told you that, you lying little—"

Boom! Shayhidi shot al-Yamani in the right foot. He fell on the floor and began holding his foot and rocking back and forth, groaning the entire time. "I didn't do anything wrong," he said, in a small, whimpering voice. "I just did what I was told."

Shayhidi gave al-Yamani a cold, hard stare. "Look at me, you two-faced weasel. Look at me or I'll shoot you again!"

Almost in tears, his lips trembling, al-Yamani looked up.

Shayhidi flashed a menacing grin. "One more lie from either one of you and you'll die a slow, agonizing death."

Recalling the anger, the absolute rage he had felt when he left Phnom Penh, Shayhidi lowered his voice and looked at Hafiz al-Yamani. "Why didn't you return my calls and answer my e-mail?"

There was a long silence.

"Answer me or I'll blow your other foot off!"

"Musashi told me he was taking control of the company and he would make me an executive. I had to be faithful to him."

Shayhidi turned to Musashi. "The two of you have *really* been faithful to me after everything I've done for you, haven't you?"

Neither man said a word.

Musashi was reeling in pain when Shayhidi fired a shot into the divan between his thighs. He leaped straight back and then fell sideways.

"So, let me understand this. I was a liability to my company—*your* company, that is—and you had to terminate me."

Musashi was bathed in salty sweat. It trickled down his forehead and into his eyes, stinging them and causing tears to well.

Shayhidi continued in a relaxed voice. "As I recall, you said I was an international fugitive—with no money, no access to money, and no access to power—and no lawyer would associate with the likes of me. My life was over and you were going to make sure it stayed that way." He pointed the 9mm at Musashi's face. "Is that about right? Speak up, or I'll finish you off right now!"

"I was only trying to help you and save your business for you after things calmed down. I swear that's the truth—"

Boom! Shayhidi shot Musashi's other foot, prompting a spasm of howling and cursing.

Shayhidi smiled and then chuckled. "You lying piece of trash, trying to play in the big time. But the game is over—finished, done, the end—and so are you."

Hafiz al-Yamani began sobbing. "I was going to keep you informed about everything—I didn't trust what was going—"

Boom! The other foot was useless. Al-Yamani screamed at the top of his lungs, but it made no difference. No one outside the villa could hear anything.

Shayhidi leaned forward with his elbows on his knees and smiled with pleasure. "Do you want to be buried alive or the alternative?"

"Don't do this," Musashi begged. "I'll do anything you ask, anything you want. Just give me a chance to prove myself."

"I don't want you to do anything. I have lots of things to do today. Which will it be? Dead or alive?"

Shayhidi waited a few seconds and smiled. "Time's up. I've made the decision for you. Buried alive is a better way for two *real* weasels to leave this planet. Next question: Who goes first?"

A few more seconds passed. "Time's up. Al-Yamani goes first so the person who tried to steal my company can watch."

"Please don't do this," Musashi said, bathed in sweat and blood. "You've taught me a real lesson."

"What about you, weasel?"

Hafiz al-Yamani could barely talk above a whisper. "I feel the same way. I'll never doubt you again, I promise."

Shayhidi belly-laughed. "I had you two going, didn't I? You'll think twice next time before you screw me, right?"

Al-Yamani closed his eyes and sobbed. "Right—that's right."

"Yes," Ahmed Musashi said, with a deep sigh of relief. "We just want to be faithful to you and to the business—your business."

"Well, that's certainly the right attitude. Glad to know you're back on board," Shayhidi said, and then shot both men in the head.

He put them in body bags and placed them in the deep graves he had hired a transient to dig. Next, he broke the divan into pieces and picked up the bloodstained throw rugs. He buried them on top of Musashi and al-Yamani and then covered their graves with dirt and tree limbs. Shayhidi went inside, washed his face and hands, rested for a few minutes, and then called the hotel. The duty limousine would pick him up in ten minutes.

Gulf of Mexico

The stars were still shining brightly when the attack submarine USS *Scranton* rose from the depths to fire four Tomahawk cruise missiles. The weapons were aimed at the Military Air Base Number 1, located at Santa Lucia in the state of Mexico. Flying low at a speed of 550 miles per hour, the Tomahawks would take thirty-four minutes to reach their target. After the first missile exploded, the others would arrive in staggered order.

Seventy-three miles south of *Scranton,* the attack submarine USS *Newport News* was in the process of launching four Tomahawks at Colonia Federal Air Base southwest of Santa Lucia. The flight time to the target would be thirty-six minutes. Both submarines returned to deeper water to await further orders.

In the Pacific Ocean off Baja California Sur, the attack submarine USS *Jefferson City* was in the process of launching four Tomahawks at the Zapopan Air Base. The flight time would be nineteen minutes.

Off the coast of Baja California Norte, the USS *Columbus* launched two Tomahawks at the El Ciprés Air Base and then launched two missiles at the La Paz Air Base. They also launched two missiles at the Guaymas Air Base. One of the Guaymas missiles malfunctioned as it cleared the surface, forcing the submarine crew to fire another Tomahawk.

A total of six U.S. Navy surface combatants, equally divided between the Pacific Ocean and the Gulf of Mexico, launched a dozen Tomahawks at the Santa Gertrudis Air Base, the Culiacán Air Base, the Chihuahua Air Base, the Monterrey Air Base, the Hermosillo Air Base, and the Tampico facility.

The results were good, but not 90 percent as hoped. Space-based assets indicated that Santa Lucia was now inoperable and two of the F-5E Tigers had been destroyed. Another F-5E had been heavily damaged, and the runway was going to need extensive repairs. Most of the other airfields were badly damaged, but a few could still support air operations.

Owning the skies over Mexico, U.S. Air Force and Navy fighter/attack aircraft quickly finished the assault on the air bases with a variety of precision-guided missiles and bombs. The Tijuana Air Base was spared, barring any attempt to use it for hostile purposes.

Unfortunately, eight people were killed during the attacks and another twenty-one were injured, three seriously. The news flashed around the world in a matter of minutes, causing rioting and anti-American demonstrations in many distant countries and cities. The entire country of Mexico was in a state of calamity, and angry mobs were taking to the streets to burn American flags. U.S. citizens were fleeing the country as quickly as possible.

The U.S. embassy in Mexico City was a central target of the irate crowds. Located on Avenida de la Reforma, the fortresslike building was locked down and barricaded. Two companies of U.S. Marines had been flown to Mexico City prior to the destruction of the Mexican air bases. They reinforced the embassy security team already in place.

San Diego, California

The Mexican Navy Knox-class frigate *Mariano Abasolo* (the former USS *Marvin Shields*) was five miles due west of Point Loma. A sister ship, the *Ignacio Allende* (the former USS *Stein*) was 300 yards abeam the starboard side of *Mariano Abasolo.* Ballast Point in the Point Loma area was home to the San Diego Naval Submarine Base. The San Diego Naval Station and the North Island Naval Air Station were in close proximity. On high alert, the military facilities presented a target-rich environment.

In response to the early morning attacks on the air bases, an angry Mexican admiral had ordered the ship's captains to stand off the southern California coast. The frigates were cruising slowly as they continued on a northerly heading.

Attempting to appear calm, both captains were nervously waiting for an order to return to the safety of the closest Mexican port. Considering what the Americans had recently been through, and their amazing performance in the liberation of Iraq, the captains had no doubt the U.S. Navy would sink them at the slightest provocation.

Three F-14 Tomcats from the USS *Abraham Lincoln* battle group had been launched to encourage the men-of-war to return to Mexican waters peacefully. One of the VF-31 fighters was clean (no bombs, no missiles, and no external fuel tanks) but had a full complement of rounds for its M61 20mm multibarrel cannon. The other pair of F-14s carried four 2,000-pound bombs, two Sidewinder missiles, 20mm cannon rounds, and two 280-gallon external fuel tanks.

An E-2C Hawkeye vectored the Tomcats to the Mexican frigates while a marine corps KC-130 Hercules orbited overhead to provide fuel for the fighters.

Lieutenant Commander Dallas "Hollywood" Houghland was leading the trio in the clean 'Cat, the fastest fighter in the U.S. Navy. Flying at an altitude of 21,000 feet over the Mexican ships, Houghland initiated the first phase of their mission.

"Hollywood One is outbound," he radioed to his two wingmen.

"Two."

"Three."

They would remain in a high holding pattern to await the results of the first flight demonstration.

Heading straight south, the clean F-14 began a gradual descent that rapidly increased. At ten miles from the frigates, Houghland initiated a steep 180-degree turn passing 11,000 feet. Rolling wings level, he was heading toward the fantails of the frigates.

He engaged max blower, and the dual afterburners quickly accelerated the Tomcat as it descended through 6,000 feet. The wings were swept back, making the F-14 look like an overgrown lawn dart as it dropped from the sky like a slab of iron.

Leveling the fighter at seventy feet above the calm ocean,

Houghland was approaching the ships at the speed of heat. He had disappeared from the Mexicans' air-search radar.

Dash Two keyed his radio. "Look at Hollywood scoot. Leaving a rooster tail!"

"Those boys are gonna have the shakes," Dash Three replied. "Hope no one's shaving."

Transonic vapor was flickering off the aircraft seconds before it shattered the sound barrier 150 yards behind the frigates. Houghland passed between the two ships and snapped the Tomcat's nose skyward.

The teeth-rattling sonic boom rocked the Mexican frigates. Sailors spilled their coffee; others dropped to their knees. Most thought they had been hit with a bomb.

Both frigates went to general quarters, but it was clearly not in their best interests to engage the Americans. They increased their speed and continued north on a straight course.

Houghland had one more option to try. Then, if the ships refused to turn back, he would contact the Hawkeye. A mission systems operator would check with the admiral on the carrier and then give the F-14 flight leader his orders. Houghland reversed course, approaching the frigates head on.

"Hollywood's in hot," he radioed, as he armed his cannon.

Flying slower than the speed of sound, Houghland waited until he was a few hundred yards from the ships. He squeezed the trigger and laid down a curtain of cannon shells between the frigates.

Houghland was climbing in afterburner when Dash Two keyed his radio. "Message sent—message received."

"Say again," Houghland said.

"They're coming about, heading home."

Hollywood turned his head to look at the ships. "Good decision."

The two F-14s closed on Houghland's Tomcat.

"It's time for a lunch break," Two radioed.

"You have the lead," Houghland calmly radioed back. "Take us home to Mother."

The White House

After a fairly short conversation, Cord Macklin placed the phone receiver in its cradle and turned to Hartwell Prost and Brad Austin. "President Cárdenas is fully supportive of our grounding his air force. He seemed relieved that only eight people were killed. He understands the gravity of the situation and the urgency of our conference. He'll meet with us early tomorrow afternoon in Corpus Christi."

"Did he balk about restructuring his military?" Prost asked.

"He knew what I was alluding to, but he glossed over it."

Austin looked up. "I have a sense he will give the idea serious consideration. He left me with the impression that he would truly like to reform his country, but he can only tinker at the edges as long as the corrupt generals are calling the shots. The military star chamber has to be toppled. The culture in the military and in law enforcement has to be changed before anything meaningful can happen."

Macklin glanced at his watch. "We'll deal with that after we have the border problem completely under control. I know this is a spur-of-the-moment trip, but I want to keep a lid on it. We'll use a smaller aircraft and a skeleton crew—no press and no leaks."

"We'll take care of it," Austin said.

The USS *Nimitz* battle group was close enough to the North Arabian Sea to launch long-range strikes on a number of targets. Terrorist facilities were being pounded in five countries, and more targets were being added to the list.

The sailors and marines aboard the ships in the *Nimitz, Washington,* and *Stennis* battle groups had little time for recreation or breaking news stories. When they were not working eighteen-hour shifts or eating three or four meals a day, they were sleeping.

The relatively few who had time to pay attention to world events knew about the howls and shrieks emanating from the United Nations headquarters in New York, the International Criminal Court, European capitals, Human Rights Watch, and

U.S. "allies" and diplomats from every nook and cranny on the planet. The U.S.–led war on terrorism was being characterized as "unilateral imperialism."

Predictably, after the bombing of the Mexican Air Force bases, the die-hard media had gone into hollow-eyed shock before responding in unity. There was a massive eruption of name-calling and derisive attacks directed squarely at President Macklin and his administration.

Mexico City

The primary units of the Mexican Army consisted of a handful of brigades based around the Federal District that encompasses the Mexico City area. Along with independent regiments and infantry battalions, the brigades were preparing to move north to the U.S.–Mexico border.

The destruction of the air bases had set off a frenzy of anger within the military. Chaos reigned for the first few hours until senior officers began arriving in the Federal District.

A majority of Mexican generals and admirals had a sense of trepidation about hostilities with the United States. Many viewed the call to arms as patently stupid and suicidal. Others, political aspirants in general's uniforms, argued that personal and national pride should carry the day.

The debate mattered not. The secretary of national defense, a corrupt active-duty army general appointed by the previous president, had made his decision. The only way the general could protect his power would be to confront the Americans. President Juan Cárdenas had not been consulted, a deliberate insult that was intended to convey a message.

The Mexican military would confront the United States, the country that had stolen the southwestern U.S. from Mexico. The Mexican armed forces would defend the country's honor and protect her borders. The senior general would accomplish two goals: protect his future fortunes in drug trafficking and render Cárdenas impotent.

29

The Winslow Estate

Scott parked his rare Ferrari 275 GTB Spider, stepped out, and walked around to open Jackie's door. They were two minutes early when he rang the doorbell. Each was surprised when Hartwell Prost personally opened the massive door.

"Come in," Hartwell said, as he shook hands with Scott and Jackie. "I trust you've had dinner."

"Actually," Scott said, "we're planning a late dinner in Georgetown."

"That's good, because I had to dine on leftovers this evening."

"Where are Zachary and Molly?" Jackie asked.

"Zachary is on holiday, and Molly had to take a few days off to tend to her mother. Let's go out to the veranda."

Jackie and Scott followed Hartwell and took a seat on the lounge. Their host poured each of them a glass of wine.

"The president and I want to thank you—congratulate you—for your efforts in capturing Khaliq Farkas and finding the nukes." Hartwell raised his glass. "We're grateful."

"Glad we could help," Scott said.

Jackie placed her glass on the table. "Did he survive?"

"Barely. He's in critical condition. We hope to begin questioning him in a few days—at least by next week."

Prost paused to light a cigar.

"It was coincidental that President Macklin and I were discussing a new course of action when we received your message about Farkas. As you may know, the CIA has created a new super-secret hit team to target terrorists abroad. It's a paramilitary unit that conducts covert operations directly under the command of the Agency's counterterrorism center. The number of people on the team, their weaponry, and the location of their base are highly classified."

Scott had a question. "No congressional oversight?"

"Very little. The president's signed intelligence order, including the authority to use lethal force, expands a previous presidential finding. If Congress knew, it would be leaked, no question about it, and the lives of many brave people would unnecessarily be placed in jeopardy. Therefore, briefings are limited to the two ranking Democrats and Republicans from the intelligence committee of each chamber."

"Will the unit be able to operate anywhere in the world?" Jackie asked.

"For the most part. They will be free to disrupt, capture, or destroy terrorists in over eighty countries."

Scott had a question. "Does this have anything to do with the new assignment you mentioned?"

"Yes, one I hope you'll consider." Prost smiled reassuringly. "We believe you could bring another dimension to the covert operation: the ability to gather the ground truth from human sources. We don't want different factions competing on the same mission."

"I'm not sure I understand," Jackie said.

Prost looked her in the eye. "We want you to track Saeed Shayhidi, find him, capture him, or kill him."

Jackie and Scott were quiet for a moment before Scott spoke. "You want us to assassinate Shayhidi?"

Prost shifted uncomfortably in his chair. "Well, let's say we want you to find him and give us his coordinates to allow precision air strikes."

Jackie looked up, her eyes quizzing Prost. "Do we have any idea where Shayhidi is, the last known contact?"

"We've traced his charter flight from Siem Reap, Cambodia, to Geneva. A chartered jet left Cambodia a short time after our people went to the hotel where Shayhidi had been staying. He left so fast he didn't check out or take his clothes." His tone of voice hardened. "Shayhidi has been making a fool out of us. I'm embarrassed for the CIA, and President Macklin is beyond being upset, to put it mildly."

Prost paused and gazed across the grounds. "Geneva, his business headquarters, is where we would like you to begin. We, the president and I, *need* you to find him, whatever you have to do."

He turned to Jackie. "Your thoughts?"

"This may sound strange," she ventured, "but as a fighter pilot, if someone was shooting at me, I'd shoot back—doing my job. But morally speaking, I don't fit the profile of an assassin."

"I fully understand," Prost said quietly.

"I feel the same as Jackie," Scott admitted. "However, I'm willing to go after him. We'll leave Shayhidi's future to someone else after we've found him, unless he tries to take us out."

Scott looked at Jackie. "You okay with that?"

"Sure, as long as we all agree on what our role is."

Prost smiled with relief. "No argument from me. The two of you have the talent, training, and tenacity to accomplish things most people wouldn't even consider. The president and I deeply appreciate everything you've done."

"Thank you," Scott said. "Any problem with using our plane, carrying our personal weapons and all the gear we need?"

"None that I can think of." Prost considered the options. "You have a legitimate business conducting safety audits for corporate flight departments, including major companies overseas. In addition, you have your FBI and CIA credentials along with current passports. That seems to cover all the bases."

U.S. Air Force Global Hawk

Flying at 63,000 feet above Mexico City, the unmanned surveillance craft relayed the movement of four army brigades heading north at 11:25 P.M. The brigades comprised one armored, two infantry, and one motorized infantry. Their olive-drab "deuce and a half" cargo trucks with canvas tops were, for the most part, Korean War vintage. Once established on Highway 85, the caravan advanced toward Ciudad Victoria, a transportation center east of the 13,300-foot peak of Cerro Peña Nevada.

If the brigades stayed on 85 after passing Ciudad Victoria, that would take them through Monterrey to Nuevo Laredo, across the Rio Bravo del Norte from Laredo, Texas. If the convoy took Highway 101 at Ciudad Victoria, they would arrive at Matamoros, Mexico, across the border from Brownsville, Texas. Regardless of the caravan's planned destination, the president of the United States had a decision to make.

The White House

President Macklin was awakened at 1:05 A.M. and had coffee with Dave Timkey, Brad Austin, Pete Adair, and Les Chalmers. After a secure phone conference call with Hartwell Prost and a conversation with the senior officers at NORAD, the president and his aides went to the library on the ground floor. Macklin closed the door and everyone took a seat.

"First thing," the president said, "I want to make sure they don't get anywhere close to our border."

Secretary Austin glanced at Chalmers and then turned to Macklin. "I respectfully yield to Secretary Adair and General Chalmers on military matters. Having said that, I am convinced that a firepower demonstration would halt the convoy and turn them back like the Mexican frigates."

Macklin removed his reading glasses. "What makes you so sure?"

"These troops are not kamikazes," Austin said with conviction. "When they see what they're up against, they'll know this is an exercise in futility. They aren't a tough, well-disciplined, well-equipped, seasoned fighting force. Besides, they've seen the results of Operation Iraqi Freedom. They'll turn back."

Pete Adair spoke up in support. "I agree with you, but as a backup let's destroy the highway so they can't continue. Give them time to think about it."

"Les," the president said, "what's your view?"

"I would try something to get their attention short of destroying the highway. We have the assets standing by," Chalmers said. "One thing, though—we need to hit them just as the sun begins to nibble at the sky. Regardless of which highway they take, they'll be past Ciudad Victoria by that time and in a sparsely populated area. That's where we want to take action."

"What do you plan to use?" Macklin asked.

"Two AC-130 Spectre gunships, two A-10 Warthogs, and two B-1Bs. We'll also have helicopters in the area in case someone goes down."

The president nodded his approval. "If we do have to cut the highway, and it looks like they might try to find an alternative route, cut off the road behind them also. Strand the caravan in place and keep them pinned down with no way out."

"Yes, sir."

"Okay, gentlemen, we have a short night ahead," Macklin declared. "You can rest here or have breakfast here. Your choice, but let's gather in the Situation Room at five-thirty A.M."

Dyess Air Force Base

Two B-1B Lancers, affectionately known as the "Bone," taxied for takeoff under a star-filled sky. The sleek swing-wing long-range bomber was capable of carrying eighty-four 500-pound bombs or twenty-four 2,000-pound JDAMs. This morning the supersonic bombers from the 9th Bomb Squadron, 7th Wing, would be flying empty with a standard crew consisting of an aircraft commander, copilot, offensive systems operator, and defensive systems operator.

Cleared for takeoff, the B-1Bs took off in interval and climbed to altitude en route to Mexico. They checked in with the E-3 AWACS to receive the latest coordinates of the Mexican military caravan. The brigades were on Highway 101 approaching Santander Jiménez, and Global Hawk was keeping a watchful eye on the procession of vehicles.

Carboneras, Mexico

Orbiting over the Gulf of Mexico twenty-three nautical miles east of the small town of Carboneras, two AC-130 Spectre gunships from Hurlburt Field, Florida, waited to turn on course. The ground-attack aircraft were armed with a stunning array of firepower that could be concentrated on a small area.

The relatively low-flying Hercules gunships were equipped with two 20mm Vulcan cannons, one Bofors cannon, and one howitzer that could fire 100 rounds. The new "U" model aircraft had replaced their 20mm cannons with a rapid-firing 25mm Gatling gun. Known as one mean flying machine, the AC-130 was one of the weapons most feared by enemy ground forces.

Over Harlingen, Texas

Two A-10 Warthogs from Barksdale AFB, Louisiana, were refueling from a KC-135. The close-air-support aircraft were each armed with eighteen conventional Mk-82 500-pound general-purpose bombs. Their showcase weapon, a powerful 30mm Gatling-type seven-barrel rotary cannon, was capable of destroying any tank. The Warthog put cold fear into the hearts of enemy soldiers who witnessed the cannon fire.

After topping off their fuel tanks, the lead pilot checked in with the AWACS for vectors to their holding pattern. The senior pilots had been thoroughly briefed about the mission and looked forward to playing a role in discouraging the Mexican advance.

The White House

The president and his advisers quietly filed into the Situation Room and took their seats. There was little conversation while they waited to monitor the firepower demonstration. They paid rapt attention when the AWACS cued the first event, the B-1B supersonic Mach 1.2 reveille call. The second bomber would remain at altitude as a spare.

Ready to step onstage after the 900-mph B-1B pass, the lead AC-130 Spectre gunship was orbiting two miles north of the Mexican caravan. The second ground-attack Hercules circled six miles to the east. The A-10s would roll in together after the AC-130 departed the immediate area.

Three U.S. Air Force HH-60G Pave Hawk combat search-and-rescue helicopters formed a triangle around the caravan. They were ready to snag any downed crew members. Along the entire length of the U.S.–Mexican border, other AWACS and fighter aircraft continued to fly combat air patrols to stop any threat from the ground or from the air.

The B-1B aircraft commander was beginning his run fourteen miles east of the Mexican brigades. Since the target was moving, the bomber crew would have to make a few minor heading corrections during the pass. The last five miles would be flown supersonic at treetop level.

San Fernando-Matamoros, Mexico

Moving at a steady pace on Highway 101, the Mexican military caravan was getting closer to the U.S.–Mexican border. Most of the soldiers were asleep as the first light of day began to engulf the line of olive-drab cargo trucks. There was little traffic going north and practically no vehicles traveling south. The highway crossing the Rio Grande at Brownsville, Texas, had been closed for hours.

Some of the Mexican soldiers were beginning to wake up and stretch their arms and legs. Others who had been awake for a while smoked cigarettes and discussed how far their senior officers and their government were going to take the military charade. Even though it embarrassed some of the veteran soldiers, they figured the Americans were laughing out loud.

In reality, few people north of the border even knew the Mexican convoy was approaching the border of Texas. Certainly, no one was laughing at the Pentagon or in the White House Situation Room.

While the Mexican soldiers were discussing what was going to happen when they reached the border, a black dot appeared in the eastern sky. It rapidly grew larger as it hugged the terrain with its wings in full sweep. There was no sound, no warning.

Flying faster than sound travels, the "Bone" could drop 7 tons of 500-pound bombs in a concentrated path of destruction. Before anyone on the ground would even know what happened, the B-1B could lay waste to a large concentration of troops and their equipment.

That was the bomber's mission: to rain astonishing destruction and then disappear in the blink of an eye. The psychological impact of not being able to see or hear death coming had a debilitating effect on infantry soldiers.

Making a slight course correction a mile from the caravan, the aircraft commander intended to pass directly in front of the lead cargo truck. All four General Electric turbofans were in full afterburner, each generating over 30,700 pounds of thrust.

The driver and the colonel in the first truck never saw the bomber coming. They never heard anything. A huge, dark object flashed past the hood, startling them. A second later, the quiet of the early morning was shattered by an explosive sonic boom that cracked the truck's windshield in three places. The eardrum-splitting roar of the four afterburners topped the aerial demonstration as the B-1B steeply climbed and turned north.

The copilot of the bomber keyed his radio and spoke to the orbiting AWACS. "Adios, partner."

"Good job."

On the highway, chaos ensued as the army vehicles lurched to a stop in accordion fashion. No one remained asleep, not in the convoy or anywhere within a twelve-mile radius. Shock and fear permeated the ranks. They had never seen anything that even vaguely resembled the weapon that had just shocked them. While the officers huddled, the soldiers stopped traffic in both directions. The troops not on traffic detail gathered in small groups and speculated about their march toward the U.S. border.

Watching the scene through the eyes of Global Hawk, President Macklin was growing impatient. "I don't think we should let the shock wear off. Show them another example of why they don't want to pursue this machismo madness."

SecDef nodded.

"Off alongside the road," the president suggested. "Give them an opportunity to wake up and start thinking straight before we have to destroy the damn highway."

General Chalmers gave the order. It was immediately transmitted to the orbiting AC-130 gunship.

The aircraft commander of the Hercules had the convoy in visual contact. After carefully adjusting the power, he set up a left-hand orbit around the caravan of army vehicles. The object lesson began at the edge of the highway approximately 100 yards from the lead truck.

A combination of unbelievable firepower, accurately concentrated in one small area by the onboard fire-control radar system, dug a hole six feet deep in a matter of seconds. The thunderous noise and total devastation stunned the people on the ground.

The soldiers on traffic detail lost control as the myriad civilian drivers frantically made U-turns, some bumping into each other, and roared off in the direction they had come from.

Within seconds the frightened officers made a decision while the Spectre gunship continued to orbit overhead. Forget what the generals and politicians were going to say. Continuing northbound would be suicidal. The convoy would return to their quarters near Mexico City.

While the caravan was reorganizing, the AC-130 gunship departed the area and returned to its holding pattern. The spare B-1B bomber was granted permission to make a low supersonic pass over the convoy and then return to Dyess AFB. It was a final warning for those who might harbor second thoughts.

After the aircraft shattered everyone's nerves and tortured their eardrums, the bomber pulled up in a steep climbing turn to the north. Still in afterburner, the number-three engine exploded. The pilots went through the procedures to shut it down and extinguish the fire, but the number-four engine soon began to show indications of trouble.

Major Jared Townsen, the aircraft commander and mission

commander, slowed the airplane to 300 knots and broadcast a Mayday radio call. Two F-16s from a nearby combat air patrol rendezvoused with the stricken bomber and reported a long trail of fire emitting from the right engines.

As the aircraft began suffering multiple malfunctions, Townsen was having problems controlling the plane. He tried to salvage the situation and find a suitable airport, but the B-1B finally pitched up and rolled to the right. As hard as he tried, Townsen could not arrest the roll. He ordered the crew to eject and all four crew members exited the bomber.

The sleek aircraft crashed in a field six miles south of Reynosa, Mexico, across the border from McAllen, Texas. Once the crew was on the ground, the F-16s flew cover for the men until an air force HH-60G Pave Hawk rescue helicopter arrived.

Although the final demonstration proved costly, the end result was worth the price. A potentially deadly conflict on the border was avoided and there were now scores of true believers in the Mexican Army. They would be spreading the word to their cohorts. Provoking the world's only superpower was not a sound idea.

When news of the army's humiliating confrontation with the Americans was made public in Mexico City, it provoked more demonstrations and riots. The U.S. Marines at the embattled embassy had been ordered to hold their fire unless the perimeter of the grounds was breached.

Later, when a story broke about the army shooting down the American supersonic bomber, the crowds began cheering and chanting. Less than an hour later, the radio stations and television outlets were reporting that two American warplanes had been shot down. The news fueled more celebrating and flag waving. The Mexican military had indeed acquitted themselves well.

The White House

Acting on General Chalmers's orders, the lead AC-130 gunship reduced the crashed B-1B to rubble. There was nothing left to give anyone a single clue about its offensive and defensive capabilities.

Relieved by the turn of events, Chalmers faced the president, the only other person in the Situation Room. "The flight crew has been checked. No broken bones, just bruises, minor cuts, and abrasions."

"That's definitely good to hear." Macklin was filled with relief over the outcome of the standoff, but he didn't want to show any elation. "Do they have any idea what happened? Missile, maybe?"

"The pilots believe they might have ingested some birds just as they pulled up. At any rate, the crew is on their way back to Dyess, and I'm headed to the Pentagon."

The president rose to shake hands with Chalmers. "Great job, Les. Thanks for coming through for me."

Chalmers finally cracked a smile. "The folks flying the airplanes deserve the *real* credit."

"Well, at least part of it." Macklin's voice reflected fatigue. "Why don't you take a few days off and go fishing."

"If you'll go with me."

"Wish I could, but I have to be in Corpus Christi in a couple of hours."

Chalmers's smile slowly faded. "Cord, I hope you don't mind an old friend being honest. You need to get some rest, some quality sleep."

"I just might do that when we get back this evening."

30

Corpus Christi International Airport

Thunderstorms were building in all quadrants as the C-32A (Boeing 757) from the 89th Airlift Wing began its descent into the Corpus Christi area. The ride was not too bad, but the aircraft commander went ahead and slowed the jet to mush through the turbulence.

The U.S. Navy F/A-18s accompanying the president matched the Boeing's speed and maintained their position. They would stay with the gleaming blue-and-white 757 until it turned on final approach at Corpus Christi.

In the cabin, President Macklin was going over strategy with Secretary of State Austin and National Security Adviser Hartwell Prost. Because of the mounting friction between the United States and Mexico, they had decided on a bold recommendation for President Juan Cárdenas.

Now in radio contact with Corpus Christi Approach Control, the busy flight crew was coordinating their arrival with that of President Cárdenas. The senior pilots from the 89th had been instructed by Secretary Austin to follow the Boeing 727 from the Presidential Transport Squadron based in Mexico City.

After a series of radar vectors and two visual turns to circumvent thunderstorms, the Boeing 757 was finally vectored into position behind the 727. Both aircraft landed in a heavy downpour and taxied to a secure area.

The Secret Service was out in force and quickly shuttled the two parties to a portable air-conditioned conference room parked only yards away. Cárdenas and Macklin had agreed to have only the principals in the meeting. The various political aides and the Secret Service agents remained outside underneath shelters.

Avoiding any reference to the military confrontation that morning, the men shook hands and sat down. President Cárdenas and Secretary of Foreign Affairs Antonio Ferreira were on one side of the table. On the other side of the table, President Macklin was flanked by Brad Austin on the right and Hartwell Prost on the left.

After a few pleasantries, Macklin broke the ice. "President Cárdenas, Secretary Austin and I have had an in-depth conversation about the core problem that exists in your administration: the corruption in the military and in the law-enforcement branches. Please take the time to tell me how ingrained you think the problem is."

Even though he had known the question would be coming, Cárdenas paused to craft his answer carefully. "The primary problem is the military. Six generals and one admiral have the military in their grip. They are clever mobsters cloaked in uniforms who recruit servicemen in their image.

"Without them in the picture, there are two generals and three promising colonels who want to help me take the steps to form a system on the U.S. model. Otherwise, we will be forever mired in graft and corruption. The crooks in uniform at the top have the weapons, the power, and the money while the citizens are defenseless."

Secretary Ferreira's eyes were downcast.

"These people are morally corrupt and totally ruthless," Cárdenas said, speaking quietly and slowly. "They rule by using fear and hard-core intimidation. They will go to any length to destroy their opponents' credibility, destroy their ability to make a living, destroy their personal lives, or worse."

"Or worse?" Prost asked.

"If they don't comply, members of their family or friends disappear or turn up dead. Many of the deaths are claimed by the medical examiners to be suicides. These examiners are on the military payroll as full colonels."

A few silent moments passed while Cárdenas had a drink of water and regained his composure.

"President Cárdenas," Secretary Austin began, "you mentioned the senior officers recruiting in their image. I take it that's the way this corruption has carried on for so long?"

"Absolutely. Carefully planned ascension. Less than a month after I was elected, one of the senior generals promoted his twenty-four-year-old nephew, who had never served in the military, to lieutenant colonel. The nephew, who has a criminal record ranging from extortion to murder, is surreptitiously laundering drug money in the United States and taking care of his uncle's offshore bank accounts."

Macklin glanced at Secretary Ferreira and then focused again on Cárdenas. "Do the seven men—the generals and the admiral—ever get together?"

"I know they occasionally congregate at various resorts, but the outings are random and always secret. We don't know the location of the meetings until after they return to their military quarters."

"Let me suggest a course of action," Macklin said matter-of-factly. "You don't have to make a decision now, just think about it for a while. The details can be worked out later. If you want these criminals to disappear, we have the capability to do it."

Macklin glanced again at Ferreira. He was definitely nervous.

Macklin continued. "The question, President Cárdenas, is basic, but fundamental to our success. Are you certain the officers you have confidence in will in fact remold the military as *you* see fit?"

There was no hesitation. "Yes, I'm confident. There are many fine officers and soldiers who want to see the corruption weeded out of the military. It taints them and their profession, but they know the consequences if they try to change things."

Ferreira's mouth was agape but no words came out.

"How would we explain their disappearance?" Cárdenas asked in a guarded but clear voice.

Macklin paused, frowning slightly. "They were killed in a plane crash at sea, in the Bahia de Campeche, en route to a military conference in Cancún."

Cárdenas mulled the proposal. "I deeply appreciate your consideration, President Macklin."

"We're here to help *both* our countries; we're no stranger to corruption. As you said, sometimes we have to do some weeding, be it in the military, the corporate world, or the political arena."

"President Macklin is right," Secretary Austin chimed in. "What's good for Mexico is good for our country."

Cárdenas nodded. "I do want to take time to contemplate your suggestion and its consequences. It's a lot to digest."

"Think about your contribution," Prost said. "This could fundamentally change the course of Mexico."

Cárdenas turned to Macklin. "Thank you for your generous

support. I am deeply indebted, but I have to think about this for a while."

"We understand."

Cárdenas and Ferreira rose to shake hands with the Americans. Out of respect, Macklin walked with the president and his senior statesman to the 727. He waited until the airplane began taxiing for takeoff before he boarded the 757.

"Well," Macklin said to Austin and Prost, "we might see a *real* change in Mexico's future. At least there's hope."

USS *Constellation*

Now in a position to join the war on terrorism, the carrier's air wing was tasked with bombing specific terrorist training camps. The complexes had been clearly defined by space-based assets and unmanned aerial vehicles. Some of the sites were new and had a multitude of weapons stockpiled, including mortars, rockets, and missiles. Other sites that had been destroyed were being modestly refurbished to use as storage facilities.

The first wave of strike aircraft launched at 5:40 P.M., to be over their targets after dark. The second strike launched at 6:30 P.M., and it would follow groups of planes from *Stennis* and *George Washington.* The wide-ranging air raids, which would continue to first light, were designed to flatten several terrorist facilities. Buildings, supplies, munitions—everything would be destroyed before daylight.

Geneva, Switzerland

Saeed Shayhidi was back in his familiar element. Although he was confident about his disguise, he avoided going to his office building. His executive assistant, Gamaa al-Harith, was his go-between. The CIA agents watching the office had no idea who al-Harith was or what he did. He was just one of the many anonymous employees who came and went during the course of the day.

Living in a modest dwelling until his new home was built, Shayhidi was selling the remaining cargo ships and tankers in his fleet, consolidating his resources into long-term investments that could not be sunk or blown apart. Yes, life was pleasant again and he still had a plethora of assets to use against the infidels.

The company lawyers were fighting with the insurance companies while Shayhidi, using his new identity, was negotiating for a new airplane. He smiled every time he thought about Macklin and the CIA. Now, after putting his life back together, he could concentrate on continuing the attacks on the United States.

Chevy Chase, Maryland

Brad Austin was shaving when his wife, Leigh Ann, walked into the master bathroom. "I'm sorry to bother you, but you have a phone call."

"Tell them I'll call back in a few minutes."

"I tried that," she said with a smile. "It's urgent; someone from your office."

He wiped the shaving cream off with a hand towel and walked to the phone beside the bed. "Austin."

Leigh Ann, sensing something important was developing, brushed her teeth while she listened to her husband's phone conversation.

"What's up?" she asked, when he walked back into the bathroom.

"It looks like the bombing campaign is having an adverse effect on the hosts of the terrorist groups. Syria and Lebanon are particularly incensed about the American, Israeli, and British warships standing off their coastlines. It seems that shipping has been effectively halted."

"That sounds like good news."

"You bet." He applied fresh shaving cream. "Iran, Syria, Lebanon, and Sudan, collectively, have requested a secret conference with us at a neutral location. They want us to stop the bombing now and then make a decision about where to convene for the talks."

She looked at Brad's reflection in the mirror. "Sure. After all the attacks we've suffered, please stop the bombing—then we'll talk."

"Well, the president makes the final call, but I'm going to recommend we continue the bombing—intensify it, if possible—until they are begging us to come to the table."

"How much damage are we *really* doing?"

"A lot. Bombs are literally falling round the clock."

"Do you believe the leaders of the host nations can actually control the terrorist groups?"

"Not completely, too many zealots are operating on their own."

"Then it just goes on?"

"Probably so, but greatly diminished." Brad turned to Leigh Ann. "Every time we have an act of terrorism perpetrated against American citizens, we will flatten terrorist compounds. They can live in rubble all their lives or stop this madness."

"You'd think it would dawn on the terrorists that they can't win."

"They'd rather die than come to their senses, and we can certainly accommodate them."

Leigh Ann reached for her coffee cup. "Do they really have to be pulverized, bombed into submission?"

"Yes, eradicated; not on this planet anymore."

"I see." She was shocked by his honesty.

Kennedy Space Center, Florida

After September eleventh, the majority of U.S. intelligence data indicated the space shuttles were high-value targets for terrorists. The greatest concern was not an attack from the ground, or from the sea, but a suicidal terrorist attack from the air. Even a relatively small general aviation aircraft could destroy a fueled orbiter on the launchpad.

Having carefully analyzed the risks, the NASA administrator and the White House had decided to increase security to wartime conditions and continue the launches. To ground the remaining space shuttles would give the terrorists another huge moral victory and delay placing critical military satellites in orbit.

Atlantis was poised for a late-afternoon launch on Pad 39B. Fueled with 1.3 million pounds of liquid oxygen, 225,000 pounds of liquid hydrogen, and 2 million pounds of solid propellant, the 4.4-million-pound shuttle was scheduled to launch a new spy satellite.

All general-aviation aircraft operating under visual flight rules were banned from a thirty-mile radius of Pad 39B, beginning twenty-four hours before the proposed launch time.

Atlantis was being protected by Florida Air National Guard F-16s vectored by AWACS and FAA radars. The fighters would cover the central and eastern areas of Florida, while Air National Guard F-15s would patrol the immediate area around the Kennedy Space Center. Kansas Air National Guard KC-135 tankers would supply fuel for the fighters.

One of the key surveillance elements for the fighter aircraft was the portable USAF/Northrop Grumman radar with a 240-nautical-mile range. The radar could track objects with a cross section of only nine feet. The unit, from the 728th Air Combat Squadron at Eglin AFB, Florida, was deployed to Cape Canaveral, several miles south of the space shuttle pad. The radar also supported USAF Avenger/ Stinger surface-to-air missile batteries located nearby.

Army Apache attack helicopters worked with NASA Huey helicopters to form a low-altitude ground security ring. Air force reserve HH-60 helicopters from Patrick AFB, Florida, patrolled for any sign of trouble and would perform rescue duties if necessary.

On the ground, scores of Humvees with 50-caliber machine guns patrolled the launch complex. Off the coast of the space center, two armed coast guard cutters provided surveillance at sea in the restricted area. Light antiaircraft guns and shoulder-fired surface-to-air missiles were deployed close to the launch site.

* * *

Anticipation on the orbiter's flight deck was building as the shuttle commander, Navy Captain Owen Paddock, and the mission pilot, Air Force Lieutenant Colonel Gavin Dinsmore, continued with the extensive preflight checks.

"Control, *Atlantis* shows cabin pressure nominal," Paddock reported.

"Roger, nominal."

At T-minus-thirty minutes, the ground crew secured the white room and retired to the fallback area.

Paddock and Dinsmore completed their voice checks. Paddock copied the weather for a return-to-launch-site abort and for the Transatlantic Abort Sites at Morón and Zaragosa, Spain, and Ben Guérir, Morocco.

Four marine corps AH-1W Super Cobra attack helicopters made a pass down the beach and began a wide orbit around the shuttle facility. The gunships would remain in the pattern until T-minus-two minutes.

Paddock and Dinsmore continued the countdown with Mission Control and Launch Control, including the abort check.

After a mandatory hold to catch up before beginning the final phase of the countdown, the clock resumed at T-minus-nine minutes.

"Control, *Atlantis* event timer started."

"Roger, *Atlantis*."

At T-minus-seven minutes the crew-access arm retracted. Paddock and Dinsmore secured all loose personal items.

T-minus-six minutes. "*Atlantis,* initiate APU prestart."

"Roger, Houston."

At the five-minute mark, Paddock keyed his radio. "Control, *Atlantis* is powering up the APUs."

"Roger."

"APUs are looking good," Paddock radioed.

"*Atlantis,* you're on internal power."

"Roger."

At T-minus-three minutes the orbiter's main engines swiveled to their launch position.

"*Atlantis,* main engine gimbal complete."

"Roger."

One minute later, the marine attack helicopters departed the area and flew to a distant holding pattern.

As they continued through the checks, Paddock glanced at Dinsmore. "Are you ready to light the burners?"

"The sooner the better."

"*Atlantis,* H-two tank pressurization is okay. You are go for launch at this time. Good luck."

"Go for launch," Paddock replied. "Thanks."

At T-minus-twenty-five seconds the shuttle countdown switched to the onboard computers.

"Fifteen seconds and counting."

"Here we go," Paddock said over the intercom, to the rest of the crew. "Going flying now."

Precisely at 3.8 seconds the computers commanded the three space shuttle main engines to start, each producing 375,000 pounds of thrust.

"We have main engine start—two, one, zero."

At T-plus-2.64 seconds, the orbiter's two powerful solid rocket boosters ignited, each creating 2,650,000 pounds of thrust. There was no turning back now, no shutting down the rocket boosters. The space shuttle was committed to at least a partial flight. Propelled by over 6 million pounds of combined thrust, the orbiter levitated off the launchpad.

"We have liftoff! We have liftoff of space shuttle *Atlantis*!" Seconds slowly passed. "The tower has been cleared; all engines look good."

Paddock keyed his radio. "Roger, Houston, looks good from my view."

"Beginning the roll," Houston reported.

"Roger, rolling."

Belching billowing clouds of gray smoke and shaking the ground, the huge shuttle began a slow roll to the "heads down" position. All eyes were glued to the magnificent orbiter.

No one saw where the missile came from. The mushrooming clouds of smoke from the solid rockets obstructed the wisp of telltale smoke. The missile hit the shuttle's main engines, destroying two of them.

"*Atlantis,* we show two main engine failures!"

"We have trouble!" Paddock said excitedly. "We're returning to launch site, two engine failures."

The RTLS option was used if the main propulsion system malfunctioned in the first four minutes and twenty seconds of flight.

Paddock and Dinsmore could not begin the critical RTLS maneuver until the solid-propellant boosters burned out and were jettisoned. On the flight deck, Paddock and Dinsmore were going through the emergency checklists and trying to figure out what happened. Other systems were affected by the emergency, but the orbiter was intact and pressurized.

The rest of the stunned crew was preparing to go into the water if Paddock had to ditch the shuttle.

There was a constant stream of dialogue with Houston, but no one had any idea what happened. Visions of *Challenger* and *Columbia* flashed through the minds of most support personnel. The news from the launch site was blood-chilling for the controllers in Houston. A number of pieces from the shuttle's main engines had impacted close to Pad 39B.

The mission controller elected not to say anything to the flight crew. At this stage of the emergency, the information was not helpful and the controller didn't want to distract Paddock and Dinsmore.

Continuing on its trajectory, the orbiter finally jettisoned the two reusable solid rocket boosters. The space shuttle and external tank would continue down-range on the power of the one main engine, both orbital maneuvering engines, and the four aft-firing maneuvering rockets.

Paddock would wait until he had barely enough propellants in the tank to reverse the direction of flight. This would be a "rabbit's foot" moment during the difficult maneuver.

On the ground, emergency vehicles of all types were converging near the runway. Rescue boats were standing out to sea.

With Dinsmore backing him up, Paddock began a 5-degree-per-second pitch. *Come on—don't blow this maneuver.*

Time seemed to go into slow motion until the orbiter was almost headed toward the landing site. That's when the exotic propellants were exhausted and the main engine expired, followed by the separation of the huge external fuel tank.

Paddock turned to Dinsmore and shook his head. "Well, I hope everyone brought their swim fins along."

Dinsmore nodded. "Looks a bit low on energy."

"I'm going to have to improvise: aim closer to the end of the runway and then wrap it up tight."

"Yeah, only option to make the runway."

Paddock talked to the crew and kept them apprised of where he was in the evolution. He also conferred with the controllers at the Kennedy shuttle landing facility and was given the current winds.

"We're not making the numbers," Paddock said in a dejected voice. "Just shy, maybe four or five percent."

"*Atlantis,* Houston."

"Go, Houston."

"How does it look?"

"Not promising, but we still have a chance."

"Roger."

With eighty-five seconds to touchdown, the crippled orbiter was descending on a steep 22-degree glide slope through 13,100 feet, 420 mph, 7.6 miles from the 15,000-foot-long and 300-foot-wide runway. The landing strip had a 1,000-foot overrun at each end for improved safety.

Not wanting to use the speed brake, which doubled as the rudder at the back of the shuttle's vertical stabilizer, Paddock concentrated on maintaining the optimum glide slope to make the runway. He keyed the intercom and spoke to Dinsmore. "Rocket Two, what do you think?"

"Maybe we should have talked with one of our *real* rocket scientists."

"No time, have to make the call."

Thirty-three seconds to touchdown, 2.1 miles from the runway, 356 mph out of 1,700 feet.

"We're not gonna make it," Paddock announced to the crew, as he banked the orbiter in preparation to ditch offshore. He initiated the pre-flare. "Brace yourself for ditching!"

Paddock glanced at Dinsmore. "We leave the gear up; don't touch the landing gear."

"You can bet on it."

"Call my speeds," Paddock said, as he began the flare to 1.5-degrees nose up, "and altitude."

"Three-hundred-five, altitude one hundred thirty feet."

Using his considerable flying skills, the former navy fighter pilot nursed the shuttle lower. Fortunately there were no boats in his path.

"Two-sixty-five, eighty feet."

Paddock began bleeding off airspeed.

"Two-fifteen, twenty feet."

Holding the orbiter in ground effect—in this case, water effect—Paddock slowed *Atlantis* and eased it down. He deployed the split-rudder speed brake and made a slight adjustment in attitude.

"Two hundred, maybe ten feet."

The water was reasonably smooth, and the shuttle skipped a couple of times before it made solid contact. Paddock held the nose up as long as possible before it fell through and contacted the surface, sending a wall of water washing over the orbiter. The deceleration to a full stop was fairly benign and the pilots scrambled to get out of their seats.

"Let's go!" the shuttle commander ordered. "Out the hatch!"

The crew removed the left-hand overhead window near the aft crew station behind the flight deck. They grabbed the life raft, draped the thermal curtains over the side of the vehicle, and tossed out a rope to descend to the water.

In less time than it took to get all seven of the crew in the life raft, rescue boats began arriving. Everyone thought the orbiter was floating until they realized it was resting on the bottom.

At the same time the space shuttle had jettisoned its external fuel tank, the mystery of what happened to the orbiter was solved. A NASA Huey helicopter carrying heavily armed security personnel was slowly flying along the beach looking for debris from the damaged shuttle. When they spotted suspicious items, they radioed the location to searchers on the ground. They in turn marked the item and left a guard at the site.

One of the observers in the helicopter noticed a slight movement along a low beach ridge. The helicopter made a 180-degree turn, approached the spot, and descended to land. Like a phoenix rising from its own ashes, a young bearded man rose from the sand and shot himself in the head with a small 22-caliber handgun.

Upon further investigation, the security personnel discovered a partially buried man-portable surface-to-air missile launcher. The SA-18 Grouse missile was manufactured by the Machine Production Design Bureau, Kolomna, Russian Federation. It had been hermetically sealed in an opaque shrink-wrapped plastic container.

The identity of the suicidal terrorist was uncertain. The Middle Eastern man had no ID, but given the fact that so many Russian-made military items were turning up in Iran and Iraq, there was a good chance he was from one or the other country. It made no difference; all countries that hosted terrorists were going to pay for the attack.

A tattered wet suit, dive mask, snorkel, and the plastic container for the SAM were buried a few feet away from the slant hole the man had dug with a compact entrenching tool. He also had a tan-colored sixteen-inch-long, two-inch-diameter plastic pipe he used to get fresh air when he was completely covered with sand.

From the two empty canteens and the seven energy bar wrappers, security personnel figured the terrorist must have come ashore at least three nights before the launch date. Many of the searchers wondered if there were other terrorists hidden under the sand. Armed ground parties soon began combing the beach in both directions.

Three boats and a group of divers searching offshore from where the terrorist hid found a Diver Propulsion Vehicle. The DPV was anchored to the bottom in seven feet of water. The tow vehicle was a battery-powered propeller-driven scuba diving accessory that eliminates exertion on the part of the diver or swimmer. The discovery explained how the terrorist had managed to bring so many items ashore. Where he launched from was anyone's guess.

The terrorist had almost destroyed the orbiter. It would take time to refurbish *Atlantis,* but she would fly again. Security at the space center would increase even more, especially when Congress got involved and the television cameras permitted unlimited face time.

31

The White House

President Macklin was playing golf at Burning Tree when he was informed of the attack on the space shuttle. With exasperation showing in his eyes, he returned to the White House, showered, changed into a suit, and went to meet with Timkey, Prost, Adair, and Chalmers in the Oval Office. The men had already seen replays of the shuttle incident several times.

"Gentlemen, keep your seats," the president said, as he walked briskly into the office and sat down at his desk. The atmosphere was oppressive: no smiles, no pleasantries, all business.

Macklin shook his head in disbelief. "As we've learned the hard way, Cold War thinking doesn't apply when we're up against fanatical terrorists. During the Cold War, the logic of mutual assured destruction taught us that rational people would not commit suicide."

The president glanced at his colleagues. "Painfully obvious to the entire world, that assumption does not apply with this enemy. They still don't get the message. We're going to have to strike at terrorist targets by any means available to us. First strikes with everything in our inventory—including nukes, if we have to."

The comment raised a few eyebrows.

"Pete, I want you and Les to choose at least eight sites where we know bunkers exist, more than eight if you think they're worthwhile. Our space-based assets, along with Predator, Dragon Eye, and Global Hawk, have cataloged over twenty sites built since the Gulf War in 'ninety-one. Choose a variety: bunkers where they're hiding command and control centers, and weapons labs."

Pete Adair's face was without expression, emotions tightly controlled by years of military training. "I'm assuming you want to go with our newest bunker buster?"

"Absolutely. Make a *loud* statement."

The weapon was a long thin bomb designed to burrow through forty to fifty feet of earth and concrete before detonating. The resulting explosion would destroy everything in the bunker, and the ground above it would collapse.

"When do you want to deploy them?" Adair asked.

"As soon as you have them ready. No rushing; keep it safe."

Adair was about to reply when a military aide opened the door and profusely apologized for interrupting. "Mr. President, Secretary Austin is on the phone, insists on talking with you, sir."

"Thank you, I'll take it." Sensing more bad news, Macklin picked up the phone. "Hi, Brad."

While the president listened, his head slumped forward and he closed his eyes for a few moments. When he looked up, Macklin caught the attention of Hartwell Prost and then thanked Austin. After placing the receiver down, he swore to himself.

"President Cárdenas is dead," Macklin announced, in a steely quiet voice. "Died about thirty-five minutes ago."

"Died?" Prost was in disbelief. "From what?"

"They aren't sure."

The evasive answer did not fool Prost.

The president rose from his chair and walked around the end of his desk, signaling the end of the meeting. "Hartwell, if you don't mind, I'd like to discuss another matter with you."

"Yes, sir."

Macklin thanked Timkey, Adair, and Chalmers for dropping their dinner plans and rushing to the White House, ushered them pleasantly out of the office, and sat down across from Prost.

"You may want a drink," the president suggested, walking to the enclosed bar.

"I'll take you up on the offer." Prost watched the president's demeanor.

Macklin fixed two straight scotches and sat down. "Brad said the word from Mexico City, actually Los Pinos, is that Cárdenas was taking his usual afternoon nap before dinner and passed away in his sleep."

The normally calm Prost was incensed. "That's a bald-faced lie," he snapped. "He was murdered. There were only five of us in the conference room, and it had been sanitized before we arrived."

"That's exactly right." Macklin's patience was whipped raw. "Antonio Ferreira, the secretary of foreign affairs, was the informer. He is in collusion with the Mexican generals."

"And now the generals know what we intended to do."

The president remained quiet, contemplating the situation. "If you think about it, that's not bad. We can keep them looking over their shoulders, always wondering what might happen . . . and when it might happen."

"Right," Prost said as he sampled his drink. "Has the Mexican Congress designated an interim president?"

Macklin nodded. "Yes, Marco García Fernandez, Cárdena's former commissioner for northern border affairs."

"Can he be trusted?"

"Austin says he can, but he'll have to eliminate Ferreira." Macklin took a slug of scotch. "I'll ask Brad to see if the new president needs any assistance with that task."

Dulles International Airport

After a morning of shopping for supplies, Jackie and Scott were in the hangar stockpiling their Gulfstream 100 for the long flight to Geneva, Switzerland. They had no idea where their quest to locate Saeed Shayhidi would take them, but they wanted to be well prepared for any contingency. Geneva might be the first of many stops during the hunt for the elusive terrorist supporter.

Because of the complexities of international rules and regulations, they were not going to carry any firearms except their personal 9mm handguns. The CIA and FBI identification they carried would take care of most questions or problems with foreign customs.

Although their new jet had tremendous range, they were going to take a conservative approach to their first Atlantic Ocean crossing. After departing Dulles International, they would stop for fuel at Gander International Airport in Newfoundland, Canada. The next stop would be London-Luton Airport, Bedfordshire, England, and then on to Geneva.

While unloading Jackie's packed Ford Explorer, they were catching snippets of the morning news reports on their portable television in the hangar. A huge barge with an attached crane was on its way to retrieve the space shuttle *Atlantis,* and the chaotic situation on the U.S.–Mexican border was finally under control.

The situation at Mexico's presidential palace was a different story. The sudden death of the popular president left the country in a state of shock. There were more questions than answers surrounding his death.

An elaborate public funeral was in the final planning stages. The rioting had stopped and media outlets from all over the world were descending on Mexico City.

Closer to home, thousands of people and hundreds of companies were donating their time and services to help clean up the mess left by the deadly flood in the Colorado River. Assorted trucks of every variety, bulldozers, backhoes, and other heavy equipment were arriving from the four corners of the United States. Other trucks, many of them from Canada, were spreading fresh water and food supplies along the length of the river.

When the last boxes of personal gear were neatly packed in

the Gulfstream's cavernous luggage compartment, Jackie and Scott went into the cabin and sat down in the leather club seats.

"I was just thinking about Shayhidi," Jackie said.

"And?"

"His remaining ships are being sold—at least they're up for sale. There has to be a broker or an attorney involved, someone to go between Shayhidi and the prospective buyers."

"That's a good place to start," Scott admitted. "But I'm concerned that he's completely disappeared, vanished. Hartwell said the CIA is clueless, lost in a fog."

Jackie leaned back in her seat. "Someone has to be running the business on a daily basis. We know Shayhidi isn't showing up at his office and no one has intercepted any messages from him."

"Well, there's one thing the CIA knows. Two of Shayhidi's close associates flew to Crete and disappeared. One of them was Ahmed Musashi, who was acting as Shayhidi's company CEO. The other was a new hire named Hafiz al-Yamani, a longtime friend."

"What's the Agency's take on the disappearances?" Jackie asked. "Kidnapping, ransom?"

"They don't know. Witnesses saw the men arrive on the island, and others saw them at the Elounda Beach Hotel. They never returned to Geneva and have not been seen since."

She accepted a glass of tomato juice from Scott. "If memory serves me, that's one of those resorts where you have to take out a second mortgage to spend a night."

"That's right."

"Elounda Beach is Shayhidi's kind of place," Jackie remarked. "They may have gone there to meet with him."

"That may be true, but the surveillance cameras show Musashi and al-Yamani walking into the hotel and coming out with a man who wasn't Shayhidi. Plus Shayhidi wasn't registered, and no one resembling him checked in."

"It doesn't make sense," she said. "We need to see the tape, find out who walked out with Shayhidi's employees."

"Hartwell is having still photos made for us. He'll send them over to our office this morning."

"Well," Jackie began with a suspicious look, "there's something strange about the disappearance of Musashi and al-Yamani."

"That's right. It didn't happen by chance."

"Shayhidi doesn't do anything by chance." She waited until a Falcon 2000 taxied by. "New subject?"

"Sure."

Jackie caught Scott's eye. "After we finish at the office and get the photos from Hartwell, how about an old-fashioned backyard cookout this evening. Something special before we head for Geneva?"

"Sounds like a winner."

When they stepped out of the airplane, Jackie walked to their portable television while Scott went to the Explorer to get their Jeppesen international trip kit.

She reached for the ON/OFF switch and froze when she saw the Fox News Alert logo. Jackie stared at the familiar woman anchor, carefully listening to her every word.

"Scott, you're not going to believe this," she said, when he walked back into the hangar. "He's free—escaped this morning from a Phoenix hospital."

Dalton was confused. "Who's free?"

"Farkas. They mentioned him by name."

Transfixed, he raised his hand. "Start from the top."

"Farkas escaped," she said, exasperation in her voice. "They referred to him as an international terrorist who had been injured in a helicopter crash."

"Damn! How could he escape?"

"I don't know."

Scott shook his head in total frustration. "I thought he was in critical condition."

"Apparently not anymore." A pained look crossed her face. "They reported that he killed a doctor who was making rounds, the same doctor who saved his life."

"That sorry, worthless bastard," Scott said angrily.

"And he severely injured a security guard posted outside the door. The guard heard a commotion and rushed into the room. Farkas took the guard's gun, shot him twice, and then commandeered a car in the hospital parking lot. He's still at large, and a manhunt is on."

Astounded, Scott was speechless for a moment. "Did they say anything about his condition?"

"No, just that he escaped."

Scott's jaw went rigid. "I'm tempted to finish it, kill the worthless bastard before he kills another few thousand innocent people."

Jackie turned off the television. "They have a widespread alert out, and every law enforcement agency in Arizona and the surrounding states is hunting for him. Let's not get sidetracked from our primary mission."

Her words prompted Scott to inject some calm into his emotions. "You're right, we've done everything we can. I just get frustrated."

"Let's relax, unwind, and enjoy the evening."

"I think we'll start early." He shut the door to the jet and locked it. "Let's go to the office, see how Mary Beth is getting along, check our mail, and pick up the photos."

A smile appeared on her face as she tossed him the keys to her Explorer. "You drive, and I'll work on the menu."

Whiteman Air Force Base, Missouri

Five stealth aircraft from the 509th Bomb Wing were taking off at staggered intervals to bomb carefully selected underground bunkers throughout the Middle East. Other air force bombers, including B-1Bs and B-52s, would hit military targets and terrorist infrastructure. The conventional bombers would be augmented by night-attack F-117 stealth aircraft armed with two 2,000-pound Saddam Special laser-guided bombs. Seven of the aircraft were on their way to strike terrorist complexes in Libya. Three other F-117s were bound for Sudan.

Sixteen F-15 Strike Eagles were tasked with various missions and carried a wide variety of ordnance. Considered by many to be an F-4 Phantom on steroids, the versatile F-15 Strike Eagle was adept in both air-to-air and air-to-ground roles.

Over 140 carrier aircraft from the combined forces of *George Washington, Stennis, Constellation,* and *Nimitz* would contribute to the largest bombing campaign to date. This was an all-out effort. The navy and marine corps flight crews were primed and ready to terrorize the terrorists and their hosts. U.S. attack submarines and surface combatants would launch multiple Tomahawk missiles at highly defended sites before manned aircraft attacked them.

Over two dozen helicopters were providing combat search-and-rescue support. Other CSAR assets, including air force HH-60G Pave Hawks and navy HH-60H Seahawk strike-rescue helicopters, were standing by to launch on a moment's notice.

Georgetown

Scott and Jackie had closed their office early, allowing Mary Beth extra time to get ready for a date. When they arrived home, they decided to leave the television off. The continuing air strikes on the terrorist groups and their hosts were receiving wide media coverage, but Scott and Jackie wanted to kick back and take it easy. They had had enough bad news for one day.

They briefly studied the man in the photos with Shayhidi's two missing employees and then packed the pictures in their luggage. After loading most of the last of their personal items into the Explorer, they were ready for their early morning flight to Gander.

"If you'll fix the cocktails," Scott said with a lazy smile, "I'll light the grill and set the table."

"You're on."

When they were finished with the smoked medley of lobster, shrimp, and salmon, Jackie and Scott cleared the patio table and loaded the dishwasher. After charging their glasses with wine, they reclined in chaise longues under the stars.

"Should we go to Crete first?" Jackie asked.

"I've considered it, but I think there are more answers in Geneva. For whatever reason, my guess is that Shayhidi had those two people killed."

Jackie stared at the heavens. "If that's true, and I don't doubt you, it must have been one hell of a falling out."

"Must have been." Scott turned to her. "We have to concentrate on Shayhidi, and I think Geneva is the key to finding him."

"Well, we'll be there tomorrow to get the lay of the land."

They remained quiet, each deep in thought. So much had happened in such a short period, in the United States and around the world. So many things Americans had taken for granted were now damaged or destroyed. The United States was bombing terrorist-harboring nations round the clock. When would logic prevail? When would reason again be the benchmark of civilization?

Jackie turned on her side and faced Scott. "If you don't mind, I'll take the first leg tomorrow."

"That's fine with me." Scott sat up on the edge of his chaise. "How about a stroll around the block?"

"Why not? Need to burn off some nervous energy."

The White House

All the players and their aides were gathered in the Situation Room while the first of five B-2s made their bombing runs using the new penetrating weapons. When the last stealth bomber completed its mission, nine out of the ten bunker complexes had been completely destroyed.

President Macklin, Dave Timkey, Brad Austin, Pete Adair, Hartwell Prost, and many others were monitoring the imminent press briefing at the Pentagon. The media hounds were in full whine and tugging on their leashes. Many of the reporters appeared to be salivating, waiting to sink their fangs into any of the knuckle-dragging Australopithecus cretins wearing a military uniform. They were about to meet the new "chief cretin" at the Pentagon.

Marine Corps Major General Walter "Wally" Connaught stepped to the podium for his inaugural news briefing. Handsome, tall, choirboy smile, wide shoulders, and not an ounce of fat on his rugged frame, Wally was a highly decorated F/A-18 fighter pilot.

Brad Austin looked at President Macklin. "This should be worth the price of admission."

Macklin smiled, humor in his twinkling eyes. "I think Wally will hold his own in his first briefing at the day-care center."

In a clear, resonant voice, Connaught introduced himself to the frenzied crowd. The introduction elicited only harsh looks and unfriendly stares.

He placed his hands on the edges of the podium. "To answer the obvious question first: Yes, we used ten super-bunker busters on targets recognized as not friendly to the United States."

The place erupted.

General Connaught raised both hands to calm the riotlike atmosphere. "Okay, folks, we're going to have to inject some order and discipline into these exchanges. If everyone talks at once, it sounds like a foreign language: gibberish. The art of communication works best when we employ a pattern. You talk, I talk, you talk, et cetera. The concept is tried-and-true. I'll select the questioners, and the rest of you give them a chance to be heard."

From the indignant glares, Connaught was confident he had struck a collective nerve. He calmly pointed to a young woman who was beet red in the face and deeply frowning.

Her voice was high pitched and strained. "Why are you using these super-busters on countries, on—on—on people who can't defend themselves? Violence only leads to more violence."

Connaught maintained an air of detachment. "Before I answer the question, please take a few seconds to relax. Don't want anyone to faint," he deadpanned. "We are using super-bunker busters to penetrate deep underground fortifications containing weapons of mass destruction and/or the laboratories producing them. Violence *does not* always lead to more violence. However, ineffective, halfhearted, limp-wrist violence is *guaranteed* to lead to more violence."

He paused a couple of seconds, gazing at the sea of wide eyes.

"Overwhelming, concentrated, well-executed violence never leads to more violence because the enemy is *dead.* All of them are *graveyard dead*—end of the violence. No rehabilitation, no reeducation, simply *dead.* You get the picture?"

Another reporter raised his hand and was acknowledged. "How can you justify the use of secret superweapons in a—"

Connaught cut him off. "It's simple. Think of it as a game. They're trying to kill us. The object of the game is to kill them first."

He pointed to another reporter, a young man with long wavy hair. "You said you used ten super-bunker busters."

"That's correct," the general said pleasantly.

"How many casualties were there as a direct result of . . . of using the super-bunker busters?"

The general paused a moment. *I can't believe this. Many of these people are too stupid to know they're stupid.* "We're not sure, won't ever be sure." Connaught smiled. "The casualties all occurred fifty to sixty feet underground."

His audience was stunned.

The next question was about racial profiling, and the general almost laughed out loud. "Let me ask you a question. Who do you think is trying to kill us: New Zealanders, Icelanders? Of course we're profiling; we'd be fools if we didn't. Next question." *And I thought flying a jet at night from a carrier deck was scary.*

The general closely refereed the remainder of the question-and-answer period. Order and discipline were maintained, but Connaught had learned as much as, if not more than, the questioners. He knew he had experienced a microcosm of society that truly astounded him.

In the quiet Situation Room, it was clear to President Macklin and his staff that world opinion and the media hounds would be yapping at his heels. The president was not the least bothered by those lacking willpower or resolution. The handwringers would always be held hostage to blackmail and appeasement. He would continue thrashing the terrorists and their sponsors until they surrendered unconditionally. He would settle for nothing less. Until then, Macklin vowed to continue terrorizing the terrorists.

32

Dulles International Airport

The day was dawning under cloudy skies and brisk winds when Jackie and Scott arrived at the Signature Flight Support executive terminal. Their witty, sometimes bawdy, Irish-born taxi driver placed their luggage next to his cab and wished them well.

Scott handed him a crisp folded bill. "Keep the change."

A glint of appreciation flashed in the driver's twinkling eyes. "Thank you, sir. Very generous of you."

"My pleasure."

After they entered the building, Jackie checked the en-route weather and filed an instrument flight plan to Gander, Newfoundland.

With the help of a friendly customer service representative, Scott loaded their luggage and supplies into their new Gulfstream 100 jet. With fresh coffee, warm pastries, water, and plenty of ice on board, they were ready to get under way in their search for terrorist mastermind Saeed Shayhidi.

After Jackie started an engine, Scott listened to the ATIS and called Clearance Delivery. He copied the instrument clearance and then read it back for verification. Switching to Dulles Ground Control, Scott requested permission to taxi to Runway 19-Left. When they were cleared, Jackie added power and began taxiing. Clear of the parking ramp, she started the second engine.

Completing the before-takeoff checklist, Scott rechecked the flap setting and then called the tower as they approached the runway. Granted permission to take off, Jackie pulled onto the runway.

"Ready to go?" she asked.

"All set."

She added power and tracked straight down the centerline of the 11,500-foot runway. The aircraft rapidly accelerated, and Jackie made a smooth transition to flight at the calculated rotation speed.

With the landing gear retracted and the flaps raised, the tower handed Gulfstream 957GA off to departure control.

Scott changed frequencies and keyed the radio. "Uh, Dulles departure, Gulfstream Nine-Five-Seven Golf Alpha out of fifteen hundred feet climbing to five thousand."

"Gulfstream Nine-Five-Seven Golf Alpha, departure, radar contact, turn left, proceed direct Baltimore, climb and maintain one-one-thousand."

"Left, direct Baltimore, climb, maintain one-one-thousand, Fifty-Seven Golf Alpha."

After a short delay, Dulles departure switched the flight to Washington Center and Scott changed to the new frequency. He checked in, and the controller cleared them to climb and maintain 37,000 feet.

Climbing through 18,000 feet Scott and Jackie reset their altimeters to the standard setting of 29.92 inches of mercury. Passing 33,000 feet and cleared to climb to 41,000 feet, Scott climbed out of the cockpit and went into the cabin to turn on the Airshow direct-broadcast satellite television. He selected the Weather Channel and waited for an overall view of their route.

Keeping one eye on the screen, he handed Jackie a cup of coffee and a pastry. He munched on a Danish and watched the current weather patterns. Satisfied with the en-route update, he finished his coffee and returned to the cockpit. He strapped into the right seat as the Gulfstream leveled imperceptibly at 41,000 feet.

"The weather still looks fairly reasonable to Gander, but after that it may be a bit dicey. Showing thunderstorms with tops up around mid-forty range and growing."

Jackie's voice was emotionless. "We can climb above it."

"Not if they're up to fifty thousand feet," Scott said, knowing he was being tested. He casually rolled his eyes toward her. "The higher we climb the more dangerous the atmosphere. Not to mention that we'd be close to our aerodynamic ceiling. Only a few knots of separation between an aerodynamic stall and Mach buffet . . . possibly experiencing Mach tuck. The early jet pilots learned that lesson the hard way, losing a lot of good planes and good pilots."

"True," she said, without looking at him.

He glanced at the engine instruments. "I'm staying at flight level four-one-oh until I'm comfortable with this machine."

"I've never seen you intimidated by an airplane."

He raised an eyebrow in good humor. "What's that old saying about truly superior pilots?"

She laughed softly. "They use their superior judgment to avoid those situations where they might have to use their superior skills."

He turned to her and smiled. "And, I might add, the test pilots have already set the limits for this airplane. We don't need to experiment."

"No argument from me."

Gander International Airport, Newfoundland

The flight from Dulles International was smooth and uneventful at FL410. Jackie made landfall over Burgeo, Newfoundland, on the final descent into Gander. As usual, she made the landing look effortless and then taxied to the Century Aviation facilities.

While Jackie closely observed the refueling, Scott again checked the weather and filed an instrument flight plan to Luton Airport, located thirty-five miles north of central London. They enjoyed a snack and a soft drink before investigating the duty-free shop.

"Time to move on," Scott said, as he reset his watch to local time. "This is the long leg."

They walked out of the FBO and headed toward their immaculate red-and-white Gulfstream 100.

Jackie studied the sky to the northeast. "You haven't said anything about the weather. What's London like?"

"London isn't a problem." He glanced at her and shrugged his shoulders. "There's a huge system, thunderstorms, from the southern tip of the Reykjanes Ridge to the Newfoundland Basin."

"That's all the way to the Azores," Jackie said with growing concern in her voice. "Maybe we should wait until morning."

He ignored the suggestion. "We can probably skirt around it to the north. Pilot reports from the low flyers indicate moderate to heavy rime ice from eight to fourteen thousand feet. The jet drivers are reporting the tops at forty-five and above."

"What about going south?" she asked.

"We don't have the fuel reserves if it drives us too far south, have to land at Lajes. I believe we can find a place to get through."

She raised an eyebrow. "Okay, but let's leave our options open, come back here if we have to."

"I agree. We'll give it a try."

They climbed aboard and strapped in, and Scott started the engines. Jackie handled the checklists and radios while Scott gave a crew brief. They were soon airborne, climbing to FL410. They picked up moderate rime ice but rapidly climbed through the clag. Two hours into the flight, they could see dark clouds stretching from horizon to horizon. Flying away from the setting sun was rapidly enveloping the jet in total darkness.

"Want to go up to forty-five?" Jackie asked.

"Not yet," he mumbled. "Just not comfortable pushing it that high if we encounter severe turbulence."

"Coffin corner?"

He glanced at her. "Yeah, we don't need an upset in the middle of a thunderstorm, bad for the adrenal glands."

They could see dim lightning flashes in the distance. The radar was beginning to paint the enormous series of storms.

After another fifteen minutes of anxiety, she stared into the midnight-dark sky. "We're going to have to rely solely on the radar, can't see a damn thing outside."

He studied the radar screen for a few seconds. "It looks like a possibility, an opening at eleven o'clock . . . coming left ten degrees."

"What if it isn't?"

"Then it's going to be a bumpy ride."

The turbulence was intensifying by the minute and lightning was beginning to blind them. A few splattered raindrops announced the beginning of a wild ride. A sense of unease stole over Scott when a huge bolt of lightning flashed directly in front of the jet.

"Tighten your straps," he said evenly. "Continuous ignition."

Jackie engaged continuous ignition for the engines and rechecked the icing switches.

"Let's slow to maneuvering speed," she suggested, when they flew into heavy rain and menacing lightning.

"Okay, easing the power, let's go with all the lights," Scott said, in a calm voice. *Maybe we should get out of here . . .*

Jackie quickly responded. Their darkened cockpit was suddenly brightly illuminated to help stave off flash blindness.

"That's much better," he said, keeping his eyes on the flight instruments. "Almost like daylight in here."

An awkward silence filled the cockpit for the better part of a minute.

"This is not good," Jackie finally said. She watched the weather radar and suppressed a twinge of panic. The screen was one large blotch of solid red. "What about diverting to Iceland, to Reykjavik?"

Scott started to reply as the Gulfstream was swallowed by an extremely severe level-five thunderstorm. The fierce weather system was immense, creating storms of colossal proportions.

"Do you want the strobes off?" Jackie asked, in a tight voice.

"Sure, kill all the exterior lights."

The exterior lights reflecting off the clouds were distracting. The turbulence quickly became severe, forcing Scott to hand-fly the airplane. The lightning was the worst either had ever seen. It was almost continuous and blinding, forcing both pilots to squint.

Seconds later the heavy rainfall turned into pounding hail. The airplane was taking a beating and the engines were ingesting large amounts of ice. Scott was concerned about losing control of the jet and overstressing the wings or tail. A deafening thunderclap, accompanied by a crackling flash, shocked them. Jackie's windshield popped when hail cracked the lower right corner. *That's enough—this windshield could go at any second!*

"Scott," she said, urgency in her voice. "This is a huge, powerful system. Let's make a one-eighty and get the hell out of here."

They were inside a killer storm and their situation was definitely serious, a life-threatening experience over the middle of the North Atlantic.

Focused on keeping the jet under control, he nodded quietly. "Yeah, might be the best course."

A double flash of intense lightning made them wince.

With fear in her eyes, she glanced at Scott. "We just took a lightning strike. The left engine is rolling back, losing power!"

Gripping the control yoke, Scott turned left toward Reykjavik. Fighting the extreme turbulence, he lowered the nose and thought about broadcasting a Mayday message. "As soon as we're in the parameters for an air start, give it a try."

Before she could answer, the G-100 took a mind-numbing lightning strike that literally knocked out the entire electrical system. It was like tripping the main circuit breaker to a home.

"Both engines are spooling down," she said in a frightened voice. "We've lost everything!"

"Grab the flashlight!" Scott said, focusing on his three small, dimly lighted basic instruments. "Put on your mask!"

They quickly donned their oxygen masks while Scott initiated an emergency descent. Without the electrical system, they could not communicate with anyone.

With her mask adjusted, she snatched a flashlight from her flight bag and trained it on the emergency primary instruments. "We're in deep trouble," she said in a muffled voice.

"Check the circuit breakers," Scott said, when he smelled the pungent stench of burned electrical wires. He adjusted his mask to fit tighter.

Jackie made a quick sweep with the flashlight and felt a cold chill run down her back. "We have smoke in the cockpit."

"Keep the extinguisher handy."

"I have it."

Scott remained unusually quiet, concentrating on flying the airplane and facing reality. *Most aircraft accidents are the result of a chain of events leading to a disaster. I dismissed all the obvious warning signs, all the flashing neon lights.*

The emergency instruments were powered by an independent battery that lasted a half hour or less. The radios did not have a separate battery. Scott and Jackie had to find a place to land or risk losing control of the battered jet. Making matters worse, there was no way to declare an emergency or broadcast a Mayday call. They were alone and descending through the maw of a violent thunderstorm.

Scott centered his attention on flying the plane as smoothly as possible in the severe turbulence. "Stay on oxygen until we're out of fifteen."

Jackie nodded, as she stared at the primary instruments.

They focused on the basic survival instincts. Don't lose control of the jet during the rapid descent. Passing through 17,000 feet, Scott couldn't wait any longer.

"Jackie, try the sat phone—get off a Mayday!"

She slowly shook her head. "They're packed in the external luggage compartment."

"Great."

She ripped off her mask and handed Scott the flashlight. "I'll check the satcom in the cabin." She hurriedly unbuckled her seat restraints and then rushed into the darkened cabin. The turbulence knocked her from side to side and caused her to trip. Jackie checked the satcom and lurched back to the cockpit door. "The phone in the cabin is fried."

"It just keeps getting better." Scott yanked his mask off. He could feel the Grim Reaper's hand resting on his shoulder. *We can't make land—have to ditch at night in a thunderstorm . . .*

"Jackie," he said, in a controlled voice, "grab one of those glass tumblers from the bar and fill it half full of water."

She fumbled in the dark, found a glass, and guessed at the amount of water she drained into it. Jackie steadied herself and then handed the glass to Scott. She braced herself on the glare shield and fell sideways into her seat, banging her head on the side window.

Scott set the flashlight on Jackie's lap. He carefully placed the water glass on the glare shield directly in front of him. Although the water continually sloshed around, it stayed in the tumbler. "If we lose our emergency battery—our primary instruments—shine the flashlight directly on this glass."

"A homemade artificial horizon?"

"It'll keep us right side up."

"We're going to have to ditch," she said, fear creeping into her voice. "No options—no place to go."

They exchanged knowing looks in the faint illumination of the flashlight. The mental illusions of denial were rapidly being displaced by the stark reality of their situation.

Scott paused and drew in a deep breath. "Yeah, we don't have any choice—my fault—*huge* mistake." He picked up the flashlight. "Break out the life raft and two life vests."

Without saying a word, Jackie went into the dark cabin. She stowed the carrying case containing the nine-man life raft in the aisle between the emergency hatches. The right and left exits were over the leading edges of the wings. Swaying in the aisle, she donned a life vest and staggered to the cockpit with another one. She handed Scott his vest and then strapped into her seat. "I'll take it."

"You have it." Shining the flashlight on the instrument panel, Scott wiggled into his vest and cinched it tight. "After we descend through five thousand feet, remove the starboard hatch and stow it in the lavatory. Remove the raft from its carrying case and secure the restraining line to something solid in the cabin—we don't want the raft to blow away."

He flinched when a jagged bolt of lightning hit the left wing. "As soon as we stop, set the raft on the wing—but don't pull the lanyard until I reach the hatch."

A sudden silence fell over them while Jackie trained the light on the emergency instruments. "If we live through this," she began slowly and deliberately, "we need to discuss a new operating protocol."

"Integrated steps in decision making."

"Yes. Exactly." She stared into the darkness. "We've been operating at the far edges of the envelope, sometimes over the edge, for a long time. We've been lucky. We think it's normal to push everything to the limit and beyond to see if we can reel it back in." She paused and glanced at him. "We may have gone too far this time."

"There's ten thousand feet," Scott declared. "We'll discuss it later; time to strap into your seat in the cabin. Take all the sharp objects out of your pockets and take off your shoes."

Jackie made her way to the cabin and sat down in the aft-facing club seat on the right side of the jet. The stomach-churning turbulence, combined with the heavy rain and lightning, made a true believer out of her. She would never again fly through a thunderstorm, at least not on purpose. Jackie knew this was one of those experiences she would remember in great detail all her life, and the ordeal wasn't over.

Passing through five thousand feet, Scott turned around and peered into the dark cabin. "Stow the emergency hatch."

"Working on it."

With confidence the emergency battery would hold out, Scott placed the flashlight on the right seat and cinched his restraints as tight as he could. Out of 3,000 feet he began slowing the jet. He could intermittently see whitecaps when the lightning flashed.

"One thousand feet," Scott announced. "Brace yourself!"

"All set."

The controls were beginning to feel mushy. Scott scooped the water glass from the glare shield and tossed it on the floor in front of the copilot seat. *Don't stall the airplane . . . where's the surface?*

Descending through 400 feet, he had a peek at the ocean during a mighty flash of lightning. The huge frothy waves were only 100 feet below him.

Oh, my God! he said to himself. *The altimeter was off—not set properly in all the confusion.* Scott eased the control yoke back. Hoping for another flash, he realized there wouldn't be time to align the airplane parallel to the swells.

Scott nursed the yoke in an attempt to bleed off speed. He was holding his breath when the Gulfstream smacked the first towering wave. The right wingtip plowed into the water and violently yawed the jet to the right. The aircraft plunged through another giant wave, and its forward motion suddenly stopped.

"We've stopped—toss the raft out!" Scott was out of his harness in a heartbeat and scrambling for the open hatch. "Pull the lanyard," he yelled, as Jackie stepped on the wing.

She yanked and the raft was automatically ejected from its carrying case. It began inflating and Jackie jumped in a few seconds later. Scott followed suit after the raft was fully inflated. He frantically searched through the raft's equipment bag and found a utility knife as the Gulfstream slipped beneath the waves. Scott slashed at the retaining line attached to the jet. The airplane was about to pull the edge of the raft underwater when the partially severed line snapped.

It was too windy to attempt to raise the canopy. Cold and dripping wet, they would have to huddle together until the storm system moved on. The swells were gigantic and they were concerned about capsizing. After a couple of failed attempts, Scott managed to deploy the sea anchor. It helped stabilize the raft.

"Wouldn't it figure," Scott said after taking inventory of the equipment bag. "No emergency radio and no ELT." The emergency locator transmitter transmits simultaneously on 121.5 MHz (civilian) and 243.0 MHz (military), the search-and-rescue homing frequencies.

"Well, let's look on the bright side," Jackie said, in a relieved, upbeat voice. "We're not injured, and someone is going to be looking for us fairly soon, if not already."

Scott looked at her sheepishly. "There's a lifetime of lessons to be learned from this—from *my* unmitigated bonehead move."

"Don't worry, you won't do it again. Trust me."

Scott nodded quietly and lowered his head. *So much for superior judgment to avoid having to use superior skills.*

33

The White House

Completely redecorated with donated funds, the elegant state dining room was surrounded by English oak paneling and highlighted by crown molding around the ceiling. The room was designed to seat 130 guests comfortably, but this evening President Cord Macklin and Maria Eden-Macklin were entertaining 80 of their close friends and family members.

The president and the first lady were greeting their dinner guests, many of whom were long-standing friends from their military days. The occasion was their quarterly dinner party, always known to be lively and replete with colorful stories. After the gentlemen and their ladies gathered in the elaborate dining room, Hartwell Prost discreetly approached Macklin.

"Mr. President," he said in a barely audible voice, "may I have a brief word with you in the family dining room?"

Macklin could tell from Hartwell's solemn expression that something was amiss. "Sure, lead the way." The president maintained his casual smile as they left the room.

When Macklin closed the door to the private dining room, Prost sadly shook his head. "Jackie and Scott are missing, overdue in London."

"What happened?"

"I don't know," he said grimly. "They would've been out of fuel a couple of hours ago. There were no distress calls, nothing; they just vanished between Gander and London."

The president was visibly shaken. "Has this been verified?"

"Yes, the plane was registered to their aviation consulting

company. The FAA contacted their secretary and she called my home. They had given her my number in case of an emergency. My butler relayed the news to me about fifteen minutes ago."

"What about a search?"

"It's under way. The weather along their route was bad—horrendous would be a better description. How about using some of our military assets to help in the search?"

The president nodded. "Anything you need. Take charge and pull out the stops."

"I will, Mr. President."

U.S. Coast Guard Air Station
Elizabeth City, North Carolina

Less than an hour and twenty minutes after the conversation between the president and Hartwell Prost, two coast guard HC-130H Hercules departed from Elizabeth City to look for the missing aviators. Another coast guard C-130 on a training flight from San Juan, Puerto Rico, to the Azores had changed course and would soon be assisting in the search. In addition, a marine corps KC-130F from MCAS Cherry Point, North Carolina, would be joining the growing rescue effort.

Two coast guard cutters, the Hamilton-class WHEC 721 *Gallatin* and the Famous-class WMEC 907 *Escanaba,* would be supplemented by three U.S. Navy ships and an E-2C Hawkeye early warning aircraft from the aircraft carrier USS *Harry S. Truman.* Civilian airplanes and ships in the general search area were also notified to be on the lookout for the downed pilots.

Naval Air Station Brunswick, Maine

Four P-3C Orion land-based maritime patrol aircraft from squadrons VP-8 and VP-26 were tasked to join in the search for Jackie and Scott. The long-range four-engine turboprops would be joined by two P-3Cs from VP-64 at NAS Willow Grove,

Pennsylvania. Each aircraft would be assigned to a particular search pattern by the E-2C Hawkeye.

The Raft

The raging, icy seas were becoming less violent by the time Scott noticed the first hint of daylight. Numb from the cold water and gusty winds, he could barely move his stiff limbs. He turned on the flashlight and struggled with the canopy poles. Awakened by the beam of light darting around the raft, Jackie opened her eyes and blinked a couple of times. "I'm frozen solid. How can you possibly move?"

"Trust me, it isn't easy." Scott extended the flashlight to her. "If you'll hold the light, I'll see if I can get the canopy up."

"Happy to help. Ready to start the oven and fix breakfast."

It was an unwieldy wrestling match, but Scott finally placed the water-activated strobe light on top of the canopy and closed the flap to the entrance. The wind chill factor immediately dropped to nil. He arranged the whistle, signal mirror, dye marker, bailing bucket, first-aid packet, and flare kit by the water and rations kit.

"Here," he said, handing Jackie an emergency space blanket. "Crawl under this and warm yourself."

"Thanks."

She curled up under the blanket and Scott draped another blanket over her legs. Jackie accepted a tropical chocolate bar and then had a long drink of water from a plastic canteen. "Well, one thing's for sure, it's nice and cozy with the canopy up."

Still shivering, Scott managed a half smile. "Yeah, spending quality time together in the great outdoors."

She swallowed another drink of water. "The alternative could've been a lot worse: lying on the bottom of the Atlantic."

They remained lost in their thoughts while the life raft bobbed up and down in the choppy waves. Late morning saw the beginning of the end of the downpour. When the sun began peeking through occasional holes in the low overcast, Scott picked up the bailing bucket. He opened the canopy flap and methodically began scooping water out of the raft. *What a stupid and dangerous thing I did.*

Finally, he used the sponge to drain the last of the water out of the raft and then shut the flap. "Home sweet home."

She stared at him thoughtfully. "If you could be anywhere right now, where would it be?"

He looked up, his eyes quizzing her. "That's a loaded question. I'd choose to be in Gander yesterday and stay on the ground."

"I said right now, not yesterday."

Scott's voice was even and matter-of-fact. "Under the circumstances, I'd say in the Rowes Wharf Bar at the Boston Harbor Hotel, thinking about the dumbest thing I've ever done—not counting yesterday."

She smiled and shook her head. "Even though I think you walk on water, pun intended, I have a couple of other suggestions for the dumbest category."

He looked at her suspiciously. "You have a mean streak."

"Let's see: for starters, parachuting onto a Chinese Communist ship in the middle of the night in the middle of the Pacific Ocean."

"I was trained to do that."

"You were trained to fly, too. A naturally gifted pilot who successfully flew jets from the decks of aircraft carriers."

Scott didn't blink an eyelash. "New subject?"

Feeling a sudden pang of guilt, Jackie nodded in agreement. "Sure." *He has to live with this for the rest of his life.*

"Let's set up watches," he suggested. "Four hours on, four off."

"Sounds fair." Jackie glanced at the two collapsible oars. "We can sit next to the open hatch and slowly rotate the raft."

He reached for an oar. "An unrestricted view of the ocean and the sky."

"Yup, we sure don't want to miss anything."

Scott raised the flap and glanced at the horizon. "And we don't want to be sunk by some ship we didn't see coming, spoil our vacation."

"Just keep the flare gun handy."

He unfolded one oar and locked it in place. "I'll take the first four and you try to get some sleep."

"I won't argue with you." She made herself a comfortable lair and curled up under two space blankets. "Wake me if a cruise ship stops by."

"Count on it." Scott mindlessly paddled the raft in a slow circle, scanning the horizon and the sky. *My flaw is being too mission-oriented, too eager to press on under any circumstances. There wasn't any time line—no need to rush to Geneva. A night in Gander would have saved a lot of grief. Fortunately, no one was killed or injured.*

Scott allowed Jackie to sleep an extra hour before he began dozing off. Reluctantly, he woke her and waited until she was fully roused. He consumed some chocolate and water before stretching out and closing his eyes. Although he was exhausted, Scott was tormented and embarrassed by his serious lapse in judgment. Finally, after twenty minutes, the gentle undulation of the raft rocked him to sleep.

Jackie settled into a slow, methodical routine of paddling and searching. The low overcast began to dissipate and the sun was appearing more often. By late afternoon, Jackie's eyes were playing tricks on her, or so she thought. *Is that an airplane low on the horizon?* She scanned back and forth. *That has to be a plane, but there isn't any sound—probably a turboprop with the power pulled back.*

"Scott, wake up!"

Startled awake, he rubbed his eyes. "What is it?"

"It's a plane—look! It's just under the overcast!"

He scrambled to the opening and took one look. "Damn!" He reached for the flare gun. "Watch out."

She rolled out of the way and looked over his shoulder.

Scott pointed the flare gun up at an angle and squeezed the trigger. The bright flare quickly reached its apogee while Scott reloaded the gun. He fired the second flare and they stared at the plane.

"It's a P-3 Orion," he said, as the sun suddenly bathed them in its warm glow. "They're either hunting subs or searching for us."

"Let's hope it's the latter."

They watched for fifteen seconds as the aircraft continued on course.

"Come on," Scott said impatiently. "Hell-*o,* is anyone awake?"

After another ten seconds, their hopes were dashed.

"Well," he said, meeting her gaze, "we know people are look—"

"It's turning, banking toward us!" She grabbed the dye marker and tossed it to Scott. "Might as well use it."

He quickly deployed the vivid yellow dye and watched it spread over the sea. "Between our international-orange canopy and the dye, I don't think they'll have any problem locating us."

Jackie raised a hand to shield her eyes from the bright sun. She could barely hear the low deep-throated sound from the four turboprops. "Question is, how long before a ship or helicopter arrives?"

Scott held his answer while the antisubmarine-warfare plane flew low past the raft. They waved at the crew of the P-3C as it pulled up in a gentle climbing turn to the left.

"Who knows? It shouldn't be too long."

"I hope you're right."

The big maritime patrol plane slowed and began a wide holding pattern around the raft. Thirty minutes later, the tall mainmast of a vessel under sail appeared on the horizon. The gleaming ninety-two-foot crewed charter yacht was headed straight for the raft.

Scott smiled reassuringly. "Things are going a lot better today than they were yesterday evening."

A sixth sense compelled Jackie to look beyond Scott. Another aircraft was approaching from the southwest. "And we have more good news," she announced, pointing to a low-flying C-130.

Even at a distance, Scott immediately recognized the white aircraft. "The coast guard is here."

Low on fuel, the navy P-3C rolled wings level and departed to the southwest. The sound of the engines became louder as the airplane climbed through the broken overcast and disappeared.

The coast guard HC-130H slowed and passed close to the life

raft. A crew member standing on the open aft ramp tossed a bright orange object into the ocean. It landed within ten yards of the raft.

"A radio," Scott said excitedly. He reached for an oar and plopped on his chest at the entrance to the raft. With long smooth strokes he propelled the raft to the orange container.

"Got it," he said, unwrapping the survival radio. It was already tuned to the emergency channel. "Coast guard, it's good to see you guys!"

"What's your condition?" the pilot asked.

Scott keyed the radio. "We're in great shape."

"Excellent, stand by."

"Roger."

The C-130 began a wide left-hand orbit before the aircraft commander again keyed his radio. "The Good Samaritans in the approaching yacht have graciously agreed to host you until our helo arrives. Recommend you keep your raft for the helo pickup, easier than lifting you close to the mast. Copy?"

"Roger that," Scott said, and then laughed with Jackie, relief in their voices. He rubbed the stubble on his cheek. "From a life raft to a sailing yacht, can't beat it."

With the tension now subsiding, Jackie turned sober. "We had an *extremely* close call, but the real fun begins when we visit with our insurance company."

"Yeah, that's going to be ugly."

When they were helped aboard the luxurious yacht, Scott and Jackie were surprised to see a Union Jack ensign. The British crew and their Italian passengers were friendly and hospitable to the two Americans. During their short visit, Jackie and Scott were given dry clothes, food, and all the bottled water they could consume.

They were escorted on a tour of the impeccably maintained teak, brass, and mahogany vessel. When they reached the dining room, highlighted by bird's-eye maple panels and oriental carpets, the ship's skipper gave a champagne toast in celebration of their rescue.

Minutes later an HH-60J Jayhawk helicopter from the coast guard cutter WMEC 907 *Escanaba* arrived over the yacht. After profusely thanking their hosts, Jackie and Scott boarded their life raft and cast off. The helicopter crew quickly plucked them up. The captain of the yacht recovered the raft, deflated it, and stowed it belowdeck.

Scott and Jackie were flown to the cutter and greeted warmly by the commanding officer. Following explicit directions from coast guard headquarters in Washington, D.C., the captain made arrangements for the pair to have privacy in order to contact a government official.

Hartwell Prost was thrilled to hear from them as they explained what happened. As usual, he came right to the point. "Let's be thankful you're safe and on your way home. What happened is in the past, can't do anything about it. Look to the future, and don't worry."

Prost was cheerful. He told them to take a few days off and then contact him. He had been in touch with Mary Beth and she was deeply relieved to know Jackie and Scott were okay. After their call to Prost, the friendly skipper insisted on bunking them in staterooms. Jackie and Scott were reluctant to ask the officers to give up their quarters, but the captain insisted.

Unable to shake the memories of the accident, the couple spent the following two days discussing their aircraft insurance options. The morning of the third day, when *Escanaba* was drawing close to the East Coast, they were flown to Washington, D.C.

Georgetown

Once home, Jackie instinctively turned on the television and stepped into the master bath to shower. She was rinsing her hair when she heard howling and clapping coming from the family room. Next, there was banging on the bathroom door and muffled shouts of elation. Jackie turned off the water and reached for a towel. *What is wrong with him?* She opened the door to find Scott holding a bottle of champagne and two flutes.

"He's dead—they killed him!"

"Who?"

"Farkas. It's confirmed; he's in a morgue."

Jackie was skeptical. "What happened?"

"He tried to run a roadblock outside of Prescott—they nailed him on the spot!" Unusual for him, Scott let out a wild shout. "Hell, it's on Fox so it *has* to be true!"

Jackie threw her arms around Scott's neck, almost dislodging the champagne bottle. They celebrated the news and decided to follow Hartwell's advice: to take a few days off to enjoy one of their favorite getaways for relaxation and privacy. Scott, who had been planning a surprise for Jackie's birthday, was especially excited about the respite.

34

Wequassett Inn Resort & Golf Club

Located on Cape Cod's picturesque Pleasant Bay in Chatham, Massachusetts, the secluded waterfront Wequassett Inn was one of Jackie and Scott's cherished hideaways. The twenty-two wooded acres offered a relaxing atmosphere in a quaint and intimate setting. The resort was well known for its wide variety of facilities and services. The main dining room, for example, was constructed in the early 1800s and featured a view of the bay.

After checking into their preferred suite the evening before, the couple played a sunrise round of golf on the eighteen-hole course. Refreshed by the exercise, they enjoyed a light breakfast and then decided to go sailing.

Repairing to their suite, Scott and Jackie changed into nautical attire and Topsider boat moccasins. They packed their mesh boat bag with supplies and headed for the dock.

"What a beautiful morning," Jackie noted, as she studied the puffy clouds and blue sky. "The temperature is perfect and the water is calm."

Brimming with anticipation, Scott gave her a brief smile. "Couldn't be better, a Chamber of Commerce day."

After lounging and sightseeing under the warm sun, Scott anchored the sailboat in a small, quiet bay guarded by dozens of curious seagulls. The resorts kitchen staff had supplied a sumptuous picnic for the sailing excursion. Jackie and Scott enjoyed the fare at leisure and relaxed with a glass of wine.

Scott took in the scores of moored sailboats in the small harbor across from their location. He locked his fingers behind his head and stretched out on his back.

Jackie placed her wineglass in the picnic basket and propped herself up on one arm beside Scott. "I want to capture this picture in my mind and be able to recall it anytime I feel insecure and need to be in a peaceful place."

Scott took in a deep breath of sea air and slowly let it out. "I know what you mean."

"Speaking of insecurity," Jackie deadpanned. "What about us?"

Scott raised an eyebrow. "Our business?"

Jackie suspected Scott was teasing her but she wasn't sure. "Our future, you and me. We can't keep doing what we're doing until we're senior citizens. We won't live that long."

Scott nodded. "We're committed to finding Shayhidi. Agreed?"

Jackie smiled knowingly. "Yes."

"After we locate him, we'll concentrate on our aviation consulting business and safety audits and step away from the clandestine operations."

She tilted her head up. "Do you mean it?"

"Absolutely," he said firmly. "We have plenty of money and we don't need to take the risks."

Jackie sat up, surprised. "No more Commando Crazy adventures in the middle of the night?"

"That's right."

"Strictly legitimate, safe business operations?" she asked.

"That's the way I see it—already used seven lives."

She paused a second, schooling her voice to be calm and assertive. "What about us, our personal relationship? Where do *we* go from here?"

Scott chuckled quietly and looked her in the eye. "This is really coincidental."

"What?"

Scott's cell phone rang.

"I thought we agreed to banish the phones," Jackie protested. "At least for this trip."

"Sorry," he said, reaching into the boat bag, "but after our latest experience I feel safer with a phone around."

The conversation was mostly one-sided, with Scott saying "Yes, sir," a lot before he tossed the phone back into the bag.

"I detect trouble," Jackie said, disappointment in her voice. "What's the problem, Hartwell?"

"Yes," he said grudgingly. "There's something in the wind—couldn't say much over a cell phone. He wants us on a plane to Geneva as soon as we can be ready."

"Shayhidi?"

He nodded, concealing his disappointment. "They want him *now*—one way or the other."

Scott briefly touched the engagement ring in the pocket of his nylon water trunks. *This is not the opportune time.*